Picked as a Book of the Year in

The Times
Guardian
Sunday Times
Daily Express
Spectator
Scotsman

~

'A story so original and so fully imagined. Meek shows the era as alien, which it is, and doesn't falsify it by assimilating it to ours. But his characters are recognisably warm and human'
Hilary Mantel

'An astounding linguistic fantasy about the advent of the Black Death'
Philip Hensher, *Spectator*

'Meek brilliantly creates a variety of voices, and a language appropriate to the fourteenth century, for a story of the distant past with unsettling echoes of the present'
Sunday Times

'I was incapable of ripping myself away from this novel once I began it. James Meek is the bold creator of a world that I felt I could see, hear, smell and taste with complete clarity. What an excellent storyteller he is'
Charlotte Higgins

'A triumphant medieval fable . . . At the centre of this beautiful novel is an exploration of the difference between romance and true love, allegory and reality, history and the present'
Guardian

Also by James Meek

Fiction
McFarlane Boils the Sea
Last Orders
Drivetime
The Museum of Doubt
The People's Act of Love
We Are Now Beginning Our Descent
The Heart Broke In

Non-Fiction
Private Island
Dreams of Leaving and Remaining

TO CALAIS, IN ORDINARY TIME

JAMES MEEK

CANONGATE

For Kay and Sophy

This paperback edition published in 2020 by Canongate Books

First published in Great Britain, the USA and Canada in 2019
by Canongate Books Ltd, 14 High Street, Edinburgh EH1 1TE

Distributed in the USA by Publishers Group West
and in Canada by Publishers Group Canada

canongate.co.uk

1

British Library Cataloguing-in-Publication Data
A catalogue record for this book is available on
request from the British Library

ISBN 978 1 78689 677 3

Typeset in Perpetua by Palimpsest Book Production Ltd,
Falkirk, Stirlingshire

Printed and bound in Great Britain by Clays Ltd, Elcograf S.p.A.

MIX
Paper from
responsible sources
FSC® C018072

God is deaf nowadays

— William Langland, *Piers Plowman*

OUTEN GREEN

'CUT ME THAT rose,' demanded Berna of the gardeners. She pointed to the most finely formed flower, coloured the most brilliant crimson.

'A prize surely intended for your marriage,' said her cousin Pogge. 'Weren't it sufficient provocation to take your papa's book without consent?'

Berna embraced the volume she carried. 'Papa offered me the fulfilment of my desires in the garden, in lieu of my preference for a liberty general.' She turned to the younger of the two gardeners. He had default of height, but was formed pleasantly, with puissant shoulders. His freshly razed face had an appearance of attentive tranquillity. 'Will Quate, cut me the rose.'

IT WAS SUNDAY, St Thomas's Day eve, and there wasn't no garden work to be done nor no other work neither. Will Quate wasn't no gardener. He came to help Rufy bear home a heap of rose sticks for his fire. But the lady Bernadine happened to come by and bade them give her the best bloom on the bush, and they mightn't say no, so Will hewed the rose with his knife, plucked five thorns of the stem with his fingers and gave it her. She took it and led her kinswoman through the door in the garden wall to her father's wood.

My COMMISSION TO annotate the abbey's property case is complete; I am obliged to transmit it to the advocates in Avignon. Nothing detains me in Malmesbury except the difficulty of leaving. It is not terror of events that obstructs my return to France, but the practicalities. It is impossible to be a solitary traveller in these times. I must find company for the journey, yet the roads to the southern ports, previously dense with viators, lie vacant.

I suspect the prior has more intelligence about the progress of the plague in Avignon than he divulges. I have received no communication from the city since Marc's brief note in March, informing me that the pestilence was general there, and that on the advice of his doctor the Pope now defends himself against the pestilential miasma by habitation at the median of two enormous fires.

Written at Malmesbury Abbey, sixth July anno domini one thousand three hundred and forty-eight, of ordinary time the twenty-seventh, the Sunday preceding the festival of the translation of the relics of my name saint, Thomas martyr, by Thomas Pitkerro, proctor of Avignon.

BERNA AND POGGE passed a line of village children who foraged in the husks of last year's beechmast. They followed a path to the foot of a tree, sat on a blanket and placed between them the book and the rose. From a pouch she carried, Berna took a bowl and a bloodletting knife and demanded that Pogge bare her arm.

'I prefer not to,' said Pogge.

4

'It is simply to demonstrate the method, that you might at some future point apply it yourself.'

Pogge lifted her arm, rigidly enclosed in linen. 'It's sewn in,' she said.

'I advised you to permit your limbs liberty of movement.'

'I desired to accustom myself to sewing in, in advance of your marriage ceremony.'

'It is my opinion that you contrived this excuse. You doubt my ability to bleed.'

'You know I admire your numerous virtues, but you are a knight's daughter, not a surgeon.'

'It is notorious in our family that I possess a plethora of blood.' Berna rolled up her own left sleeve till it was above the elbow. 'Regard,' she said, demonstrating the faint marks of previous cuts in the crook of her arm, and one more fresh. 'Are they not finely accomplished? I chanced to see my friend sanguinary, the barber, in Brimpsfield last week. He advised that should the advertisements of the clerks prove true my former comfort would be a form of defence. My chaperone left me unobserved for a moment and the barber supplied me with the knife.'

'I would have held you too determined in your gentility to have acquaintance with barbers.'

'I ne strain for gentility,' said Berna, raising her voice a fraction. 'It is courteous amiability towards such classes as barbers that distingues our relations with them from their relations with each other, determined, as they are, by money.'

The pique left her, though not the ardour with which she spoke, accompanied by a certain generality of address, as if Pogge were only one of a number of listeners. 'While my mother lived she conducted me to the barber to be bled once a month. My humours were of so special a nature. She would lie on a couch, supported by a cushion, I would lie against her in the same position, and she would fold me in her arms while the barber opened my veins. The cut would be pursued by silence, apart from the respiration of my mother in my ear and the gutter of the blood in the bowl. I have never known such contentment.'

)

SIR GUY CAME and saw the rose was gone. He chewed the inside of his cheek.

'Was my daughter here?' he asked the men.

They ne said nothing.

Sir Guy beheld the heaps of rose sticks Will and Rufy had bound in bundles.

'A heap of Sabbath-breakers,' he said. 'Would you have the murrain sent us sooner?'

Rufy said it wasn't work, he and Will only gathered the sticks for his hearth, as his lord had behest him the boot of the rose tree when he shred it.

Sir Guy cut one of the bundles with his knife and took of it a thick, well-shaped length of rosewood, bent at one end in a handle, as it had grown. He held the handle, let the other end sit on the ground and leaned his weight on the wood.

'A kind walking stick,' he said.

Rufy said the tree would grow that way, and his mum was lame.

'There's sap in your old dam yet,' said Sir Guy. 'I saw her hop about the pole two month ago.'

Rufy said her bones were bad, and he ne thought it him no harm to take a good strong stick to help her walk about.

'I'll learn you otherwise,' said Sir Guy. 'I'll have bad bones one day. Why would I lack a good stick of my own rose tree to help

6

your shiftless mother? All hold me soft and reckon they might have what's mine without no afterclap. I was robbed of a gown, and now you'd rob me of a walking stick.'

Will said they mightn't say no to the lady Bernadine when she bade them give her the bloom. He took a handful of little brown spikelets of his belt-bag and, with bowed head, offered them to his lord.

'Eh? What's that?' said Sir Guy.

Will said he hewed them from the rose branch. They were the thorns, he said, that must also rightly be Sir Guy's.

A COMPANY OF archers pervenes to Malmesbury imminently, on its way to France. It is suggested I go with them.

When travelling towards the pestilence was a theoretical possibility, I had fortitude. Now I may actually go, I am terrified. My mind cannot accommodate my own mortality, yet is capable of engendering an infinite series of images of colleagues and remote acquaintances who have succumbed. I remember Brozzi, the Rota lawyer with the enormous jaw. I have been visited repeatedly by a vision of him recumbent in a pit in his court robes, his face corroded by marauding dogs, the bone of the jaw protruding nude and white, while my baker asperses soil over him with a flour scoop.

BERNA STROKED HER cousin's cheek and told her how fortunate it was she'd come. She'd been about to take her own life.

7

'How?' demanded Pogge.

'Thrown myself into the moat.'

Pogge shook her head. 'Your moat's not profound enough for drownage. You'd kill several frogs and break your arm.'

They disputed the best way a woman should contrive her death. Pogge favoured poison. Berna preferred a tumble from a high window. Pogge said she couldn't have done it anywise, for suicide was the mortal sin that mightn't never be absolved, and Berna were certain to go direct to hell, to burn till Judgement Day.

'The King of Heaven will absolve me,' said Berna. 'He will perceive the purity of my soul and the sincerity of my ardour. He will see that by forcing me to marry an old man in place of my amour, my father left me no alternative method to preserve my honour. I shall be raised to heaven as a martyr to love.'

Before Pogge might reply she was arrested by a noise of approaching pigs. The place Berna had chosen was a hollow between two roots that rose higher than their heads, hiding them from most of the forest. They could hear the beasts grunt, step through last year's dry leaves and dig in the ground with their muzzles. They heard the voice of Hab the pigboy. Pogge lifted her head and looked round.

'Please ne regard these villainous animals while I explain the misery and joy that contest for possession of my heart,' said Berna.

'I have a despite of pigs. They are large and hairy and have a displeasant odour,' said Pogge. 'I beg your pardon. I am yours entirely. Let's consider your state in a manner proper.'

'How well-tempered you are,' said Berna. 'How many times at night I've wished you were in bed with me that I might wake you and be solaced of your reason.'

'How old is your affianced?'

'Fifty! Fifty years! As old as papa!'

'Have you met him?'

'He has hunted here. I call him Sir Hennery, because his face is like to it was pecked by chickens.'

'But he isn't otherwise disfigured.'

'No.'

'He's of fair height, sound in body.'

'It's a husband, not a horse! He becomes my master, till the end of his days!'

'Of estate substantial.'

Berna shrugged. 'Three manors in Somerset-Somewhereset-Nowhereset.'

'You'd be secure.'

'He has hairs growing out of his nose.'

'Encourage him to pluck them.'

'He's illiterate, hates music, and considers an evening well spent disputing the best hound to catch a hart in grease.'

'England's unloving husbands and wives may find relief of matrimony,' said Pogge. 'There's a town in France where so many lay in the street they couldn't neither bury them like Christians nor dig a pit to hold them all, and they burned them there, in front of the houses they were carried from.'

'Who told you this?'

'A Gascon who came to Bristol with merchandise for my father.'

'I very much doubt the French have been burning people. In general we are too phlegmatic as creatures to burn well. Anyway, it ne troubles me. I'd rather the world perish than that I live without my amour.'

'By "amour", I suppose you refer to Laurence Haket?'

'Ne speak his name,' said Berna. 'It's discomfortable to me. Say "he" and "him".'

'Ah. Then I suppose you refer to he-and-him.'

The church bell rang in the village. 'Oh, for a priest romantic,' said Berna, 'who might say, for example, "Death is sent by Love

9

to make us sensible how few hours remain to he who is desirous of the Rose, once the Rose has flowered."' She placed the rose on her lap. 'Pestilence or no pestilence.'

'To imagine Laurence will rescue you from your future husband will make you suffer more. Laurence is departed and won't return. You live in a manor in Gloucestershire, not in Paris among the poets.'

Berna laughed and touched the corners of the book. 'How measurable you are, dear Pogge. Like the Lover in the book you pass too much time listening to Reason. Why not France? Calais is joined to England now, and Laurence is promised tenure of a grand manor outside the city. Why should he and I not voyage there together, and love and be secure?'

'The pestilence.'

'We're all mortal.'

'Your eyes are feverous, Berna. How might he come for you, if he's in Calais, and you're here?'

'He's not in Calais. He's in Wiltshire for Saturday's joust, and leaves for France next day.'

Pogge folded her arms. 'Only account for this,' she said. 'Your father would marry you to his friend. Yet your Laurence is, by your description, an excellent young man of a good family, with prospects for advancement. If he loves you, why not ask your father if he may have you?'

'He requested, and was refused. Laurence has no daughter marriageable, whereas Sir Hennery does. And my father judges himself, like Sir Hennery, a widower in need of a wife.'

'Berna!'

'I wouldn't tell you, it's so dishonourable. Their intention is that Sir Hennery arrive, we marry on Saturday, we journey to Somerset with my father, and there, after harvest, celebrate a second wedding, between my father and my new husband's daughter.'

Pogge bared her teeth. 'Outrageous,' she said.

'Is it not hideous? I and this other poor maid are our own dowries.'

'Can the clerks allow such a bargain?'

'You see why I speak of martyrdom. I've never prayed more than now, and if the archdeacon will hear my confession, let him make himself comfortable for a long duration.' Berna opened the book and placed her finger on the page. 'Listen how perfectly the Romance descrives him: "Il m'a au coeur cinq plaies faites." Love has pierced him with five golden arrows: Simplicity, Courtesy, Company, Beau-Semblant and Beauty.'

'Your beauty?'

'Pogge, you ne understand allegory, just listen. In being pierced with these five arrows, love has crippled him.'

'Certainly it is a great inconvenience to a man going about his affairs to have five arrows sticking out of him.'

'Shhh! No more interruptions. He is crippled by love, he is love's vassal. When he was here, in Outen Green, he told me even were his will otherwise, he couldn't but love me par amour. He's all that love demands: courteous, free of pride, elegant, light-hearted and generous. Yet he suffers terribly from the pain of those five wounds. How he suffers, most of all when we parted, try to conceal it as he might. Five wounds, Pogge!' Berna touched in turn the palms of her hands, her feet, and one of her ribs. 'Cinq plaies! Pogge, you ne know what it's like to love and be loved. Believe me when I tell you that to see his face when he regarded me for the last time at the moment of his departure was like seeing the very face of Christ on the cross.'

Pogge wrinkled her nose. 'I ne think it proper to know Christ's love in a sense romantic.'

Berna leaned forward, took Pogge's hands in hers and pressed them tightly. 'Might you joy the sentiment of true love, as I have, you see it like to a sphere with many aspects.'

Pogge squealed, leapt to her feet and backed up against one fork of the tree roots. The glistening snout, pointed tusks, stiff bristles and small black eyes of an enormous boar depended of the top of the root opposite. Over his ears hung a garland of mallow-flowers and from his half-open mouth fell threads of silver slime.

Berna got up and scratched the boar on the cheek. 'Enker,' she said, 'you frightened my cousin.' The boar narrowed its eyes and snorted.

Hab the pigboy appeared beside Enker and bowed his head to Berna and Pogge. Berna commanded him to keep the swine at a greater distance, and Hab bowed again, and answered, and they spoke for a time.

He was a meagre brown youth in a patched tunic of undyed linen, barelegged, with shining black hair down to his shoulders, large black eyes and full red lips that gleamed as if he'd raised them from the surface of a spring. He spoke a word to Enker, the boar wheeled and they disappeared. There was a clatter as the herd moved off.

'I lack your courage,' said Pogge in a trembling voice.

'I knew Enker as a piglet. They're gentle beasts,' said Berna, sitting down, 'and cleaner than you suppose.'

'The city pigs are nastier,' said Pogge. She stayed on her feet and crossed her arms. 'I can't understand your villains. What did the pigboy say?'

'It's Cotswold,' said Berna. 'It's Outen Green. As if no French never touched their tongues. I ne know myself sometimes what they mean. They say steven in place of voice, and shrift and housel for confession and absolution, and bead for prayer. He said he hoped they'd catch the thief who stole my marriage gown.'

'It's marvellous that your villains have such familiarity with the privy troubles of their lord's family.'

'It's not so very privy no more,' said Berna. 'After the gown was stolen my father looked to recover the expense of replacing it by raising their amercements. Well, one of them must have taken it, and they might easily have saved themselves the trouble by informing us as to the person of the thief. We must go. If anyone from the house sees us in the forest sans guardian we'll be punished.' But she ne moved to part, and ran her finger over the painture of the Lover in *Le Roman de la Rose*.

'And punished again for taking your father's book,' said Pogge.

'He knows I read it.'

Pogge knelt down close to her cousin. 'The Lover is a man,' she whispered. 'It's a book to guide men. If the Lover is a man, what are you?'

'So you've read it,' said Berna. 'And you'll know the response.'

'I suppose you are Beauty and Simplicity and all the other arrows that have pierced him.'

'It's Love, not I, who shot those arrows.'

'This was his sole desire,' said Pogge. She took the rose and held it in her palm. 'You refused it him, and he departed.'

Berna's face turned crimson and she stood. She picked up the book and the blanket with impatient gestures, seized the rose from Pogge's hand and threw it away. She began to walk towards the village, and Pogge hurried after her.

ON THE LEAVINGS of housewives' stockpots the children laid owl pans and rotten crow, rib of vole and otter, a deal of brock rigbone, some small-fowl carrion and the shells of things that crawl in mould. All it ne gladdened us the pans of nightingales webbed with rat leg and snake rib in one mound of bone, Nack the hayward said a bonefire cleansed the air like no other, and held the saints their noses, their ears were open yet to beads, their gold eyes open to our candles' light.

RELATIONS BETWEEN THE abbot and the prior having degenerated so severely (the abbot now completely separated from administrative matters), the prior has assumed responsibility for the emergency. He is content to have me here as a distraction, until he remembers I have no capacity for music, and is dissatisfied. He suspects horror of the plague, rather than, as I insist, practical obstacles, postpones my exit.

'I RECOGNISE YOU from the book,' said Berna. 'You're she who imprisons Warm Welcome and the Rose together in a high tower that the Lover ne approach.'

'Jealousy?' said Pogge. 'I'm not Jealousy. If I'm in the book it's as you say, as Reason.'

She looked over her shoulder at the pigboy Hab, who hadn't moved away with the swine, but remained sufficiently close to the tree roots to hear what the cousins said. He caught her eye, laughed, winked, clapped his hands together, dropped his head back and let a squeal. The swine trotted to him.

'Reason,' said Berna, 'is merely Jealousy in disguise.'

Pogge pleaded that she not be angry and took her by the hand.

They passed the foragers and Berna demanded of the children their purpose. The oldest girl, who carried a baby asleep on her back, said they gathered bones for the Thomas's Day bonefire.

'You made that stinking smoke once this year already, on John Baptist's,' said Berna. 'There aren't but small bones here.'

The girl said they'd burned their best bones the first time, and Nack the hayward told them they must have a second fire, for Death bode for a fair wind from France, and must be met with bone smoke. They gathered what they could find. She took from her apron a bird's skull of an apricot's bigness. It was small, she said, but they'd been bidden not to come home till they'd got bones to the weight of her baby brother.

The demoiselles continued on their way. 'Concerning the stories of the clerks,' said Pogge, 'is there any doubt of the verity of what they say? In Bristol we're sure. It's inevitable. Everyone's afraid.'

'Here most people believe it's a ruse to enrich priests,' said Berna. 'And deny such a malady could cross the sea to England. But it pleases Cotswold peasants to pretend obedience. And some do believe. Our hayward, for example, and he has power here. Hence the bonefire.'

THE OLD PIGSTER Dor farrowed Hab, and none knew the sire. Dor spent her death pennies on Hab's christening, so when God called her forth she hadn't aught left for the fare, and Hab was left alone in the world, without no gear nor silver. He kept our swine and we kept him. As we to the high and proud, so Hab to us. He was knave to any churl. In winter he bode in Enker's cot, in summer a wattle shelter in the woods, and was deemed true enough that twice he'd driven swine to a buyer in Melksham, and come again with the silver. He danced naked in the bourne, dark as any eel, and sang and rolled in the mud with the grice.

QUERY: HAVE I been honest? Response: No. In perscribing this commentary I create a substitute for my faith in the continued existence of home.

Today I went to the feretory. Six pilgrims had risen from the pavement to press their noses to the crystal aperture protecting the nail with which the Romans fixed Christ to the cross. I imagine they who buried him cared more for his corpse than for the ferrous fragments perforating it, or for the spiny crown with which his executioners derided him, a part of which is also supposed to be in the abbey's possession. These are false relics, I suppose; yet I do not doubt that Christ was crucified. So do I not doubt that my villa outside Avignon is securely insulated from plague, even as I create these textual ephemera. The pilgrims would connect with Christ de facto did they remain at home in a state of piety and virtue, in patient expectation of his resurrection and their transmission into paradise. Yet they doubt paradise is their destination, they suspect damnation, and so prefer to frequent sanctuaries, to touch with their hands the luxurious fallacies of the cult of sacred objects.

So it is with me. It is my creed that, as I perscribe this in Malmesbury, the chanting of the fraternity perpetually audible, Judith and Marc move around the villa in Avignon in the chanting of the cicadas, picking basil and lavender, lighting the lamps, setting out wine and a volume of Ovid for my return. This is the paradise I expect. But instead of proceeding there with maximum velocity I retard myself here, perscribing. In the mode of the pilgrims, my horror of damnation intervenes with false objects. My creed is the paradise of home, but the pestilence that has not yet infected England has afflicted Avignon, and my terror is to arrive there to an absolute post-mortal silence, pure nullity, except the accumulation of cadavers, the putrefaction of familiar faces. The terror is not of my own mortality, but the mortality of those I care for, that they might perish before me, and I would be in solitude, like Adam without Eve. Best is to be certain they have not perished. But to be uncertain is better than to be certain that they have.

THE COUSINS AMBLED towards the church. 'There'll be free and villain, no gentry, just us,' said Berna. 'A place is kept for us, although my father attends mass elsewhere. It's a mean church, with an indigent curate.'

The church was so full it would have been difficult for the demoiselles to push through the entrance had the villagers not pressed themselves against the walls to let them pass. Some of the better-arrayed free women tried to meet their eyes; the rest acted as if they mightn't see them, or oughtn't, save that they stepped aside to open a way through to a bench close to the jube. There wasn't enough incense lit to cover the scents of sweat and newly laundered cloth. All talked.

In front of the jube stood a group of young men with bowstaves against their shoulders. Among them was Will Quate, who sensed the demoiselles' regard and turned his face towards them. On perceiving them he lowered his eyes and turned away.

'His is the second face out of a painture I have seen among

your common people,' said Pogge, 'although the pigboy's reminds me of Lust among the sins, whereas Will Quate looks simple and honest. There is some assurance there that all men aren't inevitably beasts, even among that sort.'

Berna regarded her cousin uncomprehendingly, and laughed. 'You favour him? He's no gentleman.'

'My father says a family that ne breeds in a peasant every third generation grows away from its proper nature.'

'Pogge, as you see, I converse with one as low as a pigboy, even cherish the boar he guards, but I wouldn't marry it. Quate ploughs and weeds for a penny a day and lives with his mother. She's villain-born, and the father free-born, so by his father's blood he should be free. But his father went to be an archer and died at Sluys, so as far as my papa is concerned, the Quate boy is unfree again.'

'And does Quate think he is free?'

'He would be free. My father prefers him to be unsure. He tells him he's at liberty, then offers him villain land to farm.'

'Is that a bow he carries?'

'After Crécy, they all practise archery after mass.'

'He follows his father.'

'Papa is supposed to send an archer for the Calais garrison, but Quate is to marry the village beauty, Ness. She lost a child in March, probably his, so he's not such an angel. Anyway, Quate mayn't go to France, so that beefy person next to Quate, the miller's son, he's going.'

Pogge whispered in Berna's ear: 'You should go. You desire to go to France so fiercely, and have already pierced the heart of a man with five arrows.'

'Par amour, par amour,' whispered Berna. 'It was Love that shot those arrows; all I may do is make him apprehend the value of the pain.'

Hab came of the wood at noon and made Enker, by his craft, bide at the lichgate. He came in the churchyard and went to the outer door of the church, which stood open, the inner door wedged wide by us that thrang there. Hab listened a handwhile to the priest through the open doors. The qualm would come to Gloucestershire, the priest said, to pine lewd folk for their sins.

Hab came away from the church door to where the Fishcombe women had left their gear ready to sell their wares after mass. He put the market boards on their trestles under a tree and sang

> To whom should I, the wolf said,
> Tell of my sins ere I am dead?
> Here ne is nothing alive
> That me could here now shrive.

The women came out of church with baskets of cheese and orchard stuff. Hab said he'd set their boards under the tree so they'd be in shade and they gave him a garlicle, a thick long stalk with fat red cloves below. He took it to the bowman's field and sat on his haunches to bide till the bowmen came.

It was the first Sunday since the field was mown, the best time for bowmen, when the weather was good but they wouldn't lose time looking for untrue arrows in the long grass. Four came from church to shoot, and chid each other as they went.

Those days, with Calais won for England, high folk lacked Lord Berkeley that he ne met his due of fresh bowmen to man the walls of the town so the French ne take it again. As the high folk stirred Berkeley, so he stirred his under-lords, and so Sir Guy stirred us for a bowman to join Hayne Attenoke's Gloucestershire score when it went by Outen Green, Calais-bound.

Will Quate was our best with bow, but he was to wed Ness Muchbrook. Some gnof had got her with child, and she went to Santiago de Compostela with her mother, and came back a fortnight after, not great no more, with a likeness of St Margaret stamped on a littlewhat of tin. We ne knew how long it took to wend to Spain and back, but we believed it to be further. Maybe, the godsibs said, she ne fared to Spain. Maybe she went to see a woman in Bristol who knew how to make the unborn never-born.

Some of us reckoned Will Quate the sire of the get, as we'd seen them hop together at other folk's weddings, but most of us reckoned it was Laurence Haket, Sir Guy's kinsman, who was his guest when the get was gotten.

Anywise, Will and Ness were betrothed, and besides, the greater deal of us ne deemed Will a free man, so us thought Cockle, the miller's son, was the man for Calais. He was free and full barst to go, to wear the iron cap and drink wine and know the French maids. When he told his father he was going, his father called him a dote and smote him on the ear. But now Cockle'd shifted his mood. He'd met a pedder of Bath who told him the qualm was right fell in France, and all the French were in hell anywise, without his help. So he wouldn't go. And when he told his father, his father called him a canker and smote his other ear.

Sim, the master-bowman, who lost an eye to one of Despenser's churls when we weren't mostly born, said Cockle was a wantwit.

'I'm a free man,' said Cockle. 'I'll live as it likes me.'

'It needs find a bowman by Michaelmas, and I'm too old,' said Sim.

'I'd go,' said Whichday Wat, 'only my wife's got great, and the youngest is sick, and the ox is lame.'

They looked at Will.

'He mayn't go,' said Cockle. 'He's not free. He's bound to the manor.'

They heard a stir in the middle of town, over by the green. The priest flew out of the church in his mass-gear and ran toward the hooting, followed by his altar boys. The bowmen went to see, out-take Will, who bode in the field and shet an arrow at the mark.

THE MARK WAS a gin of straw and wattle meant to be in the likeness of a French knight, and the arrowhead blunt. But when the arrow struck the mark a keen cry of sore seemed to come of it, and a long, low moan. Will looked round and saw Hab on his haunches in the shade of the yew tree. Hab dropped his hand off his mouth and laughed. 'Mind when I made Bob Woodyer think his cow could speak, and the cow told him she was the angel Gabriel, and God had hidden a golden crock in her arse?' he said.

'And Bob went about all week beshitten to the armpit,' said Will.

Hab held the garlicle out, the stalk thick and right and the cloves red and full.

Will unstrung his bow, set it against the tree and sat by Hab. He took the garlicle, ran a thumbnail down the garlic sack and slote the rind. He bade Hab put out his hand and pushed the cloves into it. He told seven, white and clean. Hab did six in his bag and one in his mouth. He chewed and said: 'I lack sweet meat to clean my breath.'

'There's none,' said Will.

'There is, would you give it me. A kiss.'

Will laughed and shook his head.

'I showed you where the white owl nested,' said Hab. 'You helped me when they'd tie me to a post and throw sticks at me like to a Shrovetide cock.'

'We aren't little knaves no more,' said Will. 'Find a maid to kiss. She'll share your bed and cook for you.'

'If we're all to die ere Martinmas, as the priest says, those as have sins to sin must sin them soon.'

'The priest will say aught to sell candles.'

'Am I not dear to you?'

'You aren't so dear to me as you'd like, not nearly.'

Hab narrowed his eyes. 'I saw you kiss Whichday,' he said.

'I kissed him on the cheek when he'd been to Tewkesbury. I hadn't seen him a week.'

'So then you may.'

'When I meet a friend I lack.'

'My old friend!' said Hab. 'I haven't seen you for so long. Kiss me!' He dabbed at Will's mouth with his. Will laughed, curled up like a hedgehog and trendled himself away.

Hab thrust out his underlip. 'I wouldn't that you leave our town, and I left alone,' he said. 'I'd swim with you again, and dry in the sun with you, my head on your chest.'

'That's gone.'

Hab mirthed again. 'It needs do better than Ness,' he said. 'Her eyes aren't in a right line, and her neb's whirled like to the full moon. Would you not take me, take my sister.'

'You haven't no sister.'

'I have a sister, and the sight of you gladdens her. Her name is Madlen, and she'd leave town with you and not come again, even to France.'

'You haven't no sister,' said Will again. 'You haven't no kin. You bide alone with Enker in the wood.'

'Madlen's fair like May morning, and you'll meet her, and she'll prove your bowmanship.'

Will said he wouldn't talk to Hab no more. He left him in the churchyard and went to the green.

THE STIR WAS made by two friars of Gloucester. One drove a cart and the other banged a drum. The priest came to fight them, for none but he had the right to shrive the folk of Outen Green, and he'd rather die than see Christ's love sold cheap, or for a halfpenny less than he sold it, anywise.

But the friars, unwashed and deep yet bright of eye, came to sell other than forgiveness. Their cart was heaped with wood and tin likenesses of our Clean Mother. They showed us how to fill a likeness with holy water that the water seep from holes in her eyes, and she weep two days on our threshold till spent, and how, were a candle put in the hole in her womb, the tears would shine as jewels to shield us of night-death, and how it was our last hope to get a likeness, for the friars wouldn't come again. They'd sworn to bide in a hermitry in the Malverns, eating not but dry bread while they prayed to God to forgive mankind. The fee was a bare sixpence, eleven pence for two, and any that took three likenesses, the friars said, might pay but a penny for the third.

Most folk, out-take Nack, reckoned the qualm was a tale the priests wrought up to wring out our silver. We ne thought us Christ so stern as to slay us by sickness when he took so many in the

23

great hunger thirty winter before. But we wouldn't that the priest weened we unworthed him, so we bought likenesses.

The friars said they had an errand from Hayne Attenoke in Gloucester. Hayne bade them tell town and manor his score of bowmen would fare by Outen Green early on Tuesday, the day after next, and they looked to meet their new man on the Miserden road that same afternoon.

THE MANOR SENT Anto the reeve to Will. Anto found him in the high half of the top meadow, shooting mark arrows at rags dropped by little knaves. When Will hit a rag at one hundred yard the knaves walloped out over the stubble, yall as them thought French knights would shout with an arrow in their gullet, and threw themselves on the ground, merrily slain.

Anto said their lord must send a bowman to Calais, and none might go but Will.

'I'd go gladly,' said Will, 'but I mayn't. I'm needed at harvest, I'm to wed Ness Muchbrook, and Sir Guy ne deems me a free man.'

'They'll crop the fields without you,' said Anto. 'You'll wed Ness next summer, when you come again from France, laden with silver.'

'I mayn't go unfree,' said Will.

'Your lord deems you free,' said Anto. 'I heard it from his own mouth.'

'Deemed he me free, he wouldn't offer me no bound acres to farm.'

'You ne know the stead you stand in,' said Anto. 'You've no thank for the blessings the Almighty and Sir Guy send. You've not but eighteen winter and you've two worthy brothers to keep your mother, you're betrothed to the sweetest burd in Outen Green, and your lord, out of the kindness of his heart, bestows on you a cot and ten good acres to farm when you're wed. And here you're offered the speed of a fare to fight in France, such as any bold young man would yearn for, and it's sikur Sir Guy deems you free. How else might he let you go?'

'A bound man on his lord's errand is bound yet, fares he to the brim of the world,' said Will. 'Go I to France, come home again and farm those acres, I were still bound to Sir Guy, for I still owed him two days' work in six.'

Anto's face lost hue and he no longer seemed to have himself in wield. He asked Will, in a steven like to he was choked, what then he'd have his lord do.

'Let him give me an inch of hide with the words of my freedom written in ink and sealed with a gobbet of wax, for me to show all kind living clerks, that they believe my freedom true and not a tale I tell. Then I'll go to France.'

'You ne know your lowness in God's read,' said Anto. 'You'd threaten all. The higher the ape climbs, the more he shows the filth of his arse.'

ONCE, THE EXCITING friction between the textual accumulation of old wisdom and the vivacious inquiry of a new generation was to be found in monasteries like this. That vigour has moved to the universities now.

'You have a mind,' said the prior. 'Why remain a proctor, and not be a scholar or an advocate?'

'When Oxford desired me for a doctorate,' I explained, 'I expected Paris, and when Paris offered to adscribe me, my finances were debilitated. When I had saved sufficient money, I submitted myself to the preliminary examination of Paris, and was rejected.'

The prior smiled. 'You are bound for purgatory,' he said. 'You are excessively humid for infernal incineration, insufficiently lucid for celestial jubilation. On the margin of destroying humanity, the Deity created a homo novus, and you are the archetype. You are a non-decider. You neither reason nor instruct. You observe without participation. You do not reflect on the sacred mysteries. You comment on action as an alternative to action. You investigate pagan books in the library. You scribble on furtive parchment – and what do you scribble? Is it useful, or to the glorification of God?'

'Ephemera,' I said.

THE SERVANT ASSIGNED by Sir Guy to confine Berna to her chamber on her return from church admitted Pogge and closed the door behind her, permitting the cousins their privacy, if not their liberty. Pogge discovered Berna with her face pressed to the narrow ouverture that offered a view into the southern distances. She approached her and placed her hand on her shoulder but Berna ne turned, as if cloyed in the window's stone surround.

'Does your father's emollience not surprise you?' said Pogge.

'Have they persuaded you to join their party, in contravention of our bonds of amity?'

'I shall be loyal to you for eternity,' said Pogge gently. She sat on the bed. 'Your father promises to restore your usual liberties tomorrow. He permits you to retain the book in the chamber, for your consolation.'

Berna detached herself from the window. The sun had set and

the chamber was sombre in the blue afterlight, Berna an indistinct form pacing to and fro, her hands in constant motion, now on her cheeks, now combing her hair, now on her hips.

'He considers me a fine animal he has already vended, and desires to maintain in good condition till the purchaser arrive,' said Berna.

'You are extremely severe in your judgement of his motives.'

'This Romance he so generously lends me,' said Berna, seizing the volume of a table, 'isn't even finished.'

'Berna, I doubt there is another demoiselle within three hours of here who is literate, and would have any non-ecclesiastical reading matter if she were.'

'This Romance,' repeated Berna, 'is not the finished article. Our poor family possesses only the first part, the part by Guillaume de Lorris, which concludes with the imprisonment of the Rose in Jealousy's castle. The greater part of the book, its completion by Jean de Meun, is absent.'

'From what I hear,' said Pogge, 'de Meun's so-called completion is a displeasant addition to another poet's romance, excessively proud in its own ingeniousness, replete with irreligious mockery and the misprizement of women. I have never comprehended who gave him the authority to declare after another poet's death that his rival's verse was unfinished, and that he should complete it.'

'So it is with people,' said Berna. 'Some girls consider themselves finished because they're comfortable with whatever base rewards their parents offer. A Bristol merchant's daughter may easily be satisfied with an allowance and a merchant's son to marry when she lacks the imagination to realise how incomplete she is.'

The chamber was still for several moments, save the evening chants of the birds and Pogge weeping. Berna returned to her place at the window, blocking what little light remained.

'I mayn't attend my amour no longer,' said Berna. 'I shall journey to him.'

27

'I know I haven't your courage and imagination,' sniffed Pogge. 'I ne present myself as no example.'

Berna went to the door and demanded a candle of the servant. She took the light and went to sit with Pogge. 'Pardon me my cruelty,' she said. 'My rigour towards you is a sign of my inquietude. Will you aid my escape?'

'I would prefer to aid you in a change of heart,' said Pogge. 'Your severity to me bears a greater resemblance to your real nature than your acceptance of the role of the lover's Rose. I'm not persuaded by your reliance on poet's language to justify your strange intentions. To say Love's arrows have crippled Laurence, to say he is Love's vassal, has the odour of Guillaume de Lorris, not Bernadine. As I remember, Love possessed a sixth arrow, one he never used.'

'The arrow named Frankness,' said Berna.

'That arrow is more characteristic of you, I would judge. The arrow that issues of a rose with a voice.'

'I am best placed to judge my own sentiments.'

'As my mother says, one is often the last to know one's own roof is on fire.'

WILL SHET TILL the shadows were long. He unstrung his bow, put the arrows in his belt, plucked a cluster of loving-Andrew and went down the hill to town. He went by the fields to the back road and in through the Muchbrooks' orchard gate. Ness's deaf eldmother Gert, who when she was young had seen the king ride by at hunt like a giant, on a white horse, with gold stars on the harness, sat and span by the back door. The sun had set and the new moon shone. Ness came out bearing one of the friars' likenesses, with a candle set in it. The Holy Mother of God wept. The light of the candle made a loop of hair between Ness's forehead and her head-cloth's hem gleam gold. She set the likeness down next to Gert and came to Will. He gave her the blossoms.

'Do you truly go to France on Tuesday?' she asked.

'Does Sir Guy give me a deed of freedom, yeah. To come again next summer with silver, a free man, and we'll be wed.'

'Your dad ne came again.'

'I ne go to fight as he did. I go to hold a town already won.'

The blue leaves of the blossoms shook. 'If you so yearn for freedom, why bind yourself to me?'

'I need a wife, and you're the best I know, and the fairest, and go I to France, to Italy, to Jerusalem, I won't find better.'

'Freedom's dearer to you than I,' said Ness. 'You would I were your chattel, like the silver you hope to win in France.'

'Why so wrathful?' asked Will. 'Aren't you my sweetheart no more?'

Ness looked into his eyes and smiled unevenly. 'My heart yearns for sweetness of you, and you ne give it. Last year you ne heeded me, so I went with Laurence Haket, to egg you on with a show of liking another. And Haket was weary of playing the lover to the lady Bernadine, so he hungered for it. But he japed me.'

'I was ashamed to live so meanly,' said Will. 'I'd better my lot before I asked to wed you.'

'Laurence Haket sang to me in French,' said Ness. 'He told me truelove things, and made me laugh, and I would kiss him; but to kiss him were wrong. And it was like to when I was a little girl. Mum made an apricot pie, and left me with it, and forbade me eat even one deal of it. But I ate one deal, because it needed me a sweet thing, and after I'd eaten one deal, I was already damned, and might as well eat the whole pie.'

'I forgive you all that,' said Will.

'Am I to owe you everlastingly for forgiveness?' said Ness. 'Your forgiveness is but another name for the right my sin gives you to wed me without loving me, to have a wife and freedom at the same time.'

'My brothers told me maids were unkind and dizzy, but I ne believed it before,' said Will. 'I won't burden you no more.' He went to the gate.

Gert, who maybe wasn't as deaf as folk said, got to her feet, pulled the headcloth off Ness's head that her gold hair glew in the candlelight, and said: 'Would you leave such a hoard to go to France?'

'I mayn't take her with me,' said Will, and went home.

His brothers were awake. They chid him that he vexed Sir Guy with his proud asks, when the lord had almost forgiven the town for the theft of his daughter's gown, and was about to feast them all for her wedding. Went Will to Bristol, they said, he'd see the street thick with men of the land who'd gone seeking freedom and found it begging at a merchant's door. Any dog, they said, was free to starve.

The stir woke their mother, who saw Will and buried her neb in her hands.

Will left them, clamb the hill and sat in the top meadow, looking down on the town under the moon. All had lit candles in the likenesses they'd bought, and filled them with holy water, and from one end to another the town sparkled with the bright falling tears of the Holy Mother.

Feet trod on the cropped grass behind him.

'I know you, Hab,' said Will, but he ne turned.

A mouth breathed on Will's neck, a side crowded his back, and a hand reached inside his shirt, where it lay against his chest.

'How may you know I'm Hab, and not Hab's sister Madlen, or some other?' came a whisper.

30

'I know your walk, and your steven, and the feel of your hand.'

'Hab and Madlen are brother and sister,' came the whisper. 'You mayn't know which I am.'

'It's one of two?'

'Yeah.'

'You haven't no sister.'

'Likes you my hand on your skin?'

'It ne baits me.'

'My hand may hold your pintle.'

'Ding you bloody if I feel it.'

'Yeah, were I Hab. And were I Madlen?'

'I'm betrothed.'

'You wouldn't ding me if I were a maid?'

'It ne likes me to ding no maid.'

'Let there be such a qualm as the priest says, and all die out-take you and I, and we be the only folk left in the world – would you take me then, as you say you would take Ness?'

'Never, so long as you be Hab.'

'And as her sister, the fair Madlen?'

'Look!' said Will, showing the sky and the town with his finger. 'Like to the town be a great lake, and all the Holy Mother's tears the folk have bought the likeness of the stars come again of the water. I would see the sea at night. Dad said the sea's so great the light of all the stars come of it again.'

'You speak as if the thing you yearned for more than any other were to leave this town. And yet you didder about with Ness and deeds of freedom like to you lack the strength to have your will.'

'Ness said freedom was dearer to me than she.'

'She's right.'

'I wouldn't hurt her.'

'Then stint at home. But if you would go and know the world

and the sea, you must hurt her, and it were better you hurt her hard and quick than long and steady.'

'I would not.'

'It's more kindly. Have her and walk away without a word, if you're bold enough. Let her deem you a wretch, that she ne care so much you're gone.'

MARC, EVEN IF this is not humanity's final hour, it is improbable that you and I will survive the imminent calamity. If these texts have been transmitted to you, it signifies that I have expired; as I perscribe it, you may already be entombed. We here in Malmesbury – the clerics, if not the common people – accept that the pestilence has devastated Avignon, and Provence, and Italy, and must inevitably perflow to this insular location. In the event that I succumb and you survive, transfer these commentaries to the library at Senanque. All other post-mortem instructions are to be invented in my final testament, located in the signed scrine in partition vii of my analogium.

PS Examine my Latin for errors of syntax and vocabulary and make the necessary corrections. Reject the temptation to edit.

PPS Purge my debt to the fishmonger – iii sols, as I remember, or the equivalent in candles if he has perished – and apologise to him or his heirs for my intemperate assertions on the quality of his sardines.

My regards to your wife. I have a presagitation that Judith is secure.

Thomas

On Monday, the holiday, it seemed to us Will had lost everything, for we heard he'd fallen out with his betrothed and his kin, and no word had come from the manor about his proud ask. Folk said Sir Guy would withdraw his offer of land. It seemed Will's pride would leave him worse off than before, without a bride, without acres, without the speed of a fare to France. He'd lost the freedom he'd always had, in his fellows' eyes at least, by seeking to get a clerk to write it down.

All liked Will, but we were glad to see him lowed. We would not that he got his deed. Most of us that were free hadn't no deed to say so; got he one, would that make us less free than he? And what of the bondmen? Got Will a deed, were it like to he deemed all bondmen worthless churls that they ne durst ask for one themselves?

Will ne looked ever so alone as in church, for Ness ne seemed to mind him, but kept her eyes to the ground and her fingers knit together with a string of beads. The Muchbrooks ne looked at the Quates, and the Quates ne looked at the Muchbrooks, out-take Will, who turned his head her way at the saecula saeculorum.

After mass the priest led us out of church and downhill. We bore the likenesses of St George, St Andrew and St Michael, and Rob the deacon bore the oaken rood with the likeness of our Maker nailed to it, and Whichday and Cockle and Tom the smith and Bob Woodyer bore the likeness of our Clean Mother in her blue kirtle with her fair white face shined with wax and lambswool and lips hued red. The knaves rattled sheep knuckles in boxwood cans and we sang

> *Domine Maria I have in mind*
> *Whereso I wend*
> *In well or in woe*

We came up to the bonefire and the priest bade us kneel and hold up our hands to heaven. The priest stretched his fingers over us and spoke in Latin and then a bead in English asking Christ to ward us of ferly death.

Then Nack came forward and un-knit the cloth around the horsepanthing and set it on the pole pitched in the middle of the heap of bones. No smith of Outen Green hadn't made no horse-panthing since the ill crops of the old king's day, and most of us hadn't seen one. Tom put a little nail in the horsebone for each soul in Outen Green, edging the eye and nose pits with nail heads as to make it seem the horse were undergirt with iron when it was quick in our fields.

We tinded clouts soaked in pitch and cast them on the bonefire and it was fired and burned and black smoke ran off the bones. It stank all day and darkened the sky. Evening it dwined to ashes, and though we ne yet knew would Will outgo, the ploughmen set up a board for a bowman-ale in the churchyard, and some of our shepherds came.

It ne fetched but six shilling for Will's shrift, and we ne knew would it be spent, for there wasn't no word of Sir Guy, and none nad seen him. Whichday fetched his pipes and Buck the warrener his gittern and they played Guy Came Out of Warwick, The Maid of Cardiff, Three Strings and a Reed, The Mirthful Sparrow, Green Grow the Rushes, The Fiend and the Gleeman, My Love Yed to Fair Gloucester, The Oak Is Hoar and The Ram Would Have Good Wether. A few maids came by and we hopped with them.

When the moon was high, Whichday and Will ran and fetched Whichday's ox and hitched it to a plough and they began to plough the duck pond, saying when they'd ploughed it they'd sow it with duck eggs, and in a fortnight crop baked duck.

'Pogge. Pogge! Are you asleep?'

'Yes.'

'I'll take bread with me, and a veil for my face. And a blanket. It may be necessary to sleep in the forest.'

'You won't sleep in no forest, for you won't go nowhere, and on Saturday you'll be married.'

'Pogge, I have no money. I mayn't travel without money.'

'All the more reason why I shouldn't lend you none.'

'One night's lodging on route, and stabling for Jemsy.'

'Your father's horse?'

'Two florins should cover it. I'll repay you double when we're safe in Calais.'

'The larger part of femininity, if they may not marry him they love, will take the marriage, then try to return to their amour in secret once their social and financial position is secure.'

'Pogge! How can you make such monstrous pronouncements? You evidently consider the larger part of femininity to be a branch of the sorority of prostitutes. A woman who permits a man she ne loves to possess her as a secret route to her real amour? Haven't sufficient virgins been martyred rather than surrender to such advances?'

'You summon the saints to justify your aversion to marriage, and the poets to justify your passion for the lover who provokes that aversion. You ne permitted me to finish. I spoke of the larger part of femininity. There is another part, whose members will

joyfully allow themselves to be stolen from their families by a
gallant lover before they may be married to a lubber of their
parents' preference.'

'Yes! That's I!'

'No, Berna. Laurence hasn't come to steal you. When he was
here I'm sure he played the lover par amour very well. You ne
know to whom he played before, nor to whom he plays now.'

'You won't make me cry, Pogge, although I know you wish it.'

'He hasn't come to steal you, so you've determined to steal
yourself, and deliver yourself to him, wherever he is.'

'Wiltshire,' came Berna's voice, small and rageous in the darkness.

'I shan't lend you no florins, but so long as you're disposed to
steal, you may have one of my gold nobles.'

'Where are they?'

'In my purse. Remember, I am measurable.'

Berna laughed and stretched, holding her arms straight back behind
her head and clenching and unclenching her fingers and toes. It was
hot and they lay on the bed without covers. 'I shan't never let no
one measure me,' she said.

TODAY I INQUIRED of the prior if he sensed the pestilence were
the Deity's final act with respect to his human creation. Would
humanity be extinguished?

'I predict,' said the prior, 'that you will perish. So Deuteronomy.
And the music will cease, and the candles of the abbey will be
extinguished, and its columns ruptured, and the Deity will abolish
light, so that were a single member of humanity to survive, he
would not possess the means to testify to its ruin.'

'What of the last man?' I said to the prior. 'Who will receive his confession?'

'We assume the final human to be male, but man's was the prime nativity,' said the prior. 'Why should man be the last to die? Why should the final human not be female? Why should Adam not perish before Eve, and none remain except Eve for him to confess to? Eve's was the primal vice, the rapture of the fruit. Were not it just for the last person left on earth, unconfessed, unabsolved, to be female?'

'A terrible solitude for any human,' I said, 'to have no society except their conscience.'

'Terrible and anticipated,' said the prior. 'Be cognisant that Canterbury determines the situation to demand an exceptional regulation, that in extremis the female may take confession from the male.'

NB Marc, the Dante by my bed belongs to one Konrad Schadland of Mainz. Do all in your power to return it, with a request that he absolve me.

IN THE MORNING Will asked his brothers if there'd been word from the manor, and they told him no, he must earn his bread with his back bent like any poor man, for it was a working day.

He took his weeding bill and stick, went by the back road to the demesne land, whet his bill and set to cropping golds and poppies in Sir Guy's acres under corn. We saw him there hooded against the sun. He went inch by inch along the rows, set the fork and swung the bill and cropped the weeds one by one, right and steady. Behind him went a heap of small girls who gathered the blossoms that flew of his blade, and two thack-pot knaves to scare the crows. He ne saw nor heard Anto till the reeve was nigh behind him and spoke his name.

Anto asked him sharply why he was bent over the dirt in the sun when he must be on the highway to France that afternoon.

'I mayn't go till I hear from my lord,' said Will.

'Thinks you he comes out to the field in the sun to make his ends known to a hired man?' Anto turned and went again to the manor house, fetching dust of the ground with his busy steps.

Will stood still and beheld him, tools hung from his hands.

Over his shoulder Anto called: 'Would you be a free man and go to Calais, or sweat a scarecrow's steading in the corn?'

Will ran after him to the manor house. The knaves followed and banged the pots, and the girls held up their barmcloths filled with blossom heads, but they stinted at the bridge across Sir Guy's ditch, while Anto and Will went through the gate.

THEY WENT THROUGH Sir Guy's hall, through laths of sunlight that came in through the narrow windows. The hall looked sluttish still after the masons of Coventry came the year before, took Sir Guy's hearth off its old stead in the middle of the floor and set it under a brick pipe they called a chimney. A wonder gin it would've been had they fulfilled it, and two more chimneys at either end of the manor, but they went away when Sir Guy stinted the silver, to buy his daughter's gown that was stolen.

Anto bade Will leave his tools outside and led him through the new door at the west end of the hall and into a room. It hadn't no stead for bed nor dogs nor food-stuff, only a board and chair and chests and a cherrywood rood with a likeness of our Maker pined by his own weight. Sir Guy called it his privy chamber, chamber being room or cot or steading, and privy being that none of his household was to go in out-take him. When we'd asked Anto why Sir Guy would make a room to be alone in, if he ne slept there, Anto said he read the leaves of books, of which he had three or more, and wrote letters, and drank wine with the priest, and played dice with the high-born, and hid him from his daughtren.

Sir Guy sat on the chair at the board in hunting gear with one hand on his morning wine-crock and the other on the neck of the old alaunt, Canell. Nack the hayward stood on one side of him and Anto went to stand on the other. Will stood before them with his hands clasped, and bent and lifted his head. The three mole-hued greyhounds, Fortin, Pers and Starling, crope about like to one dog with three tails. Behind Sir Guy was a window scaled in glass and iron and at his left hand a brass box.

'Ruth to lose a good ploughman ere harvest,' said Sir Guy. 'Worth it yet, do the French learn a Cotswold man can draw a bow as deep as any. The English archer's the best on God's mould, all be one in two a thief, and one in ten a murderer. You need to be quick, though, to be on the road by afternoon.'

Will said, always calling Sir Guy his lord, that he mightn't go without a deed of freedom.

Fortin squatted and laid a turd in the nook and Sir Guy got up and went to him and pressed the dog's nose to it. 'Is that my thank for the rabbit liver you get of your master?' he asked.

Anto said if Sir Guy would yield to Will's ask, the fee mightn't be less than five pound. The Muchbrooks nad paid the two pound owed by Ness, the lord's bondwoman, for lying with Will when they weren't wed; and to wed her Will must then pay his lord another pound for the loss of the bound children she wouldn't never bear the manor.

Sir Guy straightened and pulled his lip. 'The kind bonds that knit men together should rather be meted in love than ink and silver,' he said. 'The old wise me liked, when the lord feasted his men and shielded them with his sword arm, and they wrought the lord's land for faithfulness alone, like the bond between father and son, when each was thankful to the other, and each gave the other worthship.'

Anto said Will was a thankless churl. The world was up-half down, and kind wit ne need look far to see what drove God to loose the pest.

'Man ne owes to deem his maker,' Sir Guy said.

He sat and opened the box. He took out a calfskin scrow, a feather and an inkpot and laid them on the table. He set the feather at Will.

'Anto was wrong to say five pound was the fee for your freedom,' he said. 'You may hear me say you're free for nothing. But ink and wax and calfskin is law, and law costs silver. Do you have five pound?'

Will said he hadn't.

'How then might you buy the deed?'

Will said he couldn't buy it, and would go back to weeding Sir Guy's field, and Hayne Attenoke would lack one bowman.

'I hope you're no stirrer,' said Sir Guy. 'That's the shortest way to the gallows.'

Will said he ne stirred aught but the salt in his peas.

Sir Guy gave a kind of laugh, like to a pig found a fresh acorn. 'I mayn't give you the deed shot-free, but I'll send it to my kinsman Laurence Haket, who's been enfeoffed near Calais. Enfeoffed, understand? They gave him land. I'll give you a letter for him, to bid him give you the deed once you've earned enough to buy it. You'll find five pound and more in France. An English archer in France gets silver as lightly as a knave getting apples of a widow's orchard.'

He held out his hand to Will and Anto bade Will kneel and kiss it and Will did as he was bidden.

Sir Guy said to rise, and lifted him, as if it were Will's wish to bide on his knees. 'Do me one errand on the way,' he said.

He took a mouthful of wine and opened the box and dalve in it, but couldn't find what he looked for. He went to the window and turned a key and the scales of glass set in iron swung out like a door. There was a garden beyond with green grass cropped short and a spring-well. Sir Guy's younger daughtren played there with Bridget the housekeeper and the lord's nift Pogge. Sir Guy called out to Bridget and in a handwhile a wench put through the window a stitch of cloth that gleamed where the sun caught it.

Sir Guy laid it on the board. On a white field were sewn scarlet roses and white lilies in silken thread. One hem was sewn in gold, and golden blazes ran through the field.

'It was of such cloth my daughter's gowns were made,' he said. 'The gown that was stolen and the second, that she'll wear for her wedding. Keep your eyes and ears open, and get you tidings of the stolen gown, send word back to Outen Green, and we'll muster men, fetch the thief and hang him.'

They sent Will out and in a stound Anto came to him with the letter, folded to the muchness of a hand and sealed with a grot of wax. Anto thacked him on the shoulder and said it was done, and he must be on the high road for France in three hour, and to gather his gear and ready his sins for church.

NACK STINTED US at the church door and let Will in and the priest's knaves stripped him naked and washed him with holy water while the priest sang Latin and swung a crock of smoking reekles.

On the eve, Nack had gone to our women and told them we

owed to see Will geared such that we not be shamed if he went forth, for whatever weird bode him in the south, in him wasn't his worth alone, but ours. Now Nack came in with fresh clothes the women had sewn for Will, a shirt and breech with rood stitch on the hem, a grey kirtle, red hose and a red hood. We cleaned his shoon, that he'd bett with thick leather under-halves for a far fare, and we thrang into church.

Each of us was there. Even Sir Guy and his folk, that took their mass at Brimpsfield Priory, were in their stead by the south wall. We lacked only the lady Bernadine, who, us thought, would rather hight herself for her wedding, and Hab, who minded the pigs.

The priest came away from the altar and we kneeled for the confiteor. The priest called Will near and Will kneeled at his feet. The priest bade him clasp his hands together, bent to whisper in his ear and listened while Will whispered in his. We'd hear Will's sins, but couldn't, for he spoke too soft. He got shrift, and was shriven clean, and came away from the priest with his cheer clean and shining, and the women wept.

The priest came down from behind the rood-pale and led Will by the wrist to the likenesses on the north wall. On any other day we ne heeded the likenesses. We knew them too well. Yet now, tight together in the candle stink, it were as if we'd seen what they showed. When the priest spoke of Christ it were like to he told of a kinsman who'd gone out of Outen Green and fell in with uncouth churls that ne knew his worth, and scorned and slew him. It were like to we stood in the garden in Jerusalem, and smelled onion on false Judas's breath when he kissed us in the murk, and felt the chill on our bare backs when the shirt was torn of it, the smart of flesh when the knotted rope struck, the uncouth spit wet on our faces, the weight of the rood like to a house-cruck, the hawthorns that pricked our brows and the nails that went between our hand-bones and foot-bones. It were like to we were pitched in the wind to hang like flesh on the butcher's hook. And we saw him rise to heaven, like lightning shotten upward of the earth.

The priest went again to the altar. When the sacring bell rang we shoff up against the rood-pale and went on our knees and lifted our hands. Some of us saw our Maker in the priest's hands and they at the back yall at the priest to lift our Lord higher. Buck and Whichday took Will by the arms and lifted him up out of the heap of folk, that he got good sight of Christ, for he that saw the Lord was shielded were he reft ferly of life. Then the priest ate Christ's flesh, and drank of his blood.

After mass Will went from hand to hand, for each of us would wish him well, and give him some thing or useful word. His mother dight her hands on his cheeks and made a show of a smile, for she'd sworn to hold back her tears till he was gone.

Will walked away up the road with his pack on his back and his bowstaff in his right hand, the children after him. They stinted at the top field wall, and Will clamb over it, and ne looked again, and we couldn't see him afterwards. That was how Will Quate left Outen Green.

When he'd gone we minded how mild he was with the old and children, how good a neighbour, how right he sowed and ploughed and sheared, how it comforted to see his cheer behind an ox-gang in the rain and hear his feet breaking ice in the puddles on the back road on a winter morning. We felt bare shame to let such strength and manship go, with his neb like an angel's. And we felt bare glad the Green had such an offering to make. It lightened us to think us strong enough to send so handy a man away to where, the priest said, the Fiend had free hold. Let the world see, we kept no jewel back.

SOMEONE CRIED THE pigs were loose, and we ran to shield our orchards, and called for Hab, but he wasn't there.

Whichday and Cockle bode at the church, and when the priest came out, Whichday went to him and said the night before he'd had a dream of Will walking through a cornfield ahead of him, but Will wouldn't turn when he called, and did the priest know the meaning?

The priest was a ploughman's son like us, who'd gotten Latin of the Gloucester monks. He said many men dreamed of their corn before harvest, and Whichday most likely feared hail.

Whichday said it wasn't that. He lacked Will, and wished they hadn't let him go. He'd know where he was, and what he did, and how he fared. Wasn't there, he asked the priest, a way to ward dreams, to reach what you sought of them, not to be at the dream's bidding?

The priest said man's lot wasn't to choose his dreams, nor win of them, and dreams fell upon us, like wild deer in darkness, while we slept. Yet there were some folk who warded their dreams, as shepherds warded sheep, and kept them as easy by day as by night, and won of them, as of their herd shepherds won wool. These folk, he said, were called writers, and they were close to the Fiend.

Yet, he said, there were holy among them. He told us he'd met a book in the getting of his priest-lore, a book by a man of Italy, about the life of Christ, and in this book was written of deeds by our Lord that weren't in the gospel.

Like for one the gospel told how the Fiend tempted our Maker in the desert, and how Christ fasted, but the gospel ne told whence came the meat with which Christ's fast was broken. So the man of Italy wrote a thing that seemed what our meek and simple son of

44

God might do, that Christ bade angels fly to his mother's house and fetch meat of her, and Christ, wrote the man of Italy, ate alone in the desert, with angels to serve him.

Whichday and Cockle were astoned. Cockle asked had Christ in truth sent home for meat to break his fast?

The priest said we mightn't know, for the man of Italy ne wrote of what was true, nor what wasn't true, but what might be true, by his conning of the lifelodes of men, and the things and deeds he minded, that he crafted with his mastery of dreaming into a likeness of truth.

Cockle said the man of Italy was a liar.

The priest pulled Cockle's sleeve and asked was the seamstress who made it a liar, for making a thing out of flax in the likeness of another sleeve, and calling it a sleeve?

Cockle said he'd like to see a man ride to Brimpsfield on the likeness of a horse.

The priest bade Cockle beware to call those who made likenesses liars, for the gospel told us how our Lord made man in his own likeness. And Cockle shouldn't rue the way he was, for God had made so many likenesses of himself, it wasn't no wonder his fingers slipped once in a while.

All this time Whichday stood and stared about and played with the two hairs on his chin. He said he would ward his dreams that night. He would make a likeness of Will Quate.

THE WORLD

WILL WENT THROUGH the wood beyond the wall till Outen Green was hidden from his sight. The sun's light beshone the path in flecks. The boughs of the trees were still and the only sound was birdsong, Will's feet on the earth and the creak of the pack straps on his kirtle.

Deep in the wood, the shapes of a man in white and a great dark deer seemed to go ahead of him, and he stinted, and they weren't there, and he went on.

Feet came quick behind him, twigs cracked, and Ness came, neb red of running. She threw her arms around Will and bade him bide longer.

'I must go,' said Will. 'I'll come again in a year, if you'll have me.'

'I'll have you,' said Ness. She took him by the shoulders and looked him in the eye. 'Swear you won't be killed by no French. Swear you won't sicken of no qualm.'

Will swore it.

Ness fumbled in her barmcloth, took out a tin token and gave it to Will. 'It's St Margaret,' she said. 'She was swallowed by the Fiend in the shape of a firedrake, and after it swallowed her the firedrake barst, and Margaret stepped out of the skin unhurt, with every hair in its stead, and the Fiend was ashamed to have been beaten by a maid.'

'I would you kept her,' said Will.

'She's done her work for me,' said Ness, and shut Will's fingers on the token. 'I got her in an uncouth land, where I went with a child in my womb, and I came back heal without it. Where's your freedom?'

Will showed her the letter, and Ness turned it in her hands, and rubbed the seal against her lips to feel the smoothness of the wax.

'It's but the deed of a deed,' said Will. 'The freedom will be redeemed by one in Calais.'

He took her hand and led her off the path to a dim stead under a low oak branch, horseshoed by holly. He set down his bowstaff and took off his pack and stroked Ness's tits through her kirtle. She kissed him and put her tongue in his mouth and reached under his kirtle and into his breech for his pintle and stroked it. She lay on the ground on her back and pulled up her barmcloth and kirtle and shirt and pulled down her breech. Will let down his hose and breech and his pintle swung out stiff and thick. 'It's a fair one,' said Ness. 'If you ne put it in my cunny quick as a wink, I'll die.'

Will knelt between her legs and shoff his length in and out and Ness squealed and thrashed her head about on the leaf-mould. Once Will dight, twice, thrice, four times, five, six, ten, and he stinted, and a sigh came of him.

He stood and righted his clothes and put on his pack.

'Likes you my cunny?' asked Ness. She bustled to him on her knees and put her arms about him.

Will ne spoke. He shoff her away roughly. His neb was red and he might not meet her eyes with his.

'What's wrong?' said Ness. 'How did it ne like you? Won't you say nothing? Won't you say you care? Won't you say goodbye?'

'I must go,' said Will. 'I'll come again next summer.'

He turned and went away. Ness might not see his tears, for he ne looked again, and she might not hear how he wept, for she sobbed so loud herself.

WILL FARED TO the high road. He wiped his eyes and nose with his sleeve. He looked one way and the other. Flies stirred about his head. He sat by the wayside, pitched a twig in the dust, looked up at the sun and made marks near the twig the length of its shadow. The shadow nad crope to the first mark when a pig grunt in the trees behind him.

Under an elm stood Hab. He wore a high-born maid's gown, made of the cloth Sir Guy had shown Will, gold and white and sewn with blossoms, and a maid's white headcloth. By his side the boar Enker cast his snout about balefully. The pig was shod for a far fare.

'You'll hang,' said Will.

'You greet a maid roughly on the first meeting,' said Hab.

'You're no maid. You're Hab the pigboy and you wear a wedding gown you stole of the lady Bernadine.'

'You mistake,' said Hab. 'Hab's not here. I'm his sister Madlen. My brother gave me the gown and went away. Ne deem you me winly in silk and gold?' He spun about with his arms stretched wide.

'I've woned in Outen Green as long as you. You haven't got no sister. You've got Hab's neb, Hab's steven and Hab's shape. You're Hab.'

'We're alike,' said Hab. 'So alike man can't know one by the other. Hab speaks high for a man, and I speak low for a maid, so we meet there. But my brother hasn't no tits, and I do, as you see, good ones.'

'You stuffed it with moss to make it seem you've got them.'

'If you ne true them, feel them,' said Hab.

Will reached with his hand.

Hab thacked his wrist hard. 'Ne be so bold, you know me but a handwhile,' he said.

'For the love of Christ, take it off and hide it in the wood before you're seen, or you'll be lolled up by morning.'

'I go out of Outen Green today,' said Hab.

'What for?'

'I go to Calais.'

'You mayn't go and you know it.'

'Why may you go and I not?'

'I'm a free man and you're bound to the manor.'

'I ne came into the world with no chain about my neck. I'll come with you to Calais. How might you go so far without a friend? Tell the bowmen I'm your wife.'

'I'm bethrothed to Ness Muchbrook.'

'She's all arse and tits. I saw you ride her and I saw it ne liked you. You were like to the woodpecker makes fast to peck a hole in a tree only so he might rest the sooner.'

'You were wrong to bid me fuck her and walk away without a kind word,' said Will. The tears came of his eyes again. 'Now my heart's sore, and so is hers, and the guilt's all mine.'

'I ne bade you do nothing,' said Hab. 'I've never met you before. That must have been my brother.'

'Fiend fetch you, you're a liar, and besides, you've no right to behold while I do to Ness what's lawful in God's sight.'

'If I ne beheld, who would? God has better things to do than see a Cotswold churl and his burd go five-legged in the woods.'

'Who learned you to deem the swive of others?'

'Hab,' said Hab.

'To learn his own sister how to swive, there can't be no sikurer way to the fire.'

'So you own he has a sister,' said Hab.

'There's no Madlen, you're Hab in the likeness of a maid, and

52

if you dare follow me, I'll ding you and fell you and leave you to lie for Sir Guy's men to find.'

He reached for Hab, like to he'd snatch the headcloth of his head, but Hab stepped back and said in a sharp steven: 'Your bowmen are coming.'

Hab ran back into the woods, Enker behind him. Hooves rang on the road.

A SCORE HORSEMEN rode toward Will. The sun found the gleam of harness in the dust they made. They rode long grey horses, tall, lean, right-boned men with fair faces, clad in grey shirts and white kirtles marked with red roods. Swords hung of their belts and each second man bore a bow on his back. They ne spoke and their eyes rested on the road ahead, like to their only longing were for the fight to come. Among them was one horse without a rider, and behind them, at the same great speed, came a two-wheeled cart hued with the likeness of St George and the worm, driven by a knave with blue eyes and a golden beard, who stood upright, gripping the reins.

Will stepped into the road and lifted his bowstaff. The bowmen ne slowed. Neither the horsemen nor the driver of the cart looked at him as they clattered by and Will must press back against the hedge not to be struck by hooves or a wheel. Will picked up his pack and ran after them, calling into the dust that he was the bowman of Outen Green who was to go with them to France. He stumbled and fell. When he was on his feet again the riders had gone behind a crook in the road. The noise of hooves and harness and the chirk of axle wasn't to be heard no more.

BERNA CONDUCTED HER horse from the forest. She hadn't had time
to assemble no baggage for the journey when she escaped from the
manor. She possessed a saddle and harness, a blanket, and the clothes
she wore when she departed.

She apperceived Will Quate by the roadside. He regarded the
distance with visage dolorous.

'Quate,' she said, 'you attend your archers, I suppose.'

He stared at her. She wore a white wimple, a veil covering her
face, and her marriage gown, gold and white and sewn with flowers.

'I would you ne looked at me in that way and manner, Quate,'
she said. 'How I choose to go about my kin and family's land is
not for you to deem or judge. I bid and command you not to tell
no one you meet on the road that you saw me here.'

Will Quate approached her, closer than a villain had ever stood,
so close she took a pace back. At first, when he saw her, he'd
appeared surprised, but now there was menace in his eyes.

'Get away from me or I'll have you beaten,' she said. But Will
Quate paid no attention.

'Thinks you,' said Will, 'you might as well be hung for a horse
as a gown?'

'How dare you address me as an equal?' said Berna.

'First you steal a gown, then you steal a horse, then you steal
the tongue of the manor. You took their words to make yourself
sound like a high-born. Or was it your swine taught you to say
"equal" and hack your speech into trim gobbets?'

'You're a lunatic,' said Berna.

'I warned you not to follow me, and now I'll ding you, but I'll
have the moss of your false bosom first.' He plunged his hand inside
her gown and firmly enclosed one breast.

Berna screamed. Will pulled his hand of her and his mouth fell open. He blenched, retreated and stammered his incomprehension; he was sure Hab had no sister, he said, he ne knew how she might be a maid.

Berna took her chance to mount her horse and ride away southward. The last she heard of Quate was of him crying for her pardon.

'Is this what happens when we leave the places we were born?' she demanded of her horse. 'That a noble lady is deprived of her authority, and a villain transformed from an obedient servant into a savage, senseless beast?'

SOON AFTER THE sound of the horse's hooves had faded, Will heard song. Four men came down the road from Gloucester in breech, shirt and thick shoon. They were white of dust, with packs and bowstaves on their backs. The singer sang in Welsh and wore a straw crown webbed with reed, pitched with stalks of pig's parsley. He had long black hair in rings, and a nose like an axe-blade, and a string of onions hung of his belt. Beside him came a short freke, thick of body, with a deep wem aslant his neb, like to his head had been cloven and put back together; and the third was a sweaty man, crooked of his burden, his mouth hung open and his eyes turned down.

The fourth was a giant, as long as two of the others together, in a hide hat under which brim his neb was shaded. Hung from his neck by a thick silver chain was a great rood bearing a likeness of the Lord of Life nailed up. The likeness was hued so wonder like a man, the pale flesh sucked in between the ribs and blood that oozed of his wounds, it seemed Christ might ferly stir and call out to them for help.

They went by Will and ne stinted. Will went after them. He asked was one of them Hayne Attenoke.

'I,' said the giant, and his steven was like to thunder in the womb of a hill. His neb was as a rocky hillside, with eyes set deep within it like coves.

'I'm the man you look for,' said Will. 'The bowman of Outen Green. I'd be of your score, and go with you to Calais.'

They ne shortened their stride. It was like to they ne heard him.

'I'm a free man,' said Will. 'Strong, heal and I shoot well.'

The bowmen ne stinted. 'We shan't take you,' said cloven-head.

'Why?' said Will. The bowmen ne answered but strode on.

'I've seen one band of bowmen go by already, and I shan't miss the second,' said Will. 'I shan't go home again but if you show me to be no bowman.'

'What band of bowmen was the first?' said cloven-head. Will told them and the Welshman laughed.

'He mistook the players for us,' he said. 'Maybe you were better as a player than a bowman. You've the face for it.'

'I'll show you I shoot true, and not in play, if you let me,' said Will.

'Have you arrows?' said cloven-head.

'I ne brought none,' said Will.

'The moon,' said Hayne, who ne slowed, and ne beheld Will.

Still ne stinting, cloven-head strung his bow, took an arrow of a cocker on his back, nocked it, found a mark to his left and shot, all in one swift stir. The arrow hit an oak stump two hundred feet away in the sheep field above the road.

'Fetch that arrow,' said cloven-head to Will, 'and if Noster ne shifts your mood, and you may shoot the arrow and hit the moon so it spins about, you can be of our fellowship.'

Will began to run toward the stump, and while he ran called out 'How can I hit the moon?'

The bowmen ne turned and ne answered, and by the time Will had gone up the field, fetched the arrow and come again to the road, all the bowmen were gone, out-take the sweaty man, who sat on a stone, drank from a flask and cursed.

HIS NAME WAS Noster. 'I'm done,' he said. 'I shan't be a bowman no more. I'll go home to the works of Dene. You owe to go home, too.'

'I shan't go home. I'd learn how I might shoot at the moon with an arrow and hit it so it spins about.'

'Mad was right,' said Noster. 'You're better fit to play a bowman than to be one.'

'Ne unworth me till you know me.'

Noster's mouth stirred like to a man who'd smile but had lost the lore. 'You ween I worth you too low,' he said. 'No, you worth us too high.' He ran his finger down the middle of his neb. 'Does the sight of Longfreke's wem ne tell you to shun the life of a soldier?'

'What's a soldier?' said Will.

'It's a French word that tokens a fighting man, who fights for silver, far from home.'

'I'd be a soldier, then,' said Will. 'I'd see uncouth lands, and win silver for my deed of freedom. My lord says an English archer in France wins silver as lightly as a knave gets apples of a widow's orchard.'

'Why so eager to steal of widows?'

'Were it so fell to be a bowman, why are you one?'

'None was there to learn me the truth when I cleaved to the score.'

'If Hayne will take me to Calais, I'll go.'

'You ne know the shape of things,' said Noster. 'Hayne's a vinter, which is to say the head of one score bowmen. Can't you tell how far Hayne falls short of twenty? Without me they're three. They've five more to pick up along the way. That's eight. Where's the leave?'

'Maybe they fear the qualm.'

Noster laughed, shook his head and spat and said: 'There's one bowman. His name is John Fletcher. He goes by the ekename Softly. In a cart he keeps a stonemason's daughter, a Frenchwoman he reft of her maidenhood in Mantes on the way to the fight at Crécy. She ne gave it willingly, nor did her kin leave him to take it but that he had to quell them first. Would you have such men as fellows?'

Will asked where Hayne stood.

'On the side of right,' said Noster.

'Then I'll stand with Hayne, and shun this Softly.'

'But Hayne ne hinders Softly. So you fare to France in a body with men who keep a stolen Frenchwoman against her will.'

'Anywise, I'll go,' said Will.

'You make your choice,' said Noster. He bade Will godspeed, and went again the way he'd come, on the road to Gloucester.

'How can I hit the moon with an arrow?' yall Will after him, but Noster ne answered. Will ne stinted no more and set off on the heels of the other bowmen.

IT IS TEMPTING to believe, as do the majority of common people here, that this island is immune to the pestilence. This island, that is, of England, Scotland and Wales, but also this island within an island, the abbey. Locally the foundation of hope is the prior. Calamity, it transpires, is the veritable patria of this inconspicuous man, who in normal times resembled an exile – obscure, ignored, uncomprehended. His firm actions give us confidence that no matter how intolerable the onus of authority, he will not fracture.

In consequence of the preceding period of extreme laxity under the abbot – was there a better example of the clerical corruption that provoked God to initiate the plague? – it was facile for the prior both to assume control from his nominal superior and to curate a restoration of the Benedictine rule, the perfect opposite to the abbot's discredited ministry: simplicity, humility and traditional discipline. The prior prohibited absolutely the consumption of quadrapeds, except to the genuinely infirm, with bipeds and fish prohibited Monday, Tuesday and Saturday. Fornicators, masturbators and sodomites to be flogged for the prime offence, excommunicated for the second, expelled for the third. Pilgrims to be admitted gratis, but to approach the feretory prostrate. Monks to remit sumptuous vestments to the almoner. Monday and Tuesday, a procession of the fraternity around Malmesbury, with urban clergy and the lay.

Most significantly: incessant music. The prior has extended the liturgy to its ancient duration. He has constructed a fortress of sacred music, in which psalms, antiphonae, versicules and responses concinnate in aural simulation of the lapidary defences of a castle.

NB Marc. Many years ago Otto requested that I transmit a petition to Cardinal Roux, and I averred to Otto that I had done so, but I did not, out of some sordid malignancy – envy, I suppose. It is an insignificant matter, certainly, but it appeared important to Otto at the time, and it perturbs my conscience. Inform Otto that I repent sincerely, desire remission, and am prepared to make restitution.

I had an important question for Judith, but I cannot now remember what it was.

WILL CAME TO an ale house, a long cot of white stone. Three goats cropped the grass by the pale and Hayne, Longfreke and Mad sat in the yard with food and drink set before them. They ne greeted him but ate and drank like to he wasn't there.

Will stood at the yard gate, strung his bow, nocked the arrow and shet it at a board hung over the ale-house eaves. The arrow struck the board with a mighty thock and the board span around twice on its pole before it came to rest.

The bowmen hearkened to the strike. Hayne rose, reached up and wrenched the arrow from where it was pitched in the board. The arrowhead had throughshove one eye of the likeness of the moon that was wrought there. Hayne smoothed the splintered wood with his fingers, dropped the arrow in a cocker and showed Will a free seat where he might sit with them.

'Sweetmouth found that likeness in France and named his ale house the Moon,' said Mad, 'but the One-Eyed Cheese likes me better.'

The brewster came and put before Will a can of ale and a bowl of eggs and peas. Will said he bore his own bread, for he lacked the silver to buy aught else. Longfreke told him fall to and they'd stand him the fee.

'What did Noster tell you of us?' asked Longfreke.

'That you'd meet more bowmen along the way,' said Will. 'One named Softly.'

'Noster told the youngster all, yet he came,' said Longfreke to Hayne.

'Let him come another mile down the highway and be founded in flight,' said Hayne.

Out of the house came a man with a full beard, naked out-take white breech with green bars. It was the bowman they called

Sweetmouth. Two little knaves followed him bearing rods of hazel. He sat on a log, straightened his back, knit his arms tight to his ribs, clenched his jaw, and said: 'Begin.'

The two young knaves, his sons, of eight or nine winter, began to hop about him and beat him with the hazel rods. Soon his skin was streaked with red weals and the knaves were breathless. They stinted often to rest and to read them which span of skin to smite next, while the man cried he was ashamed to have begotten such weaklings, and egged them to beat him faster.

'Beat him on the head!' cried Mad to the knaves. 'Let it find a use at last!'

They heeded him and whipped fast Sweetmouth's noll till it bled.

'His wife the brewster hasn't the time to beat him herself and must leave the chore to the children,' said Mad to Will.

When Sweetmouth's wife came to fill their cans and behold the children's work, Will asked what her husband had done to earn such blows.

'Nothing,' said the brewster. 'But if we ne beat him now for all the wrongs he'll do while he's away, who will?'

Sweetmouth fell on his knees on the grass and his sons dipped their hands in a stop and sprinkled water on his noll.

He rose and came up to the board with blood and water dripping of his beard. He shook hands and asked after Noster.

'Went to the iron-works of Dene again,' said Longfreke. 'Home to his mum and his burd.'

'He's a whore bitch's whelp, damned to hang by his whore tongue from the Devil's inmost arse hair,' said Sweetmouth.

'Sweetmouth means he wishes his even-bowman well,' said Mad.

'May the Fiend fuck me in the arse till my eyes weep shit if that were my meaning,' said Sweetmouth. 'Who's the featous knave? He looks like he came down of a church wall. Are you in the score? I need a fellow like you.'

61

'We're to found him betimes down the road,' said Longfreke.

Sweetmouth went into the house and came out later with the blood cleaned of him, a pewter St Christopher hung of his neck over a blue shirt, and a pack on his back. His wife stood in the doorway, the end of her barmcloth held to her mouth, her eyes sore of weeping. One of Sweetmouth's sons handed him his bowstaff. Sweetmouth rubbed the knaves' scalps with his knuckles and turned from them and the four men at board rose, nebs reddened by ale, and went on their way down the southward road.

The low sun gave the hayshocks long shadows in the cropped fields and made the bowmen squint. As they went by, the culver fowl that picked at the earth between the sheared stalks took fright, and flew into the sky, threshing the wind with their wings.

'I saw a wonder thing,' said Sweetmouth. 'A maid flew by on a dear horse like to the Fiend was at her heels. She'd hidden her neb with a cloth and wore a white gown sewn with flowers, like a king's daughter would wear to her wedding, and she was alone, without friend nor kin to shield her. A handwhile later I saw the same maid walk by through the woods near the road, in the same dress, but with her neb not hidden no more, and instead of a horse she had with her a much boar.'

'How did she ride?' asked Mad. 'Legs astride or hung off the side?'

'It walked beside her,' said Sweetmouth, 'with her gear on its back.'

'A witch,' said Mad.

'I ne spoke to her for fear of that. A maid who may craft a horse into a boar might hurt a man. But now it seems to me she looked too fair to be a witch.'

'Now we get to it,' said Mad.

'She's dark as a bourne on a summer's night, and when I woo her it must be dreadful, like to the sun nears the moon and so heats her she's bound to shed her gown and let him shine within her.'

'A Saxon man outdoes my song,' said Mad.

'I ne know her name, nor where she goes, but she has a lickerous mouth and silk blossoms on her tits, and I'd spend the leave of my days in a monastery, with my flesh under a knotted rope, could I kiss her cunt but once.'

'Sweetmouth likes to kiss a maid on the lips in such a way she may sing at the same time,' said Mad.

'A boar,' said Longfreke, 'is a right hard deer to break to burden, and a maid alone on the road with blossoms on her dress is not but a whore or wit-lorn.'

Sweetmouth's eyes widened and shone. 'My pintle would be to her cunny like to a naked king slid inside a bearskin on a winter's night, a bearskin fit for a king, made of the smoothest, youngest bears, tight to his shape.' He put his arm around Will. 'I wived too soon. The dark maid is she our Maker wrought for me alone. I'll meet her on the road, you'll help me win her. There's none better than me in the greater deal of wooing, but to draw a maid's eye, man would have a fair neb, which I lack. So I'll have you be the bait, to draw the maid in.'

'Ne heed him,' said Mad. 'Sweetmouth speaks so much of maids only that none might know his shame, that he's true to his wife.'

They went on, and Will and Longfreke fell behind. Will learned they were to fare on foot through Wiltshire as far as Westbury, where they'd meet one of the English lords who held Calais, who was to get them horses, and take them through Dorset to the ship that would bear them to France.

'Then Hayne's not our chief, this lord is,' said Will.

'This high-born fellow's no lord. He's lower, a squire or some such. He does the bidding of the lords that hire us. Laurence Haket by name.'

It appeared to Berna an over-eager suitor kissed her. She opened her eyes and regarded the salivating mouth of Enker, with Hab beside him. The boar pressed his nose to Berna's cheek and grunted pleasurably. He was shod and had a sack tied to his back. Hab wore his usual patched tunic.

The lady was far from home, said Hab, her wedding was soon, and her folk would lack her.

Berna stood and brushed grass and leaves from her person. 'Where I travel and fare isn't yours to know,' she said. 'It's not your place to wake a lady, sleeps she in her chamber or a forest. Who gave you leave and permission to quit my father's manor?'

Hab said he sought his sister Madlen.

'I know the names and faces of each of the servants and bound folk on my family's estate, and even of servants' servants like you,' said Berna. 'You have no sister. There's no Madlen.'

There was a Madlen, said Hab, but she was shy, and versed in concealment.

'Were you to have a sister indeed, why would she be here, half a day on foot from her right and proper stead and place?' demanded Bernadine.

Madlen had left Outen Green that morning, said Hab. She loved Will Quate and sworn to follow him wherever he went, be it to the ends of the earth.

Berna laughed. 'My poor pigboy,' she said. 'Your kind hasn't the time, nor the letters, nor the fineness of mood and sentiment for love. Drink ale with your friends, wed and marry your sweethearts, bear and carry children, the Almighty won't ask and demand no more of you. It's only we of blood must endure love's smarts.'

Hab's face crinkled with subtlety, and he addressed Berna with a sudden directness, as if they were of one estate.

'Is it for love you sleep in the wood, instead of being at your father's side to meet your new husband?' he asked.

For a moment Berna was incapable of response. She turned her head in esperance of aid, in vain; they were alone.

'You may not speak to me in that familiar way and manner,' she said, attempting to give her voice authority. 'Depart from my presence this instant.'

'In your sleep I took you for Madlen,' said Hab.

'How is that possible? Your sister mayn't afford a cloth as rich as this,' said Berna, holding out the flowery stuff of her marriage gown.

'She stole it,' said Hab.

Berna put her hands to her mouth, then to her cheeks. 'Why, my dear Hab,' she said with sincere pity, 'if your sister is the thief who stole my first gown, she'll rightly be caught and hung.'

The menace of penalty mortal failed to provoke the proper response. Hab ne trembled nor blanched. He regarded her disdainously. 'You fear you won't outshine Madlen unless she's dead,' he said.

'Outshine?' said Berna. 'You demonstrate a marvellous ignorance of our different natures.'

'Demon-straight a what?'

'You see, pigboy? We scarcely speak the same tongue and language. You're incapable of comprehending that were your sister to able herself in my gown, it wouldn't change her into no demoiselle. The qualities that mark and distingue our kinds go deeper than outward seeming and appearance. Her lack of gentilesse, her coarseness of movement, the roughness of her shape, are in harmony only with dull colours and cheap cloth. In my gown, she would become discordant and odd. She would seem still lower and meaner than she already is.'

Hab beheld Enker and scratched an ear in thought, only instead of his own ear, he scratched the boar's. 'You ween Madlen ne look fairer than you, though she wear the same gown? How may you know, if you've never seen her?'

'I ne say your sister's not fair,' said Berna more gently. 'A daisy may be wonder fair, and never as lovely as the humblest rose.'

'I saw Madlen in the gown she stole,' said Hab. 'She hight herself right winly. I saw her come again of the still water at the foot of the bourne and she seemed to me as fair as any rose. Truly, when I beheld you asleep, I took you for her.'

Berna coloured. 'You lack the sense to apperceive and know the clear signs of my nobility,' she said.

'You're like to her in other ways. She's a thief, and you're a thief, for you stole yourself from your own wedding.'

'I lose all rule by which to measure your offensiveness,' gasped Berna.

'And you're like her that you fare for love, Calais-bound. Madlen yearns for Will Quate, and you, I guess, for Laurence Haket.'

'Shut your mouth!' cried Berna, so furiously that her horse, tethered nearby, reared and whinnied. 'I shan't accept no comparison of my fare and journey to no errand of a pigboy's sister.'

Hab shrugged. 'High-born as you are, you're alone in the wood without friend or kin to help.'

'Ne harm me,' said Berna, 'or you'll be pined and made to suffer.'

'How?'

'I am imaginative,' said Berna.

Hab's demeanour changed again; the familiarity that had so troubled Berna disappeared, and his consciousness of the lady's superiority seemed to return. Humbly he proposed to accompany the lady on her journey, that she might appear to have an entourage. Together they would attempt to travel under the protection of the archers.

Somewhere on the road to Calais, Berna was certain to encounter Laurence Haket; while Hab, if he kept close to Will Quate, would surely catch his sister.

. 'But Will Quate will know me,' said Berna. 'He'll see I've fled my marriage. He will betray me to my father. I already know he's not to be trusted. I met him as I left Outen Green and he behaved despicably towards me, without honour or worth, like to we were equals — as you did just now, but worse.'

Hab said no doubt the lady's face had been veiled; no doubt Will, thinking like Hab that the lady was occupied with marriage preparations in the manor house, had mistaken her for Madlen.

'Another one?' said Berna. 'Do I seem so like a low-born woman?' She examined the backs of her hands. 'Is it because I've let the sun brown my fingers?'

She could turn it to her advantage, said Hab. The other bowmen would accept her as she was, as the lady Bernadine, but providing she went veiled, Will would assume she was Madlen.

'That Lady Bernadine should pretend to be Madlen pretending to be Lady Bernadine?' said Berna. She laughed. 'You're imaginative.'

Hab said it was her second usage of the word, but he ne knew what it signified.

'As you may understand it,' said Berna, 'it is the sleight of mind that gives the speed to know things not as they are, but as they might be, were God or man to work them otherwise. Have you any food?'

WILL AND LONGFREKE next came upon their even-bowmen in the cool shade of a wood. Hayne lay stretched on the leaves, eyes shut, the likeness of Christ flat on his chest, while Mad and Sweetmouth made a rope fast to the crown of a young birch, drew it down and knit it to the trunk of an oak.

'It's a proud young birchling, and we'll learn it to know its stead in the forest,' said Longfreke.

'We'll make of it a bow, bound to its lord the oak,' said Sweetmouth.

'We haven't no arrow, and it needs us a true one,' said Mad. 'Where in this wood might we get such?'

They turned to Will, gripped him with firm hands and tore the pack of his back. Will strove to free himself but the other two were stronger together and they laid him down with his rigbone flat against the bowed birch.

'An ill token he ne struggled much,' said Mad.

'I ne used but half my strength,' said Will.

'A proud arrow that backbites,' said Longfreke. 'We'd best found it. Shoot!'

They loosed the knitted rope and let Will go. The birch whipped and Will was flung upwards. He flew through the air and came to earth through a holly tree. He fell on his shoulder and cried out once, then cried no more, but ne rose, and lay still.

'He flew true,' said Sweetmouth.

'He flew crooked,' said Mad.

'True,' said Sweetmouth. 'I took the holly as the mark.'

'Crooked,' said Mad, 'I took the nettles.'

'Player!' called Sweetmouth to Will. 'You'd best have shielded your neb from scratches, for I need it whole.'

'How did the world look when you saw it as the birds do?' asked Mad.

Will groaned and stood up. Hayne loomed over him and said: 'Would you be a bowman in my score, and come with us to Calais?'

'Yeah,' said Will.

Hayne clasped Will's head in his great hands and looked at it from this side and that like to he'd made Will out of straw and sticks and rags, and would see he'd made him right. He stepped away and bade Longfreke take the oath.

Longfreke took Will's wrist and put his bowstaff in his hand and bade him swear by the blood and bones of Christ, by their Clean Mother, by St Sebastian and by St George, and by his bow, to be true to Hayne Attenoke and to his even-bowmen of the Gloucestershire score, to do the bidding of the master of the score faithfully and without backbiting.

Will swore it.

Longfreke bade Will say after him:

> Feathered tail but I ne sing
> I rise high without a wing
> I am but a wooden freke
> Yet I have an iron beak
> As a falcon so my flight
> Of my master's will and might
> Ne to think on flying's end
> Free in air to while and wend
> Faring far in light and dark
> Blind to my high master's mark.

'What are you?' asked Longfreke.

'An arrow,' said Will.

'Who is your master?'

'The bowman.'

'And who is that bowman?'

'Hayne Attenoke.'

'It is the Lord God Almighty,' whispered Longfreke. He took a flask of his pack and gave it to Will and bade him drain it to the bottom. It was a Scotch drink, he said, of frozen ale. Will drained the flask, sat on the ground, shut his eyes and slept.

Now it is night, when under the abbot's regimen the monks would have been asleep. Under the invigorated rule, one third of the community chants, insomniate, sating the vacuum of tenebrous nocturnal silence between Compline and Matins with adamantine clarifications of the divine.

The abbot and his pomp are not part of this. The abbot, formally the monastery's most senior cleric, celebrates mass in his private secretarium, absents himself from chapter, does not participate in processions, and has separated himself from the chanting of the liturgy. I have become the sole inhabitant of both abbeys, the decadent abbey of the abbot and the austere abbey of the prior.

Accordingly, I divide my hours. After Vespers I exit the nave and transit the area to the abbot, who tells me that the prior is a fanatical dictator, a usurper, a depraver of regulations, that he is ignorant of the furious verities of public administration. It is the abbot's opinion that only the fatuous would find it credible for God to damn the carnivores and offer the herbivores and pescivores salvation, or exterminate humanity because an abbot in Malmesbury wears coloured velvets. 'Are we to accept,' the abbot says, 'that God may perceive true fidelity only through the rags of penury, the habits of opulence rendering it invisible?'

But before Vespers, and at night, I regress to the nave, ambling between the pilgrims pressed to the pavement, supplicating miserably as they reptile to the sanctuary. I resonate with the chanting of the choir. The chancel exhales an incensed nimbus, mollifying the flagrant ardors of the candles, while the immense columns of pale native stone simulate the trunks of celestial arbors.

NB Marc. I should have conducted you with me to England, as you requested. I confess I was directed by an irrational resentment which is difficult to explain: I resented the contrast between your superior (in respect to me) command of Latin and your inferior command of rhetoric, which resulted in the more erudite of us – you – being subordinate to the more sociable, me. You remained my servant, when you might with facility have found an alternative master who honoured his dependency on you in terms more amiable than finance alone. I request that you absolve me.

PS The request for absolution to be extended to your wife – Judith having indubitably suffered indirectly from my resentment.

WILL WOKE ON a sack of straw in a hot dark room. Evening light came of small windows pitched in the wall and around him were the shapes of other men asleep.

His pack was by his bed-sack. Someone had taken the shoon of his feet and left them nearby. Will rose and did on the shoon. He'd go out the door, but a tall lean freke with a rood written on his forehead in blackneedle stood in his way.

'By what right do you behold me?' asked the man.

'I'm thirsty,' said Will. 'You stand between my thirst and my whole hope to quench it.'

'Would you go by me?' said the man. 'Would you? See how far you go.'

'I wouldn't strive with a man and ne know why,' said Will.

'For one, you behold my forehead like to you ne worth the holy rood of our Lord and Saviour, Jesus Christ,' said the man. 'For two, your face ne likes me. I would work it to a better shape with the sharp end of my bollyknife.'

SOMEONE CALLED TO the man in a soft steven and bade him come away. 'Your wrath were more worthed did you hold it back, my Dickle, that it mightn't be fare for all, as bread, but doled out in shreddles, as saffron,' said the soft-spoken one.

'I wasn't there when they made this gnof a bowman,' said Dickle. 'I'd have sent him home to his mother's lap with his neb slit.' He shoff by Will into the room where Will had been asleep and shut the door.

It was Softly John Fletcher who spoke. 'Dickle Dene's a fell man with knife, but ever holy,' he said. 'He fared the last fifty mile to Jerusalem on his knees, and had the rood written on his forehead in blackneedle that all might know his holiness.'

'I'm ill of head and dry of mouth,' said Will. 'I ne know where I am nor how I got here since I drank the Scotch.'

'You drank enough to make you blind,' said Softly. 'This is Rodmarton, a morning's fare from Malmesbury. Hayne bore you on his back.'

He led Will to a long telded cart, with a ladder hung on hooks on one side, in one hern of the guesthouse yard. The moon had risen and the stars shimmered and cans of fleabane smoked at the doors. A light was lit in the cart and someone went about inside with a sound of clay and iron and thin timbers that knocked against each other.

Softly called into the cart and a woman brought out a can of ale, which she gave to Softly, who handed it to Will. Will drained the can and they filled it again. Softly bade the woman bring light and the woman brought a flame that gleamed in an ox-horn cup.

'Behold, Cess, Player Will Quate,' he said. 'Isn't he as fair a young freke as you've seen?'

Cess ne lifted her eyes to see. 'I shan't behold no other man but you,' she said.

'She makes a show of meekness for me, but she's as all French maids, wanton and sly,' said Softly. 'Find you her fair?'

Will said he mightn't deem the fairness of any woman but his own betrothed.

Softly laughed. There was gold in his teeth. He put his arm around Will's shoulder, led him to the board and bade him take an old barrel-half for his seat. He was friendly, and asked Will many asks, and Will answered.

'I'll help you,' said Softly. 'I'll learn you what's what, for though Hayne's leader, him ne likes the other bowmen to know what he knows. He leaves it to each man to choose his way, and if that way ne answers Hayne's read, woe betide him, in war or frith.'

'What's war?' said Will. 'Is it a fight?'

'War's all the fights together, and all that betides on the days between the fights, which is the greater deal of soldiery,' said Softly. 'A man who lacks but war makes a poor soldier.'

'I lack the sight of the sea,' said Will. 'I lack silver for my freedom.'

Softly nodded. 'You're right to seek your freedom in France in wartide,' he said. 'The English soldier has such freedom in France as no king ne gets in his own house.'

SOFTLY JOHN WOULD have Will know he was a God-fearing man.

'I was a seafarer,' he said, 'and met a holy man, who gave me a golden rood, but I lost it. The holy man gave it me, for he saw in me an angel-light.'

Softly had sailed on a ship out of Weston took flour, ale, apples and candles to the holy man, an anchor who lived alone on an island. The anchor wone in a house made of stone and wood he'd gathered of the strand, and sat there all summer and winter, bidding his beads and writing. There wasn't none more holy, said Softly, though his teeth were rotten and his feet bare and he hadn't but sea-calf skins to wrap him in. Lord Berkeley was bound to send him goods twice a year, but it ever fell short, and Softly went about the staithe begging stuff of folk for the leave, so the holy man ne storve. When the ship landed and was unladen, the holy man would kiss Softly's hand and weep and tell him he was a true Christen, and read to him golden tales of the saints from a book, and behest that should he die, Softly might have his golden rood.

One winter, when they were to go to the island, a snowstorm came, and blew for a fortnight. After the storm had gone they sailed forth. They found the anchor in his house, sat at his writing board as if he were yet alive, a feather in his hand, his eyes open and his skin clear, pale and dry, like to a skin cut for a book before it's written on. A sweet stink came of him, like to reekles on smoke in church, and when they came to lift him, he weighed no more than a sparrow, for his ghost was so great that when it left him there wasn't but a shell left. He'd burned his books for to heat him, out-take the book of golden saints' tales, of which the greater deal was left, and Softly minded the holy man's behest and took the golden rood, which he'd since lost.

TWO MORE BOWMEN, Holiday Bobben and Hornstrake Walt Newent, came into the light, sat down and began to play at dice. The dice belonged to Hornstrake, yet it was Holiday who won most throws.

Hornstrake was a lank freke, shaved in patches and bald in patches, whose clothes hung loose, and who sat bent, with his head lower than his shoulders, and sniffed and rubbed his nose.

'Hornstrake bought a set of weighted dice,' said Holiday, 'but they cheated him. The sellers were so false the dice they sold him were true.'

All Holiday wore was of the newest and best, like to a rich young knave from a much town, out-take that his kirtle was sewn with hooks and straps and slit with leather mouths for hidden bags. One leg of his hose was red, the other black, and he'd oiled his hair. He had fat whirled cheeks and sharp quick eyes.

'A Player must play,' said Holiday, showing Will the dice. 'I'll lend you sixpence against your first week's fee if you lack the silver to lay on a game. Or would you be read to from a book?'

'Have you truly a book?' asked Will.

Holiday reached inside his shirt and drew out a bundle hung from his neck on a cord. He brought it up to the light. 'I keep it for Softly,' he said.

'I can't read bookstaves, but Holiday learned himself,' said Softly. 'It likes me to hear of a saint's deeds with my ale.'

Will asked to see the book, and Holiday took the cord of his neck and gave it him to hold.

It was made of dry, stiff leaves of thin calfskin bound together, with bookstaves written in, and likenesses of men and fowls and worms of many hues around the hem. One hem was burned black, like to it had been pulled of the fire, and the first leaf was spotted with brown.

Will stroked the first page with his fingertip. 'I ne know how a man might get words out of these little black bookstaves,' he said.

'Each staff tokens a littlewhat of a word. The first staff, that's like to a snake, tokens "s", as the hiss of an adder. The second, like to a house on two floors, tokens "a", as comes of your mouth when you fall of the upper floor. The third is "i", like to a shut

75

eye, the fourth, "n", like to the house on two floors, but it lacks floors, and the fifth is "t", like to a crossbow, and like to the sound when the bolt is let. T-t-t. And next comes an empty spot, that tokens the end of the word. Now you read it.'

Will spoke the letters in their turn. 'Sss-a-eye-ne-te,' he said.

'Go at them quicker, like an arrow through five rooks on a branch,' said Holiday.

'"Saint",' said Will. '"Saint!"' he said again, and his face was lit with mirth, and he looked blithe from neb to neb around the light.

'"Saint",' said Holiday, 'and the word after it is "Agnes".' He could read it, he said, but the pith and marrow of it was that Agnes was a holy young Christen maid in Rome who wouldn't take the hand of the knave that would have her, and the knave's father, that was constable there, stripped her naked to shame her in front of the townfolk, but God made the short hair on her head grow long, so all her limbs were hidden from their eyes. So the constable put her in a whorehouse, and bade the men of Rome have their will with her as them liked. But God filled the house with light, that none might see her, and when the knave came to reave her maidenhood, he dropped down dead. And Agnes was dight saint.

'There it is in the book,' said Softly. 'See you we know God's ends better than Hayne?'

Will showed by his stillness he ne understood.

'There was one,' said Hornstrake, 'on whom no hair grew, and there wasn't no light from our Maker, and God ne stirred himself to kill the reavers. So it was reft, and she wasn't dight saint.'

All three men looked on Will, like to they bode some words of him in answer, but he sat still and beheld the flicker of the candle in its horn.

'I told you he'd be of Hayne's mind,' said Holiday to Softly. 'Now Hayne'll have five, and we but four.'

Softly said, in his low sweet steven like to a busy beeskip, that it was the hour for Holiday and Hornstrake to go to bed. The two of them nearhand ran from the board, and Will and Softly were let alone, out-take that at the nigh end of the cart, Cess sat and sewed a glove in the moonlight.

Will yawned. Softly took a woollen from the cart. He nodded at Cess.

'Would you have her tonight?' he asked Will.

Will beheld the ground and ne answered.

'You're right,' said Softly. 'I ne sell her cunt to no one. I'm bound by oath to gut the man who lays a hand on her. I might have left her there but now she's my burd and burden for ever.'

Cess murmured something, and Softly bade her go in. 'There's nothing worse than pride in a maid,' he said when she'd gone. 'It's the first thing to take of them.'

He held out the woollen. 'Take it as a gift,' he said.

'I mayn't. It's too dear,' said Will.

'I bought them to great cheap of a ship in Bristol,' said Softly. 'Take it.'

'It's warm,' said Will. 'Now's harvest weather. I ne need it.'

'Come winter you'll sleep in a cold Calais harbour. Take it. If a man withsay a gift a third time, the giver might think himself unworthed.'

Cess cried out in French from the cart, and Softly turned. Will took the woollen, thanked Softly and went to bed.

Emerging from the abbot's house this evening I was asperged with holy water by a trio of masked monks chanting 'Sicut tabescit cera a facie ignis pereant impii a facie Dei,' as if the abbot were a centre of evil and I must be instantly isolated and purged in my transition from his location to that of the prior, lest the army of demons encamped outside the prior's musical fortifications conceal themselves on my person, secretly enter the abbey and destroy it from within.

NB Marc: In infancy I contrived to attribute culpability for the destruction of a valuable crystal reliquary to my younger brother Gavin, who was, in consequence, gravely battered by our father. In fact it was I who fractured the object. I have never admitted this to him.

WILL WAS WOKEN by snorks and cratches outside. He got up and went to the window that looked out on the orchard side of the guesthouse. Enker dug there at the roots of an apple tree.

The other bowmen ne stirred. Will did on his shoon and went out into the yard. The first cock nad sung and the sun wasn't but a fallowing of the darkness on the dogs asleep and on the wakeman who slumbered at the timber-haw gate, his cheek pillowed on his fist. Will came through the gate and went round the back to see Enker come out through the gap he'd made in the orchard hedge.

He followed the boar out of town and into a wood, till the first light of morning glimmered in a ridding. There he found Madlen in the lady Bernadine's gown, sat on a tree stump, at work on her fingernails with a little knife. She looked up when Will came towards her and bent to her nails again.

'Why won't you let me alone, but follow wherever I go?' she asked.

Will sat at her feet in the grass and looked up at her. 'You're so like to Hab, God's bones I'd swear you were he, had I not put my hand in your gown and found tits instead of moss.'

'You nad no right to grip a maid there without her leave.'

'You were full of high French words when we met before. Who learned you?'

'A maid learns by listening,' said Madlen.

'Where were you when Hab and I were children?' asked Will. 'Where were you when we swam in the bourne and caught fireflies?'

'I was there, but you ne saw me,' said Madlen. 'Would you keep me with you now?'

'I'm still betrothed to another, and a sworn bowman, and you still wear a stolen gown. Bury it and go home.'

'Is that your last word?'

'Yeah.'

'You'd truly go to the ends of the Earth alone, rather than have me with you?'

'I have my even-bowmen.'

Madlen stuck out her lip and plucked at the silk flowers on her barm. 'Then I'll leave you for ever,' she said. 'But first, while the ridding's heavenish, and the birds sing and there are pearls on the grass, tell me what kind these bowmen are you go among.'

'The leader Hayne is a giant who barely speaks, who wouldn't take me to France and ne worths me. Yet it was he bore me the last mile to Rodmarton after I'd drunk a flask of strong Scotch wine and went asleep witless, when he could have left me in the wood. And Hayne's first underling is a free handy gome called Softly John who seems to be my friend, yet keeps against her will a maid he stole in France.'

'Is she fair, the French maid?' asked Madlen.

'It was too dark to see.'

'Oh.'

'One of my new fellows learned me to read words,' said Will. 'Of a book.'

'How nimble you are!' said Madlen.

'He learned me a bare five bookstaves, but it was enough to read a whole word.'

'Shut your eyes,' said Madlen. 'Bide a handwhile and open them and I'll be gone.'

'Light as that?'

'Shut your eyes.'

Will shut his eyes. The grass rustled and feet trod the earth. 'God be with you,' Will said. 'I'll see you next year.'

He opened his eyes. Madlen's eyes stared into them from six inches away.

'It wouldn't be right for me to go,' she said. 'You ne sold me to our lord, when you might have done it lightly, and won of it. This tokens that in the dern hollows of your heart, you care for me.'

'I wouldn't never sell no man to nobody,' said Will. 'That's my own worth I love, not you. You showed yourself too late to get love of me.'

'Without me, you won't have no kin to tell of the wonders you see.' She came to sit by Will and laid her head on his shoulder.

'I'll come home again and tell everyone,' said Will.

'You won't come home again. The priest said so. All will sicken.'

'I told you, the qualm's a priest's tale to win silver,' said Will.

'Oh, loveman,' said Madlen, and held his cheek in her hand. 'I ne durst leave Outen Green but that I believe the qualm will slay us, every one. When all must be quelled I ne fear no gallows, for you and I may love and die and go on to the next house together.'

'It mayn't be.'

'Two nights ago, my brother asked if you would take me, were you and I the last folk left on earth. You ne forsook me.'

'I ne said yeah.'

'You ne said no.'

The first bell rang in Rodmarton.

'I'm a soldier now, and must go,' said Will. He freed himself from Madlen's arms.

Madlen caught his wrist and bade him give her one kiss before he went as token, but Will wouldn't. Madlen looked in his eyes, dight her head at his neb like a cat on a mouse, and smote him on the mouth with her lips.

'When you understand,' she said, 'I shan't be far away.'

'I would you were.'

'On the far side of Malmesbury, Hab and I will cleave to you and your bowmen.'

'Ne dare.'

'I'll wear a cloth on my neb and use French words and make a show that I'm the lady Bernadine.'

'I'll tell them otherwise.'

'If you do they'll send me back to Outen Green to be hung as a thief.'

'Won't you let me be?'

'I may only let you be with me.'

WILL CAME AGAIN to the guesthouse. The other bowmen were at board, their dishes nigh to empty. Will came up to Hayne and asked to be forgiven his late. He'd risen early, he said, and gone out to see what kind of town Rodmarton was, for he hadn't never seen it. But Hayne wouldn't behold him.

There was a free stead next to Hayne on the bench, and a stead free by Softly, and Softly called to Will to sit by him, and Will took his seat there.

A maid came from the guesthouse and set before Will a can of ale and a dish of hot collops. He put egg and pig-flesh on the bread with the flat of his knife and fell to as one hadn't eaten a fortnight.

Hayne spoke, and it was like to a hill shook. It was his law, he said, that all must be together in his sight at cock-crow, and all must be together in his sight at sundown, and Will Quate had broken this law. When one of his score broke this law by going his own way, said Hayne, those as hadn't broken the law would be hurt.

All the bowmen fell still but Softly, who spat on the ground.

Hayne rose and bade them gather their gear and get on the road.

THE LAND ABOUT them fell away. Ahead of the bowmen to the south lay a wide flat wold, and at the far brim of their sight, a line of hills. Between them and the wold a great dark blade reached into the sky, like to a giant under the ground had pitched his spear through the world's hide. Longfreke saw Will stare and told him it was the spire of the church of the abbey in Malmesbury. In all England, he said, only Sarum's was longer.

They came to the Fosse Way, that marked where Gloucestershire and Wiltshire met. After a mile's fare they met a gooseherd and his knave, who drove a flock of geese northward. The gooseherd went in the midst of the geese, and greeted the bowmen as they went by. The knave walked last, at the end of the flock, and when Hayne went by him, he smote him in the head with his fist, and the boy fell to the ground without a sound.

Hayne struck his blow so quick and true that the gooseherd, in his dreamy fare, ne saw nor heard, and walked on, and the knave lay still in the road.

Will opened his mouth but before he could speak Holiday had

dight his hand over it, and Holiday and Longfreke between them held him back from going to help the knave. They made him go on till they were out of hearing of the gooseherd, then let him turn his head to see the knave sitting up with his noll in his hands.

'Mind what Hayne said,' said Longfreke. 'When one of us breaks Hayne's law to go his own way, one that ne broke no law is hurt. Smarts it to see the gooseboy, who hadn't done us no wrong, struck down by Hayne?'

'It smarts,' said Will.

'Mind it next time you're out playing the ram and the sun comes up.'

Will turned and caught the eye of Cess. No light came in her grim cheer, and she dight her headcloth lower on her forehead.

'I would that they who made the laws might learn me what they are before I find a way to break them,' said Will to Longfreke.

'Hayne's laws are such that the man who breaks them knows them in his heart, whether he's told or not,' said Longfreke. 'But I'll tell you one.' He nodded at the spire. 'In half a mile we leave Gloucestershire. After that you mayn't go home again out-take by France or in a shroud. My read's to turn now and go home.'

Will ne heeded him. He went with the bowmen when they turned from the Fosse Way, and crossed from Gloucestershire into Wiltshire, and all, even Hayne and Dickle Dene, shook Will's hand, and said Player Will Quate was of their fellowship, ale, bed, board and threepence a day. From there they went the last mile to Malmesbury.

I DISCOVERED THE prior at his usual post in a recess near the choir, considering with the precentor a table on which coloured wooden symbols on a chart depict the disposition of the choristers – those who are singing, those who are absent, asleep, in the refectory, in the infirmary. Other symbols signify the sites of suspected eruptions of evil and the commitment of mobile anti-demon choirs to counter them. The mental labour is immense; the prior must continually visualise his invisible defences and his invisible opponents, assisted only by the chart, by reports from the perimeter, and by his divinely-inspired vision, capable of detecting the Satanic multitudes projecting themselves against the monastic harmonies with teeth and claws and red eyes, and, worse, calling to their compatriots whom they have previously inserted in us, telling them that now is the moment to surge out and join the assault.

The prior was exhausted, unrazed, red around the eyes. Extraordinary that he should have organised such music with the debilitated instruments his community offers, the senile and the juvenile, the crapulent and the insane, the tone deaf and the mono-lingual, ignorant of the significance of the words they chant.

The precentor, conscious of the uses of Paris, disposes triple organa of tenor and descant – a minimum of forty-eight choristers for the tenor, twenty-four for the vox organalis and twenty-nine for the vox principalis. He and the prior have decided that should the descant and tenor combined fall below ninety-six, the integrity of their exaltation will erode, and God will project pestilential affliction through the ruptures in their vocal edifice. Every hour, determined by an horarium, spent choristers depart the choir, to be replaced by rejuvenates.

When I arrived, the grains in the superior part of the horarium had almost descended into the inferior. Simultaneously each of us around the table detected a diminution in the vigour of the music. Panic manifested itself in the fraternal faces. Their terror commu-nicated itself to me, and I sensed, with them, the fracture and rupture of our defences, the strident ululation of the demons as they triumphantly surged through the fissures between the diminishing chords and prepared to feast on our souls.

Only the prior remained calm. He admonished a novice, who ran off and revened with the alternate choir, recently sleeping, their faces engraved with fatigue. The precentor urged them to the chancel. One by one the voices of the revived monks integrated with those of the attenuated brothers, the sound of the psalm expanded, the density of sacred incantation firmed our fortifications, and we relaxed.

The magnitude of sound oppressed our ears and forced us to clamour in order to be heard.

'The archers have arrived,' exclaimed the prior. 'I desire that you go with them. Their dux Hayne Attenoke requires a cleric in the company, to take confession should the plague erupt tumultuously when they are far from any chapel.'

'I am a proctor, not a priest,' I said.

'In extremis there is no requirement for confession to be heard by an ordained priest. In the circumstances of proximate pestilence, as homo literatus with a pulse, you are super-apt. Spend tonight in the library with the penitentials and you will comprehend the scheme better than the greater number of vicars. Nobody demands that you celebrate the eucharist. They will demand your services only in the ultimate exigency.'

'The choral obstacles you have erected against Beelzebub are so magnificent, so splendid,' I said. 'Let me remain and record for posterity how the demonic legions were repulsed by the power of Malmesbury.'

The prior inspected me sternly. 'Do you not have friends, colleagues, valued servants in Avignon?' he said. 'Are you not anxious to discover their fate?'

His aspect was so terrible I could not face it directly. 'Were you to offer me some evidence that the suffering in Avignon is as severe as rumour reports,' I murmured, 'I would go immediately.'

'That is your promise?'

I assented. Immediately he gave me a letter from the city that he had previously kept secret.

It was a difficult text. Some phrases appeared to resist vision, others to lacerate it: *Sixty-two thousand corpses buried . . . all the auditors, advocates and proctors have either left, or died, or plan to leave immediately.*

'This letter declares that the papal court is suspended until the feast of St Michael,' I said, attempting to conceal my desperation. 'I should not progress south prematurely.'

The prior studied my face as if at the prime encounter with a new animal. 'You would annul your promise with such temerity?'

'The circumstances have altered,' I babbled.

'You have no purpose here. You do not contribute to the defence of the abbey. You associate with the corrupt. Introduce yourself to the archers as their itinerant confessor, go with them tomorrow.'

Marc, I must request that you share these notes and ephemera of mine with Judith. To know that you perused them together, even with contempt for my pusillanimousness, would be of enormous comfort.

I ENCOUNTERED THE archers at the pilgrim hospital, where they had been assigned accommodation. With what terrific creatures was it proposed I itinerate! Their dux, Hayne Attenoke, is a giant, silent, intractable, with a gigantic, ornate crucifix suspended from his neck on a silver chain, and his comrades are percussors, brutes, squalid homicides. One has a cross sculpted in the skin of his front and a self-induced stigmata; another, the clement-voiced John Fletcher, alias Softly, gold dentistry, with sufficient oral opulence for a papal candelabrum; Gilbert Bisley, alias Longfreke, whose face is on a plane with my scapula, has a fissure dividing the dexter and sinister parts of his face, a cicatrix so profound it appears he has been formed of dual semi-humans, conglutined into unity. Their lingua anglica is dense, turbulent, spined, immune from the tactus of Gallic or Latin. They are squalid, rude, with a sanguinary odour. There is an exception, a novice archer, William Quate, alias Player, solid of form, pectorally muscled, but with the face of an angel, a tranquil gestus and an intelligent aspect.

With them is a vehicle containing their armaments, and in it a captive female, Cecile de Goincourt, of uncertain status. The closure in her face is redolent of violence and abuse, yet she has a residual core of dignity.

I erupted to the prior and explained that it was not possible for me to navigate with these predators to the pestilential, meridional territories that were our destination. They were as horrid as the prospect of the plague; and I was perplexed as to what mode of confession to accept, and what form of absolution to offer, when the archers itinerated with the permanent substance of their nefarious conduct, viz, a woman they had violated in France and subtracted from her family.

The prior offered no alternative. 'Investigate the circumstances of this alleged violation,' he said, 'congruent with your confessorial position, and care for her spirit as well as theirs. Confession is not an exact science; it more resembles the cultivation of fruit than the design of a cathedral. As terrible as the archers are, they are ab utero materno, like you, and ultimately as timid in the face of damnation.'

Marc, Judith, I comprehend now how miserly I have been with my gratitude to you since my advent in Avignon decades ago. How vastly you improved my Latin and my French! With what grace you tolerated my vehement insistence on amicable dialogue with you and my conflicting desire to subordinate you, to dominate you, because I was your master and you my servants!

◡

WILL ASKED THOMAS the shriftfather if the monks ever stinted their song.

'They reckon holy songs a wall to ward them of pestilence,' said Thomas. 'To stint were like to they lowed the stones between them and the Fiend.'

Will said in his town they worthed the smoke of burned bones.

'Bones outburn,' said Thomas. 'A bonefire's not but work to an end. This holy song has at once an end and a lovely endlessness. Man likes any work that helps him forget his ghost's bound to his body by a thread.'

Will leaned his head back and said him thought he wouldn't never tire of the awful might of the great stone posts that held the roof so high above them. Was there in the world, he asked, a bigger church than Malmesbury?

'Behold, an uplandish scholar,' said Thomas. 'Offered a wonder, you seek another more wondrous. My namesake Aquinas would say a man like you won't stop till he reaches the wondermost.'

Will asked Thomas what he meant, but by now they were out of the church and saw Sweetmouth and Longfreke, who beheld the likenesses corven about the door. Will would stand to wonder with them, for to look on the doorway with its many hues and gems, and the likenesses of Adam and Eve, Moses and Noah, Christ and God and the angels, was like to the tale of the world went by.

The bowmen couldn't guess Thomas's kind. He was long and lean, with sharp cheekbones, close-cropped grey hair and skin that ne feared the sun. He'd seen forty winter, and was rivelled about the mouth and eyes from laughing. When he spoke he smiled often, in such a way that those who listened smiled with him, till ferly his face went hard and cold, and listeners felt they'd misdone to smile. His clothes, rich, dark and plain, were more like to a dealer's than a priest's, and he wore no ring, nor spoke to them as priest to flock, but man to man, though he was learned, and gave them to understand he read books, and knew the gospel. His English tongue wasn't southern nor western nor midland, not Kentish nor Cornish nor Yorkshire, but somewhat Scottish and somewhat French.

'Shall I tell you of the likenesses?' said Thomas.

He showed them with his finger on the doorway where red-kirtled God lifted Adam from the slime of the earth, breathed into his neb the breath of life and pitched him upright, like to a ploughman set a new-born calf on his feet in the spring field. He showed where God took Eve out of Adam's side when he slept, and God bade Adam and Eve not to eat no apple of that tree. Where the serpent wound about the tree and told Eve she might not die by death, for God woot that in whatever day she ate the apple, her eyes would be opened, and she might be as God, to know good and evil. Where an angel with a golden crown sent Adam and Eve away from God's garden, and they wept that they must step out into the cold world with but one mean sheepskin each.

Thomas showed where God told Noah how the Earth was full of wickedness. That he would bring great flood on Earth, and slay each flesh in which was the ghost of life under heaven, and waste all things on Earth, and how he bade Noah make a ship, and fill it with birds, work-deer and creeping deer, all living deer of all flesh, and his own kin.

'Here's Noah again,' said Thomas. He showed the next likeness. 'He shapes a beam with his adze. Behind him are the black clouds that bear the rain.'

Sweetmouth said Noah mightn't afill his work before the flood.

'He afilled it,' said Thomas, like to a man who brought news of a thing that happened last Friday. 'He made the ship. Then all the wells of the great sea were broken, and the windows of heaven were opened, and rain was made on Earth forty days and forty nights. And look, here's Noah and his kin stood in the ship, warded from the flood, with a roof over their heads to keep them from rain, and one of Noah's sons steers with an oar. Now, you reckon the folk in the ship.'

Longfreke told them on his fingers: Noah, his burd, his three sons, and their wives, eight in all.

'Right,' said Thomas. 'Eight of mankind and womankind left alive in all the world. The masters that corve these likenesses chose their gospel tales well, for Noah was forefather to Abraham, and look here, next to Noah in his ship, in a green kirtle, you have Abraham. Abraham kneels on the ground before God, and tells God he'll be childless, and God for his answer shows him the night sky and the stars. Look, you can see it, the dark hue of the sky and the fires of the stars within. And God asks Abraham if he may tell how many stars there are, and Abraham mayn't; and God tells him his seed will be such on earth, like stars, more than can be told. Do you see what it tokens?'

The bowmen were still.

'The meaning is that when the Lord would be wreaked on mankind for the wrongs we do, he won't kill all. He lets enough folk live to seed the world again. Be there eight folk left on one bare ship when all the leave are drenched to death, it were enough, and the children of the eight and their children's children and all their kin afterwards will be untold as the stars in heaven. So owes it to be with the pestilence. Let the Lord slay folk in their thousands on thousands; be a handful left, or only two, like to Adam and Eve, they might spread mankind again, after the pestilence is spent.'

Longfreke said God must be more angry than in Noah's time, for he pined them with pestilence, not flood; and what kind of ship might keep a good man from that evil?

'On the road, each must build a ship out of rue for his own done wrongs,' said Thomas, 'which is a better ship than Noah's, for Noah's ship fared safe but on this world's seas, while the ship man makes of the beams hewn of his own heart's wood bears him safe from this world into the next.'

The pestilence was a priest's tale, said Sweetmouth. Even were it true, he said, Thomas's read was horse-dung. The good of Noah's ship was that all his kin was in it, and if they overlived the flood, they overlived together, and if they died and their ghosts went to the Lord's house, their ghosts went together. Let the wayfarer make of his heart the cleanest ship there was, he was alone in it, and his dearest weren't with him. They might be drenched while he yet float, and he mightn't know.

Now Thomas was still, and sorrowful again. He was about to speak when Hayne and Hornstrake came from the church with the infirmarer, a weary monk with glass yolks fastened to his eyes on hide string. Hayne bade the other bowmen go to the infirmary, and hear what the infirmarer would tell them, for he'd speak with Thomas alone.

SWEETMOUTH'S FACILE DESTRUCTION of my argument humiliated me. It was not my intention to deliver a sermon. I desired to demonstrate to my new companions an incidental mastery of priestly matters, even though I stated to them candidly that I was not a priest; a point I repeated when Hayne and I sat adjacent in the church porch, his gigantic head inclined and mine facing up.

Among the archers, said Hayne, were obstinate spirits who had not attended confession for many years, yet whose spirits were gravid with crime. The conditions of our itinerary were such, the moment of mortality so unpredictable, that one of our party might perish when we were a considerable distance from a church. It was important to him, he said, that the archers under his command confess before they were exterminated. He made this lamentable prediction with such tranquillity – 'before we be quelled' was the English expression he used, a very severe form – that I had to verify he referred to the plague. He did; I apprehend that he considers the archers' deaths from the pestilence, and mine, to be quite inevitable.

I reminded him that I lack the clavial power to absolve an individual of crimes. I can only obtain an account of those crimes, to adduce a person's conscience out into the light, to probe and ameliorate it till it attains a state acceptable to God. Perfect contrition, I explained, was visible to the Deity, but the penitent could not assess his contrition for himself. He required the assistance of another, i.e. the confessor.

Concerning crime, I said, I had expected him to make some reference to the archers' captive, de Goincourt, whose presence among them under duress perturbed me. I said I had originally intended to commence my penitentiary work by attending to her confession.

Hayne advised me that Softly, de Goincourt's custodian – he referred to her as Softly's possession – was not convinced of my bona fides, and any attempt to converse with her prematurely would be fatal.

Would he not protect me? I inquired. He did not respond. This was characteristic, I discovered. Colloquium with Hayne cannot consist of question and response; all one can do is to move into proximity with him and speak. Statements may issue from his lips, or not; when they do, they may appear to be responses, or not.

In terms of the events of Mantes, two years previously, said Hayne, he had not been in the vicinity of the house from which de Goincourt (the archers refer to her as 'Cess') was abducted, and precise details of what occurred might only be obtained from the archers directly responsible. Certainly Softly had been involved, and certainly none had disputed his control over her person since.

As an account of what occurred, this is evidently unsatisfactory. Yet as frequently as he failed to respond to my interrogation, he anticipated a question I had not articulated. It had been his intention since the company's foundation, he said, to select such archers as would benefit from maximum liberty to act in accordance with their consciences. Even though matters had not evolved as he desired, he could not now restrict those liberties, or dissolve the company, without assisting their evasion of the just retribution towards which their actions inevitably led.

'And Will Quate?' I inquired.

Here Hayne did respond. He turned his eyes to me; and his attention was so much more terrible than being ignored by him that I regretted my question. He said only that he had provided Quate with the necessary terms on which to base his decision to join the company.

I remain convinced that Quate's conscription disturbs him.

Hayne said that responsibility for the company's actions were ultimately his; yet this did not absolve the archers of culpability for what they did.

I trembled. In his crude English diction he had enunciated, unconsciously, the precise paradox that led to my rejection by the magisters of Paris after their initial audit of my capabilities. Requested by them to discuss the contradiction between God's omniscient omnipotence and man's liberty of action, I was expected to summarise and comment on the perspectives of Augustine, Aquinas and

Boethius. In place of this I questioned, and speculated, and advanced my own peurile ideas. Accordingly I was not admitted to the faculty.

Marc, in privileging you with the occupation of copyist, and you, Judith, with the occupation of domestic servant, I desired not only to alleviate tedious labour, but to create in our common domicile a miniature form of the scholarly paradise, university, from which my mistakes excluded me. I expected you to alternate between labour and academic discourse to my benefit. I have confessed as much to you previously. I am impelled at this hour, however, to confess a novelty, that in attracting you to my service there was a third factor, your affection towards each other. I confess that I envied it. I could not acquire that love for myself, but I desired to contain it, as a bottle may not imbibe wine, but must satisfy itself with preventing its escape, and protecting it from corruption.

THE SICKHOUSE STOOD east of the church. In the sickhouse yard, twenty feet from the door, stood a wicker stall with a roof of rough cloth. The stall had four openings, one on each side. None might go in the sickhouse, said the infirmarer, but that they go through the stall first, to be undersought for sickness.

Afterwards they might come out three ways — one door to the sickhouse, if they might be helped; another door to go again whence they'd come, if they were heal; and the third door for those too far gone to be helped by any doctor.

'What owe those unhappy dogs to do?' asked Longfreke.

'Seek a priest,' the infirmarer said, 'or a friend or kin to comfort them, or at worst a lonely stead where they ne have none near to spread the pest further.'

Longfreke asked how long the stall had stood, and the answer came, a fortnight.

'Have we missed news?' said Longfreke. 'Has the pest reached England?'

'It must come soon,' said the infirmarer. 'Too many of our brethren in France and Italy have gone to Christ for me to ween otherwise, and I'd be ready.'

Each bowman went into the stall, one by one. Within, the infirmarer and two knaves tied handfuls of wool soaked in vinegar to their mouths and noses, groped under the bowmen's arms and between their legs, pinched their necks and looked at their tongues. They asked each bowman where he was born, and on what day, and wrote it down in a great book. All deemed heal, the infirmarer led them into the sickhouse. He stood them about a board where lay pots of treacles and sheaves of dried worts and glass flasks of many hues. Behind him in the hall were a score empty bedstraws, each made with good clean linen. In the middle of the hall a knave let fall leaves into a smoking fire. The sickhouse stank sweetly of vinegar and rue.

The infirmarer coughed, clasped his hands together, made a steeple of hi. first fingers and lifted them to his lips.

'The qualm, or as it is rightly called the pestilence, pest or plague, is airborne, as a sickly mist, and spreads from stead to stead when the wind blows from the south,' he said. 'Once it lights on a town, it spreads between folk like to fire in a dry wood. It may reach England in two ways: in clouds, blown by the south wind over the sea, or in ships, either from bad air caught in the sails or in the bosom of the ship, or in the bodies of the seafarers. Comes it thus, it'll most likely be through London, or Bristol, or Kent, or one of the southern havens, Southampton or Plymouth. Where d'you ship for Calais?'

'Melcombe in Dorset,' said Longfreke. 'There's a cog, the *Welfare*, that looks after us a week hence.'

The infirmarer shook his head. 'I wouldn't overgo the Avon this tide.'

'That way leads to France, and that way we must go.'

The infirmarer told how they might shut out the pestilence. Sanguinary bodies that were hot and wet, he said, had most to fear, for their sweat-holes were most open, giving the sickly mist of pest a way into the body. Yet even the coldest and driest of them was in plight, were they not to follow the right path. They owed not to work too hard, lest they get hot and their sweat-holes open. Nor should they know women in fleshly lust, or bathe in hot water, or go more than a day without that they purge their bowels. They owed to shun honey, garlic, onions, leeks and hot spices; to eat cucumbers, fennel, borage, bugloss, spinach and sour fruit, to drink water with verjuice or vinegar instead of wine, and season food with strong vinegar. Dung heaps, gongs, middens and like stinking steads of filth must be shunned, and it were well that each one took sweet-stinking blossoms with him wherever he went, to stop his nostrils with.

'When the pest's nigh, if it be summer, the sky darken by day but there ne be no rain at first, only thunder in the south. At night, lightning, or falling stars. If the wind begin to blow strong of the south, wherever you are, find shelter and be sikur to shut the doors and windows on the southern side.'

Were the pest to reach them, the infirmarer said, they ne felt it when the foul damp air went into them through their noses, mouths and sweat-holes. It passed through the blood to the brain, the heart and the liver, each of which fought to drive out the evil. Those taken first felt chill and stiff and a pricking in the blood and their head ache. Maybe they coughed and felt sleepy. A hard botch in muchness between a pea and an egg grew under the skin, in the groin if the foulness gathered in the liver, in their armpit if the heart, in the neck or under the tongue if the brain. In some, black marks or spots showed on the skin. Either way, death came in three days.

In others, the evil took a shorter path. It fastened on the lungs, which mightn't then cool the heart, and to shield the heart the brain sucked the sickness into itself, but the brain mightn't win, and the sickness either barst out through the ears with a roar that deafened, or, which be worse, through the eyes. For this hapless sinner died the same day; but while he lived, it were enough for him to behold another and the sickness went from his eyes into the eyes of whoever saw him, and from there into his heart, or brain, or liver.

'Thus,' said the infirmarer, 'the first most needful thing when one falls sick of the pest is to bind a cloth over their eyes, that the sickness mayn't get out and spread to those who help him, or to the priest who sends his ghost forth clean. Any asks?'

Hornstrake, whose face had shifted to white while the infirmarer spoke, said he'd know if there were ways to heal those who sicked, or did all who caught it die?

'It gladdens me you asked this,' said the infirmarer. 'Though the best weapon against the pest lies in a right life, I, too, with God's send, may help any man with the will to help himself. Having looked deep into the health of each of you, knowing when and where you were born, I am able to offer you what in Paris is called a course complete of treatment medical and personal, that is, in English, a read of leech-craft good for each man alone, shaped by knowing the stead of the planets and lights when he was born, the lie of his humours, the hue and wetness of his tongue and the clearness of his piss. With the read comes a bag of worts, cunningly minged to hold off the pest with a spoonful a day; a box of Emmanuel plasters, to lower the swelling; and a pot of Bethzaer. Nor is this all. The read also comes with a steel blade, made best for the letting of pestilential blood. And should the sickness be so strong that neither the worts, nor the bloodletting, nor the Bethzaer heal you, I'll throw in a mouthful of a treacle made for kings and cardinals alone, that has in it violets, roses, sandalwood, pearls, oranges, gold leaf, ground silver, emerald and bone from the heart of a stag. All these things together, in London or Paris, mayn't be had for fewer than twenty pound; but I'll give the whole read to any bowman, made for each man's needs, worts, plasters, Bethzaer, bloodletting blade, king's treacle and all, for two score English silver.'

Will would bide, but Longfreke took him by the wrist and led him away.

LONGFREKE, WILL AND Sweetmouth sat at board. A knave brought them fish pies and ale and small hard sour green apples. While they ate, Mad came and sat with them. He told them he'd taken the infirmarer's stead among the singers.

'You haven't no Latin,' said Sweetmouth.

'Credo in Deum patrem omnipotentem, et in filium eius unicum,' said Mad.

'What's it mean?' said Sweetmouth.

'Dum-diddle-dee, dum-diddle-day,' said Mad. 'I tell them I ne know why it needed God to make Latin when there was already Welsh, a better and an older tongue. Latin's as green to Welsh as English to Latin yet they ne dream to sing to God in English. But I tell them I'll sing for them in Latin if they will, if they give me the words. And they say even knaves with quick young minds take days to learn a psalm by heart. So the songmaster gives it me, and I sing it back to them word for word, and they behold me like to

I'm an ape in a mass-hackle, but they mightn't withsay me, so I cleaved to them and sang a spell.'

'You ne wrought a full shift,' said Longfreke.

Mad drained a can. 'I mayn't sing for them no more,' he said. 'I feel the Latin carve shapes in me, like to it takes the rough ridges of my heart, where seeds might take root, and smooths and edges them to floor a church. How was the sickhouse?'

'England's doctors have slain more folk than England's bowmen,' said Longfreke.

'It's the same, priests, doctors, stars,' said Mad. 'If they'd know the true wellspring of this qualm, they owe to know the story of Branwen, daughter of Llyr, and how her brother Bran fought for her worthship in Ireland and lost, and bade Pryderi cut off his head, and how Pryderi did his bidding, and Pryderi's men drank in Harlech for seven years, and for four score years in Penfro, with the head beside them, then went to London and buried the head under the White Tower, with its face toward France. As long as the head be kept underground, no evil may come from that side.'

Sweetmouth said they were weary of the story of Bran's head.

'I haven't heard it,' said Will.

'We've heard it a hundred times,' said Longfreke. 'Ask we Mad who dug up the head and when, he says there's no when, when is for clerks, and as for who, he ne knows, maybe King Arthur, but it must have been a giant, for Bran walked to Ireland through the sea, and the water came no higher than his shoulders.'

'No qualm won't come,' said Sweetmouth. 'It's a tale.'

That night Will mightn't sleep. He rose and went out of the guesthouse in the half-light of the early summer morning. Hooves drummed on the high street and a score horsemen rode by on black horses, and with them a two-wheeled cart hued with the likeness of St George and the worm, driven by a knave with blue eyes and a golden beard. They went north on the Gloucester road.

Will went again to bed and in the morning said he'd seen the players go again the way they came, like to they'd gone home ere their work was done; but his even-bowmen told him he'd dreamed it, for they'd heard nothing.

⌣

NEXT DAY THEY left the abbey and overwent the Avon early, when there was dew yet on the wayside leaves.

'I ne gave a leek for the monks' song when I was in the abbey,' said Sweetmouth, 'but now I'm without it, there's not between me and the eyes of all the devils aroam in Wiltshire.'

They looked over their shoulders at the spire and town of Malmesbury on its hill above the stream. Though it was in Wiltshire, it marked the south edge of Cotswold, couth to them, and now their road was through uncouth land, flat where theirs was hilly, cow-land where theirs was sheepy, rid of trees where their woods ran for miles without a ridding.

In the fields by the road the crops were nearly ripe and bondmen and their wives bent to the weeds, hilling their heads with straw hats, and their children, half storven while they bode on the new bread, lay in the shade with their mouths open and their tongues lolling like dogs in the heat, lacking the strength to cast stones at the birds as they owed to.

The bowmen went as before, on foot with Cess driving the cart, out-take that now Thomas the shriftfather rode among them on a lean brown mare, gazing at each of them in turn, like, said Mad, to a glee-master picking which piper would best play first at the hop, for all must play, but he'd open with a lively one.

Dust rose of the road as they went, and in fields further of the stream the ribs of the cattle showed clean under their hides, and the grass they cropped ne greened the hard pale earth. Far away, in another cloud of dust, the sun shone on a thing of gold, and Will, whose eyes were keenest, saw a heap of folk bearing a likeness of the Clean Mother to the stream. The bowmen read whether it were a going against the pest, or against drought. Longfreke and Holiday spoke of the hunger of their childhood, when there wasn't no harvest three year, and the priests made all bring each child to mass, that folk might know no man kept his kin alive by butchering the least of them.

The road was mostly empty of folk, but after an hour's fare two came up to them from behind: a young swineherd driving a great shod boar, and, on a fair black horse, a maid in a dear white gown, with a white headcloth that hid her hair and her neb.

THE MAID SAID she was the lady Bernadine Corbet, daughter of Sir Guy Corbet, a knight of Cotswold. Will Quate, she said, had wrought her father's fields.

All turned to Will, whose neb reddened. He bowed his head, and said he knew her by her steven.

Lady Bernadine told the bowmen she was on the way to the joust at Edington, but the men her father had hired to shield her on the road, together with her maid, had fled for fear the qualm had come to Wiltshire. Her only help was a faithful swineherd, who drove a boar as a gift for one lord. She asked if she might fare with them as far as Westbury, that she be kept from harm along the way.

Hayne said she might ride with the shriftfather if she would, had she the silver for her own bed and board in Melksham, and ne hampered the bowmen, and minded they were their own men and not hers to bid.

They went on together. Lady Bernadine rode alongside Thomas, and Hab and Enker wandered behind. Sweetmouth came to Will and upbraided him that he ne heeded the doings of his own town well enough to know the lady from Sweetmouth's tale of two days before.

'She's too high-born for me to have her, but she'll be drawn to you, a sweet crumb blown of her dad's larder, and I shall know of you how it feels to run your rough ploughman's hand down her bare back, that's known but feather beds and sweet oils,' he said.

Will smiled and shook his head.

'Ne spurn this godsend, you thankless dog,' said Sweetmouth. 'We're on the road, and the road lies between the end of one life and the beginning of another. That life where you were a filthy Cotswold rat-fucker, up to your neck in your lord's dung-heap and behest to some cross-eyed hagspawn witch with two sheep farts and a bent penny for a dowry, that's two nights behind us, and the life of a soldier in Calais is yet to come, and on the road between you're a free man, who leaves his bed at night to seek cunny, and ne comes again till breakfast.'

'It's not so,' said Will.

'So, so, right so,' said Sweetmouth. 'As I mayn't learn the smack of high-born cunt, you'll know it for me, and tell me be it as I dream: like to the sweetest, ripest cherry about to burst on the bough, like you take the tip of your blade near and it ne reaches the mark before the cherry cleaves of its own tightness and a narrow slit opens up, and spits a drop of sap onto your tongue.'

Will laughed and said it wouldn't be.

'No?' Sweetmouth pilt Will in the ribs with his elbow. 'Look, she comes.'

QUATE SPOKE WITH another bowman, who grinned and winked and sprinkled spittle in his talk. Berna told this other she'd speak to Quate alone, and he bowed his head and fell back. It seemed to Berna she saw him of the corner of her eye flicker his tongue vilely at Quate, or at her.

'Are you glad to see me?' she demanded of Quate, in what she took for a common manner of speech, as a sister of Hab might employ.

'What should I be glad about?' said Quate. 'Each time I see you you're deeper in the mud, and when you sink, you'll draw me and your brother with you. First you steal a gown, then you steal a horse, now you make out you're a lady.'

'I would be a lady,' said Berna. 'My dearest wish is to be like the fair Bernadine in all things. But I am too low, too slow-witted, too rough. I lack her learning and her feelings. I lack the softness of her heart and her sharp wit. Were you to set me and her beside one another, even in the same gown, it were like to a gem beside a wall-stone.'

'I ne know aught of that.'

'But isn't she right fair?'

'Not that I marked.'

'You say so to spare my feelings.'

Will snorked.

'Poor Bernadine,' said Berna. 'How sad she was when Laurence Haket went away and her father made her wed an old man.'

'I wrought her dad's land,' said Will. 'I hadn't no time to see no sorrow in no daughter of his.'

'I saw,' said Berna. 'I saw how Haket wooed her and I envied, that is nithed, them. I wished I might have their dear clothes and clean well-shaped hair and their playful ways with each other. It was ruthful to see how the lady Bernadine was pined when he went away. The hearts of all who saw her were melted.'

'Not mine.'

'As her sorrow deepened, she wouldn't eat, and grew thin and wan, and her eyes were much and bright. I saw that as one near death, Bernadine had been so near the unearthly bliss of love her soul had risen to her neb. I overheard her kinswoman Pogge say to her, "Terrible as your suffering is, it has conferred on your appearance a touch of the divinity of the martyr."'

'Too much French there for me to know.'

'And me, but the sound of it liked me. And the lady was so fair in lovesickness I would have my own likeness of true love. And since I mightn't have no gentleman, but only a churl, I fastened on you, and stole her wedding gown.'

'I'm no churl. I'm a free man. You were better to forget the lady and work out how you might get yourself off this gallows road you're on.'

'Yeah! I believe you're right, my friend,' said Berna. 'After two days on the road I understand my wrong. I know now I mayn't rise above my kind. I'm a pigster's daughter, not made for love. I'm of the earth, as are you, and Bernadine is made of other pith, less earthly, more fire and air.'

Will frowned and looked up at her. 'You're a dote, Madlen,' he said.

'I know,' said Berna.

'But now you've shifted your song I'll say I worth you more than the lady Bernadine. You've come far, and put your life at stake for something you won't never win, while that one only stints at home and meekly does her father's bidding.'

'You ne know what the lady Bernadine does or thinks or feels,' said Berna hotly. 'Hers is a higher and harder way than we can hope to follow, for we know not of the world but through our eyes and noses, rather than, as she, through heart and soul. I reckon when I left Outen Green she readied for a fare of her own. Against hers mine's but a bound girl's foolish game. There mayn't be no love between us, Will. You're betrothed to Ness, and when you come again from France, you'll go behind the plough, and Ness'll cook and keep house and bear your children and bring your ale, and you'll hop on the holidays till you lame, and if she ne do as you bid, you'll beat her, and your backs'll bend like two old trees, and you'll die and have a little house in heaven together.'

'Go home, then,' said Will. 'I ne wanted no love of you. I ne asked you to come after me. Go home with Hab and make out some other stole the gown.'

'I shall. And I shall seek some filthy villain to breed with, more meet to my kind.'

Will laughed.

'Why do you laugh?' said Berna.

'You mirth me.'

'You owe to be more sorry I ne love you no more. Tell me truly, am I not fairer now than when we last met?'

Will keeked at her and shrugged. 'Yesterday in the ridding you nad no cloth on your neb, and now you do, so I mayn't deem your fairness.'

'Am I not wiser, then?'

'Yesterday you were steadfast in your wishes. You knew what you would have, all that I wouldn't let you have it. Now you've lost your boldness. It's like to you ne know what you'd have or where you go or who you be no more.'

'The lady Bernadine . . .'

'And I ne understand why you're so sweet on your lady Bernadine when you know what a dizzy twit she is.'

'In what way?'

'Busied she less with her heart and soul, and heeded more her eyes and ears, she'd have learned what Laurence Haket would do with Ness Muchbrook when she thought him at hunt. Then I wouldn't be betrothed to a maid already gave herself to a high-born in the wood, and wouldn't have to seek my deed of freedom from the man who swived her and got her great.'

ALL THE STRENGTH flowed of the lady Bernadine, and she fell forward onto the neck of her horse, and would have fallen to the ground had Will not hent her.

He laid her by the side of the road. Breath came of her, so the bowmen knew she lived, but they ne durst lay a hand on her, even Thomas, even to take the cloth of her face. They asked Will what he'd said to fell her like to a knight shot of a steed. He said they'd talked of doings in Outen Green, and he mightn't guess what made her sicken so ferly.

At the word sicken Hornstrake got on his knees, took a glass ball of his shirt and began to say a broken paternoster.

'Leave me here,' said the lady Bernadine, with her eyes shut. 'I die. It is my heart.'

'My guess is lovesickness underlies this,' said Thomas.

'We owe to leave the harlot where she lies, as she asked,' said Dickle. 'We ne owe her nothing. She's no lord of ours.'

Lady Bernadine began to sob.

Will looked for Hab, but the pigboy had gone on down the road, and whistled while he plucked blossoms of pig's parsley the muchness of trenchers and fed them to Enker.

Hayne came up and bade Softly get Cess to help the lady Bernadine into the cart. Softly said Cess wasn't to be shared, nor his cart neither. They were soldiers, he said. It wasn't their lot to keep knights' children.

Hayne took three strides and stood against Softly, his shoulders a good inch higher than Softly's head. Softly ne shifted his ground. The two stood clammed together.

'I may over you,' said Hayne, 'and you ne may over me.'

A handwhile went by when all was still, out-take that Dickle set his hand on his bollyknife, Longfreke cracked his knuckles, and the lady wept to herself.

Softly laughed, clapped Hayne lightly on the cheek and stepped back.

The lady Bernadine was laid on a heap of woollens in the cart, and Cess bidden to see to her while Hornstrake drove. Will was given the lady's horse to lead. Will would speak to Hab, but when he called to him, Hab ne answered, and ne came near.

AT ABOUT NOON they came to Chippenham. A bridge bore the highway from Bristol to London and Canterbury over Avon stream and through the town, the greater deal of which was on the far side. The bowmen hadn't no need to overgo the bridge, for theirs was the southern road to Dorset. They stinted to rest and eat where a warrener hucked brad hare at the meeting of the roads.

'We owe to go into Chippenham,' said Hornstrake. 'There's a stall in the shambles there sells the best hot cow's feet in England.'

'I mind what happened when we last came through Chippenham on the way from France,' said Longfreke.

'We ought to have fired their stinky cots,' said Dickle.

'I ne know what stirred them up so much,' said Sweetmouth. 'I did but spill a drop on the alewife's bosom.'

'It wasn't the spill but how you cleaned it,' said Mad.

Sweetmouth opened his mouth, let his broad tongue loll of it and tapped it with his finger. 'You owe to learn of the cat how well a tongue may wash a kitten,' he said.

'It ran out of hand,' said Longfreke. 'You let so much of their ale into their trough our own horses got drunk.'

Hayne told Hornstrake he might go, were he back within an hour. None would go with him, so he went alone.

'They'll know you,' said Longfreke.

'It was more than a year ago,' said Hornstrake. 'They won't mind no more.'

Off he went. An hour went by and he ne came again. A flock of grim men came out of town bearing baskets full of stones. They set the baskets down at the far end of the bridge and beheld the bowmen with their arms folded. Hayne went to deal with them.

LONGFREKE BADE THE bowmen gather by him and be ready. Will made to string his bow, but Longfreke took his bowstaff from him and dight it with his own in the cart, and their even-bowmen did likewise. Softly whistled to Cess and she handed each bowman a bat of willow wood, an iron cap and a wicker shield. Behind her the lady Bernadine could be seen only as a lump under a woollen.

Longfreke learned Will how to knit the leather strings that held the cap on his noll and how to hold the shield.

Softly bade Will follow him, and learn how to fight, and how to win by it.

'Ne heed him,' said Longfreke to Will. 'This is a small fight, not soldiery.'

'Follow me, lest you live as meanly as Longfreke,' said Softly. 'The greater deal of soldiery is to learn other folk their lack of might. If they fear for their goods and their women, they won't fight no more, and the war ends quicker.'

'But Chippenham folk are English folk,' said Will. 'We haven't no war with them.'

'They're no kin to me,' said Softly. 'All know Wiltshire churls are milksops, and spend their holidays pining their bulls to take them up the arse.'

'I thought me to fight the French,' said Will.

Longfreke said Will would do as he was bidden.

Cries came of the bridge and Dickle yall that the Wiltshire churls had blooded their vinter. He took off his shirt and let it fall to the ground. On his bare chest in blackneedle for all to see was the likeness of two legs in armour, with spurs on the heels, in the teeth of hell-mouth.

Hayne came of the bridge like to naught had happened, but a stone had hit his forehead, and it dripped blood. The townsfolk had known Hornstrake, and took him and put him in the stocks and wouldn't let him go out-take that the score gave them five pound silver against their losses from last year's fight. When Hayne bade them let Hornstrake go, they cast stones at him.

Holiday smeared treacle on the wound, and Hayne dight the bowmen as he would have them go into Chippenham: Dickle, Longfreke, Softly and Holiday foremost, Sweetmouth and Hornstrake in the middle with the ladder, Mad, Will and the priest behind. Cess would mind the cart with the lady Bernadine, and let the swineherd see to it that none came near.

'I'll bide here with the cart,' said Thomas.

Hayne said Thomas must leave his horse behind and go with them, and they'd keep him from harm.

'Free Hornstrake, do no more,' Hayne told his men. 'Ne handle these folk as their like in France. Ne steal, ne fire no house, ne spill no goods nor guts, ne lay no hand on no maid, wife nor child. Use no weapon with an edge. Fight clean, look to each other, keep your eyes on the swivel, and ne shame the name of Gloucestershire.'

Hayne took a shield and an iron cap and went to the stream's brim, near the bridge. He lifted the shield over his head and strode into the river. Deep and fast as the Avon was, it reached no higher than the giant's waist, and he fared through the stream as lightly as a man who walked on land through the wind.

The Chippenham folk howled and hooted with scorn and glee and began to stone Hayne. But they mightn't hit him, for he was shielded. They ran onto the bridge and leaned over the water to let fall their stones the better. When they did this, Longfreke led the bowmen over the bridge toward them.

The townsfolk stood frozen with fear to see Dickle come at them with the token of the Fiend on his bare chest and the holy rood on his forehead, Longfreke, with his cloven face, by his side, and six handy young gomes with them. They ne knew which way to turn, for the giant Hayne came on through the stream, and clamb up the town half, and the other bowmen neared them quickly. A few made shift to let fly slingshots, but none hit their mark, and the greater deal of them let fall their stones and fled.

Hayne caught two Chippenham knaves, gripped them by the throat, lifted them like to they were hens, carried them to the bridge and let them fall in the river. The lanes that led of the high street rattled with the snackle of locks and bolts and shut doors, and those few shopkeepers yet selling made fast to put up their boards. A cheesemonger's board, held flat of his window by two strong chains, was laden with ripe wares, and seeing the bowmen near he made to lift the board, cheeses and all, that the window might be shut with his goods inside. He was a bald red fellow and his neb shone of tears and sweat. The brim of the board nearly met the wall but one thick round cheese withset him, like to the bailiff's foot in the bondman's door, and he began to mew with fear. Dickle dang him on the back of his shoulders with his bat, the old gome fell on his knees in the street, and the cheeses, let free, trendled toward the bowmen's cart. While Dickle thrashed the cheesemonger, and the women of his house screamed from the windows above to spare his life, Softly and Holiday hent the cheeses that went by and stowed them in sacks on their backs.

Longfreke would drag Dickle away from the cheesemonger that the man not be killed, but Dickle smote him yet. A housewife emptied a pot of filth and piss on the bowmen from a high window. Sweetmouth and Hornstrake reared the ladder to the house, clamb up, leapt in through the open window, broke open the shutters of the other windows and began to cast down cloths, cups, cats, bags of pepper and shoon. Three knaves ran out of a lane and would overthrow the ladder, but Mad and Will smote them on the legs and drove them away. Holiday hopped about the cart, catching pepper in his iron cap, and a pewter flask full of wine let fall by Sweetmouth struck him on the head. Wine and blood ran down his neb into his mouth, and he licked his lips, and Mad held the priest by the wrist and bade him look on a holy thing, wine into blood.

Longfreke got Dickle from the cheesemonger, who dragged himself away by his elbows, and yall Hornstrake and Sweetmouth down of the house, and Hayne came out of a lane, and the score went on to the market ground. It wasn't a market day, or maybe it was and fear of qualm kept the sellers away, but anywise nobody sold and the shambles was empty, out-take an old buck goat with one good eye bound to a post, and Hornstrake, locked in the stocks.

'Ne rue,' said Sweetmouth. 'You ne got your hot cow feet but you kept your great much donkey head.'

'They knew me early,' said Hornstrake. 'It was hue and cry.'

Softly broke the lock with a tool he bore, set Hornstrake free and, while Hornstrake rubbed the smart of his wrists, struck him a blow across the side of the neb to learn him to be wiser. Holiday washed the blood and wine of his neb with water of the trough.

The empty market about them was still and no sound came of the houses at its brim. Nothing was to be heard but the cratch of the priest's pen on a littlewhat of calfskin and the creak of the rope as the buck goat stretched toward the water.

'What do you write?' asked Dickle.

'Letters,' answered Thomas, 'to them as come after us.'

'Who's after us?'

'Our children.'

'I haven't got no children.'

'Nor have I.'

'You're a liar, then.'

'Anyone's children, I meant.'

'You're a liar. I never met no child as could read. Ne write nothing of what we do or say, or I'll quell you,' said Dickle.

'I shan't, I swear,' said Thomas.

'What was the last you wrote?'

'"The intangible sensation of terror I have experienced in proximity to this squalid militia manifested itself today in violent action."'

'What's that in English?'

'"I fare well to France, haply met with a score or thereabouts handy fellows of Gloucestershire on their way to Calais, who keep me from all harm."'

Dickle went to the trough and splashed water on his face and chest.

'Write my name,' said Dickle, 'and I'll quell you. I shan't tell you the wrongs I've done, not you nor any man. I ne fear the fire.'

He dight his whole head in the water. The old buck goat heard the sound, wrathed, found strength, broke its rope and hurled at Dickle while he was bent over the trough-side. Before any bowman could lift a hand the goat's head and horns struck Dickle in the arse and he flew over the trough and landed flat on his back in the dirt.

All laughed, out-take Hayne. Dickle lay still while the goat drank. The back of Dickle's noll had struck the brim of the trough and he'd been knocked witless. Holiday and Hornstrake lifted him and pitched him up against the trough to wake when he was ready.

Softly whispered to Holiday and Hornstrake and they went over to where the goat drank. They gripped the beast, Holiday the horns, Hornstrake the hind legs, and wrestled it over on its back. Softly took out his bollyknife and came up to the goat and asked it sweetly if it rued that it had hurt their friend Dickle.

The goat bleated.

'That's no answer,' said Softly. 'I asked an ask, and if you ne answer, it means you ne worth me, or my friend Dickle.'

Softly turned to Will and held out the knife to him.

'Come help learn the goat worthship,' said Softly. 'Hew its legs off at the knee, one by one, until it rues its deed.'

'While the goat still lives?' asked Will.

'How else would it rue? Let it be your christening into the score.'

'I was christened already,' said Will. 'I shot the moon, I was shot from a tree as an arrow, I drank Scotch and I took the oath.'

Softly shook his head. 'I wasn't there,' he said. 'Anywise, those games are for green bowmen. I'd know you were good for the true bowman life. He that holds goat legs higher than one of his fellows isn't fit to bear a bow to France.' He held out the knife to Will again, and smiled, and bade him come.

Will opened his mouth, but before he could speak, cries of 'Wiltshire!' and 'George!' came of the town.

ONE OF THE lanes that led onto the market ground shed a stream of Chippenham knaves weaponed with mattocks, flails and iron poles. Among them was a priest in a white robe bearing a wooden rood in one fist and a blackthorn cudgel in the other.

There were two or three to each bowman, and it seemed the Gloucestershire men must be overcome. Some of the Wiltshire churls were handy fighters, and they set half their strength on Hayne alone, like to they thought if the giant were felled, the others would sikurly fly. This made it lighter work for the other bowmen to beat their foes. Hornstrake broke heads, kneed bollocks and spat in the eyes of the priest. Sweetmouth and Mad fought back to back, Softly and Holiday shivered bones with each clap of their clubs on Chippenham hides, and Will stood over Thomas, who cowered on the floor with his hands on his head. Two of the Wiltshire knaves would lay hands on Will, thinking to wrestle him instead of smiting, but ne reckoned with the strength of the Cotswold freke's arms; Will dragged them down, head foremost, pinned them with a knee on each throat, and took of one his weapon, an iron-topped pole.

He saw that Softly was beset by more foes than he could handle. He ran to him with the pole held to one side in both hands, like to he were about to smite a great tree with an axe, and swung overthwart. The iron tip of the pole dung three Wiltshire knaves at knee height and one after the other their legs crumpled, they cried at the smart, and they fell, rolled about in pine and grat.

The last rese of the Wiltshire men ended. Softly went to where the goat had gone back to drinking at the trough, twisted it to the ground, pinned it with his knee, hewed off one of its legs at the shoulder, dipped his fingers in the blood and smeared it on Will's cheek.

'Deem yourself christened,' he said.

Without a word, Will went to the maddened, screaming goat, ended its life and turned his back on Softly.

~

THE BOWMEN WERE all heal, out-take wems and weals. Softly told Hayne they must spill the town a little that it worthed Gloucestershire bowmen so low.

'Let's fire the market, at least, and have some goods,' he said.

But Hayne bade them go over the bridge again and fare to Melksham. He lifted Dickle, not yet woken, onto his shoulder, and led the way.

Will tarried on the brink of the water-trough with his head hung down, tears in his eyes. Sweetmouth and Mad stood nearby. They beheld each other, and turned to Will.

'It's of a knave of Gloucestershire,' said Sweetmouth, 'who cropped other men's fields for a penny a day, till his back ached and each bone smarted. But on holidays he shot with his bow, for he'd be a bowman of the king, and fell the French chivalry like his father, and like his even-English did at Crécy, by the strength of his arm.'

'And by a wonder hap,' said Mad, 'he was taken into the score of Hayne Attenoke, better was there none. But how unlike to the bowmen of his hopes these bowmen were.'

'Murderers and thieves,' said Sweetmouth, 'and one with hell-mouth on his chest in blackneedle. One that wasn't English, but Welsh.'

'One that babbled of not but the dern hollows of women,' said Mad.

'And when this young knave first saw his even-bowmen fight,' said Sweetmouth, 'it wasn't like to tales of Crécy, but like to when both halves of Stroud play each other at football, only worse, for in football the halves ne break into houses, nor hew the limbs of live goats.'

'So though this young bowman fought manfully,' said Mad, 'he was sick at heart.'

'But his even-bowmen wouldn't let him stew in wanhope,' said Sweetmouth, 'and besides, he'd sworn the oath. So they told him how it went at Crécy, for they were there, and they fought truly.'

'THE KING GATHERED us on a hill in ox-shape,' said Mad, 'with his son at the head, the king in the body, and Thomas of Durham, bishop, in the tail. And the horns of the ox were thousands of bowmen, dight in two lines of two each horn, meeting at a keen tip, so that were the French chivalry to come at the sides of the host, they'd suffer all the arrows of one side of the horn, but if they came at the head, they'd fall between the horns, and suffer arrow-shot from either side. And that the head of his host might withstand French blows, the king bade his carters shackle their carts together to make a hedge around it, with but a narrow opening at the front, and bowmen dight on each cart.

'It rained in the afternoon, but we kept our bowstrings dry.

When the French were ready to fight, the sun shone. On his way down in the west he warmed our backs, and blinded the French, who must come at us with the light in their eyes. That light came again to us of the French armour and spears. The French were so many, and their weapons so bright, that when we looked on them it was like to a bourne of silver flowed of the hillside to the valley floor, and in this silver stream, like to amel, floated the banners of the French lords, the four lions of John of Bohemia, blind of an ill doctoring, the silver band on blue of the proud house of Blois, the red fret on silver of the great house of Soyecourt, the banner of the old house of Coucy, that was to token aquern fur, and the black lion on gold of Louis of Nevers, whose lands a man wouldn't overgo in a week. King Edward rode by before the fight began, to egg us on, and as he went by the shouts of "Edward and St George!" roared like to the sea striking a broken cliff. When the king came to our score, he saw Softly's gold teeth, and bade the herald call down to the French that they should come and help themselves, for there was a duke's ransom in the mouth of every English bowman.

'In the early evening the French sent crossbowmen of Genoa toward us, but they shot their bolts too soon, and they fell short. Our gunners fired the powder in their guns, which as all said sounded like to thunder, but while men did hear thunder only with their ears, they heard the guns with ilk bone in their bodies.

'At the clap of the guns, we bowmen began to shoot. There were many thousand of us, and all could fetch, nock, aim, strike and loose in the time it took to say it. The Italians were hidden under a swarm of arrows. They fell and their bodies lost their kind, pinned in uncouth shapes, black with wooden shafts and goose feathers. Those that weren't slain ran away, and the French chivalry cut them down, their own hirelings.

'The French chivalry began to come. We heard the hooves of ten thousand fighting horses beat the ground, the yells of the French knights and the strakes of their trumpets. The grass of the hillside was oversprad with the blue and gold of their coats and the silver of their spear tips. It seemed to us a handwhile we stood like to deer in a blind slade, made to bide on the hunt come to spill us. The world hadn't never seen such a hunt, a mile wide and deep of men-at-arms on horseback. All the lords of France full of mirth and thirsty for blood all at once, the foremost row clinching the saddle, spears down, they in the last row so far behind they yet laughed, told tales, wiped the wine of their lips and bade their knaves watch their hounds. And in the rows between, sheaves of ostrich feathers yellow and purple wagged of steel helms, knights shoff to be nearer the foremost, as much to see and be seen as to fight the sooner. Soft hands that two days erer stroked the white wombs of their ladies put on steel-ring gloves and smoothed their horses' silk coats.

'They yearned to kill us and win the fight, but like to a hunt, it was their holiday. They ne knew for sikur which were the right end of a hunt, the slaying of the deer, or how they were seen by others as they slew, how the sun shone on their harness, how sweetly their sword arm hewed, and did the bard see it to sing of afterwards? Even a king that wins his fights needs to sing of it, and not only to sing of his winning, but to sing of how he won in some way folk mind always. That under him were killed three horses, or he fought with an axe like to a bound man, or he fought without a helm that his golden hair might show the better.

'The French chivalry went into that storm of arrows and began to die. Under the hiss of the shafts and feathers in the air the bowmen heard a sound like to hail as thousand on thousand needle-sharp arrowheads pitched through the steel of the French knights' harness. The foremost would shape themselves into right rows, the better to drive and harrow us, but as fast as they made a row, it was broken by the fall of men and horses.

'Among us were those that had seen great hunts in England, and minded how those heaps of proud folk are so light and easy and well together while the sun shines through the trees, how they behold each other's dear clothes and falcons and hunting gear and worth each other right high. Then a storm comes up, the wood darkens and the hunters' silk, leather and feathers are sodden, and the hunters mayn't find their way, and their horses stumble and cast their riders in the mud, and they as would keep to the hunt go one way, and they as would find shelter go another, and each with his horse's hooves overtreads the bodies of his hirelings, and the anger of each rises, and all the while the rain beats down. So it was at Crécy, with arrows for rain, and blood the wet that soaked their clothes and harness.

'Otherwhiles, out of the seethe of dying chivalry, a ragged row of knights would shape and rese toward us, only to melt before it reached us. Those few that overlived to ride between the rows of bowmen and in at the gate of the hedge of carts were slain by the English knights there.

'Had the English chivalry stood its ground, and let each row of French be winnowed by our arrows before the scattered leave fall to the Black Prince's men, the fight might have ended sooner. But the English high-born mightn't bear to stand by and let a heap of lewd churls with bows and arrows steal the worth of winning the fight. They must rese out of their haven and set upon the French in the open field, where the foe was stronger. And once the English and French chivalry fought together shield to shield, spear to spear, sword to sword, we must let of shooting, that we ne butcher the followers of our own king. Blind King John, the French king's friend and best of all their chivalry before he lost his sight, had himself and his horse knit to two of his knights by ropes, that he might be led into the fight. He mightn't see the foe but whirled his sword about him like to a windmill. Afterwards it was said he was throughshove with English iron by one of the Prince's high-born followers, but others said he was found with arrows in him. The truth was that none looked after a king's death in a fight, be the fight ever so great, and the high-born on either side couldn't bear to think them that a low-born churl had done the slaying. But none of the high-born would take the death on himself, so they told each other he'd died fighting another of the chivalry, and the name of his foe wasn't never spoken.

'Without the sikurhood of the carts and bowmen, the Prince and his followers ne withstood the French, and were thrown back. But when the French went forward, they laid themselves open, and the bishop came from behind with men from the hindmost deal of our host, and smote the French in the side. And the French broke and fled. It was all but night, and by the light of the moon and stars and an on-blaze mill King Edward had bidden be fired on the hilltop, we saw the gleam of steel of many thousand helms and sets of harness as the living crope away, and saw the shadowlike rough lumps of the dead and wounded they left behind, like to the sea that ebbs and leaves on the strand empty shells and the timbers of drowned ships.'

ABOVE BERNA WHEN she opened her eyes was a ham, black except where a morsel had been cut off. Three flies were busy about the rosy cut, like to they played a game: if one lighted on the ham, the other two must be in the air. Next to the meat hung an iron pan, a bunch of garlic and a cleaver. All were suspended from one of the wooden hoops that supported the cart's sailcloth cover. There was an odour of oiled tools, spilled ale and stale bedstraw.

Berna rose to her knees. Cans, bundles and handles shifted under her. In a basket lay a knife, its greased iron blade worn hollow by long grind. She took the knife in her right hand and let the fresh weight of the blade rest on her wrist. She replaced the knife and took out her bloodletting blade. She removed the veil from her face, rolled it into a ball, pulled up her sleeve and, with her tongue stuck out in concentration, added a fresh cut to the existing array. Attentively, like an infant studying the movement of ants, she regarded the line of blood course into the veil.

When she had finished, the bleed staunched, the cut compressed with tape and her sleeve rolled down, Berna crawled to the front of the cart. The shafts rested on a patch of bare earth. Between the shafts, in the shade, Cess washed men's shirts and breeches in a tub. Her grey coverchief came down to her eyebrows and up to her chin. She could not have been much older than Berna. She had prominent cheekbones, a gap between her front teeth and lines under her eyes.

'I'm thirsty,' said Berna. 'Fetch me something to drink.'

Cess ne looked up. She said she wasn't the lady's servant.

Berna swung her legs out over the end of the cart and allowed them to dangle.

'Es-tu Française?' she demanded.

Cess let a stream of French of her lips. Though Berna knew some of the words she couldn't interpret the whole. 'I thought me I knew your language, but I ne comprehend you,' Berna said. 'Perhaps it's because you're a servant. My French suffices to read *Le Roman de la Rose* in the original. I suppose you're unfamiliar with the text. I suppose you haven't your letters.'

Cess regarded her. She saw the sanguinary veil in Berna's fist. She got up, dried her hands on her apron and gently touched Berna's arm where a spot of blood had coloured the tissue of the gown.

'I find a gentle purge to be of assistance in balancing my humours,' said Berna hesitantly.

Silently Cess took the veil from Berna's hand, plunged it into the tub and began to frot it clean.

'Are you familiar with Paris?' said Berna. 'I wished to go there. I have heard it is rather large compared to our London. All my favourite poets found their voices in that city. It must be a marvellous place. I think it is a terrible pity the French king is our enemy at present.'

Cess attended more to the lavendry than to Berna. She poured the water from the tub and began to wring out the clothes and hang them to dry on the arms of the cart shaft.

'I suppose I mayn't journey to France no more,' said Berna. 'I imagine I shall probably expire as a suicide.'

A trace of a smile passed across Cess's face.

'It is ungenerous of you to mock me without taking account of the exceptional gravity of my position,' said Berna. 'You haven't suffered as I. You haven't such cause to consider self-murder. I chose love over marriage to my father's choice, a dull old man, only to discover, with my course already set, that my paramour is false.'

Cess finished hanging out the clothes and commenced to mingle hashed leeks and green cheese in a bowl.

'My cousin judged it risible that I couched my tenderness towards Laurence in terms romantic and poetic,' said Berna. 'I was very affected by the Romance. But how else, except by presenting to my senses a distant person towards whom I was attracted, might I create in myself sufficient courage to depart my family? Had my father possessed in his library the story of a demoiselle who escaped a hateful marriage to prosper and be content in a grand city far away, I dare say I would have adopted it with pleasure. I might only cultivate my imagination with the materials at hand.'

Cess regarded Berna and addressed her with that familiarity, so uncomfortable from the common people to the gentle, that Will and Hab had employed. 'Why kill yourself, when you may see a man suffer your feigned indifference?' she said. 'Would that I had such liberty.'

'You are unmarried?'

'We all have our troubles,' said Cess.

'What are yours?'

'They came to my father's house looking for valuables and wine,' said Cess. 'They killed my father and ravished me, and afterwards took me with them by force.'

'Who?' demanded Berna. 'Who did this?'

'The archers. Who else? Softly was the first, and treats me as his property now.' She pointed to the clothes drying on the shafts. 'Look,' she said, 'I wash his shirts.'

WHEN WILL CAME again to where they'd left the cart, he saw the lady Bernadine there in her wedding gown; he knew her by her neb. Hab told him she had fled her wedding and come of Outen Green all alone.

'Where's Madlen?' asked Will.

'When she saw the lady Bernadine come,' said Hab, 'she ran away. I ne know where she went.'

WE DEPARTED CHIPPENHAM with Dickle Dene still unconscious in the cart. Lady Bernadine had recuperated sufficiently to remount her horse, but had experienced a severe emotional injury. A rigidity and lack of sensibility to all that occurred around her was substituted for the inquisitiveness and nervous excitement that had animated her previously. She had removed her veil, and although I had not observed her face before, I perceived that her skin was pallid and her eyes no longer possessed the same lucidity. The contrast between the lighter skin of her face, her black hair and the carbon darkness of her eyes created an interesting and attractive effect, an effect of which she was possibly cognisant. How easily the young may transfer reverence between those terrible manifestations of the supernatural they will encounter in life – from love, that is, to death.

We alone of the company had our own mounts, and were closer in station to each other than to any of the archers. The propriety of our association – I, a person of uncertain marital status and she, a virtually unaccompanied, unmarried female – was secured by the implied ecclesiastical quality I had acquired. It seemed natural that she should turn to me for spiritual advice.

After a brief exchange of formalities and platitudes, Bernadine interrogated me as to my confessorial bona fides, at the conclusion of which, having satisfied herself that I would protect her secrets (she required that I adjure to this) and that my method was both informal and flexible, she said she would confess everything. By this she did not intend the totality of her sins in the eyes of God, but the narration of her history. She required not so much to demonstrate remorse and receive absolution as to create a channel by which her recent experiences, venemous when confined within her, might flow out and be dissolved in the more expansive containment of two. In brief, she required confidence in me.

Accordingly she acquainted me with her misfortunes, that she was fugitive from an odious forced marriage, and that, as she had just discovered, Laurence Haket, the amator on whose protection she now depended, had secretly fornicated with the serf woman to whom Quate was affianced; this in the context of the relevation of Cess's rape and abduction by the very company Berna had selected to conduct her to salvation.

I would have supposed that this sequence of male atrocities must combine in Bernadine's mind to create an idea of the world as nothing but the scene of an unequal male–female conflict in which the female was interminably vanquished. I would have imagined her surveying the region for a nunnery. Not so. Her discovery of Haket's perfidy did not deprive her of emotional power over him, or over her father; to her mind, it simply redirected that power from the romantic's to the martyr's pole. She proposed that if Haket rejected her as his lover, she would go to him as that which he could not ignore, a corpse.

I advised Bernadine that suicide as a method for the restitution of a lover's attention had significant disadvantages. She would gain but a minuscule advance against the satisfaction of his remorse, with the principal entirely lost; and rather than forcing the lover to comprehend the magnitude of his error, the facility with which the demoiselle extinguished her corporeal substance might only confirm him in his previous conclusion that she had been too insubstantial a creature on whom to fix his future.

'If your intention is to force him to recognise his lack of devotion,' I said, 'if you desire to disturb him from his arrogance and have him prostrate at your feet, isn't it preferable to demonstrate how minimal his power to injure you? Go to the joust and let him see you delighting in the revelry, as if he ne existed.'

'That is what poor Cess advised,' said Bernadine.

She pitied Cess, and resented her own capacity for pity, when she so desired pity from others. She resented, too, that she defected from a quality generally native to women of her status, namely the ability to assume common people, like beasts, did not possess mental faculties of sufficient delicacy to permit the injury of an organ as subtle as the mind or heart. That one would no more discuss non-consensual fornication between commoners in terms of rape than when a stallion covered a mare.

'Will her family ne ransom her?' inquired Bernadine.

'Ransom is for nobles,' I said.

'Then she has a duty to herself to escape, as I escaped my father.'

'You're a knight's daughter, in your own country, and even you demand protection on your journey. How much more difficult would it be for a solitary female foreigner of low estate to vagabond around without being used more severely than now?'

'The cart is full of knives. Had it been me I would've exterminated my tormentor long ago.'

'Might it be that she attends the proper moment to act?'

'What would you know about action? I'm not sure you've ever acted. You've clearly attained a marvellous perfection in the study and description of a state of affairs from every aspect; and the more aspects you observe, the more content you are with a state of affairs as it is, and the less you desire to change it.'

She silenced me. I desire my defects be obscure, visible only to super-perceptive observers rather than protruding flagrantly, luminous to all. I directed her to Hayne, who alone among us had power over Softly. She went to converse with him, and encountered a silence more impenetrable than mine.

Marc, Judith, have you discerned the nature of my concupiscence? I despise my failure to act decisively, to intervene in the existence of others, and yet had I acted towards Judith as directed by my demons, how miserable the consequences would have been. Yes, an extra cause for self-abomination: only the proximity of the plague forces me to admit to you that I have committed the crime of desire for Judith more times than I can enumerate. With the maximum of humility I petition you, Judith, and you, Marc, for absolution.

ON THE WAY to Melksham, Will would speak with Hab. Hab said he would speak to him later, when they could be alone.

Before they came to the town Will lost sight of him in the dust and when he asked the others if they had seen him they ne knew where he was.

WE TRANSITED THE plain in a nimbus of pulverised soil that irritated every orifice of man and horse. It appeared to me that I was in purgatory, where all colour is attenuated, all motion retarded, all sound strangled, and my destination and that of my companions perpetually receded.

I regretted the conclusion of my discussion with the acute and impatient Bernadine. She distracted me from the violence in Chippenham and from Dickle's condition. He is indubitably a confederate of Softly's, whose instinct tells him I am, by my nature, his enemy. How terrible my initiation, should an archer die unconfessed even before we encounter the pestilence.

How had I positioned myself so horribly? Was I obliged to go to the cart and attempt to extract a confession from the savage Dickle against his demise? Might he not abruptly recover and see in me an apt object for retribution? If I kept my distance, and he perished unconfessed, he was sure to be damned for eternity, and the culpability would be mine. If I neglected to act till we arrived in Melksham, and he was as close to death as I suspected, the archers would summon an actual priest, and my status as confessor would come under scrutiny.

Judith, Marc, do you remember how one night a single phrase of Cicero's excited us and we debated it with such intensity that only the dawn interrupted us?

THE KEEPER OF the inn at Melksham wouldn't take them at first when he found one of them sicked. Holiday showed him Dickle's wound, and said he'd only fallen, and hadn't no ague; his forehead was cool and dry, his breaths steady.

The innkeeper knew Hayne, and said if he would sleep in the same room as Dickle, they might bide at his inn. So a room with four beds was got for Hayne, Dickle, Longfreke and Softly, and beds would be made later for the other five bowmen in the hall.

The innkeeper withsaid again when he learned that the lady Bernadine was unwed and alone, till Thomas in a strong steven, more like to a stern priest's than he'd shown before, said he'd speak for the lady's worth, and gave the innkeeper the names of mighty folk who fared on that road to and from Avignon, who were his friends; and besides, the lady bode for a maid, who must come soon. The innkeeper yielded and gave the shriftfather and the lady good rooms on the upper floor.

Nobody knew of no doctor in Melksham, so Holiday sat with Dickle while the other bowmen ate. Before the meal ended Hornstrake got up, said he was weary, and got a knave to bring him a sack of straw to lie on in the dark hern of the hall where the bowmen would spend the night.

Hornstrake kept dried figs and nuts in his bag, Sweetmouth told Will, and him ne liked to share. Some nights on the road he'd go early to bed, lie alone and cram his mouth with food, which he loved more than cunny, for he wouldn't never come to the bath-house with them.

When they rose from the board, Sweetmouth bade Will listen. From the stead where Hornstrake lay came a sound like millstones at grind. Sweetmouth said he'd go to see their friend was well. He went to the dim hern, bent down over the still shape that rose and fell with each snore, and came again in a short while. Hornstrake was deep asleep, he said.

Longfreke minded them of the read of the Malmesbury doctor, but they ne heeded him, and Sweetmouth led Will and Mad to the bath-house, and Longfreke came with them anywise.

THE BATH-HOUSE STOOD a short way from the inn. It was timbered of the bigness of a barn. It lacked windows and dimmed with a stream of smoke the sun that set over the roofs of Melksham. The bowmen went inside to a small room where they gave money to a long great-wombed man in a dirty white kirtle. They left their knives and the man gave each a tin token. He let them through to another room where they took off their clothes. Two young knaves took them and gave them linens to wrap about their middles, and would sell them soap, but Sweetmouth shooed them away with his token and they went through a curtain into a dark, hot hall filled with steam.

The hall was floored in stone and lit by grease-lights in glass pots hung on the walls. In the middle of the hall stood a tub of hot water, filled by knaves with buckets who ran in and out from the fire room. Men stood spread through the murk. They washed themselves, let water of dippers onto their bodies, whitened their clefts and groins with soap, straightened their hair under falling water and sat on benches about the side to dry themselves with linen, or sat still, as if asleep, arms on their knees, head bowed. The dippers splashed and clanged against the rim of the tub, water hit the floor, feet slapped on stone. None spoke.

'Behold the poor sinners,' said Mad.

They went to the far side of the hall, to where a fellow with a stick and a maid's face corven of whalebone fastened to his neb instead of a nose made them show their tokens. He unlocked the door for them and they went through. The door closed and they were in darkness. They heard a maid sing under a gittern:

> And love is to my heart gone with one spear so keen
> Night and day my blood it drinks.

'Hell harrowed,' said Mad.

'Here's Eden before they crammed their guts with apple,' said Sweetmouth.

They pushed forward through a heavy sheet into another, narrower hall. It too was hot and filled with steam, yet lit with twice as many lights, and these were beeswax, not grease. The steam gave of sweet stinks as of blossoms and church reekles. On either side of the hall were three tubs, each half hilled with hoods of sailcloth hued with likenesses of fish and sea-elves, half fish, half maid. In the tubs, in water up to their chests, sat naked men, eating and drinking wine of white linen on boards laid overthwart the brims. Fresh water was brought by naked women, who also fetched the food and wine, and who stepped in and out of the tubs, washing the men, laughing with them, feeding them and letting their tits be felt.

A woman came up to the bowmen. She bowed her head and smiled like to she knew them all, though Will hadn't never been further than ten mile from home, and never to a bath-house. Her hair was bound behind with red silk tape and she wore a silver ring on each finger. Sweetmouth said they'd brought a fresh young bowman and the woman put her hand on Will's cheek and told him her name was Lisa, and the bowmen had been room-hearted to bring such a featous gift for the girls on their last night. The abbot had told them the house needed to be shut, she said.

Longfreke asked why and Lisa shrugged and said for the same why there were so few on the road.

'Look how still it is,' she said. 'The bath-house in Chippenham's shut a week already, and it does twice our business.'

'It's wearisome how the clerks speak of a thing that's about to end the world, yet it never comes, till all think it a wile,' said Sweetmouth.

'An ill wile for the abbot if so,' said Lisa. 'It's his bath-house, and he loses two pound a week when it stands empty.'

She took them to a tub and they took off their linens and clamb in and women began to come and go with hot water while others laid out a board with wine and dishes of small sweet pies.

They sat and drank and spoke of the fight, and were it Christ or the Fiend sent the goat to smite Dickle, and whether a bowman, Will, might swive a lady, Bernadine, and hope to keep his bollocks. Once the top of the water reached their middles a woman stepped into the tub and sat between Will and Longfreke. She put her arms on their shoulders and turned her eyes from one to the other.

'Likes you the maid, I'll stand you the fee, as you're a green young fellow,' said Sweetmouth to Will.

'It's a false offer,' said Mad. 'Sweetmouth'll seek afterwards a tale of the swive so much longer than the swive itself that he'll get more mirth of it than you ever might. Sweetmouth likes more to listen and to speak of swiving than to swive. He's always first to the bath-house, but never yet went with a woman in one. He only has to see a woman naked to have in his mind all he'd do to her in so full and bold a likeness that when it comes to the deed he's already spent.'

Sweetmouth threw a dipper of water in Mad's neb. 'Mad gets

wise in the ways of whores by being one,' he said. 'He'll never come out in the evening without selling the whoremistress a song she must buy with her cunny.'

'No shame to be a whore of song, nor to be a whore who may be bought for one,' said Mad. 'Truth is, the swive is less of a fee than the tales they tell me afterwards.'

Will said the woman, whose name was Jul, him liked much, but he was betrothed.

Jul asked Longfreke how it was with him.

'I was betrothed,' said Longfreke, 'but when I came again from France with my neb corven atwain, my burd went to another.'

'I'll be yours for sixpence,' said Jul.

Sweetmouth let a roar. 'And how much to be Will's?' he said.

'Sixpence,' said Jul.

'But that one's got a neb like an angel, and Longfreke's is like to a devil on a rainspout.'

'Owe I to take less from Will, or more from Longfreke?' said Jul.

'Nothing from neither,' said Sweetmouth. 'Will's too fair for you to take silver of, and Longfreke's too wretched.'

'All men who come to the bath-house are alike to me,' said Jul.

'I ne believe it,' said Sweetmouth.

'Do you mind all the arrows you shoot?' she asked. 'There are so many, and all the same.'

'But when a bowman shoots a man in war,' said Longfreke, 'the bowman fucks him, and in swiving it's the man who fucks the woman, not the woman who fucks the man.'

'In the bath-house, I'm the bowman,' said Jul. 'I shoot and shoot and shoot, and all the arrows are the same to me. But to him I wound, there's only one arrow, the arrow that hits, and he'll never forget it as long as he lives.'

Longfreke laughed. He took her hand and drew her out of the tub and away.

Another maid began to wash Sweetmouth and talk with him. Mad leaned toward Will and murmured that if he sought the swineherd, he'd find him in the far tub on the other side of the hall.

~

HAB WAS WITH an old man who wore a gold St Nicholas on a chain nested in his white chest hairs. The old man held a glass cup of wine in one hand and ate hazelnuts from a dish on the board before him. When he saw Will he called to him to come into the tub with them.

Will asked the old man who he was.

'Jacob. Wool-buyer of Ghent.' They shook hands.

'Hab's a thrall without silver,' said Will. 'He's run of his manor without leave.'

'A naked arse no man may rob,' said Jacob. 'Hab's my friend, and I've silver enough for both of us for a night, and for you too, if you'll come in the tub with us.'

Hab whispered in Jacob's ear. Jacob stood up and wrapped a linen round his middle. He smiled at the younger men in turn and bade them be kindly to each other.

'Ne make me bide too long,' he told Hab. He went to the door at the end of the hall where Jul and Longfreke had gone.

'Come in if you ne fear me,' said Hab.

Will took off the linen and got in the tub with Hab. He sat at the far side.

'We weren't in the water together since we played in the bourne,' said Hab.

'How'd you know Jacob?' asked Will.

'You ne owe to have told him I'm a thrall.'

'I'll say and do as it likes me, for I'm a free man, and all the wrong's on your side for following me wherever you go.'

'You'd have all folk bide in the stead they were born, out-take you.'

'Me ne thought she'd run of her own wedding.'

'Why not?' said Hab. 'You ran of yours.'

'It's not true.'

'She ran that she not wed a dull one who'd make children and keep her at home. You're the same.'

'Ness is my burd,' said Will, 'if she'll still have me after the unkindness I did her on your read.'

Hab laughed. 'It's Outen Green says the fairest maid weds the best young ploughman. That's stale old ways. Love you Ness, you must yearn to kill Haket, be wreaked on him for what he did. But you ne yearn to kill him.'

'How might I kill a high-born man like him?'

'Loved you Ness truly, you ne recked the how. I see it ne hurt you one grot to learn she gave herself to him.'

'You ne see into my guts to know what I feel.'

'I see. I know. You only let as though you care for her. You lie to yourself that you love her for fear to learn the true name of the one you love.'

'There must be some wise pigs in the wood to learn you so much.'

Hab looked down and grope his pintle and bollocks in his fist under the water like to it were a heap of pond weed.

'A bondman's bound to bear his tools all day, but that ne means he loves with them,' he said.

He slipped off the bench and sat on the floor of the tub. The water came to his shoulders, which were near Will's knees. He looked up at Will. A woman came and poured in hot water, maffled some words to Hab and went away.

'We stood in the bourne,' said Hab, 'and plight to follow it to the sea. And you dragged me underwater and held me, and our bodies were against each other, and our lips came together. It were like to you'd rather be drenched together than let me go.'

'We wrestled as little knaves,' said Will, 'and afterwards we grew to manhood.'

'To grow from child to man's but one way to grow,' said Hab. 'You've grown from ploughman to bowman, from bound man to free, from Will of Outen Green to Will of the world. Grow again.'

Will laughed and played with his fingers and bowed his head. 'A lamb might grow to any kind of sheep, but not to an ape,' he said.

Hab reached forward, grabbed Will's middle and made to pull him down into the water. Will wrothe and Hab laughed. Will kicked with both feet and sent Hab flying back against the edge of the tub. Hab gasped, sank, rose, shook his head, stood and wrapped a linen round himself.

'Did I hurt you?' said Will ruthlessly.

'The water's cold,' said Hab. 'I'll go away and you won't never see me no more. Hab's ended, for you won't be with me.'

'I'd be your friend, do you only bide for me to come again from France next year.'

'There's no time,' said Hab. 'All of Hab there is will be what you mind of him, no more.'

He bade Will farewell. Tears stood in his eyes. Will rose, and did on his linen, and lifted his hand as if to hold Hab's shoulder, but let it fall.

Hab bade Will go to the back of the bath-house and bide there for his sister.

'You sought too much of me,' said Will.

Hab ne answered, and went out through the dark door at the end of the hall.

WILL BODE OUTSIDE the bath-house till the sun had gone and it was half dark. Madlen came out. She wore a dull-hued gown, a barmcloth and a white headcloth, and bore the bundle that'd been on the boar's back.

'Where'd you get the silver to buy another dress?' said Will.

'Work,' said Madlen.

'I ne know what you'd have me do,' said Will.

'Let me be near you. The days are few.'

'Ne give me your tales of pestilence. I ne believe that priest's swike.'

'It ne hangs on your belief. There's no time. The lady Bernadine's groom Sir Henry is come to Melksham with Cockle the miller's son, the one for his bride, the other for the thief of the lady Bernadine's gown, that I be taken home to Outen Green and hung.'

'I ne care,' said Will. 'Run away or be caught, it's the same to me. I ne asked you or your brother to leave home and be my burden. I ne need your friendship or his. I came out of Outen Green to be free. I'd be rid of you all. Do they loll you up I'll light you a candle when I get to Calais.' He left Madlen and went again to the inn without her.

BERNA LEFT HER chamber and turned the key in the lock. She pushed the door and it remained closed. She smiled and unlocked and locked it several times. From her chamber a gallery, open to the inn yard on one side, led to a stairway. She perceived a number of archers, Will among them, depart the inn through the yard gate.

She went downstairs. The innkeeper and his wife were engaged in a muted disputation. They ceased when they saw her and regarded her doubtously. Beyond them in the common hall she distingued the forms of guests, male and female, dallying over food and drink.

She held the key in one hand and her mother's mirror in the other. She desired to show the mirror to Cess, to let her use it, and parle with her, but she couldn't see her, and Softly was by the cart with the one who balmed and apparelled himself above his dignity, the one they called Holiday, and the two men regarded her. They appeared amused.

She turned again to the hall. The innkeeper bowed his head and said if her needed anything, he might send it to her chamber.

'I wish to dine in the common hall with the other guests,' said Berna. 'My maid must arrive at any moment.'

The innkeeper refused. He ne doubted she was of gentle blood, he said, but a maid on the road without kin or servants owed to count herself fortunate to have a privy chamber, his best. She'd be safer and more comfortable remaining there until morning. Or he could send a message to a nearby manor; one of the noble ladies would surely invite her to pass the night.

Berna demanded to be allowed to dine with Thomas, her confessor.

She was told he was with the injured archer, and had requested he not be disturbed.

She bade the innkeeper send up a light, some victuals and hot water, and went to her chamber.

It had a bare wooden floor and a bed with a horsehair mattress, made up with rude linen that wasn't quite dry and curtained around with heavy twill, discoloured in patches. There was a pot on the floor, a pitcher of water, a chipped basin and a towel on a small table, a larger table, and two chairs with leather seats. Berna opened the shutters on two windows that gave out on Melksham's high street. They weren't larger than a foot across but a little air blew through them and they gave sufficient light to illuminate the paintures of lords and ladies hawking and chasing hinds with dogs to the strakes of a horn that embellished the white walls.

The girl who came to her chamber wasn't more than twelve or thirteen, and Berna couldn't make her speak nor stay with her while she laved and dined. In solitude, in the darkening chamber, Berna drank watered wine and ate a cherry tart and a little sausage and bread, but left the onions. She passed time at the window, regarding the people and dogs and horses that moved with sureness of purpose below.

When the sun was almost set she placed the two candles the girl had brought her at either end of the large table and arranged her possessions in a line. The innkeeper had given her an uncountable number of pennies after she gave him her gold noble. From a purse she wore on a cord around her neck she took a ring, a chain and a nouche of gold of her mother's. She had a whalebone comb, a toothbrush, a wimple, two sets of fresh linen, silk tape for her hair, a nail file, a jar of face cream, a vial of piment, a bag of grains de paradis, her bleed-knife, the key, the mirror, and the book.

She opened the mirror. A shower of broken glass fell to the floor. She swept the shards up with the edge of her hand and put them in the purse. She lay on the bed for a time with her eyes open. She got up and began to read *Le Roman de la Rose*, sitting at the table and bringing the two candles close at either side. When the chamber was almost completely dark beyond the edges of the light, she closed the book and went downstairs. She ignored the innkeeper and his wife and Softly, all of whom cried out to her, and without knocking went into the chamber where the injured Dickle Dene lay.

Thomas sat on the edge of one of the beds. He wrote on a piece of vellum that rested on a board across his knees, with an inkhorn on one corner and a candle on the other. Close to him, on a bed by the window, lay Dickle, his eyes closed. In the obscure corner furthest from the window was a grand armoire.

'My lady,' said Thomas, bowing his head. 'I overfilled my inkhorn, or I'd greet you properly.'

'I require confession,' said Berna.

'This soldier suffers,' said Thomas. 'Let him rest while I sit with him. Please return to your chamber.'

The armoire moved; it rose and lengthened. It was Hayne Attenoke, who had been sitting still at the end of the bed. He said he would send Holiday to find a priest, and left.

Berna sat down opposite the confessor. 'I'm treated with disrespect,' she said. 'I'm a knight's daughter. A Corbet. The meanest of my father's cottagers may flee his bondage for Gloucester or Bristol and be free in a year, while I, a gentlewoman, ne move a foot without inciting suspicion of my motives, as if to be abroad without a man or servants were of itself a sin.'

'The gown advertises an incompleted sacrament,' said Thomas. 'If only others might view in it the very story, that you are in the process of exchanging one man's protection for another's.'

'This isn't so plain a story as that, which you know,' said Berna. 'Is the archer very sound asleep?'

BERNA SAID: 'I'M uneasy in the choices I've made.'

'And the choices made for you,' said Thomas. 'Your regrets are easily comprehended. Your father might have arrived at a consort better suited to you than to himself. You might have prepared more carefully for your departure. You might have been more attentive to the character of your amour.'

'You ne value speech for itself,' said Berna. 'All virtue is in the argument and the conclusion for you. But there's no conclusion here. Nothing is easily comprehended. I'm alone among strangers, without support or security, far from home, deceived by the amour on whom my whole hope rested, and in this moment, I bruise my late mother's mirror. The occasion compels me to grieve, to abandon myself to grief. I lie on my bed to pass the night in tears. Yet I feel only joy. Never before have I had my own privy chamber, with a key to lock it. To be able to lock my own door is a queen's power. And in the midst of such joy at the power to defend my solitude I am miserable because I have no one to tell how joyful I am and why. Is this how madness appears, when one sentiment opposes another?'

'Were I a priest,' said Thomas, 'I would probably advise prayer and fasting.'

'Have you read *Le Roman de la Rose*?'

'I have known the rage of the doctors that I, like so many scholars, abused my literacy to enjoy the story of a young man's dream of love for a perfect flower.'

'I haven't read the conclusion,' said Berna. 'The copy in my possession comprises solely Guillaume de Lorris's portion, with the Lover left unsatisfied.'

'The book in general, and the second part in particular, are not intended to be read by demoiselles,' said Thomas.

Berna made a gesture of impatience. 'When I lived in my father's manor house and Laurence Haket loved me par amour, I could imagine myself as the Rose. But now I go to him as if I were the Lover, and he the Rose. As if I, not he, suffered the wounds of Love's arrows.'

'And suffer you such very pain?'

Berna smiled uncertainly.

'Frankly I find a great mystery in the Romance,' said Thomas. 'It contains a male Lover, who is a single person. But there is also a female counterpart, who is divided into two personages. She is represented as the Rose: passive, unmoving, silent, vulnerable, of a value to men that is both immeasurable and transient. The Rose is the promise of sensual gratification, intense and brief. She is the embodiment of adolescence at the moment of the first stimulation of maturity. She may not act or speak; she can anticipate one of only two responses from the Lover, to be adored, or to be used. But the Lover's female counterpart is also a second personage. She is also Warm Welcome, an aspect of the female in male form: generous, honest, courteous, amicable and loyal. She, as he, acts; she, as he, speaks; she, as he, has power. She, as he, desires not to be the passive recipient of the Lover's desire, but his companion.'

'You would entice me with reports of mysteries. A poet's ruse.'

'It is clear that the Lover desires the Rose. In the part you have read, he fails to obtain her, and languishes in a state of love denied.'

'I find it poignant.'

'But in Jean de Meun's conclusion, the Lover possesses and uses the Rose, in a passage of the crudest, basest comedy.'

'How disappointing,' said Berna, wrinkling her nose. 'How unmysterious.'

'The mystery is that throughout the poem, from de Lorris to de Meun, we fail to discover the Lover's sensibility in respect of Warm Welcome. Is he pleased or displeased with Warm Welcome's company only so far as Warm Welcome facilitates his access to the Rose, or does he value Warm Welcome's intelligence and accomplishments? Would he be Warm Welcome's companion, even without the Rose?'

'I marvel at the consideration you've given to such matters. Do you discuss them with your spouse?'

'Indecisiveness and misjudgement of reasonable possibilities have left me a bachelor,' said Thomas. 'I couch with my library.'

'I judge from your response that you carry old injuries.'

'It is difficult to say without appearing to find fault with someone apart from oneself, but my encounters have been of Roses without Welcomes, and Welcomes without Roses.'

'Am I now your confessor, master proctor?'

Thomas smiled. 'Really, I doubt the deity would have created male so singular and female so plural in matters amorous. Two Lovers, two Roses, two Welcomes; the very mystery is that there is only one Love. Where does he have his habitation?'

They were silent and each turned, suddenly solemn, to regard Dickle, as if realising the impropriety of their parliament in the presence of a gravely injured stranger.

The innkeeper came to the door and told Berna her servant had arrived.

THE INNKEEPER LED Berna to the gallery outside the door of her chamber, where a maid attended. Berna let the innkeeper go, unlocked the door and prayed the maid to enter. She left the door open, stood with her back to the bed, and demanded that the maid step into the light of the candles that still flamed on the table.

Before Berna stood a meagre maid of her own height, with black curls below her wimple and a familiar face – black eyes, tawny skin and full lips, the lower of which seemed pulled down by its own plenitude.

She said she was Madlen, Hab's sister.

'You are marvellously and wonder like to your fugitive brother,' said Berna.

Madlen said they had little time. She opened her bundle and took out a wedding gown semblable to Berna's. She placed it on the table and begged the demoiselle's pardon for stealing it.

'You might ask pardon and forgiveness of the folk and people of Outen Green for all the silver my father wrung and pressed of them in amends and mede for the loss.'

Madlen said she'd brought the gown to Bernadine again, and now the demoiselle had two gowns, one to meet her lover in, and one spare.

'How very free and generous you are with my chattels and possessions,' said Berna. 'But if you hopped and danced on the end of a rope, I'd still have both gowns.'

There was a disturbance in the inn yard. Madlen went out to look over the balcony and came again into the room.

To hang her, said Madlen, Bernadine must go home to her father again, and she'd have to wed the old man. Why not make Madlen her bondwoman instead?

'And have a thief to be my maid?'

She must choose now, said Madlen. Sir Henry was in Melksham, with men of Outen Green, come to find the lady and take her home.

'Holy mother of God, protect me!' said Berna.

The demoiselle had learned, said Madlen, how hard it was for a woman to fare alone on the road, all were she a knight's daughter. Westbury was four hours' ride away, and the moon was bright. Let her ride now with Madlen as her maid, and find Laurence Haket, and afterwards they might do with Madlen as they would.

'You're mad,' said Berna.

'They're here,' said Madlen.

They heard Cockle's voice below, and the sound of a high-born fellow raising a hue and cry over a lady. Feet hammered on the stairs. Berna crossed her arms over her breast, moved back and pressed herself against the far wall. Madlen called for the key. Berna threw it to her and she closed and locked the door.

A fist beat on the door. 'God's bones, Bernadine Corbet, you've led me a dance,' came Sir Henry's voice. 'Now I've others with me, and a fine honest scourge, and your father's benison to tan your hide with it, comen't you with me to Cotswold instantly.'

'Sweet queen of heaven!' said Berna.

A cry pierced the room, not from the gallery outside the chamber, but through the floor. It increased in force and divided into phrases. It was Hornstrake, crying to the world to flee, for the pest had come to Melksham, and he was infected.

The very feet that had passed so violently along the gallery towards Berna's chamber could now be heard running in the opposite direction, and when Berna and Madlen went out, the moon was bright enough to see, amid the tumult in the yard, Cockle and an old knight attempting to push their way into the stables to recover their mounts and escape from the plague-struck inn.

WILL WALKED THROUGH the heap of folk that flew of the inn into the night, that shoff each other to be first, cried their beads and paternosters and saints' names and the names of their kin, and dragged their horses and chattels behind them in the bark and squawk of dogs and geese. He went into the hall.

When Hornstrake yall, the hall had been halfway between wake and sleep, with some still at ale, some gone to bed. A board had been overturned and shards of broken can poked of pools of spilled ale that oversprad the floor. In the doorway that led to the kitchen the innkeeper stood with his arms around his wife, who had her neb buried in his chest. He beheld Will like to a child beholds its mother when it meets something it ne understands, and bides on her to unfold the meaning.

Will took a horn lamp of the wall and went toward the sound of weeping.

Sheets and bedstraw lay where the fearful had thrown them. Hornstrake sat in the midst of a field of clothes and sacks and shoon. His cheeks were wet with tears and he'd bound a rag over his eyes. Dust of unearthly hues glittered about his lips, limed to his skin by some murky uncouth honey. His left forearm was smeared with blood. He held a small steel blade in his right hand and in his left a clear glass ball hung of a band around his neck.

He turned toward the sound of footsteps.

'Who's there?' he called.

'What ails you?' said Will.

'Is it you, Will? Ne come nearer. I'm qualm-sick, but you won't get it of my eyes, for I hilled them well with a good thick strip of linen.'

Sweetmouth, Mad and Longfreke came into the hall and stood near.

'Fly!' yall Hornstrake. 'Ne throng about me.'

'What's the dust and honey about your lips?' Will asked.

'Treacle against qualm,' said Hornstrake, 'that I bought of the Malmesbury doctor.'

'The doctor bade you bleed yourself, not hack off your arm,' said Mad.

'You owe not to laugh,' said Hornstrake. 'You might be next to die.'

'How do you know the pest is in you?' said Will.

'I woke in a sweat, and felt hard botches in my pits, of the muchness of eggs. Shield yourselves, boys, keep ten yards of me, and fetch a priest.'

'You ne need no priest,' said Sweetmouth.

'I'm at grave's brink,' said Hornstrake.

'I'll heal you,' said Sweetmouth. He reached inside Hornstrake's shirt. Hornstrake wrothe and snorked as Sweetmouth dug under his armpits and took out two of the hard green apples they'd been given at the monks' board.

Sweetmouth lifted the cloth of Hornstrake's eyes and showed him the apples. 'These are all your qualm,' he said.

Hornstrake squinted at the apples. 'How did they come there?' he asked.

'Sweetmouth put them there while you snored,' said Mad.

'A sheep turd has more wit than this dote,' said Sweetmouth.

Hornstrake gazed at the apples. He made to cut Sweetmouth with his bloodletting blade, but his fellows were too quick and held him, and when he was held fast, his sinews slackened, and he began to laugh as a donkey.

THE CONSEQUENCES OF Sweetmouth's ridicule afflicted his victim more severely than they did Sweetmouth. As extensive as the chaos was, the sense of relief experienced when it was confirmed the signs of pestilence were false was sufficiently intense to neutralise what resentment persisted. Rather than attempting to extract compensation from Sweetmouth, the hostelry's residents purged the memory of their credulity by uniting in derision of the idiot who failed to discriminate between an apple and a plague-tumour.

It was partly to secure refuge from these insults that Hornstrake came to me, and partly to initiate confession. Until this moment I have detected among the archers an absence of the potent terror of the pestilence that motivated the fraternity of Malmesbury. With the exception of Longfreke, my military companions considered the menace exaggerated, or false, a clerical concoction, or, like Hayne, had a fatalistic perspective on an imminent and inevitable apocalypse. Hornstrake was the prime exemplar of one urged to penitence by apprehension of the probability of rapid, unexpected mortality, an apprehension conceived at the time of Dickle's accident, and reinforced by Sweetmouth's joke.

Impressing on him the need for seclusion, I conducted him to the culinary area of the hostelry, where they were preparing the furnaces to cook crustula. We stood in proximity to the flames.

Hornstrake inquired if he should genuflect before me.

It was not necessary, I replied.

Hornstrake said he would make peace with God, confess his sins, do penance and be absolved.

I advised him that Holiday must soon revene with an actual priest, and he might request absolution of him, for I had no sacramental powers. I simply offered an audience, a minor form of inquisition, an assessment of the sincerity of his penitence and the suggestion of some penitential acts.

Hornstrake inquired as to the price.

The transaction had no monetary element, I said.

This caused Hornstrake to doubt. A service could not be of use if the vendor offered it at no expense, he said.

I told him I required a graver price than money.

Procrastinating, Hornstrake exhibited a sphericule suspended from his collar. He had protection against qualm, he said. They had attempted to vend him numerous parts of porcine anatomy in simulation of sacred relics, saints' digits, portions of the tibia of the martyrs, dental extractions of the major ecclesiastics, but he had rejected their frauds and blasphemies, and extended his entire pecuniary provision on a sphere containing the very exhalations of Christ upon the cross. And, in his terror, he had nearly confractured it.

I expressed relief that Christ's final respirations remained secure.

He inquired if it were very solid that I had perfect Latin and resided in Avignon, and, on my responding in the affirmative, inquired whether I had personal acquaintance with the Pope.

I told him there had been an extremely brief colloquium between His Sanctity and myself at one of His Sanctity's convivial events.

Hornstrake inquired as to his character.

His Sanctity Pope Clement VI, I said, desired that his terrestrial environs be as splendid as their prospective counterparts in heaven.

This appeared to satisfy Hornstrake, and he requested that we commence.

I said that in the circumstances I would confine myself to mortal sins. He need only confess to sacrilege, homicide, adultery, fornication, false testimony, rapine, theft, pride, envy and avarice.

There was silence. Hornstrake inquired if I had finished, as he had expected there to be at least one sin he had not committed.

I gestured to the furnace. Did he, I said, sense the fervour of the flames? Would he press his palm against the incandescent surface to experience the sensation? I did not opt, I said, to compel a confession by reminding him of the alternative, but eternity was of a very long duration.

Hornstrake began to effuse a litany of blasphemies and felonies from his youth. He had appropriated a candle from Gloucester cathedral while inebriated, and, while he and his married aunt were similarly intoxicated, they had contrived oral contact with each other's genitalia. A companion had perished several days after a tavern conflict in which he had been involved, although he could not be certain his had been the fatal blow. He had consorted with prostitutes. He and another person had attempted to separate a merchant from his property, but they had been apprehended. He envied Holiday his sartorial talent and his literacy.

I interrupted and instructed him not to focus on misdemeanours when major crimes went unconfessed. Record must be made, I said, of his actions in France.

Hornstrake protested. The archers' commanders, and such clerics as accompanied the English military in France, had promised them that their cause was just, God approved their invasion, and acts committed by the archers in the course of the war that would normally be considered homicide, or arson, or robbery, were sanctified; those who exterminated the maximum number of French, and caused the maximum destruction to their property, were to have the sins on their conscience not increased, but remitted.

Had his superiors, on divine authority, commanded him to kill Cess's father and to violate and abduct her? I inquired.

Hornstrake moved away from the furnace and curved his spine in abnegation. He was ignorant of such matters, he said. He had not injured Cess's father, he said, nor abducted Cess; she was Softly's. As for rape, he was the most minor archer, and had not desired to fornicate with Cess.

I instructed Hornstrake to give an exact account of what had happened. Having received my assurances that I would protect him from the vindictiveness of Softly by the absolute confidentiality of his testimony, he proceeded.

HAYNE'S ARCHERS, HE said, were part of a cohort assigned to cause destruction in Mantes, some days prior to the confrontation at Crécy between the French and English crowns. The labour, primarily incendiary in nature, was retarded by the city's lapidary construction, by inter-military discord on the part of the English, and by the French merchants, who positioned containers of wine on the perimeters of their property in the often-realised expectation that the crapulous English would intoxicate themselves till they were incapable of doing further damage.

At noon, Softly, Dickle, Holiday and Hornstrake were combusting a textile emporium when Sweetmouth passed by. Sweetmouth reported to them that he was in quest of Hayne, and had been reluctantly obliged to quit the vicinity of a young French virgin whom he had observed through a fissure in the portal of a sculptor's court. She was, he said, desirable and decorous, and he intended to return to Mantes post-war, for she was such as he required.

Holiday requested the location of the sculptor's domicile, and Sweetmouth told them, but as he spoke, dolour transformed his face, and when they departed, he clamoured that they not abuse his candour.

The four archers located the structure and forced entry into the court. Attempting to defend his family and property the sculptor sustained from Dickle a fatal abdominal injury. The archers entered the sculptor's domicile, extracted Cess, closed the residue of her family inside, and proceeded to violate her in sequence on a mass of marble on which her father had sculpted the preliminary designs for a magnate's sephulchre.

Cess resisted and anathemised the archers with French maledictions until they restricted her arms with cords and obstructed her mouth. Softly was the initiator, then Holiday, and Dickle was to have been next, but in proximity to the injured woman, sanguinary and suffering contusions, Dickle experienced a defect of fortitude, became lacrimose, and exited. Softly and Hornstrake discovered him behind an image of St Agatha, so terrified he had urinated inside his own vestments. Dickle could not endure the vision of a female's private parts, he told them, it provoked in him a sense of incompleteness.

They revened to the court, where Holiday had concluded his violation of Cess, and Hornstrake was to be the third to rape her. He exposed his member and positioned himself between her legs, but was incapable of performing the actions, partly, he said, out of pity for Cess, who was practically insensible and presenting obvious injuries, partly out of horror of the transformation of Dickle, whom he had known up to that point as an individual unacquainted with terror, and partly out of uncertainty, as he was unmarried and unpopular with females, and had previously coupled solely with prostitutes, whom he had generally found cooperative and amicable.

In a state of conturbation out of anxiety that he act incorrectly in front of his companions, Hornstrake decided to simulate intercourse, but it was not necessary, for Softly apprehended his collar, retracted him and declared that Cess was not theirs to use, because he was accepting her as his trophy. He said he would abduct her, and that he would not permit any man to converse with her, or to report even the most minor aspect of events at the sculptor's, on pain of extermination. There was a cart and a horse, which they took, and deposited Cess in it, and exited the area.

Hornstrake ceased. It was necessary for me to prompt him to account for subsequent events, which he did not consider relevant. Softly had tended to Cess, but had castigated her violently on the many occasions she attempted escape, communicated with potential accessories to her liberation, or refused to submit to his authority. As her original injuries were cured, new injuries appeared on her face, until the archers revened to England, and she abandoned fugitive notions.

The abduction of Cess caused a schism in Hayne's company. Some relinquished their affiliation. Sweetmouth and Mad condemned Softly, but not to his face. Only Longfreke declared to Softly explicitly that he must liberate Cess, and there would have been actual conflict between them, conflict that would undoubtedly have proved mortal, had Hayne not intervened, saying the privilege of superior powers to judge the rapists might not be usurped.

Subsequently, said Hornstrake, Softly proposed marriage to Cess, and she rejected him, and this partially removed the hostility between the two elements among the archers. Ultimately she was French, an enemy, female and plebeian, and they had not injured her permanently. Even supposing his companions had sinned mortally, he said, he, Hornstrake, was not responsible for the extermination of the father, or Cess's abduction; he had not even fornicated with her. How stood his case, he inquired?

Despite my non-clerical status, I replied, as proctor I was intimately acquainted with the ecclesiastical justice system, and I assumed divine justice operated in a similar manner. On that basis, I concluded, he was damned to demonic torment for eternity.

His mouth became an extended pescatory aperture. He implored me to advise him how he might achieve salvation.

I was not convinced, I said, that he felt genuine pity for Cess. If he had, why had he mounted her, when she had already been raped by two of his companions? Where was his compassion? Was he incapable of imagining the suffering of Christ on the cross?

With a mendacity so flagrant it provoked a certain tenderness in me, Hornstrake said he imagined it frequently.

Why then, I inquired, could he not imagine the suffering of a woman powerless to resist the soldiers who raped her, the sanctity of her person violated in proximity to the corpse of her father, a victim of homicide from the same soldiers?

He failed to comprehend the comparison.

Those who tormented and executed the martyrs, I said. Hornstrake was directly comparable.

She could not be a saint, said Hornstrake, because God did not come to her aid, and could not be a martyr, for she was not dead.

I said the simplest course of action for Hornstrake would be to place himself in a furnace there and then, as it would merely accelerate the process by a fraction. But if he desired to demonstrate genuine penitence in the audit of God, I would advise two actions. Primo, that he destroy the most precious of his possessions.

I was not required to press the point, as his hand closed instantly around the sphericule at his collar.

He did not want to concede it, I said; he would suffer if he were deprived of it. So, in the most minor way imaginable, would Cess's experience be reflected in his spirit.

Hornstrake said indignantly that I had promised to act for him without an honorarium.

I did not intend to confiscate his relic, I said, but to observe him destroy it, as Softly had not purloined Cess's virginity for his own use, but obliterated it.

Hornstrake said that without his relic he'd be undefended from the pest.

With it, I said, he would be undefended from damnation.

He removed it from his collar and projected it into the furnace, where it was immediately consumed.

I congratulated him, and informed him that he must now perform the second, more difficult action. He must egress to the court of the hostelry, go to the cart, genuflect to Cess, express his sincere contrition for his action in Mantes and plead for her pardon.

Hornstrake said Softly would exterminate him if he did. He requested that he might rather make a vow of abstinence, or renounce meat, or repeat the Ave Maria, or dedicate a multitude of candles, because it was God's pardon he required, not Cess's.

He had no option, I said. Only Cess's pardon might magnify his voice sufficiently for God to notice him and extract him from the channel of the damned flowing towards the inferno. Dickle was in his final mortal hour, I said, and I was required there; Softly and the other archers would be with him, and no one would observe Hornstrake if he visited Cess in the cart.

Judith, Marc, in my attempt to apologise and confess honestly my errors, I have probably offended you de novo. How might these notes affect you if only one of you has survived? Possibly it were preferable for me to destroy all these manuscripts. Or possibly it is incitement to immerse myself in a more profound state of honesty.

THE ARCHERS GATHERED in the room where Dickle lay. They bode on Holiday, who must come with the priest, but he'd been gone a long time.

Dickle's breath was weak and his forehead cool. Softly sat by his bed, lifted his head and brought a can of ale to his mouth. Dickle ne opened his eyes and his lips ne showed no token of life. Each archer had some kind of light in his gear, and they lit them, and it became so bright there weren't no shadows in the room, out-take Hayne, who reared over them all, like to a post that underset the roof. Mad sang the Latin song the monks had learned him.

'Dickle's dad did his mum in when he found out she'd fallen into spousebreach with a fishmonger,' whispered Sweetmouth to Will. 'And the dad took his own life, and Dickle was raised in Bristol by his uncle, and fought four stepbrothers for every scrap of food.'

'Tell Player how bold and keen a fighter he is,' said Softly to Sweetmouth. 'It was he dragged Longfreke of the field when he'd been struck in the neb by a dead man's sword and lay witless and blooded on the ground.'

'It's true,' said Longfreke. 'I thank him for it. All the same I fear for our brother's soul if the priest ne come.'

'Dickle Dene's a better man than any of you,' said Softly. 'He'll wake in the morning and not see no priest till he's ready, when his life's near to done.'

'His life is near to done,' said Hayne.

'Is there aught Hayne ne knows?' said Softly. 'Where's your false priest, Thomas?'

Thomas had come in unmarked. He said: 'If this man is near death, and there's no priest, I may hear his sins.'

Softly said Dickle slept deeply, and mightn't speak.

Thomas came up to the bed, knelt beside it, turned his head and set his ear by Dickle's mouth. 'He ne sleeps,' he said. 'There's a little voice in him may yet find a way through the dark to one with sleight of ear to listen. Dickle! Dickle Dene! Will you list your guilts to Thomas proctor, that God might hear, and know you're truly sorry for the wrongs you've done?'

Thomas seemed to listen, then lifted his head and spoke to the other archers. 'He says he will.'

Softly shoff Thomas aside. He shook Dickle by the shoulder, spoke in his face and told him to wake, for his brother archers were false, and they'd blacken his soul in the name of making it clean. He listened at Dickle's lips and said the man slept and mightn't speak.

'Let Thomas work,' said Longfreke. 'Dickle's near to forthfare, and there's none else to handle a soul on the wend.'

'I'll tell you what he says,' said Thomas, 'and if you hear me say things I couldn't know otherwise, it'll be shown I'm no liar.'

Softly beheld Thomas like to he would slay him, but stood aside. Thomas brought his ear to Dickle's mouth again.

'I listen, brother,' said Thomas. 'Good. He says all his life he's been a wrathful man, and been vexed from childhood by demons that egged him to fight those who would be his friends as eagerly as he fought his foes. All those who've wronged him he now forgives, and begs forgiveness of those he's wronged.'

The archers yeahed, out-take Softly, who said it wasn't Dickle's voice they heard, but Thomas's.

'He says he hasn't no more to say.'

Softly laughed and struck the air with his fist and said that was the Dickle Dene he knew.

Thomas's steven roughened and rose. 'Ne withhold your sins,' he said.

'"I'll withhold as it me likes, son of a bitch, and set my ghost on you of the other side."'

'But your ghost will be bound in hell for ever, Dickle, if you ne sorrow for the worst you've done in life. You'll be meat for the Fiend.'

'"I'll choke him and be free. I'll pitch a hole in his throat with my bare right arm."'

'You're a bold fighter to gab you might choke the Fiend. How many have you slain?'

'"I ne number them, shit-sucker, but each was rightly spilled."'

'Do you ne fear Christ, Dickle?'

'"I ne fear no one."'

'Do you love him?'

'"I ne worth him so high as others do. I had them nail me to a post in Germany to see how hard a man he was, and I ne died."'

'You might pay a man to take you down, and Christ ne could. Why do you have the cross corven in ink on your forehead, Dickle, if you ne worth Christ?'

Thomas was still. There wasn't no sound in the room, like to all the land about listened.

'Spoke you, Dickle? I can't hear you. You'd have the world think you ne feared God or the Fiend but the cross on your forehead says otherwise.'

'"It is the rood of England and St George, frog-fucker."'

'I ween you fear. Ne rue you the murder of Cess's father?'

'"That wasn't murder but a Frenchman rightly spilled in wartide."'

Softly told Dickle he spoke well and true.

'The French maid, Cecile,' said Thomas, 'was she rightly reft of her maidenhood while her father lay killed nearby? To be stolen from her kin, was that right?'

'"I can't speak for he as reft it from her and stole her. I ne did those things."'

'And you ne knew her against her will at that time?'

'"No."'

'I shan't let you fare to hell so lightly. Tell me the truth, did you know Cess in her father's yard in Mantes against her will?'

'"God's nails, I ne knew her. I went to another stead in the yard to be further from her cries."'

'Why? Wasn't it your even-archers will that you had a share of their glee with the maid?'

'"I was sorry. It wasn't right to do her as she was done."'

Softly reached for Dickle as if he would strike him, but the others held him back. Softly said it wasn't true, Dickle flew from Cess in fear of her cunt, and he'd pissed himself in fright, for it had always been his greatest fear.

Thomas held up his hands. 'This isn't no court of law,' he said. 'We must take Dickle at his word. He forgave all, and asked forgiveness of all, and if he were truly sorry in his heart for what was done to Cess, God will know, and do he bide a thousand years in purgatory, he has hope to be with Christ after.'

Far away they heard the priest's bell, getting louder. Some went out in the yard to see, along with many of the guests, for the word had already gone round that the Fiend, in the shape of a goat, had dealt the worst of the bowmen a deadly blow. Into the yard came Holiday, followed by a chaplain in his mass-hackle carrying Christ in the box, with two knaves behind to carry the light and ring the bell, and a third with a handcart. All fell to their knees and bowed their heads. But when the chaplain brought the box to Dickle, Dickle couldn't eat of the Lord's body, for he ne breathed no more.

THOMAS DREW THE chaplain upstairs to his room. After an hour they came down. They should have sent for a priest sooner, the chaplain said, but Thomas had wrought right, and it seemed that, at the end, Dickle had found true sorrow for his sins, and might hope to come to heaven of purgatory, and his body might be buried in holy ground. 'It's the Fiend's oldest craft,' the chaplain said, 'to make believers fear their sins too great to be forgiven.'

The chaplain oiled Dickle's body and dight ash on the rood on his forehead, and he was wrapped in a shroud and done in the handcart, for he mightn't lie in the inn. The bowmen gave the deacon sixpence, and a penny each for his knaves, and he blessed them, and bade them light candles for their friend in church before the burial. And he left, and one knave bode to wheel Dickle to the lying-in.

Here the bowmen began to wrangle. Softly said he wouldn't have Longfreke at the burial, for he ne worthed Dickle, and Longfreke said he worthed him higher than Softly, and he would come to the burial, for they were of one fellowship. He took the handles of the cart, and Softly and Holiday would have fought him, had Hayne ne come between them.

Hayne said he would go with Softly, Holiday and Hornstrake to be with Dickle at the lying-in and the burial, and to wash him, for if the clerks saw the likeness of hell-mouth on his bare chest, their mood would shift. Longfreke would bide at the inn with Will, Sweetmouth, Mad and Thomas, and in the morning they would go to Westbury, find Laurence Haket, light candles for Dickle, and bide on Hayne and the others, that they go on to Dorset together.

They asked Will if he knew where the lady Bernadine was, for she'd taken her horse and goods and left her keys. Will said he only knew she'd found herself a maid of their town, so she wasn't alone no more, wherever she'd gone.

BERNA RODE INTO Westbury in the saffron light before cock-crow. Madlen walked beside her, agitating her mistress's ankle to prevent her succumbing to fatigue and tumbling of the saddle. All the beasts and people were asleep. The sound of Jemsy's hooves on the durable terrain of the high street echoed of the closed-up shops.

Madlen beat on the door of the inn till a porter showed his face at an ouverture and effused blasphemies.

'I am Lady Bernadine Corbet, and you will instantly provide me with a private chamber,' said Berna.

The inn was full, the porter said, and the kitchen closed. In a discourteous manner he demanded to know if the demoiselle or her maid suffered from contagious maladies or fevers, and if they'd travelled from Dorset.

They assured him they were robust, if enfeebled by their journey, that they came from the north, and that they had seen no signs of disease on their route.

The porter looked them up and down, unbarred the door and said he supposed the demoiselle was on her way to the joust.

Berna hesitated. Madlen said the porter was correct.

Better that they carry on, he said. Edington was only two hours away, and those who were sans tent might rent one at sixpence a day, with beds and all that was necessary for a noble demoiselle's ménage agreeable.

'Porter,' said Berna in a trembling voice, 'tell me this. Is there in your inn a young esquire by the name of Laurence Haket? For I would— '

Madlen interrupted. She told the porter curtly that the demoiselle required a brief halt to refresh herself and her horse before continuing to Edington. He should place a table and chairs for them in the court, furnish them with wine and victuals and rouse a stable-boy.

Berna attempted to raise her voice again, but Madlen was pressing her ankle so severely that she simply cried out. The porter left them and Berna dismounted. She closed her eyes, leaned back against Jemsy and complained that as insufferable as the journey had been to her joints, it wasn't so terrible as the prospect of appearing to Laurence in such disarray.

Madlen urged her to courage. Remembered she not what they'd agreed when they sat together in the saddle?

'Was it your voice incessantly in my ear?' said Berna. 'And did I reply? I thought it a reverie.'

Having come so far, said Madlen, would the lady permit herself to fail now?

Berna opened her eyes, turned to face Madlen and crossed her arms. 'At this moment,' she said, 'I would sacrifice all my prospects to see you suspended in mid-air with a rope around your throat.'

At that moment, Madlen replied, the only person she could complain to about Madlen was Madlen, so she'd be well-advised to preserve her life. What was essential was that when Laurence appeared, the demoiselle confidently demonstrate her disregard for his requirements, and her certainty in her own intention, which was to journey on to the joust and to sojourn there at her pleasure. No matter how reasonable his objections, she must counter them, and insist on her power to choose her course.

Berna laughed. 'Why should I attend to you? Were I to examine your notions of romance I'm sure I'd discover them composed of different cuts of pork, like a butcher's counter.'

.The porter came with a table, a red-eyed maid brought a pitcher of watered wine, and a boy led Jemsy away. The porter said the inn observed the proprieties, and he mightn't allow the demoiselle to visit the squire in his chamber, unaccompanied or otherwise; but he'd informed the young man of her presence.

'Mother in heaven, he comes,' said Berna, and bit the ends of her fingers.

WHEN WILL ROSE in Melksham that morning he fetched Enker and gave the sty-ward half a penny for his keep. He thacked the pig on the arse and bade him choose his way. Enker followed him.

'How'd you come to be a swineherd?' asked Longfreke.

'Hab bade me redeem Enker and set him free, for Hab went far away,' said Will.

'Your friends leave without farewells,' said Mad. 'We should look to our silver.'

'I mayn't help if Enker chooses to follow us,' said Will. 'He does no harm.'

He hadn't no sooner spoke than the boar eked his step and went ahead.

'First the pig chose to follow us,' said Mad, 'and now we choose to follow the pig.'

'Behold his great bollocks,' said Sweetmouth, who stared at the bristly behind of the boar. 'With knackers like that, a man might go about the world shot-free.'

The air was cooler than for many days. A light wind blew from the west and made the corn ripple. Small whirled clouds glode in the sky. As they fared over the wold of Avon they saw a long hill rise steeply at the land's brink. Longfreke said it was the Wiltshire downs, that led to Salisbury. It truly seemed that Enker led them. He struck dust from the road with his shod hooves and only stinted when the bowmen broke to rest.

Each time a lark rose over a cornfield and sang, Mad sang back in Welsh, and the folk who weeded would look up. Mad made wreaths of golds and poppies for the bowmen to wear, and caught butterflies till he had a heap of them, then let them go at once, and a packle of hues flew from his hand. Sweetmouth wondered aloud that Dickle the fighter should turn out to be so fearful a baby in the end, and to fear, of all things, the fairest thing in the world.

Otherwhiles they spoke with those they met, and otherwhiles ne spoke, or spoke and were not spoken back to. It seemed they went among two kinds of folk, those that dwelt there, and those like them that fared south. The first kind were harder and more wary and frightened than any they'd met till then. They hid their faces and kept their doors shut and bore likenesses of the Mother of God and St Michael and fell to their knees to bid beads in the field in the sun. They bode on something, and beheld the bowmen go by like they were the beginning of it. They told tales of qualm that the bowmen ne believed, that it was come to Bristol, that London sicked, that it was everywhere in Kent, that a host of French soldiers had come up the Avon to Chippenham in boats and burned it, that the Fiend went about Wiltshire, now as a boar, now as a goat, that a two-headed witch in a white dress rode a black horse along the highway at night.

The other kind went laughing on horseback in bright clothes, with pipes and gitterns on their backs and apes and aquerns on their shoulders and hawks on their wrists. There were carts drawing bundles of cerecloth, white wooden posts with red bars and heaps of wooden shields. Some went in velvet, some in leather, and they cast behind them date stones and nutshells and cake crumbs. There were maids with bare heads, and high-born fellows who'd reddened their cheeks. When they beheld the bowmen, they beheld them like to their bowmanship was but a game they played, and their true kind other.

My priority in the matter of Dickle was salvation; my own. Certainly Dickle had expired before I pretended to hear him, and that is the prime defence of my conduct; I could not have assisted in a final act of contrition, had he desired to make one, as his spirit had already departed.

Despite the exhausting events of the day, I was insomniate. When I eventually slept, I hallucinated that I had paid a constructor to crucify me. The cross was erected in the desert, in the court of an edifice fabricated of nigrous, granular material. A frigid wind agitated pennants on the turrets. The sun was reflected in the wings of falcons and pelicans circling in the air. I apprehended that the pennants and the birds were in fact flames, independent of the source of their ignition. I clamoured to the constructor to liberate me, to extract the nails from my hands. He was seated at the base of the cross, manually excavating the humus without apparent purpose or progress. He was unconscious of my presence, despite the volume of my voice and my desperation. I observed that above his simple tunic, where his head should have been, was a perfect sphere, without protusions or orifices of any kind; he had no apparatus to sense my existence and my agony was, to him, inaudible and invisible.

I woke, perspiring. I remembered an object in my late father's possession, acquired in one of the Hanseatic ports: an ivory sphere comprising two hemispheres conjoined so exactly that it was impossible to detect the line of juncture. Counter-rotating the hemispheres, they parted to reveal a cavity in each. Inside the first, sculpted in miniature, was a narrative of depravity: an avaricious blasphemer is portrayed killing his rival, stealing his money and fornicating with his spouse, then descending into the infernal orifice, where he is impaled on the demonic trident. In the other hemisphere, the same person is depicted donating money to the poor, assisting the sick and performing solitary devotions, to be admitted subsequently into the eternal presence of the divine. It is fabricated so that the central figure in each narrative is bisected; one assumes that once the sphere is reassembled, these two demi-humans are united into a single entire human. But the opacity of the ivory is such that the complete human, in his contradictory nature, may never be observed, only imagined, and one may observe the person's malicious aspect, or their benevolent one, but never the two concurrently.

As an infant I pondered less over my inability to perceive the entire human, completed yet invisible within the ivory sphere; my major concern was with the predicament of the homunculus himself, conscious of his contradictory nature, yet conscious too of the fact that his complexity was invisible, and none might ever observe more than a fraction of his essence.

I reflected on Dickle as I prepared to depart Melksham. It was Softly, not I, who damned Dickle from the point of view of his comrades, if not God's, by revealing his secret, the sole crime, in their eyes, graver for a man than to have a feminine nature: to be terrorised by a woman's reproductive organs. Why, then, does the sense remain with me that I in some form traduced this violent, aggressive man? He had not hesitated to kill Cess's father. He was not concerned by Cess's suffering or her rape by his friends; his horror was in reaction to the possibility of congress, of union with Cess – the idea, he said, made him incomplete. 'Ne whole' were the English words. Dickle, I conclude, lacked conviction in the integrity of his own substance; violence was necessary to him to assert his independent existence to others, and to himself, to declare and separate his essence from all other humans. But with women he perceived an element – or the demon who possessed him made him perceive an element – that menaced his isolation. I am sure he would have been capable of any act of pure violence towards Cess except that one act of violation, which I suspect seemed to him less a demonstration of his power over her than a momentary diminution of himself, forcing him for that instant to accept that he was not one creature, but half a creature, and that he could only achieve completion by the absolute negation of the demi-human he had been, by enclosing and being enclosed by his gender opposite, becoming complex, hermetic, like the remainder.

Judith, Marc, on reflection I judge it probable that you detected my attraction to Judith and resolved to tolerate it as the imbecility of a demented senior, on condition I did not transgress from internal desire to action. I did not do so. Absolve me, if you are magnanimous, of my fatuousity.

ON THE WAY to Westbury, Will Quate interrogated me on the nature of romantic love as practised by the nobility, and why Bernadine had abandoned her nuptials so precipitately.

I dismounted so as to speak more convivially. The splendid vigour of his honest, inquiring countenance, combined with the illusion of social unity conferred by the common direction of our movement, stimulated me to abandon any concession to his ignorance. I described the Rose, and Lancelot and Guinevere; I alluded to the cult of difficulty, of how the essence of courtly romance lay in the incompatibility of irresistible desire and impossible obstacles in the way of its satisfaction. I recounted how the resolution of this contradiction lay in the cultivation of a form of secular religion based on romance, with worship, martyrs and relics, with poets for priests and the promise of paradise as its conclusion.

Presenting this in English without a single French or Latin expression exhausted me, and I was confused when, as if proceeding logically from his prior utterances, he said he had last confessed three days previously, to the priest in his vill.

If he'd offended God in some minor form since then, I said, it could be addressed by a priest at the next pause in our itinerary.

I might as well have offered to hear his confession. He responded by recounting a series of provocations to his conscience, none of them particularly infamous. On his first night away, he said, he had touched lips with a person other than his intended. He had battered the innocent citizens of Chippenham, without justification, when they defended their urb. He had joined Hayne's company, despite being advised in advance that they maintained a female French captive whom they had raped and abducted. The premature death of one of his comrades in demonic circumstances, he concluded, proved that the archers were subject to a divine malediction.

These matters may veritably have made Will Quate anxious, as he insisted they did, but the dominant note in his discourse was not anxiety; it was ire. An event or events had occurred to transform his previous phlegmatic character to choleric. He was furious and turbulent. When we spoke it was as if he desired sincerely to confess to certain crimes, while ascribing culpability for those crimes to others.

I assured him that I perceived no crimes. It was not he who raped Cess; if the behaviour of his companions troubled him, it was in his power to depart. The legal code of England permitted any serf who resided in an urban area without capture for a year to attain absolute liberty. I was acquainted with certain powerful individuals; I might secure him a position in London or Oxford. As for events in Chippenham, St Augustine himself had explained that a member of the military acting on the orders of his commander was exempt from God's censure when the commander's cause was just; and Hayne had ordered them to counter an injustice against one of their comrades, countering an injustice being, ipso facto, just.

I terminated my reassurance at this point without mentioning what appeared to me the trivial matter of his sylvan osculation, that action which in English goes by the peculiar verbicle 'kiss'. Here I erred. It transpired it was the kiss that concerned him most profoundly, or at least this was how he presented the case to me. It infuriated him particularly that it was he, the male, the archer separated from his future spouse, who had been passive, and the female, Madlen, the sister of a swineherd, who had been active in the execution of the kiss.

On my inquiring whether he was enamoured of Madlen, Will said that, on the contrary, he despised her for interrupting the successful prosecution and completion of his period of military service in France, subsequent to which he would revene to his vill and his spouse. Madlen and Hab, Will opined, represented a demonic force that had dislocated the correct position of people and objects in the world. No attempt to avoid them, or to persuade them to remove themselves from his vicinity, had deflected them from their pursuit. He insulted them as servile, demented, sordid, obscene.

I have not encounted Madlen. Taken at face value, Will's hostility to her is a demonstration of insularity – a decisive rejection of migration in favour of the less radical option of exploration. A preference for the circle which remits a person, via exotic discoveries, to his origin, rather than permitting these same discoveries to transform and recreate a person in an unfamiliar destination.

In this interpretation, Will's desire to depart Outen Green is not a sign of one prepared to depart permanently, to establish an alternative existence far removed in space from the original. He has conjured an image of his departure, and realised the image; but the image of his return is of equal importance. He has no desire to acquire his liberty at the expense of exile in Calais, or London, or even Gloucester. His concept of liberty demands his ability to enjoy it on his native terrain.

How radically the space I traverse differs from the mental chart of those, like Will Quate, whose universe might be circumnavigated in an hour. My Europe is his Outen Green; my continent his manor. As I to abbeys and cathedrals from Durham to Cluny, so he to residences, orchards and pastures in his minimal cosmos. I perform my most important transactions with a hundred individuals, and so does he, in Outen Green; except that in his case, those individuals are the entire population of familiar space, while my counterparts are dispersed over a virtually infinite area, points of acquaintance among millions of extraneous people to whom I am alien.

So I might accept his anxiety, that he desires his journey to be circular, completed in the place it was initiated; and that the advent of this Madlen complicates his intentions. But I do not give it credence. His fury is genuine, but fury, like certain forms of love, is a member of the family of the passions. I conclude that Will did not desire to leave Outen Green, or be liberated from servitude. He simply desired. He desired ardently, but unspecifically, without an object, and attached to this desire purposes of escape and liberation, to provide himself with that object.

Could it be that Madlen, enamoured with him from a distance, perceived his state of mind, and resolved to insert herself into Will's experiences at the precise moment an object of desire was, by his design, to be attained? At the instant Will passes from the sphere of limited horizons and servitude to the universal, liberated sphere, Madlen is there to personify the transition. The kiss being the medium through which the identification of Madlen with the delights of terra nova, terra incognita, is completed. Then Will's fury is not, as he claims, caused by an interruption to his circular way from home, through Calais, to home, but by the forced realisation that he deliberately deceived himself, that all along he desired transmigration and transmutation, and required a second person to give that desire form.

The question remains to be resolved: is Will capable of recognising the generosity fortune has shown to him?

Judith, Marc, I discover that each stratum of confession, once removed, reveals another. And that which appeared as the more profound honesty (that I did not so much love your mutual uxoriousness as love Judith) conceals an ulterior verity, that much as I loved you, Judith, most important to me was to be loved by you.

Laurence Haket appeared in the yard in the shadow cast by the main part of the inn, as the first light of morning fell on Berna at table. Madlen stood at a distance, a pitcher in her hand, a towel over her wrist. The brilliance of the sun on Berna's wimple and the gold in her gown appeared to pain Laurence's eyes. He advanced several paces and arrayed his disordered blond hair and shirt. He bowed and made a courteous salutation. Berna disregarded him. He repeated his address. She continued to ignore him. She showed interest only in the diversity of her victuals, which had been presented to her unreasonably with the acceptable and inedible mingled, requiring a procedure of attentive sorting.

'I hadn't no esperance of this,' said Laurence. 'Do I rave? Is my lady Berna present, or a vision, like Guillaume's rose?'

'I parled with a gentleman in my father's garden in Gloucestershire on the subject of that romance,' said Berna. 'That gentleman hadn't patience for no rose, so he picked a daisy of a dung-hill and passed on his way.'

'My very amour,' said Laurence, 'had your father consented, I would have married you.'

'But he ne consented, so you feebly departed, demonstrating your inconstancy a second time.'

Berna regarded Madlen and continued: 'I ne suffer from the memory. Should he who vowed himself my sole and very amour turn out to be a traitor, I'd prefer it were he that regret it, not I. I remain here an hour to refresh myself, my horse and my servant, then go to Edington.'

Laurence said he'd confide in her privately. Berna replied that her servant Madlen was a simple peasant too new to service to comprehend the language of nobility.

'She may comprehend this,' said Laurence. He dropped to his knees and advanced closer to Berna.

'Ne approach,' said Berna.

'Even in a state of abasement?'

'Your imitation of a painture of Faux-Semblant is very comical.'

'I was at fault to dally with the Muchbrook girl,' said Laurence.

'Adam and Eve ne averted expulsion from paradise by referring to their relations with the apple as a dalliance.'

'I was at fault to accept your father's refusal and depart. In each case my actions were guided by despair. Faced by the permanent deprivation of your company, my spirit desired to affirm its perdition by soiling its purity in coupling with a base peasant – an act, I assure you, that gave me no more pleasure than coupling with the earth. Faced by your marriage to another, I resolved to embrace solitude and peril, desiring to forfeit my life in pursuit of a cause sufficiently noble that word might reach you of how I used my final breath to speak your name.'

Berna was silenced, and stared at him. They heard the sound of water hitting the stone flags of the court. Madlen had tilted the pitcher. She said she was sorry, but the pitcher was small, and it ne could be hindered from dribbling out whatever it happened to have in it.

'I would your servant left us alone,' said Laurence.

Berna ordered Madlen to find the stable-hand and have the horse brought.

'You surely ne intend departure?' said Laurence.

'My intentions are known to you,' said Berna.

'This is a frenzy. Now you've escaped marriage to the ancient chevalier, now the achievement of our very desire is possible, you must remain with me.'

'You have proved unreliable.'

'And you, though I adore you immeasurably, incomprehensible. What do you suppose I should have done? Ravished you of your family?'

Berna was silent.

Laurence stood. 'That was your desire? That I ride up and seize you, throw you over my horse's back and carry you to France, apparently without your consent, but in fact with your approval? Pardon me, my very amour, that I ne perceived this secret wish. Pardon me, that when in your father's garden my lips reached for yours and you turned your face away, I failed to perceive in this a sign you desired me to possess you entirely. Pardon me, that when I contrived a temporary breach in your chaperone's defences, sufficient for us to joy the delights of Nature's amorous pleasures, and you refused to let me touch you, I ne interpreted it as an invitation to steal you and carry you over the sea.'

Berna sighed. 'What an insensible beast you are,' she said.

'I am a beast!' said Laurence, hitting his chest so forcefully with his open palm that it sounded as a tabour. 'A beast to have maintained the vision of your beauty within the temple of my senses, like a sacrestan tending a saintly image, since I departed your father's manor. A beast to have endured any offence of you, that I might serve you. A beast to request of you that which your father refused, the gift which in consequence you have assumed to yourself.'

Berna opened her mouth, drew breath, then narrowed her eyes. 'Could you repeat the final part?' she said.

'Marry me.'

'Now?'

'Of course — very presently. I'll arrange lodgings for you in a pleasant place close by, and you'll rest and be comfortable, and have fresh garments brought, and choice pastries, and attend my return.'

'Your return?'

'I receive a company of archers here. I have the tally for their passage to Calais. Before we depart I have affairs at the joust.'

Madlen and the stable-hand returned with Jemsy. Madlen poured water over Berna's hands, dried them, and helped her into the saddle.

'Ne go,' said Laurence. 'You're searched for. Late last night the miller's son of Outen Green was here, on a commission of your father to catch the one who stole your gown. He'd been in Melksham with the ancient chevalier. As far as I could comprehend they almost had you trapped there. Concealment and isolation is the best course till the joust is over, my amour.'

Jemsy backed and sidestepped and Berna reined him in. She regarded Laurence. 'Having failed to pluck the Rose where it grew, you find her come to you, and suppose she'll consent when you

order her to plant herself and smile at the sun, for your conveni-
ence? You presume too much.'

'Go to the joust and they'll capture you. They'll place you in a
prison of marriage to one you despise.'

'I pray this time I'm not required to effect my own rescue,' said
Berna. 'Come up, Madlen.'

Madlen mounted Jemsy behind her and the two rode away.

'How terrible that was,' said Berna. '"Terrible", you know?
Meaning "bad". "Choice pastries"? I ne trust him yet. But I would
bite him.'

Madlen laughed, and they rode the few miles to Edington, Jemsy
soaked up to the hocks in the dew of the deep grass that waved
in an endless comb down the centre of the road.

WHEN THE FOUR bowmen and Thomas came mid-morning to
Westbury, they stinted at the inn, but Enker went on toward
Edington, and they ne held him back.

They found Laurence Haket in a dreary mood. When he learned
of Dickle's death he gave them tenpence to light candles for the
bowman at the church. They came again after an hour and Laurence
told them they must shift their read. They mightn't take the high
road straight to Melcombe, he said. There was a stir of some kind
afoot in Dorset and the sheriff of Wiltshire had bidden the road be
shut south of Warminster. They must find another way. His man
Raulyn knew of a road from Edington, over the downs to Heytesbury.

'As we must go by Edington,' said Laurence Haket, 'and as we
lack Hayne and three bowmen for a while, I've a bid for you. A
set of players hired for the joust tomorrow ne came. The folk that

work the games lack players who must, as it happens, be handy with a bow. They asked me to find a few; what do you say?'

Longfreke shook his head. They were fighting men, not players, he said.

Sweetmouth said Will was a player.

Will said it was but an ekename.

'It'll mirth you,' said Laurence Haket. 'Help my friends riot for a day before we're soldiers again.'

Sweetmouth tugged his beard. His eyes were alight. He said he'd heard the maids at jousts were thick as stars.

'You heard right,' said Laurence Haket.

Sweetmouth said he'd heard that players saw more cunny in their lives than any knight.

Laurence laughed. 'Maybe,' he said.

Mad asked whose the joust was; would the king be there?

'The king jousts in Canterbury the same day,' said Laurence. 'This is a joust of another kind. The name of she who wrought it's not to be known by the likes of you.'

Will said he'd go, and Sweetmouth and Mad said they couldn't leave him to go alone.

Longfreke bade them bide. He said he knew the thought of any woman, most of all one he'd not seen, was enough to make Sweetmouth lose his wits, and Mad lived as if he was in a tale anywise, but Will was a green young fighting freke, and ne owed to be so untrue as to have his head turned by no heap of dizzy painted folk.

'Come,' said Laurence Haket, 'it's one day of mirth in the year.'

Sweetmouth told Longfreke he was bitter that he mightn't be taken as a player, for his neb would frighten the maids.

Longfreke was still for a handwhile after that. Then he said he'd bide in Westbury for the others, and he read that they do the same. But if they must go, he bade them swear they wouldn't shame the score by shooting arrows before outcome folk while they went about in shameful players' clothes, as dogs, or beggars, or, God forbid, as women. And Will, Sweetmouth and Mad swore on their bows that they wouldn't play women bowmen at the joust.

While they readied to go, Laurence Haket took Will aside.

'I mind you,' he said. 'Are you betrothed to the Muchbrook girl?'

Will nodded.

'Was there a child?'

Will shook his head.

'She's heal?'

Will nodded. He gave Laurence Haket his letter of Sir Guy. Laurence Haket read it and stowed it away.

'Look here, young Quate,' said Laurence Haket, though he wasn't much older than the bowman, 'I have your deed of freedom of Sir Guy, brought last night by the miller's son. Do right by me in Calais, gather the silver you need to buy it, and I'll let you have it, as Sir Guy bids me in this letter. Go against me and I'll burn it, do you understand?'

LAURENCE, ON HORSEBACK, led Will, Sweetmouth and Mad on foot along the road to Edington, with the flat of Wiltshire to their left and the steep cleeve of the down above them on the right. At midday they turned of the road and went by a narrow way between trees to a great green meadow between the cleeve and a stream. Beacons of bright-hued cloth flew in the wind of poles at the meadow's edge. One third of the meadow was hilled by a town of cloth, rope and timber. Telds shone white in the sun, or were whirled and barred in red and blue and gold, or flecked with the likenesses of uncouth deer, of firedrakes, swans and lions, and beacons flew of their tops. The more telds looked out on the open meadow, and the most teld of all, of the muchness of a manor house, was black sewn with silver stars.

In the middle of the meadow, marked by lengths of white tape, was a garden in pots, of blossoms, low hedges and bushes, and in the middle of the garden, a great frame of timber, with cloth and rope heaped on the ground at the bottom. Elsewhere in the garden stood the likenesses of folk wearing naught but woollens over their shoulders, and in one stead, something of about the bigness of a cornsheaf hidden by a wrap of cerecloth.

At the other end of the meadow, a timber floor had been reared of the ground, and pipers and drummers stood on it and played songs. It couldn't be seen whom they played to, for the whole stead was hedged by wattle.

The bowmen went up a kind of street between two rows of telds, crowded by sellers who'd have them buy bunches of heart's ease, baby aquerns and squabs in wicker baskets, puddings, eels brad on the gledes, saffron cakles, pomanders, clogs, silver tokens and rattles. They came to a long teld where they were told to stow their gear. Inside a gleeman walked to and fro on his hands with his dog following on two legs, and another kept five fish balls in the air at once. Sweetmouth asked him why he used fish balls, and the gleeman said it was Friday; would he have him juggle with meat?

In the teld was a board, and around it a heap of high-born young men with soft hair, with dear knives on their belts and with clothes that were both old and dear, like to they'd show they had much silver, but would that all knew they ne cared whether they had it or no. They chid each other and struck with their fingers a little-what of calfskin on the board, held by a bald weary man with a feather behind each ear. Otherwhiles one of the young men would snatch at the calfskin, and the penman would bark and hurr at him and grip the calfskin tighter.

Behind the penman, still, his arms folded, stood a long dark fellow with a wide flat hat of which a peacock feather drooped. He wore a shirt of the same hue as the eye of the peacock feather and looked on the young men like to he'd found a nest of rats in his barn, and only sought to be sikur the last had shown its neb before he stirred himself to set the dogs on them.

'Maestro Pavone!' called Laurence. All around the board stilled and turned their heads. 'Here are the archers for your revels. If they please you, I claim my part.'

The other young men hooted and whistled and laughed. The penman set his chin on his hands and stared at the bowmen. Maestro Pavone came out from behind the board and nighed them. He ne unknit his arms, but stuck out his lower lip and stood so near they could smell a winly stink of seeds of heaven and spring blossoms of his smooth skin. He came up to Sweetmouth, so near their noses almost felt each other.

'You'd be a player, would you?' he said. 'Stick out your tongue.'

Sweetmouth did as he was told.

'Wag it up and down. Side to side. You have a grand tongue.' He shuddered. 'It is very horrible.'

Sweetmouth said he ne knew what horrible meant.

'Horrible is what us needs,' said Pavone. He lifted his steven and showed his teeth. 'When you see a belle demoiselle all you do is speak evil of her.'

Sweetmouth said it wasn't true.

'You ne know aught of truth, Evil Tongue,' said Pavone. He wrathed and darkened. 'The first thing you think of when you see a woman is how to blacken her name in the minds of others. They knew what they were about when they set you to guard the Rose. Lying wretch! She mayn't take a little sun on her cheek without that you spread a tale of how she and the sun be lovers. You mayn't love, and mayn't bear that others love, and so you use your tongue to foul all that's fair and true. No more!'

With a shout, he drew his knife and dashed it over Sweetmouth's mouth, and with his other hand snatched at a deal of flesh between Sweetmouth's lips. Red ran down between his fingers and he lowered his blade and held up Sweetmouth's sundered tongue for all to see.

The young men laughed and clapped their hands together. Sweetmouth's mouth hung open, his jaw slack.

'May you speak?' said Pavone.

Sweetmouth said slowly and weakly that it had seemed to him he felt the smart as his tongue was shift of its root, yet it was still there.

'The knife is true enough, but it ne touched you,' said Pavone. 'The red's a cloth of Italy we use. It runs of the hand like to the fall of blood. Here's your tongue, a piece of old leather. When you play the part tomorrow, you'll have it in your mouth.'

He came to Mad, and nipped his black curls between his fingers.

'Who do you think you may be?' he said.

Mad said Pavone should tell him who he might be, and he would tell him if he were right.

'Me thinks you might be the God of Love,' said Pavone.

Mad said maybe he was the God of Love, but how could he be sikur?

'You'd have wings like to an angel,' said Pavone. 'But we may lend you some if you lack them.'

'I'll borrow,' said Mad. 'I left my wings at home in Merioneth.'

'You'd be able to shoot five arrows at a big much heart, and not miss once.'

'I may do that, be the heart right much.'

'And there'd be in you some lore, that those who watched you might know without words, for yours is not a speaking part.'

Mad began to sing a song without words. It was sweet and sad. 'Who learned you that?' asked Pavone.

'Queen Gwenhwyvar,' said Mad.

Pavone laughed. 'I knew you from the start,' he said. 'You may play the God of Love. But ne speak of queens here.'

Pavone came to Will. He stared in his eyes, and Will stared back, until Pavone turned to Laurence. 'This one comes with a mask already on,' he said. 'Where'd you find him?'

'He's new,' said Laurence. 'He was a ploughman till three days ago.'

'And tomorrow he will be Venus. Who only shoots two arrows, but they must not miss their mark. Your arrows ne miss, do they, Venus?'

'Answer,' said Laurence.

'My arrows ne miss,' said Will.

'Laurence Haket,' said Pavone. 'The Lover.'

Laurence mirthed and the other young high-born men looked sick.

Pavone turned to them. 'You – Wealth, you – Idleness, you – Youth. You the Lover's Friend, you Simplicity – but for Christ's love, wipe that rouge of your cheek. You three may be Delight, Joy and Gaiety, if you learn to less resemble mourners at a burial.'

'I'm pricked to play Humility, but the part's too small,' said one of the young men.

'Such parts as Venus and the God of Love shouldn't be played by common soldiers,' said another.

'Who are you?'

'Noble Heart, you said.'

Sweetmouth said he had an ask: might they, as players, go hop to the pipes on the green?

'Listen. Between you, the common soldiers, and you, the nobles, lies a cleft unbridgeable,' said Pavone. 'You soldiers are of the dirt and the dung-heap, you live of one day to the next and aren't worth no more than the bread and ale you're fed with. You haven't no wit but what you need to drive a plough and shoot an arrow and that which goads you to breed, eat, get drunk, beat each other and find a warm stead to sleep. And you, nobles, who are so much higher, all you have is dreams and clean fingernails and bitterness that the money you got of your fathers is never enough to cover the promises you got of your mothers. Here you are, yearning to go out of your kind, to step through the golden curtain into the estate of play, where anyone may be another and all may speak to anyone. Men, I ask that when you're in my domain, you set your ranks aside.'

'Maestro,' said the penman.

'Here,' said Pavone to Sweetmouth, 'we ne hop. Toads hop.' He set himself down on his hams, puffed out his cheeks and hopped like a toad. He stood. 'Here,' he said, 'we dance.' He went up to Will and set the flat of his open right hand against the flat of Will's open right hand, while he looked into Will's eyes. 'Follow me,' he said, and began to step and turn his hips from side to side. 'Here,' he said, 'there is no hopping, and Maestro Pavone will dance with Venus.'

I SPENT SOME hours in Westbury attempting to establish the nature of the emergency that had closed the road to Dorset. I could not decide whether the ignorance of the inhabitants was sincere or pretend. They responded to my inquiries with gestures. They extended their arms, they agitated their hands, as if it were a mystery that could not be solved, and did not require to be. The flow of people in the direction of Edington ceased. Westbury was tranquil. I observed individuals congregate in twos and threes in tenebrous spaces, murmuring anxiously, or standing motionless after one had spoken with particular intensity, the one ruminating, the other observing him ruminate, each uncertain how to proceed, each expecting the other to provide guidance, or to explain how his proposition was ridiculous.

Noon came and went without the arrival of Hayne, Softly et al. I sat in the court of the hostelry and subjected Longfreke to my company. While he considers himself subordinate to Hayne, he is conscious of the giant's defects – his unpredictability, his unresponsiveness to questions, his reliance on force and majesty as a substitute for persuasion. Longfreke is, in his own estimation, a translator of Hayne's commands into terms comprehensible to the simple Englishmen of the score.

Yet none of the archers can be characterised as simple Englishmen except Longfreke himself, the sole member of the fractured company who preserves the notion of common purpose. His credo is that the tension caused by Cess's rape and abduction, the hermeticism of Hayne, the malignity of Softly, the tendencies in Will, Sweetmouth and Mad in the direction of Pan and Venus as opposed to Mars – all these are distractions from the company's unalterable military function, rather than that the military function is a remnant of former ideas, as it appears to me.

His injury, it emerged, occurred at Crécy, in the nocturnal, post-combat moments when the archers had descended furtively among the cadavers of the French in quest of spoils. Longfreke was at the remote margin of that sanguinary area, where the futile clamour for mercy of the not-yet-expired French and the rude response of the plunderers was muted.

THE MOON NAD risen, said Longfreke, and there'd been not but stars and the light of the faraway on-blaze mill to see by. He walked through a wood and came to what he took in the darkness for a thick stead where two trees had grown together. It seemed to him a thing of steel or silver hung of one of the branches. He reached for it, and saw it was a spur, and then that it was still on a foot, sheathed in iron. What he'd taken for trees was a French knight in armour mounted on his horse. Longfreke ran away, tripped, fell and lay still. He listened. No sound came of the knight.

He stood. The first light of moonrise glew on the knight and his horse. They ne stirred. The horse's head hung down and the knight, in armour from head to toe, held his bare sword upright in his hand. Longfreke took a step toward him, stinted, and took another step. He came to the horse and felt its neck. Its flesh was cold. Longfreke looked up and whispered to the knight. He spoke again, louder. The knight was as before, frozen. Longfreke stood up and began to walk about the horse.

An arrow was pitched in the knight's throat, right through the middle, between the scales of his armour. On the same side, the horse had been struck by five arrows, in a line from its shoulder to its behind. Horse and man had died this way, the knight in the saddle, held upright by his armour. Longfreke hadn't been altogether wrong about the tree: somehow before it died the horse had thrown its forelegs over a bare forked trunk, and this kept it upright, the fork holding its belly, its legs locked stiff.

Longfreke read that he couldn't bear away all the knight's goods and thought to pull the dead man of the saddle that he might throughseek his gear to choose the best things. The horse was a long one, and Longfreke short, so he'd grip the knight by his armour's knee-scales, and pull him down. But when he did this, and hung on the knight with all his weight, he couldn't shift him.

He went to the knight's left side, away from the arrows, and pulled at the knight from there. It seemed to him the knight stirred a little. Longfreke took firmer hold of the knight's knee armour, leapt up and planted his feet against the side of the horse.

Horse and rider leaned and fell. Longfreke let go and hit the ground a short while before the knight. He took the blow of the edge of the dead knight's sword in the middle of his face, thrust deeper by the weight of the horse. He lay witless and bleeding till Dickle found him and bore him back to the English.

It seemed the knight's knaves hadn't sharpened the sword as keenly as they might, said Longfreke. The blade hadn't broken the bones of his head, only hacked it a little and cloven his nose. A doctor sewed the two halves of his neb together with catgut, like a seaman righting a sail, and bade him wash the cleft with watered wine and bind it with fresh linen once a day. In six month he was heal, but no saint would give him back his fair face, and his betrothed left him for another man.

'Your even-bowmen stood by you,' said Thomas.

Dickle had, said Longfreke. Folk spoke ill of him, and he'd done wicked deeds, but it hadn't been Dickle's guilt that a much devil got in him. So much a devil that he mightn't get out by himself and had to beg the Fiend to send a goat to open the way.

'Is that what betid?' asked Thomas.

Thomas had seen it with his own eyes, said Longfreke. Dickle had been great with one of the Fiend's kind, that made him seek to fight any man he met. Why else would Dickle have got himself nailed up like to the Lord of Life, and have a rood inked on his forehead, if ne to halse the evil of his soul?

'He sought to drive out the devil?' said Thomas.

Longfreke nodded. Soldiers drew devils to them, he said, for he'd seen many like Dickle.

'The other bowmen helped you,' said Thomas.

Then and then, said Longfreke, it seemed to him they only did it for mirth. They'd start to speak to him and when he answered say they ne spoke with Longfreke but with the other half, Frongleke. He had a hundred pence owed him when they landed, and Sweetmouth clipped each one in half, saying Longfreke and Frongleke must have an even share.

'Men ne like to show their love for their friends,' said Thomas. 'They fear to be deemed womanly. They hide their love under rough glee.'

Anywise, said Longfreke without bitterness, his betrothed went to another after she saw him, her ne liked his new face; he understood, for him ne liked it either.

He smiled and said Thomas looked like a priest stood over the shrift stool, hungry for a sinner's tale.

'You're a small sinner, yet I got of you a tale,' said Thomas.

Were he to seek shrift, said Longfreke, it were for the sin of anger toward Cess.

'Why are you angry at Cess?'

She forgave Softly, said Longfreke.

'Me ne thinks she forgives him,' said Thomas.

When they landed in France, said Longfreke, and the bishops told them theirs was a right war, they hadn't in mind no slaughter of holy-likeness carvers, nor the reave of maidenhoods, nor the theft of daughtren. What Softly did was wrong and after Mantes he and Longfreke had all but gone knife to knife over Cess. The others said Longfreke wanted the maid for himself, but it wasn't true, he wanted her to be set free, and ill to befall Softly, to show there was some law. Instead, Softly came again to England heal and rich, and Longfreke lost his face and his wife-to-be.

Thomas narrowed his eyes. 'Why do you say she forgave him?'

She wouldn't wed him when he asked, said Longfreke, but they lay together each night, she cooked and cleaned for him, like to a wife.

'She hadn't no choice,' said Thomas. 'Goes she against him, he beats her.'

At Crécy, said Longfreke, she fetched fresh arrows for them without Softly's bidding. When Noster mightn't shoot no more she'd asked could they learn her to bend a bow, for she'd shoot at the French too. At the French, her own kind! And in Bristol in May, when Softly had taken up thieving, she'd helped him. The woollens he gave so freely were stolen by her of a ship in Bristol haven.

'I would speak to her,' said Thomas.

Softly would kill him if he did, said Longfreke.

ON THEIR ARRIVAL at the joust, Madlen secured Berna a fine tent with a couch, a wicker table, a screen and a pot. Berna paid for the tent for two nights, for payage into the jousting place for her and her servant, and for bread and milk for their breakfast, lightening her purse sensibly. Madlen would take her gowns to be cleaned immediately, but Berna ordained rest. Madlen lay on the grass on the tent floor, close to the entrance, with her cheek pillowed on her arm. Berna removed the gown she wore, lay on the couch in her underclothes and fell into a sleep profound.

She was woken by the cry of a vendeuse, who sold her a towel, soap and hot water from a barrel on a handcart. Madlen was absent, and the gown Berna had worn had disappeared, but the stolen gown, clean as new, hung of a nail cloyed in the pole that supported the roof of the tent. Berna laced shut the entrance, laved her hair, laved her body and put on fresh linen and the clean gown. She chewed on a grain of paradise while she towelled her hair, combed and plaited it and tied it up with silk. She spat out the chewed grain in the pot, cleaned her teeth, frot her face with cream and touched her throat with pearls of piment. She put her mother's ring on her finger and her mother's nouche on the chain around her neck. She put on the poignet of red and white cord they had given her to confirm payage. She regarded her remaining possessions, took *Le Roman de la Rose* and departed.

At the entrance to her tent she encountered the vendeuse, come again for the basins she had rented her customers.

'Have you seen my maidservant?' demanded Berna. 'A long, dark, meagre girl in a blue gown and white wimple?'

The vendeuse inquired whether the servant was a maid Berna had brought from home or one she'd hired on the road.

'She's of my father's manor, as if it were your business,' said Berna.

The vendeuse said she had seen a maid creep of the lady's tent with a gown the very image of the one the lady now wore.

'Your use of the word "creep" is misplaced,' said Berna. 'My servant simply went to have the gown I'm wearing cleaned, then must have returned with it and taken the other while I slept.'

Every year, said the vendeuse, there were one or two demoiselles ran of their people to a joust, hungry for the wide world. They always came to a bad end.

'What do you mean?' demanded Berna.

Murdered, or worse, said the vendeuse, with amiable cheer. Had any of the young lady's possessions vanished along with the maidservant?

'Cease your accusations,' said Berna. 'Do you have a mirror?'

Would she know how she looked? said the vendeuse.

'There is one I'd have see me, and regret,' said Berna.

The vendeuse pointed to her own eyes with two fingers. She'd be Berna's mirror, she said, and bade Berna listen: with her neb's skin white as lily out-take the bloom in her cheek, her lips as red as holly berries, her hair like to a raven's wing and her eyes aglitter like gold of candlelight, all men would look on Berna and regret she wasn't theirs.

BERNA PASSED BETWEEN the files of tents. Pots of fleabane sent up coils of milky smoke and there was a scent of crushed grass and roast trout. Groups of young men and women in bright chargeous clothes sat in circles on cushions and blankets. They drank from bottles and ate from baskets, laughed and sang and listened to poetry. Gittern strings were plucked and reeds made to pipe, but the very music was in the distance, not there. Berna had slept late. The low late sun gave all skin a clean copper colour. Tall, pure white clouds presented in the sky like an excess of geese pressed in nets. The air was warm and moist enough to feel its touch.

She tailed four people of her age, two demoiselles and two gentlemen, who emerged from a tent in front of her and went in the direction of the music. The men were in parti-coloured hose of white and scarlet and plain white tunics and the women abled in simple red and blue gowns with tight sleeves. Their necks and the tops of their shoulders were bare and the liripipes of their dainty hoods were wound around their heads. They moved quickly, half running, the women raising their gowns of the ground, all of them talking and laughing at the same time.

Berna pursued them, maintaining her distance, to a grand pasture beyond a sort of artificial garden, and to an opening in a wattle fence, guarded by two peasants of savage appearance. Over the top of the fence Berna perceived a company of musicians on a stage embellished with paintures of roses and of hearts pierced through with arrows.

The four young people Berna followed passed between the guards. When she attempted to do the same the guards stopped the way.

'Let me pass,' said Berna. 'I am Lady Bernadine Corbet, daughter of Sir Guy Corbet of Outen Green, and I've paid what's due.'

The more of the guards bowed and told her he ne doubted her ancestry nor rank, but her poignet was the wrong colour; only those with a green poignet might pass through to the dancing, for it was a privy affair.

Between the guards Berna could perceive the form of dancers in bright clothes.

'This is an outrage,' she said. 'You will be punished.'

The second guard saw what she carried.

A maid with a book, he said to his companion. They'd be learning them to read next, then what?

'Writing is generally held to be the next step,' came a voice from behind Berna. The guards stepped back, lowered their heads and shoulders and were silent.

Their defeat issued of a dame in a gown of red silk with a jewel on each finger and hair bound tightly to her head with a gold filet. She must have had an age of fifty. She wasn't high, but cast a great shadow, and on her feet she wore a cracked old pair of men's black leather hunting boots.

'Are you the Corbet girl? Vas-y, vas-y. How they kept it fresh I cannot imagine but it's sturgeon in those tarts. They must be eaten tonight.'

SHE LED BERNA by the wrist past the dancers to a table covered in white cloth where a young man offered her a tart and a cup of wine.

'Permit me,' said the dame, removing the book from Berna's hand. Berna took a gulp of wine and pressed the tart into her mouth. With her mouth full, she mumbled something and curtseyed. A piece of pastry fell from her lips and she swallowed.

'I plead your pardon, madam,' she said, 'I was ravenous.'

The dame looked up from the book, which she'd opened and commenced to study. 'I discomfited you by guessing your name. You may call me Elizabeth.' She extended her hand and Berna curtseyed again to kiss it.

'You are very celebrable,' said Elizabeth. 'Everyone is interested in your position. Your husband-to-be, Sir Henry, was here earlier complaining piteously that he was to be married tomorrow, and his bride absent. He desired no more than to exchange his daughter for another man's, which is apparently acceptable in this world. Ne look so frightened! He departed in a rage, on a report you were seen elsewhere.'

Berna touched the shoulders of her marriage gown and looked down at it. 'How might you know I am that demoiselle?' she demanded.

'I ne intend to slander your judgement, for it is a gown magnificent, but it is precisely the gown one would expect a girl of a Cotswold manor to wear for her marriage, and you are as your affianced descrived you, except that your face is more overt than I imagined.'

'In what manner overt?'

'I can tell you, but I have discovered by experience that to

189

request a second compliment without having properly digested the first is generally taken as the sign of a glutton. Are you as ravenous for homage as you are for our tarts? You haven't no mother? You're the eldest child? An infancy of rural banquets and dances no further than two hours' ride away from home, the company of mute young farmers? Assuredly, in the countryside, beauty may perish of a famine of appreciation.'

'I passed two years in Bristol, at my uncle's. He imports wine.'

'I adore merchants. They are always so eager to improve their minds and the minds of others. And there you acquired your letters, and your French.'

'I thought me I had French, for I can read it, but a Frenchwoman I met convinced me I ne speak it as one should, so I endeavour to prove my intelligence by meddling French with English, like everyone.'

'Such unnecessary self-diminishment! Do I hear a reflection of a mordant note in my own discourse? So: your face — overt in that it ne refuses fresh discoveries. So many girls your age, having spent their virgin years in the furious pursuit of novelty, decide that their opinions are complete, and repel additions. Excuse me a moment, but ne move, I return presently.'

Elizabeth began to talk with a long, dark, quick man in a peacock-blue tunic who had approached them at the table. Berna regarded the dance. The musicians on stage played a rapid melody, the rhythm beaten out on two sets of drums and a tambourine in the hand of the singer. She knew the singer: it was Madog, the archer with the deep distant eyes, the long hair in rings, and the rich tenor voice.

The dancers were a muddle of nobles, who danced properly, in well-formed lines and circles, and others who leaped and kicked and linked arms like peasants at a church-ale, but who were dressed more strangely and richly than peasants she knew. In places, the gentle and the savage danced with each other, and Berna couldn't tell whether the nobles constrained their inferiors to their manner of dancing, or attempted to achieve, by imitation of the commoners, a liberation of their inherited formalities. Among the dancers she knew Will and Sweetmouth, in the white surcoats with red roses on the breast that several people wore.

Little by little she perceived that she and Dame Elizabeth hadn't come in unnoticed, but were observed and defended. The young men who stood with their backs to the table, apparently regarding the dance and the musicians, formed a line none crossed without consent. People pleaded with the young men to be allowed to approach. People attended patiently, apparently expecting they would be summoned in due course. They regarded Lady Elizabeth as if at any moment she might perform a marvel. They regarded Berna.

Among the dancers Berna saw Laurence. He saw her at the same time, froze with the palm of his hand against a demoiselle's, and opened his mouth. Berna turned back to Elizabeth, who displayed the book to the man in the blue tunic. They regarded Berna, the man nodded and departed, and the two women moved towards each other.

'I appreciate the value of this so-called romance to a certain sort of man,' said Elizabeth. 'It is a useful guide, I suppose, to the seduction of young women, were the sole purpose of such seduction to take the girl's virginity. Am I too frank for you?'

'Frankness is the very quality I would hope to find in one so high.'

'If it seems to you that you know who I am, please set aside my highness. It ne likes me to talk through madam, madam, madam. But why frankness?'

'Of the arrows the God of Love possesses, it is Frankness I prefer, because frankness is truly noble,' said Bernadine. 'The other arrows — Beauty, Simplicity, Courtesy, Company, Beau-Semblant — are the qualities in a woman that may injure a man's heart while leaving his pride untouched. *That* woman may get herself a lover and never open her mouth. But the man who falls in love mostly by the wound of his lover's frankness is ennobled, for he accepts her enumeration of his faults, without doubting the loving spirit in which they are given; and she accepts his frankness in return. It may be judged a demerit of Guillaume's Romance that Frankness is the one arrow Love chooses not to use.'

Dame Elizabeth stared at her in silence, then barst out laughing. 'So ingenious, and so serious! I may fall in love with you myself, be you so frank with me. Now permit me some frankness in return. You confuse love and a husband. I was widowed three times before I was twenty-six. All my husbands were shits. I was very frank with them, and they were very frank with me, and I assure you there wasn't nothing noble about it. I loved one of them, and they loved my money and my blood. They're all departed, and I'm secure. I vowed chastity to protect my property, and chastity is a vow that may be made more than once. Love is whatever remains once one has made one's accommodation with fate. What's your accommodation to be? You're to be married tomorrow, two days' ride away, and yet you're here, alone, without family, without your future husband, without a retinue, without even a decent ravisher.'

'On that point,' said Bernadine, 'there is one here who loved me par amour, and would ravish me of my family and that wretched knight.'

She recounted her story to Elizabeth.

THEY MOVED TO a wattle bay set into the fence, screened by an arch of roses. Under the roses was a small bank of turf. Just before they sat down a maidservant appeared and placed cushions on the bank.

'I was ravished by agreement, to save me from an unpleasant marriage,' said Elizabeth. 'I married John at thirteen, and when he died four years later, with my father gone, uncle Eddie removed my liberty and pondered which baron to bestow me on. I communicated secretly with my friend Theo, and we agreed that he would steal me, as if by force, and marry me. Uncle Eddie was rageous when he was informed, and demanded compensation, which we paid, of course.'

'And Theo was him you loved.'

'I loved him. I received less in return, but there's no bargaining in such matters. To demand that one's love be returned has always had the savour of usury to me.'

'I am curious to know which of you inspired the ravishment.'

'As I remember, I was the proposer.'

'Had I passed Laurence a message saying I desired him to ravish me of my family and marry me in secret, I'm sure he would have responded.'

'In such cases the ravisher's considerations tend to concern the ravishee's inheritance as much as the delights of her person.'

'Laurence knew that my family lives of a single manor when he asked my father for my hand. He ne spent a month in our house enditing me poetry in expectation of no inheritance. Besides, his valour at Crécy is rewarded with a manor worth forty pound a year.'

'The perfect chevalier,' said Elizabeth. 'Galahad with a counting board.' She caressed the book. 'This isn't no story of no marriage. Doesn't it aggrieve you that Haket disports him here, when you ravished yourself to be with him? You might be married and halfway to France by now.'

'We saw each other this morning,' said Berna. 'He promised he would marry me, but urged me to concealment while he performed some duty at the joust. I chose rather to engender his jealousy by appearing here as if I ne cared whether he married me or not.'

'Your choice was judicious,' said Elizabeth. 'I suppose he recounted to you the nature of his duties here?'

'I ne inquired,' said Berna, lowering her eyes.

'He was subtle enough to furnish us with some archers for our pageant to replace the proper players, who failed to appear. As reward he is to play the Lover.'

Bernadine blushed and regarded the older woman fiercely. 'Your pardon, madam,' she said, 'I were better to speak frankly, as I promised, and confess my ignorance. I ne know not of no pageant.'

'I wish I had a place for you in my ménage. Most of the nobles I know would sooner confess to pissing on an altar than to ignorance of anything.'

'I wouldn't be one of those nobles, yet it would be an honour to be known by you.'

'Good. Let's be amicable.' She placed her hand on Bernadine's shoulder and kissed her on the cheek. 'It won't harm your cause with your amour to be seen to be close to me. Now, this is a joust only in name, that it ne offend the clerks. It's got up by my friend Bella. She's also my aunt, though we're the same age. We've experienced sufficient combat in our lives, very and pretend, and here's a joust without jousting, but play, poetry, music, dance and wine. My friend's son, my cousin Eddie, conducts a very joust tomorrow in Kent, and permits his mother to conduct our revels at the same time, on condition she be at least one hundred miles away, and ne tempt his favourites to join her. It's more difficult than you suppose. Some marvellously savage young men-at-arms delight in attendance here, despite the absence of disports martial. It appears no man desires more ardently to prove the gentler aspect of his nature than he whose principal duty is butchery in battle.

Nonetheless I am surprised Laurence is content to play the lover in a pageant when you have presented him with such an excellent opportunity to be the lover in life. What might explain his choice, I wonder? A certain esperance of preferment of my friend Bella? A rumour of especial royal favours granted to past players?'

She paused, inviting a question, but Berna remained silent.

With a change of tone to trenchant decisiveness, Elizabeth said: 'I ne consider it proper that you should observe this spectacle with the others.'

'No, madam?' said Bernadine piteously.

'I would prefer that you play a part. I mayn't prevent from regaining you the husband your father intended, nor oblige your amour to ravish you, but I may place you close to him in play and see what comes of it.'

'I ne know the play,' protested Berna.

Elizabeth raised the book. 'Here's the story,' she said. 'It is *Le Roman de la Rose*. Maestro Pavone! Here's your Warm Welcome.'

THE DRUM BEAT faster, Mad sang of a freke who went with an elf, and Sweetmouth hopped with two high-born maids who laughed so hard they had to hold each other to keep from falling over. Will drank two cups of wine and looked about. Another maid came up to him and asked if he were an archer, and had he been at Crécy.

'Slew you many Frenchmen?' she asked. 'What was it like? Where are you from?'

Cotswold, said Will.

'D'you know the Granvilles of Moreton?'

The lady Bernadine came in among the folk that hopped. Will

asked for word of Madlen, and Lady Bernadine said Madlen had run away. She wouldn't stint to say more. She went to speak to Laurence Haket, and they spoke, and each seemed to wrath, and Laurence Haket shouted at her. Lady Bernadine took his wrist, but he shook it off and left the hop, alone. Will lost sight of Lady Bernadine after that.

Will told Sweetmouth he'd go, and Sweetmouth bade him bide longer, for he ne might swive two burds by himself. But Will bade him goodnight and went again through the meadow to the telds. The high-borns' hires and followers cooked and washed there and besought their lords' horses and falcons. When Will asked after Madlen they bade him look outside the joust field, where the hucksters, onlookers and beggars gathered who mightn't spend the night inside.

Will went out by the two outcome churls who warded the gate to the field. A bear-keeper with his bear on a rope told the wardens they must let him in, for the bear's evening flesh was with a kinsman there and the bear was hungry. The keeper's arms ached of holding him back that he ne snatch at a child. The wardens bade him knit the bear to a tree and find him a dog to sup on. In truth there wasn't no lack of dogs. Starved and big of eye, they stepped between the hucksters' cooking fires and took blows and stones to fight over bits of chewed pigskin spat in the dust. One licked the stumps of an old soldier, another stroked with his cold neb a thin, naked child in the arms of the ragged woman who begged at the gate.

The bear struck at one of the wardens with his hand and the warden clubbed him on the ribs. The keeper dragged the bear away and cursed the wardens. They cursed him back and asked him where the chain was he'd had the bear on in the morning.

He'd hired it to the Cotswold knave who'd caught the thief, said the keeper, the thrall that stole his lady's gown, and went about as a maid. The knave had thought him he'd earn of the runaway and shift what he made with the keeper.

While he spoke, and fought to get the bear in wield, the keeper nodded to a heap of folk gathered by the furze further up the cleeve.

MADLEN SAT ON the dust in the middle of a ring of folk. She was held by the bear chain. One end was knit to a leather neck-cuff, the other to a stake hammered in the ground. Her dress was torn open down to the waist and she held her arms tightly on her chest to hill her tits. She bled of a slit over her eye and had a bruise on her cheek. She saw Will and turned her head away.

Cockle stood nearby with a kinsman Will knew, Matt, who'd gone to be a stoneworker with a guild in Cirencester. Cockle egged an old woman with three cock-sticks in her hand. 'Throw true,' he called. 'It's a thief and a runaway that stole his lord's daughter's wedding gown and his hayward's boar. He goes against his kind and God's behests. A true shot's a godsend.'

Will went up and took the woman by the wrist that she ne throw. Matt came over and helped two other men drag Will away. Folk took the woman's side. They yall at Will that he hadn't the right nor might to hamper folk's games.

'Let her go,' said Will.

'Her?' said Cockle. 'There's no cunt on this, but you can fuck it in the arse for sixpence if you would.' Folk laughed. Cockle shook the chain. Madlen's head rocked and she fell on her side. She raised herself on one hand, keeping the other over her chest.

'Let me alone,' she said to Will. 'Your help ne needs me. Go. Live a free life.'

'This isn't Hab, as it thinks you,' said Will to Cockle. 'It's his sister Madlen.'

'What sister? Throw, woman.' The woman threw the sticks at Madlen. Two missed the mark. One struck her on the back of the neck. Madlen grunted at the smart and held her mouth shut.

'Who'll pitch sticks at the thief?' called Cockle. 'Penny a throw.'

'This isn't right,' said Will.

'It needs me to work him to hill the time I took to find him,' said Cockle. 'When we get him to the Green again he'll be hung anywise, and not too soon. He were better not born.'

'What harm's she done to you?'

'She! Would you learn the shed between man and woman?' He made as if to lift the hem of Madlen's gown but before he could do so a knave came forward with a penny and Cockle gathered up the sticks for him.

'Christ's love, would you take her to Outen Green, take her now, let her be deemed there without this pine,' said Will.

'And miss the show tomorrow?' said Cockle.

'They're to set a castle on fire,' said Matt. 'They're to show a tale, with players and songs.'

'So which is it, cock or hen?' asked the knave with the sticks.

'He's a thrall,' said Cockle.

'She's a maid,' said Will.

'I would it were a maid,' said the knave. He hurled the first stick at Madlen. It struck her on the nose. Blood streamed of her nostrils.

Two long fellows in dear black kirtles, with swords hung of their belts, shoff into the ring of folk and asked highly who answered for the stir.

The knave let fall his two sticks and stepped away. Cockle said he'd caught a thief who'd gone about the joust clothed as a maid.

There wasn't no sound but the snot and blood that burbled in Madlen's nose as she sniffed. The longer of the two fellows, with a hawk's nose and cold dark eyes, came up to Madlen and proked her in the side with the toe of his boot. He turned to Cockle and asked who gave him leave to take money of folk to pelt a thief with sticks in this stead.

Cockle went to a bundle and took of it the lady Bernadine's wedding gown. He shook it out and said it'd been stolen of his lord in Cotswold by this thrall, a swineherd. Five pound Sir Guy had paid for it, but it wasn't worth five pound now, spoiled of this gnof who'd worn it on the road.

The hawkish fellow dight his hands on his hips and turned to Will. 'And who are you, in the livery of the pageant?' he said.

Before Will could answer, Cockle said Will was a low bondman of his town who'd gone to be a bowman, and he'd always been homely with the thief.

'I ne asked you,' said the hawkish fellow to Cockle, in so fell a steven that most of the folk who nad left crope away.

Will said he was sworn to Hayne Attenoke's score, and the joust needed one who could shoot true. Today he was a bowman, and on Sunday he would be a bowman, but tomorrow, he would be Venus.

Cockle bade the hawkish fellow mark how Will made himself out to be a man named Vaynous, which he wasn't nowise in truth.

'It ne recks me how you handle the thief,' said the hawkish fellow to Cockle, 'but take you silver of folk here again, gobbets of you will fatten my swine. As for you, Venus, while you wear that livery, you ne stray from the players' tent.'

He led Will away. Will looked over his shoulder at Madlen. She ran the back of her hand over her neb, smearing blood over one cheek. She met his eyes and shook her head.

'Forget me,' she said.

'Shut your mouth,' said Cockle. He kicked her in the ribs and when she lay on the ground kicked her again in the head. He called to Will to ask if Will had seen the lady Bernadine. Will ne answered, and followed the fellows in black to the gate.

WHAT, JUDITH, IS the significance of my indulgent confession that
I desired to be desired by you, carnally as well as spiritually? More
profound than that transient libidinousness was an infantile urge for
security, to have a love undeserved and unconditional, without
expectation I would offer the same in return.

NEXT MORNING THE nobles went to the chase. They returned at
noon to the jousting place to rest and change. While they had their
sport, the personages of the pageant rehearsed their roles. After
noon the trumpets sounded, the noble audience assembled on benches
and the common people sat on the heights surveying the enclosed
pasture. The grand black tent was extended at the front and a
company took position there. The difference between the brilliant
daylight and the obscurity at the entrance rendered it difficult for
those outside to perceive the faces or apparel of these people, yet
ne prevented the nobles and their entourage thus obscured from
enjoying a fine view of the spectacle. The exception to the privity
of those at the tent entrance was Maestro Pavone, who stood in
advance of the company. His blue shirt trapped the light. A large
trumpet capable of multiplying his voice was mounted on a gantry
close to him.

The music ceased. A figure lay solitary in the pasture.

'In my twentieth year,' came the voice of Pavone, 'when Love
claims his tribute of young men, I went to sleep as usual one night,
and dreamed a beauteous and pleasing dream.'

The Lover, portrayed by Laurence Haket, lifted himself of the pasture and stood with his hands over his eyes. He removed his hands and marvelled at the scene.

Pavone's proclamations and the performers' enactments were aided by a choir on the stage, until the audience ceased to tell the elements apart, and even the common multitude, for whom the high language of the narrative, with its abundance of French novelties, was largely incomprehensible, fell under the enchantment of the story.

The Lover approaches the border of the Garden of Love. He enters, and after consorting with Love and his circle, passes on to the font of Narcissus (*represented by a white fountain flowing into a round white vessel*). The Lover regards the crystals that lie below the surface of the water and, through their special properties, perceives the presence in the garden of an arbour of roses. Among the roses is one bud about to flower that surpasses all others in perfection. Through the power of the font, the Lover is enamoured of it.

(*Concealed cords were employed to force paintures of roses upright. A grand veil, painted to resemble the pastoral verdure, was removed, revealing a statue of a rosebud in the centre of the arbour, the profound scarlet of the issuing flower visible through a fissure in the green that closely enveloped it.*)

The Lover approaches the rosebud and attempts to touch it but is prevented by thorns (*spines pushed out of the base on which it rested*). The Lover sighs and complains that his heart is heavy. (*He raised an archery butt in the form of a painted heart, as large as he.*)

During the Lover's tribulations, Love (*portrayed by Madog ap Ithel, a Welsh archer*) advances on the Lover from the rear. He stands couched like a hunter, an arrow primed. (*Some in the audience cried out to the Lover to have regard to his heart, for it was in danger, and the heart was so large that it entirely blocked the Lover's vision, rendering it impossible for him to perceive Love's menacing posture. Love wore a long white robe and two great white feathered wings and had a crown of roses in his flowing black hair.*) Love launches four arrows, representing the Rose's qualities: Beauty, Simplicity, Courtesy and Company (*apparently very war arrows, with trenchant steel points*). Each arrow pierces the Lover's heart, and with each arrow, the heart (*held upright by the Lover*) trembles, and he cries out piteously. (*The audience ne knew whether to admire Love's dexterity, or to fear that one of his arrows had really pierced the young man.*) The Lover appears of his damaged heart and, standing close to it, complains of the pain. At this, Love launches a fifth arrow, Beau-Semblant, into the Lover's heart.

The Lover cries out that the point of the fifth arrow causes him great pain, but that it carries an ointment which relieves his suffering. (*He laid the heart flat on the pasture and bent over the arrows in such manner that the audience might not see, then stood. In his hand was a red heart of a natural size, with five small arrows in it.*) He declares that the beauty, simplicity, courtesy and company of the Rose is torment, when he mightn't possess her; but her beau-semblance renders his heart light again.

Love approaches the Lover and the Lover prays that he be permitted to enter Love's service.

'I ne let no villain nor swineherd kiss my mouth, but only the courteous, the noble and the frank,' says Love.

'I promise you,' says the Lover, 'these qualities are proper to me.' He surrenders himself to Love, and Love locks his heart with a golden key.

Love cautions the Lover that to regard the object of his affection from a distance, in the absence of the power to possess her, would be as if to fry his heart in grease.

'Indeed, I ne comprehend how even a man of iron may survive such infernal pain,' says the Lover.

'Hope is your salvation,' says Love.

Costumed in the tunic, hose, belt and knife of a young man, Berna attended in the players' tent her summons to take part. She stood apart from, and unobserved by, a company of Laurence's fellows, similarly resting prior to engagement in the play. They ridiculed Laurence's gestures and amused themselves with mocking phrases Berna strained to hear.

'Around the garden Laurence goes . . .' said one.

'Like to he longs to pluck the Rose,' said another, seizing an imaginary person in the air before him and violently pushing his hips outwards.

'While secretly this gallant lover . . .' They all snorted now with the effort of suppressing their titters.

'Longs to pluck the sovereign's mother!'

Their verse so delighted and horrified them that they began at once to laugh in the most overt manner, to battle for respiration, and to ensure they weren't spied on; at which juncture they discovered Berna, were forced into surprised silence, then turned away from her and erupted in renewed derision.

'Bel Accueil!' called the entrancer. 'Warm Welcome, au champ!' And Berna was obliged without delay to quit the tent and enter the domain of play.

The players' teld was pitched near the garden. Two benches were set before it for the players to bide their times. Mad came of his play with Laurence Haket. He went by Lady Bernadine as she walked out onto the field, folded his wings and sat on a bench next to Will, who was clothed as Venus in a red gown and a copper crown. Like Mad, Will wore mighty wings, plump with white goose feathers.

Sweetmouth came up to them clothed as an old woman. His girth was broadened with straw stuffed in his gown and he had much false tits.

'My friends Love and Venus,' he said, 'ready yourselves for the best deal of play yet wrought in England.' He wagged his tongue at them, up and down and side to side. 'I'd get right near the maids who sit and behold our show. Let them know there's a player has the tool to lick the honey from their cunnies till they die of mirth.'

'Danger! Evil Tongue! Shame! Fear!' cried a knave. 'Go out to your steads and places!'

'The hour has come,' said Sweetmouth. He hitched up his belly of straw and ran out to Love's garden with his hand in the air, smiling at the folk who beheld the play. When the name of Evil Tongue sounded from Pavone's horn, folk hooted and whistled, and Sweetmouth wagged his tongue at everyone. He and the others went to hide in the garden.

'You ne wished our friend good hap,' said Mad to Will. 'You're down in the briars. Found you your friends from home, the swineherd and his sister?'

Will shook his head.

'This romance ne likes you,' said Mad, nodding at the garden, where Warm Welcome beckoned the Lover a little nearer to the Rose.

'Thomas would teach me what romance was, but I ne understood,' said Will.

'A love tale,' said Mad.

'I know them. A king's daughter weds another king's son.'

'A romance isn't no tale of no wedding, but of the hard times on the road to one. As, when there's to be a wedding, and the bride or groom dies. Or the bride is stolen, and the other goes to seek her, or dies of sorrow. Or when they choose to wed against their elders, for love.'

'And starve without land.'

'Or when there can't never be no wedding.'

'Why?'

'Maybe they aren't man and woman, but two men who are friends.'

Will plucked with his fingers at a stave wound about with red and yellow cloth that tokened Venus's blaze. He asked Mad: 'What's your shift?'

'I'm Love,' said Mad. He lifted his bow. 'I shoot the arrows to make the Lover sicken that he mayn't turn away of the woman, whatever his will and wit should tell him.'

'You talk like to the doctor of the pest in the Malmesbury sick-house. What's on the arrows?'

'Beauty, Simplicity, Courtesy, Company and Beau-Semblant,' said Mad.

Will shook his head. 'That's all French to me,' he said.

Mad felt Will's forehead with the back of his hand. 'No heat there,' he said. 'Some other sickness has shifted your mood for the worse. Penny to a pound says you know those arrows through their smart if not their name.'

'Who am I?'

'You're Venus. Yours is another arrow. It tokens the overspill of yearning of one to fuck, and of another to be fucked. Yours it is that tinds the fire.'

Out in the garden, Lover went down on his knees to Warm Welcome and begged permission to kiss the Rose.

BERNA REGARDED THE kneeling Laurence. She was accustomed in their encounters to be the lower of the parties. From this angle the light made gentle the firm and exact lines of his visage.

'Is it your intention to dishonour me?' she demanded.

'We aren't compelled to invent no speech,' said Laurence disdainously. 'Pavone and the choir narrate the story for us. The audience mayn't hear you.'

'My question ne comes of playing no part,' said Berna. 'I speak as Bernadine.'

'For God's sake, Berna, I advised you not to come here. I'd carry you to France and marry you, but the choice of moment must be mine, not yours.'

'And what informs your choice, apart from your native vileness? Why not marry me yesterday, in the moment of my arrivage, and commence the journey to France? What is it, precisely, that moved you to delay, exposing me to the ridicule of a grand and noble dame? Why are you content to have Elizabeth Clare, the king's very cousin, regard me as you do, as second prize to whatever you aspire to win from this pretence of French amorousness in a Wiltshire field?'

'Berna . . .'

'Might your petty young gentle-friends be correct? Might you be so simple as to imagine that Isabella, the king's mother, a pious old widow attempting to amend the errors of her youth in placid retirement, will see you gallanting about in her revels and make of you some kind of favourite?'

'Berna, you ne comprehend how valuable to us the brief interest of so potent a figure as— '

'Oh! He confesses! Odious man! It was barely in your power to seduce a peasant, and now you tilt at a queen!'

'For God's sake, play your part.' Laurence tensed for a fresh assault from Berna, but her face had changed; in place of rage was a serene anticipation. There was an alteration in the noise of the audience too. Out of the murmur issued cries of alarm. The choir was silenced. Pavone's voice could be perceived repeating 'En garde! En garde!'

'What is it?' said Laurence. Berna moved away from him rapidly.

Laurence turned. A vast boar charged at him. Enker's head was down, his tusks rampant, his eyes black points of the purest hate.

LAURENCE STOOD AND recoiled smartly out of Enker's course. But in evading the furious beast, he lost his balance and tumbled onto his face. Enker completed a circle and confronted him, preparing to charge again, his right hoof grating the earth. The young man was at his mercy.

With a courage that caused the audience to issue an audible collective aspiration, Berna ambled forward, putting herself between the vicious animal and his intended victim. She placed her hand on the beast's shoulder, calling him by name. Enker looked up at her, immediately abandoned his savage demean, frot her leg with his nose and commenced to forage peacably under one of Love's hedges.

Laughter came of the slopes. Pavone's confused hesitations were interrupted by the voice of Dame Elizabeth.

'At that moment,' came her words from Pavone's trumpet, 'the Lover attempted to counter a sudden attack by the Boar of Capricious Desire. The Lover failed to defend himself successfully, and his dignity was grievously injured; but Warm Welcome saved him from destruction, proving her concern for the Lover had more power over him than his own swinish desires.'

(*Pavone and the choir hastily resumed the narrative.*) The Lover stands and bows to Warm Welcome. Venus arrives and raises her torch over them, signalling the dissolution of Warm Welcome's resistance to the Lover's request to kiss the Rose. (*Venus guided the Swine of Capricious Desire from the Garden of Love with a gentle touch of her hand to the beast's backside.*)

IN RESPONSE TO the Lover's kiss, Jealousy enters the garden. Enraged by the presumption of the Lover, she rallies Fear, Shame, Evil Tongue and Danger, and builds a castle to imprison the Rose and Warm Welcome. (*A host of labourers, employing cords, cables, poles and painted canvas, mounted a fortress on the pasture, with four walls, four ports and a tower at each corner.*) In the centre of the castle rises a single high tower where the Rose and Warm Welcome are placed in captivity.

At this moment of the Lover's despair, Love returns and musters his barons to lay siege to the fortress. The army of Love assembles on the pasture: Lady Idleness, Nobility of Heart, Pity, Largesse, Courage, Honour, Delight, Joy, Humility, Patience, Discretion and numerous others.

A group of Love's more sinister accomplices approach the port guarded by Evil Tongue, cut out the offending organ and murder him. Love's army charges in through the breach and commences a general combat with the defenders. Though Fear, Shame and Danger are greatly outnumbered, they battle ferociously, and it appears Love's cause is lost. Love calls a truce and sends for his mother, Venus.

The Engineer (*a master who constructed the engines used by the English at the siege of Calais*) arrives and advises Love to bombard the fortress. Love breaks the truce and uses a catapault to unleash promises, represented by garlands of flowers, at the fortifications. The defenders respond with a barrage of refusals, represented by chaplets of nettles, brambles and gorse.

Venus enters. She vows she will die rather than permit chastity a safe place in any female heart. The barons of Love's army adopt the vow as their own. Finally the priest Genius, Nature's confessor, arrives with a message of his mistress. He explains that Nature labours ceaselessly to replace humans more rapidly than Death can devour them. All must employ the tools Nature has provided for the purpose of procreation; and when Love fails, the arms of Venus may succeed.

ALL THE OTHER players now turned to Will, who bore an oil-light in one hand and a strung bow in the other. On his back was a cocker with a sheaf of arrows bound with oilcloth below the heads, and bound with tin above the feathers, rubbed till it shone like silver. Will went to an iron firepan that had been filled with kindling and tinded it with the light. He took an arrow of his cocker and held it in the fire till it burned well. He nocked the arrow on his bowstring and set it in line with his mark, a black whirl of pitch on the cerecloth walls of the false castle. The mark was small, not half the width of a bondman's door, and a good two hundred feet away, and a light wind came and went. He shut one eye. It was hard to see through the flames and smoke that came of the arrow.

He lowed the arrow's tail, pitching the head two hands over

even. He felt the riff of the wind in the feathers of his wings on the left side, and shifted his aim a hand to the left. No sound came of the other players, nor the folk that beheld the play.

Will bode while the wind blew, and stilled, and blew and stilled again. When the wind rose a third time, Will struck and let with his bow hand. The arrow rose, spewing smoke, and flew like to it would go wide. While it sped, the sun came out and made the tin gleam bright as a star. The arrow began to fall, and, as it lowed, the wind took it in and steered it back onto the right way. It smote the mark an inch of the middle and in a stound flames spewed of the cerecloth and oversprad the walls.

The beholders went bare mad, like to Will had slain a firedrake. They stood and yall and hooted and slapped their hands together, and ne stinted while Laurence Haket and Mad led the high-born players in a game of running through the cerecloth walls of the false castle where they had burned away, and making out they helped the lady Bernadine from the false tower where she played at being locked away. When all were clear of the tower, Will shet a second fire-arrow at it, and it burned, and there was some play between whoever Laurence Haket and the lady were meant to be. At last Laurence Haket went over to the much likeness of a rose blossom, folded his arms around it like to it were a maid, and lifted it of its stand. Pavone's tale-telling ended, and the din of the beholders seemed enough to make all deaf.

WILL ASKED THE other players if the play were done but they ne heeded him, only laughed and made to take his hand and draw him into a ring to hop with them. The high-born folk who'd beheld the show came out onto the field. They beat their hands together and a heap of knaves came alongside bearing wine and ale. Pipers and drummers began to play a quick song.

Laurence Haket let the rose blossom down on the ground and chid some high-born fellows among the players that stood by and laughed at him. The lady Bernadine stood above with her arms folded, some yards of anyone, and proked the ashes of the burned castle with her toe. One half of her long black hair had come loose of the knots meant to bind it in a manlike shape. Will went toward her.

Thunder sounded of the south side of the downs. Will stinted and looked up. The clouds that had hung over the cleeve since the day before had thickened and grown together into one dark roof that overshadowed the field where the garden of love had been wrought.

The hopping and mirth and the din of laughter and yells and song went on, reckless of the thunder, which was still far away, but it was a handwhile before Will saw the lady Bernadine again, for she wasn't no longer where she'd stood. Three of the fellows in Love's army had taken her. One went before with his sword drawn and held by his side, that folk ne mark the blade was out; the other two held Bernadine by the arms in a tight grip and walked her. Her feet ne reached the ground but kicked in wrath. One of them thrust a hand against her mouth that she ne shout for help.

Will went to them and bade them set the lady free. But when he neared them he knew them. The two who held her were his lord, Sir Guy, and Anto the reeve. The swordsman who went before was like to the knight who'd sought her at the inn in Melksham.

'Out of the whoreson way or I'll spill you,' said the swordsman. Will stinted and beheld them, Anto and Sir Guy sweating and gasping, the lady Bernadine's eyes wide with horror.

When they'd gone by, Anto looked over his shoulder like to he hadn't known Will before and bade Sir Guy see what became of bondmen whose lords let them wander about before harvest. Sir Guy swivelled his head and knew him and bellowed: 'When I know your deal in this I'll be wreaked on you.' They went on between the telds out of sight, and no one hindered them.

It seemed that Laurence Haket ne knew the lady Bernadine had been won again by her kin. Two fellows in black had gone up to him and led him away from his friends toward the great black teld, and his friends, who had mocked him ruthlessly, now looked astoned, while Laurence Haket, who had been wrathful, had a smile on his neb.

Sweetmouth hadn't seen her taken neither. He was stood by the ropes that marked the brink of the play-field. Will went to him. A good deal of the mirth and stuffing had gone out of Will's evenbowman, and when Will came up, it was light to see why. Longfreke, Softly and Hornstrake stood on the other side of the rope. Longfreke took a clump of straw of Sweetmouth's false tits and threw it on the ground. Hornstrake laughed. Softly stared at Sweetmouth, the heel of his hand sat on the haft of his bollyknife, his fingers at work up and down. Further away beyond the rope stood Softly's cart, with Thomas and Holiday beside it, and Cess up behind the horse. Otherwhiles, Hayne sat on the grass and gazed at the thunderclouds.

Softly saw Will and proked Longfreke, who turned of Sweetmouth. 'Sworen't you me you wouldn't shoot no bow nor play in women's clothes?' said Longfreke to Will.

'Yeah,' said Will.

'Why break your oath?'

'I mayn't say.' Will shrugged and beheld his feet. 'Laurence Haket and his folk would that I did so.'

'How may we true you in a fight if you break an oath so lightly? I knew you as green, but not as a fool,' said Longfreke. 'Hayne'll deem you.'

Softly ne spoke. He beheld Will in his red gown. His eyes wrought up and down of Will's head to his toes. He clicked his tongue in his mouth and struck the iron hilt of his knife with the nail of his middle finger. He lifted the rope and showed with a nod of his head that Will should come with them.

'Venus!' The men in black who'd led Will of Cockle and Madlen the night before were behind him. 'You're called for. Let's go,' said the hawkish one.

Softly said Will was theirs, a runaway of Hayne Attenoke's score.

Will said he wasn't no runaway.

'Shut your mouth, Venus,' said the hawkish one. 'I know your golden teeth, John Fletcher, and I know the giant who's your master-archer. This lovester's in service here today to one the score may not withsay, but you may have her again before dark.'

Longfreke called to Hayne, who stood and came to them. Longfreke said their even-bowman Dickle Dene was barely cold in the ground, and Quate made glee as a maid with a bow for the world to laugh at them.

Hayne beheld Will without speech for a handwhile. He asked Will if he would sunder his bond to the score.

'I'll be true to the score till death,' said Will.

'He's the same in a maid's kirtle as in a man's,' said Hayne.

'He broke his oath,' said Longfreke.

'It's late,' said Hayne. 'A man about to be hung ne recks the ache in his shoulder.' He raised his eyes to the thundercloud and bade Softly rig the cart for rain.

Softly cursed him, and the men in black led Will away.

'What did that damned giant mean, "It's late"?' the hawkish one muttered. He led Will to the back of the black teld, where there was a dark narrow opening, warded by a swordsman in an iron shirt.

The hawkish one took Will's chin in his hand and stared at his neb.

'Do you wonder why I behold you so nearly?' he asked. 'It's to mind you well, that I find and kill you do you breathe a word of what betides inside. Understand?'

Will nodded.

The hawkish one took the crown of Will's head. 'Better not to wear that,' he said. 'If it goes well, you may ask her for something. She can be free. Go.' He shoff Will in by the swordsman.

WE PERVENED TO the festive location in medias res, the dramatic action having progressed almost to its conclusion. Softly, Longfreke and Hornstrake joined the vulgar spectators at the perimeter of the arena, while Hayne sat on the herbage, apparently preoccupied with the tenebrous nimbus condensing in the direction indicated by our future itinerary. Cess remained in the cart, and it occurred to me that if I moved into proximity with the vehicle, it would be possible to address her unobserved by Softly or his confederates. But whether stationed deliberately by Softly as custodian, or immune to the attraction of the spectacle, Holiday adopted a position that supervised any move I might execute. Even the combustion of the artificial castle, ignited by a flaming arrow, could not distract him from his post.

The performance finished, there was an altercation between the archers I had accompanied via Westbury and those who had come previously, each an actor in the spectacle – Mad personifying Love, Sweetmouth Evil Tongue, and Will Quate Venus, the embodiment of concupiscence.

The sun had traversed the zenith, and, altered not merely by its decline but by the denser air in advance of the nascent tempest, illuminated Will's candid, decorous young face with a ruby-tinged ardour, as if the solar radiance were reflected onto his countenance through rose-tinged glass. In that moment, in his Veneral tunic, Will appeared to have dissolved his sex into a more maximal, multi-sexual state, to have ceased to be exclusively masculine without sacrificing either the physical traits of masculinity or becoming feminine. Softly was incapable of perceiving this, or of imagining a human who, by a momentary effect of luminescence and complexion, appeared to transcend sex. Possibly he was capable, but resisted the report of his senses. In any case he presented himself solely as observing a male in female vestments.

As I interpret it, the focus of Softly's ire is Will's portrayal of a female combined with his public demonstration of the art of archery (it being Will who projected the incendiary arrow). Either action singularly would not provoke offence, the former a masculine joke between those whose masculinity is not doubted, the latter a demonstration of ballistic science that reflects positively on the entire company. What offends Softly is the concurrence of the two, as if the authors of the spectacle posit an organic connection between archery and femininity. Which in a sense they do: for love is the force that operates on man from a distance, a force he cannot resist with counter-force. A man in love experiences a severe diminution in his liberty, caused by the actions of another. The same occurs in physical combat, between two gladiators, for example; but in that case, each gladiator has the power to recuperate his attenuated liberty directly, by the percussion of his arms on the other's armour.

Love's victim, like the archer's, experiences physical suffering and disablement, yet, unlike the man injured by a gladiator, cannot simply batter his opponent. The origin of his injury is remote, obscure, concealed. Is it possible that what is depicted in this English version of *The Romance of the Rose* is a complex double criticism by the nobility of the common people, embodied by chivalry and archers respectively? That, primo, the archers responsible for England's victory at Crécy were womanly, in that they made men suffer indirectly, from a distance, from places of security, without exposing themselves to the peril of being injured in return? And that, secondly, the French chivalry's voluntary exposure of their actual hearts to such actual damage signifies the nobles' exclusive privilege of romantic love? Is it possible, in fact, that the entire performance was contrived as an act of confession and repentance by the English nobility before their French cousins, their crime being to have secured their victory via the treacherous deployment of vulgar archers on the pure chivalric terrain of Crécy?

It does not diminish the validity of this interpretation that Softly, when he approached me after his confrontation with Will, still incandescent with ire, subjected me to a denunciation of the event more prosaic and direct. In his view the participation of the archers in the spectacle was contrived to humiliate them. Specifically the scene of an archer in the habit of a female attempting to destroy fortifications was to Softly a conspicuous reference to the premature departure of Hayne's company from Calais the previous year, when the English still contended with the French for dominion of the city. Briefly, he judged the entire spectacle a calumny directed against him and his companions, who stood accused of female conduct, of timorousness.

But Will had destroyed the fortifications, I said, adjusting to his literal interpretations of the drama. It had been difficult to project a flaming arrow over a considerable distance in such a manner as to penetrate the castle exactly where it would ignite; the creators of the spectacle had required an excellent archer; naturally they had recruited a member of Hayne's company.

The tunic, insisted Softly obstinately. Feminisation. The company had been dishonoured.

He observed me closely. His uncharacteristically exposed ire had acted to make him temporarily oblivious of our different status. Now this momentary oblivion was removed, and he was conscious he had been addressing me as an equal. He smiled, and continued to do so, but now entirely cognisant of the alteration in our relations.

'WHERE WERE YOU born?' asked Softly.

'Leith,' said Thomas. 'The port of Edinburgh.'

'Where's your home?'

'Avignon.'

'Scottish and French is the two kind of men who most ne like me.'

'You and I are Christen folk, wherever we are born or bide.'

'I ne worth no Christen but an English.'

'Learned folk mayn't be learned if they bind themselves to one deal of Christendom. In Scotland they learned me to read, and in France they learned me to live.'

'You ne learned aught in England, then.'

'I learned to work.'

'Better if you'd learned to fight.'

'I bode on you to say "laugh".'

Softly took Thomas by the wrist and drew him toward the cart. 'Folk would have you hold me wicked, that I'd spill you lightly, go you against me,' he said. 'It's not true. I'd be your friend while we fare together. I see how nimble you are in the ask. You were sly to make out Dickle answered you when he was already dead.'

'I swear, he lived and answered.'

'Hush, hush. Ne fear. We do as we must. We'll be friends, you and I. Would you work your asks on me?'

'I mayn't shrive you out-take when there's no priest about and you're at death's door.'

'Not that!' Softly laughed. 'I wouldn't take shrift of you. No, for what you write of us on your calfskins. Ask me what you will.'

Thomas bethought him a handwhile, then asked: 'Why left you Calais before the work to take the town was done?'

'For her sake.' Softly nodded at the cart. 'The others called her a witch. Send her away, they said, or she goes as smoke.'

'The others in Hayne's company?'

'The others in the king's host. His thousands. They bleated that Softly John Fletcher stole a French maid of her folk in Mantes and since then the fight against the French was cursed. They heard I'd sought to wed her, and they'd seen her fetch our arrows, and it ne liked them. Let him fuck her as his prize, they said, but not be his even-archer. They bleated to their lords, and their lords wrathed to Laurence Haket, and Laurence Haket said we must either send her away or go back to England. Laurence Haket would that we send her away, but Hayne held to go home.'

'I ne understand,' said Thomas. 'Who was your leader, Hayne or Haket?'

'Laurence Haket is our captain, Hayne's our master. That's how it's wrought in war. Laurence Haket bids the what, and Hayne bids the how. We answer to Hayne, who answers to Laurence Haket, who answers to the Berkeleys, who answer to the king.'

'You mean Haket was with you through the fighting year in France? Crécy and Calais?'

'And before. From the day we gathered in Lechlade, took boats down the Thames, and fared to France two winter ago. Laurence Haket had the captaincy of two score, Hayne's and Tolly Whistler's score of Worcestershire. We ne saw him often. He'd ride up and bid Hayne lead us here, stand there, burn this town, that mill, and ride away again.'

'In Mantes?'

'I mind his words. I stood with Hayne when he spoke them. "Wreak the town with fire," he said. "Spare the churches, the clerks and the nuns, ne spill no women nor children, otherwise I ne care what you do."'

Thomas ran his fingers over his chin. 'Hayne ne wishes you well,' he said.

'Maybe.'

'He deems your take of Cess was wrong.'

'Maybe.'

'Why not make you give Cess up?'

'Then he wouldn't have his wish.'

'What is his wish?'

'That I burn in hell for ever.'

Softly clapped his hands and shouted at the cart. Cess showed her neb and Softly bade her set out three stools and bring ale.

'You'd speak to her,' said Softly.

'There's no need,' said Thomas.

'They told you I'd spill the man who spoke to her. It's not true. I'm not so hard as they say. Come, have a can with us.'

'Truly, there's no need.'

'May I call you Tom?' Softly cupped Thomas's cheek with his hand and stroked it with his thumb. 'I've seen you behold her like to you wonder what she knows. Come now. Ne shift my mood by unworthing me.'

They sat on the stools. Cess, in a heavy headcloth that hilled the lower part of her neb, gave them wooden cans and ladled ale of a tub. Thomas bade her drink with them and she sat on the third stool with a can held in both hands and beheld the ground.

'Do you have the French?' said Softly to Thomas. 'Ne speak it here. Speak to her in a tongue I understand.'

Thomas thanked Cess for the ale and asked if she knew English.

'She speaks it like to she were born here, which is of my hard work of learning her,' said Softly. 'It were best you keep your eyes on me when you ask your asks.'

'May I speak to her?'

'Whatever it likes you. But speak as if you asked me.'

Thomas gazed at Softly. His eyes were grey, his cheekbones high, his lips never wholly shut, so a gleam of gold always showed between them, like to he'd gulped down some hoard.

'To Cess, then,' Thomas said. 'Is it right you be here?'

'Who's she to say what's right?' said Softly.

'Let her answer for herself.'

'Listen, brother,' said Softly, 'I'll tell you what thinks her, for I know it better than she. Her father knew we English came, and it needed him to send his women away beforehand, or make sikur they were wed at least. Three and twenty winter and still a maid. Her father knew what kind of stir a kings' war is, when fighting men are far from home for months on end without their wives and sweethearts, and whores are hard to come by. Why ne sent he his women away? Pride is why. He thought him he could shield his daughter with his walls and his little knificle.'

'How may you know what he thought him? Did Dickle not end his life right away when you came in through the gate?'

Cess shuddered.

'I know, and she knows,' said Softly. 'We were four, stronger than he and pined for lack of maids, and if it hadn't been us, it were others. Look how fair she is. Thinks you no French gnof came beforehand to wive her? She owed to have been wed, she owed to have known a man already. Why wouldn't he give her to be wed when she was twenty? He was tight is why. He had a fair daughter and wouldn't lose her to a husband. Frenchmen aren't free with their goods nor daughtren, and Englishmen are free. Well, he got his mede.'

'I'd ask her how she sees it.'

'Ask her! I ne hinder you.'

'Cess— '

'Only behold me.'

'Cess,' said Thomas, and beheld Softly while he said it, 'seems it right what Softly says of your father, or was it another way?'

Cess wouldn't speak.

'She's of my mind,' said Softly.

'I ne yield that Cess's father was somehow guilty in your reft of this woman's maidenhood. But even if he were, the greater deal of guilt is on you for the deadly sin of reaving it. Do you withsay this?'

Softly's steven dimmed with bitterness. 'I ne bade you be my guest that you ask what's in my heart,' he said.

None spoke for a handwhile. Songs, drumbeats and laughter came of the great play-field. A wind blew a whirl of dust into their eyes and hair and the cerecloth pall threw and wrapped against the timbers of the cart. The clouds had hidden the sun.

Softly said: 'If the king of heaven cared about Cess's maidenhood so much, why'd he work such lust in me? Why'd he not work some wonder to shield her, like he wrought for the holy Agnes? When I first had her I ne hurt her much, and as soon as I was done, I began to sorrow, for she was young and fair and cried so loud and bit our hands when we would shut her mouth. I bethought on my mother, God keep her. But they that know me know I'm a free man, and I mayn't withhold of my even-bowmen a boon I've won. So Holiday must have his shift, and he's not so kindly in the swive as I. Then Dickle, Christ love him, went wrong. When it came to Hornstrake I couldn't bear it no more.'

'It seems to me,' said Thomas, 'that Cess ne saw you sorrowed by the way you dight her. For after you'd slaked your wants, and let your friends have their shift, you stole her from her home. That's not the deed of a rueful man.'

'I took her as my burden, for I knew what'd happen if I left her there among her own folk, without no dad nor maidenhood,' said Softly. 'They'd deem her shamed, and throw her out, and no worthy man wouldn't take her for a bride, and she'd fall to whoredom. Besides, Holiday or I might have got her great, and I wouldn't that she bear an English get there, shamed and alone among the French.'

'Those are her folk.'

'You ne know how folk can turn against you in the wink of an eye. My mother wasn't sixteen winter old when she bore me in Adam Fletcher's house in Bristol. Some queed of a seafarer had her against her will behind the roping house, and she hadn't barely begun to show when her folk told her they wouldn't feed her and a child. She'd have storve or froze without that Adam Fletcher took her in and was a good hard father to me.' Tears welled in Softly's eyes and he wiped them with his sleeve. 'She was in the street with nothing but the get she bore inside,' he said. 'She was used and thrown away. I'll not let my Cess pined like that, never. Give me.'

Cess handed him a cloth and he dried his eyes.

'I'm good to her,' said Softly. 'She wants for nothing. Clothes, food, all the gear it needs to cook.'

'He says he's good to you, Cess,' said Thomas. 'Why not be his wife?'

'She won't tell you,' said Softly. 'She won't tell me. All she says is no. I ne know what more to do. In the beginning I beat her and storve her a little, that she know what it were like without me to shield her, but now I only bide and ask. And we live as man and wife in most ways out-take in the priests' eyes. She fetched and bore fresh arrows for us at Crécy and learned to shoot in play.

When I took her home to Bristol after Calais she helped in my other work. We go to the ships with the cart and see what small loads they can't rid themselves of. She hucked in French with some Gascons at the staithe for a bale of woollens and got them for a penny each, all but shot-free. I'll give you one. Cess, fetch him a woollen.'

Cess got up and clamb in the cart.

'You're kind,' said Thomas, 'but I have all the warm clothes it needs me, and the nights are mild.'

'It likes me to be free with my goods,' said Softly. 'Take it.'

Cess brought the woollen and held it out to Thomas. Thomas kept his hands hasped together on his lap, and Cess laid it on the ground before him. It was grey, of rich, thick wool.

'A Gascon ship?' said Thomas.

'In Bristol the ships come and go by the score each day.'

'Who'd sell a twelvepenny woollen for a penny?'

'It's a gift, and my read's not to spurn it, else you unworth me.'

'I'm grateful,' said Thomas. 'Thank you. Maybe you'll bear it for me otherwhiles in the cart, till we reach France.'

'Cessy,' said Softly, 'knit the woollen to his saddle, that this learned man ne forget he has it.'

WILL WENT THROUGH dim narrow hollows of cerecloth to a teld floored with wooden tiles. In the middle was a copper tub. A great kettle stood over an unlit fire beneath an opening in the roof. On other sides were chests, corven with the likenesses of uncouth deer with much eyes, claws and feathers, where stood stops, bowls, flasks and heaps of folded cloth of churchlike whiteness. The smell in the air was like to the Melksham bath-house, but where that had been one yell of sweetness, this was like to a wood filled with birdsong, with many kind smells, each one other, yet woven in a whole.

Two women, their nebs hilled, stood there. They bade him strip naked and stand in the tub. 'Ne be ashamed,' they said. 'We've seen it all before.'

'I bathed on Thursday,' said Will.

'Then now you'll be washed away to naught.'

He stripped and clamb in the tub. The women let thick sweet oil of a flask on his head till it dripped on his shoulders and ran down his back and chest.

'Shut your eyes against the smart,' they said. Will shut his eyes. Iron clunked on iron.

'A cold bath's good for the blood,' the women said, and emptied a stop of water on his head. Will opened his eyes and gasped. One of the women showered him with water while the other scoured him with a long-handled brush. She leaned into the work like to she cleaned an ox's hide for market. Soon the oil had shifted to foam and Will's skin shone red. The women took white cloths and dried each inch of him, combed his hair, scrubbed and clipped his nails and gave him his breech, gown and shoon again.

'My right clothes are in the players' tent,' said Will.

'So she saw you, so she'll have you,' said one of the women.

'I'd be as she, to have them at my will, and leave them,' said the other.

'Were she a man, to do so weren't no wonder,' said the first. She rang a hand-bell and a bell answered out of sight. 'Go on,' she said, and showed Will the way out through another dim cerecloth hollow.

He found himself in utter darkness. A hand on his chest held him back and a man whispered to him to bide till he was told to go in.

A woman's speech came through the cloth ahead of him.

'Your tumbles pleased us,' she said. 'Have you ever considered jesting for money? It can be surprisingly lucrative.'

'Pardon me, madam,' came Laurence Haket's steven. 'Though my family be not grand, it is ancient, and though my state be modest, I would not so dishonour my name.'

'Pity,' said the woman. 'We had a purse of gold here by way of encouragement on that journey. We shall, with regret, retain it.' There was stillness a stound, and when the woman spoke again, she had something in her mouth. 'I confess, your response surprises. We were under the impression that your appearance here was influenced by a desire to achieve some form of preferment.'

'If I conveyed that false impression, madam, I apologise.'

'Influenced, possibly, by the vicious and baseless rumour current in certain circles that the exalted patron of these revels employs them as a guise to recruit young men for her intimate pleasures, to their consequent material advantage.'

'Madam! I promise ignorance of such a vile suggestion until the moment you expressed it.'

'Then why are you here?'

'For poetry. To do homage at the altar of Love.'

'Impossible. You deceive us.'

'Madam— '

'Were Love the subject of your devotion, you would pursue the paramour who escaped a vile marriage to be with you, and who has now, thanks to your inattention, been recaptured.'

'Recaptured? When?'

'It ne serves your reputation that you ne noticed her disappearance. Of course we would not condone a demoiselle's ravishment from her family by anyone, nor no secret marriages. But either it really is Love you venerate, in which case you must defy our discouragement to pursue your paramour, or you deliberately misrepresent to us your intentions, in which case our displeasure will be grave. Choose.'

There was a breach in the darkness ahead of Will. Laurence Haket came quickly of it and went by without no way to see Will was there. The one who stood with Will shoff him in the back and Will stepped forward through the opening.

$\smallfrown$

WHAT LIGHT THERE was came of many small candles dight in glass balls hung of the teld walls, which were of some cloth that, though black, glew dully in the candleshine. Before Will, on high-backed wooden seats, sat Pavone, who played a gittern, and the short thick high-born woman in hunter's boots who'd been with the lady Bernadine at the hop the night before. She ate of a bowl of cherries on her lap and spoke softly to a clerk who sat at her feet, writing in a little brass-bound book. Some way beyond them, too far to see clearly in the murk, a woman lay on her back on a small open bed before a great bed, framed by posts at each nook. Further yet into the shadows a line of folk stood still with their heads lowered.

Will bowed his head to Pavone, to the lady with the book and to the woman on her back, although her neb was turned up to the roof. He straightened. There wasn't no shift a handwhile. Pavone ne let of his song, but gazed at Will, and the lady ne let of her talk. Will went down on his knees and bowed his head again. Against his eyes the tapet on the floor was a right snarled work of knots and threads of many hues all overthwart each other.

'Madame, Venus est arrivée,' said Pavone. 'Elle s'incline. Il existe une certaine hiérarchie entre les reines.'

'Stand, Venus,' said the lady with the cherries. It was she who'd spoken to Laurence Haket. 'Voulez-vous finir, madame?'

A deep, even woman's steven came of the bed. 'Vingt livres, c'est trop?'

'C'est à vous de décider. Dix livres suffisent; douze, c'est libéral.'

'Quinze, et un petit don. Qu'aimerait-elle?'

'C'est une dame simple . . . rien de cher, quelque-chose d'inutile. Une capuche en laine.'

'Ah, c'est moi qui la choisirai. Nous trouverons un marché charmant. Notre Venus, elle est belle?'

The clerk folded his book, rose and left.

'La même Venus que celle que vous avez déjà vue et demandée, madame,' said Pavone. 'En plus propre.'

'Alors, donne lui son texte. Why do we speak in French? Does she speak French? It's absurd. Continue.'

Pavone set down his gittern, stood and came to Will. He whispered in his ear, 'Say, in a good clear voice, what I tell you. "Your Highness, noble queen, mother to our most mighty lord the king of England, I, Venus, do humbly swear to do your bidding."'

Will spoke the words, weakly, with a stammer, and even in the candlelight looked aghast.

'Dread queen,' said the steven of the low bed. The queen raised herself on her elbows. Two came of the back of the teld to help her and she sat upright. 'I prefer "dread queen".'

Pavone sighed as he sat down and took up the gittern. 'Go on,' he said. 'Again, with "dread queen" instead of "noble queen".'

Will spoke the words again.

'This Venus ne pronounces it well. "Dread" is one of my favourite English words,' said the queen.

'Madonna!' Pavone shouted, and struck the gittern with the flat of his hand. 'I advised you, madam, this Venus wasn't no proper player, but a common archer of the village. You insisted on the beau visage. Your majesty is at liberty to devise her revels without my aid.'

'Then why would I pay you? Ne broil our humours with your bile.'

'Did they tell you the king-mother summoned you?' said the lady on the seat to Will.

Will shook his head.

She offered Will a cherry, and he took it.

'You may spit the stone into that bowl,' she said. She sucked the flesh of a cherry and spat the stone. It hit the tapet and Pavone played his gittern strings like to they mocked her. Will spat his stone into the bowl. It rang like a bell. The lady and the queen laughed and clapped.

The lady leaned forward and asked Will in a low steven for his true name, and Will told her he was Will Quate, of Outen Green.

'Your lord's manor has provided and given most of our entertainment and play today,' said the lady. 'You, your lord's daughter, and your manor's pig.'

The pig was Nack's, said Will, their hayward.

'Is he here too? Did the whole village come?'

Only he, said Will, and the pigboy's sister, Madlen, and the lady Bernadine, who were both now taken to be brought home again, the one to be hung as a thief, the other to be wed against her will.

'Poor Bernadine,' said the lady. 'I would that I might help and aid her, but I mayn't.'

'What d'you murmur about there?' said the queen. 'I can't hear nor see. Conduct her to me.'

'Mind and remember, she's the king's mother, and you're nothing,' said the lady to Will. 'I would she ne wrought it as she does. Understand, our kind are given in wedlock and sent away when we're but children. To love, to fight for one's life and to play, all three are minged together. This isn't but hard play here. Do as you're bidden. Ne think you ill of her. She'll be shriven afterwards and you'll win.'

She stood and left. Pavone took Will by the elbow and led him to the queen.

'On your knees,' he said to Will.

'Oh, let her sit by me,' said the queen. 'It is Venus.' She thacked a stead on the bed and Will sat.

'Regard me,' she said. 'Look at me.'

The queen ne seemed old enough nor broad enough to have borne no king. Her skin was right white, like to it hadn't never known the sun, and where Will's mother's neb was corven deep by lines down her cheeks and on her forehead, the queen's was smooth, out-take about her grey eyes and the ends of her mouth. She'd reddened her cheeks and her lips. A net of gold wire held her nut-hued hair, in which there wasn't no white. She wore a blue gown sewn with silver-white beads. The cloth rustled like to dry leaves with her every stir.

Pavone left them, went again to his seat, took up his gittern and began to play and sing softly, with his back to Will and the queen.

'You demonstrated great mastery to inflame the Rose's prison with a single arrow,' said the queen. She stroked his wings. 'Do I appear ancient to you?'

Will said he ne understood.

'Do I seem old?'

Will shook his head.

'Ne lower yourself. We're queens.' The queen laid her hand on Will's leg. 'Speak to me as an equal. Do you know "equal"? As my even-queen. Now, how do I like you?'

'Fair,' said Will.

'I find you very sweet and beauteous. Beauteous is the same as "fair". It pleases me, which is to say it likes me, that you aren't

229

proud, which I know because you blush when I pay you a compliment. I sense that our spirits are close. It is as though we've always known each other but have only now met. I hope you feel the same. I desire that you and I share a bed tonight. This is a desire I reserve for my closest companions, those whose closeness may approach, though ne replace, my closeness to my dear deceased lord Edward, my husband, the present king's father, may the angels treat him as their own. We shall lie in each other's arms, two queens, breast to breast, share secrets, and fall together in one reverie.'

'Reverie,' said Will.

'I'm so pleased you're in accord. My final note, before you offer your response, is that as close as I sense we are, there is a surprise in your appearance. I hadn't anticipated that the very Venus would combine such masculine vigour with such femininity. Your frame is so powerful, you're browned like a peasant, yet you possess the grace and gentle face of a demoiselle.'

Without letting her right hand of Will's leg under his gown the queen set her left hand on his cheek and stroked it.

'Qu'est-ce que c'est?' she said in a wholly other steven, like to a millstone drawn over a threshing floor. 'Elle s'est rasée!' She stood and stepped back, ne far. 'Defendez-moi!' She showed her teeth. Four strong fellows in dark hoods sprang of the shadows at the back of the tent, gripped him, one to each limb, and threw him down on the tapet.

'Depouillez-le,' said the queen. They plucked the wings of Will, then stripped him of the gown, his breech and his shoon and lay him naked on his back on the tapet. He wrothe but the four knaves were too strong for him. Pavone sang on like to nothing had betid.

'You're not Venus,' said the queen.

'I ne know who Venus is,' said Will. 'I ne made myself out to be no one out-take who I am, Will Quate of Outen Green.'

'How dare you,' said the queen. 'A base villain enters my privy chamber in the guise of Venus, and when he is unmasked, addresses me as an equal. What was your sordid intention? What was it of mine you desired, or did you simply aspire to a spy's view of the skin royal?' The queen raised her gown to her knees, then higher, so her legs were bared up to the haunch. 'This?' She wore white openwork boots with long heels.

'I ne understand you, worthship,' said Will.

'I desire your comprehension,' said the queen. She lifted one foot and trod on Will's thigh. 'That is your position relative to me. Do you understand that? No?' She stood on his womb with both feet, with all her weight, and kept herself steady with her hands on the shoulders of her men. He tightened his womb as best he could. Her shoon bit into his flesh. 'Ne close and shut your eyes, false Venus. I am the queen of men's comprehension. When Hugh Despenser saw his own guts drawn out, he understood he shouldn't have come between my Edward and me. There.'

She stepped onto Will's chest and ground one heel into the flesh till it broke the skin and bled and he cried out.

'I am high,' she said, 'and you are low, and that is all you need to know.'

She stepped of his body that her feet were on the tapet on either side of his head. She gathered her dress about her waist and sat on his neb and rubbed her cunt against his mouth.

'Lick it,' she said. Will opened his mouth and licked the queen's cunt.

'Put your tongue within. Deeper. Now find the bud that lies above the cleft. Go about it with your tongue-tip like a bee that dances on a daisy.'

In a while the queen came of him and knelt beside him. 'Lâche-le,' she said, and the four knaves left.

The queen leaned down and kissed his wound. 'I ne meant to hurt you,' she said.

'That's not true,' said Will.

The queen struck him on the cheek and bit her lip. She stood, cast her gown and underclothes of her and bent over the end of the great bed.

'Now fuck the shit of me,' she said.

They swived, and it was quick, and in a handwhile Will's pintle was hard again, and the queen learned him how to fuck her in the arse, as she said it had liked the king to do, and they swived again. When they finished, for all the sound they'd made, Pavone was asleep and snoring. After the queen bade Will fuck her a third time, Pavone woke up, took up his gittern and sang on like to he hadn't slept at all.

'Is the play ended now?' asked Will.

'It ne ends,' said the queen, 'but now we make our own lines.'

They lay naked on the great bed. Hirelings came and let down the cloths between the posts till they seemed alone in a smaller room where golden walls were sewn with grim deer, lit by one hornlight. Will's hand was between the queen's haunches. The queen had her hands behind her head and beheld him.

'Am I older than your mother?' she asked. 'I've fifty-three years.'

'I ne know my mother's old,' said Will.

'A nimble answer. We should dight you an ambassador.'

'I ne know what ambassadors work.'

'Which makes you perfect. But I would you weren't nimble. I would that your face and your body were as they are, but that your soul was shallow, and your brain weak, that you were the usual sort of English villainous brute. Do you understand?'

'No.'

'Now, in this hour, I'm near to you as I have been to anyone,' said the queen. 'I'd touch and kiss each deal of you and hold it mine. Tomorrow, you'll be nothing to me. I shan't know you. Should any man say we lay together, I'll deny it and have that man killed. Were I to see you about to be done to death, for saying you fucked the king-mother or for anything, and you cried out to me for help, I wouldn't lift a finger to save your life. I'd let you die. Is that dreadful?'

'No.'

'Why?'

'You're a queen, and I'm a low-born man, without silver nor blood.'

'You ne need make it so easy for me. If you ne rue such unkindness in me, it tokens you find me a dull and unsightly old woman.'

'It's not unkind,' said Will. 'You're of your kind and I'm of mine. I know I mayn't see you again. I ne know your name.'

The queen sat up. 'How could you not know my name?' she said.

'You ne told me.'

'But there's only one king-mother.'

'I guess so.'

'I thought me all knew my name. You know the king's name.'

'Edward.'

'And the queen.'

'Philippa?'

'And the king's father.'

Will shook his head. 'Edward has been king as long as I've lived. I ne know about no king's father.'

'It was Edward! And his father was Edward before him! How can you be so ignorant?'

'Then Edward's father was Edward, and his father's father was Edward. It's like to one long King Edward for ever. How would I know of one day to the next behind the plough if one King Edward becomes another?'

'Consider your ambassadorship rescinded. Isabella! Edward and his wife, Queen Isabella!'

233

'Yeah,' said Will. 'The priest ne bade no beads for no Isabella, but now you say it I mind tales of her and the king.'

'Tell me those tales.'

'Queen Isabella was of France,' said Will. 'She came to wed King Edward, but it turned out he ne loved women, only men, so she fetched soldiers of France and took his crown, and he was locked in Berkeley Castle, home of my lord's lord, and done to death as a badling. And she was queen until her son was old enough to be king. But I thought me she lived long ago.'

'She did,' said the queen. 'She lived long ago, and lives yet. The she is I. Your tales are wrong. I ne had my husband killed. That was done by others. He was dear to me. And I to him. He loved both women and men. Edward loved all, out-take they who ne loved his loved ones as he would have them be loved. He'd fuck anyone who let him believe they would be fucked. Men took advantage of that. Hugh Despenser did.'

'You use outcome words again that I ne know.'

'So do you. What is a badling?'

'What our folk call a man who lets himself be fucked by another man. He who plays the woman.'

'Think you such men should be killed?'

'Why, if they ne harm no one? Let Christ deem them.'

'Have you a wife?'

'I'm betrothed to a maid of my town.'

'Is she your true love?'

'She went with a kinsman of my lord. He got her great, but there wasn't no child.'

'Maybe he gave her no choice.'

'She chose. She made out she did it to drive me to woo her. It's hard, for the kinsman who swived her is the captain of our score of bowmen.'

'Do you wish to be wreaked on him?'

'I find not.'

The queen laughed, took his head in her hand and turned it so they looked into each other's eyes. 'My husband knew himself, at least,' she said. 'Ne say you ne understand, for that's lightly said. Is she fair, this betrothed of yours?'

'She's the fairest— '

'Of course, she would be. You ne care whether you wed her or not. You ne care that your captain had her. All you needed when you were at home was a good wife, but now you're in the great world, you need a friend. Do you have a friend?'

'I have two friends,' said Will. 'A man and his sister. I fear they both must die soon.'

'You weep.'

'I ne weep.' Will turned on his side.

'You are so far of me in everything, and yet I know you better than you know yourself,' said the queen. 'It liked my Edward to spend days and nights with low-born folk like you, ditchers and tilers and thatchers, men strong and nimble with their hands, were they fair, and could well talk and mirth. Maids too, otherwhiles. They were as good wives to him. When I was sent of France to be his true wife I had a bare twelve years. We ne slept together till I was fifteen, and in those first years, when England was loathsome to me, he was my friend, and his men-friends were my friends, and we all danced together, and chose each other's clothes, and fished together of swan-boats by moonlight, and put foxes in the earls' rooms while they slept. I learned he was freer with his men-friends than with me; he was nearer them than me. It hurt me to know this, but I were rather a lesser friend than a mere good wife. Despenser came later. Piers Gaveston was my husband's best friend, and when the earls murdered Piers, it was the friend he wept for more than the man he dight as you did now dight me on this bed. Learn this of me if nothing else: men

235

such as you must seek and keep a friend, and all else comes of that.'

'My way's narrow,' said Will. 'I'm no king nor earl. I'm not sikur I be free. My lord, Sir Guy, and the folk in town say they deem me free, but my lord won't give me the deed of freedom unless I give him five pound, and I haven't five pence to my name.'

The queen stared at him right earnestly. 'I'm free, that you may be,' she whispered. 'How does the bed like you?'

'Wonder soft,' said Will.

'Sleep a while.'

'I mayn't.'

'Then close your eyes, I bid you.'

Will closed his eyes. The queen kissed him on the forehead, and Will slept.

WILL WAS LIFTED of the bed and dropped on the grass. The wind blew against his bare skin. It was day yet, but the cloud over the joust field was dark enough to make it seem near night. Someone threw Will his breech and shoon and Venus gown and he did them on. About him a host of hired men wrought like devils to tear down the queen's black telds and to pack her goods. While he slept, the field had been stripped of cerecloth, beacons and posts, and the hundreds of bright-clothed folk who'd laughed and drunk and hopped had gone. A line of laden wains went toward the high road. The white sheet he and the queen had lain on was pulled of the bed and billowed out before the hireling got it in wield and folded it into a trim shape for loading.

Venus's wings lay in the dust. Will bade the hired men take them away.

'No, Venus, they go with you,' they said.

A man came to him, leading a horse. Will knew him as the clerk who'd written in the queen's teld. The clerk wore a broad-brimmed leather hat and a cerecloth mantle like to he looked to fare far through hard rain.

'I owed to have been on the road long ago,' he said. 'Here.' He gave Will a purse and clamb on his horse. 'There's five pound in there. Enough to buy your freedom, my mistress told me. I wouldn't deem you worth that much.'

Will held the purse on his palm where the clerk had lain it, as if it were a butterfly that would fly away again.

'It's light for such a great deal of silver,' he said.

The clerk beheld him like to he'd lost his wits. 'It's gold,' he said. 'Fifteen nobles. Eighty pence each noble.' He held up his fingers. 'That's all your fingers twenty and one hundred times, could you tell so far. Five pound altogether. I mayn't bide no longer.' He rode away.

Will's hand shut on the purse. He turned to where the gate had stood at the joust's brink, where he'd met the bear and its keeper. It seemed that while those that came to play had gone, the heap of hucksters and beggars on the outside were still there, hoping to win of the carters and hirelings as they left.

Will began to run. At first he bore the wings under his arm, but they slowed him, and he dight them on his back again. When the hem of the gown hindered him he bunched and knit it higher. Folk hooted and laughed at him when he went by. He ran to the furze where Cockle had sold sport with Madlen and came upon the bear-keeper and his bear.

'You lag a little,' said the keeper. 'Hie and you'll overtake them. They go at the stir of the thief, and he's well lamed.'

WILL RAN UP the line of wains and came on Cockle and Matt on horseback, leading Madlen on a rope fastened to her neck. Madlen halted along with her bruised head high and her hair stiff with dust. She held the rags of her gown together with her hands.

Will shouted at them to stint. They bridled their horses.

'I'll buy the wedding gown of you for its worth new, do you let her go,' said Will. 'Five pound.'

'Where'd you get five pound?' said Cockle.

'A lady gave it me.'

Cockle snorted. 'Right.'

'Five pound gold's worth more to our lord than a marred gown and a lolled-up thrall.'

'Gold? You'd spend ten winter breaking your back in Outen Green and not get a sniff of gold.'

'Would you have it or not?'

'And have him go free, a thief? How's that right? Let's see the hue of your gold.'

Will took a noble of the purse and gave it to Cockle. Cockle and Matt looked it over nearly and bit it and muttered to each other.

'Show us the leave,' said Cockle.

Will told four more nobles and bade them let Madlen go. Cockle unknit the rope and Will took it of Madlen's neck. The skin was nesh and red where the rope had rubbed against it. She sank against the ground. Her head fell between her knees. Will told five more nobles.

'Give me the gown,' he said.

'That five pound owed to have been mine,' said Cockle. 'I should have been the bowman and tinded the players' castle and been worthed by a lady. It was the town's behest that I should go to Calais.'

He threw down the gown and Will gave him the last five nobles.

'Redeemed you your deed of Laurence Haket?' asked Cockle.

'Another day,' said Will.

'You were better to buy your own freedom than this queed's. What's he to you?'

'My friend.'

'Where will you go?'

'Calais.'

'With him? What shall I tell Ness?'

'Tell folk I'll be home again next summer.'

'You may come again. But Hab mayn't show his neb in the Green without that he be hung.'

'Tell folk I'm well, and I mind them in my beads.'

Cockle and Matt rode on. Will kneeled by Madlen and asked her if she might walk. Madlen ne stirred nor spoke.

Cockle rode up again. 'I would you came with me to Outen Green,' he said. 'You're lacked there and there'll be a wedding feast. You may ride with me.'

'I'm sworn to go with Hayne's bowmen to Calais,' said Will. 'Besides, you wouldn't bear my friend.'

'Am I not your friend?' said Cockle. 'What is it in him makes him your friend, not me?'

'I wish you no harm,' said Will.

'Come home again,' said Cockle. 'I know why all left the joust so early. The qualm's in Dorset.'

'They only fear the storm.'

Cockle shook his head, spat on the ground, turned his horse and went on his way.

Will raised Madlen, put her arm around his shoulder, held her about the waist, took up the gown and set off with her to seek the score. When they'd gone a short way there was a thunderclap nearby and lightning flashed on the cleeve. It began to rain.

A brewster had reared a house of reeds by a bourne to sell ale to those that came and went of the joust. She'd left so quickly, her stake and bush still stood. The roof and walls were strong enough to keep the rain of the inside. Will set Madlen down on the straw on the floor and fetched her water of the bourne in a broken can. Madlen drank and Will went and came again of the stream till she'd had enough.

'Are you heal?' asked Will.

'Bring me more water that I may wash my neb,' she said.

Will went to the bourne again, and when he came back, Madlen wore the lady Bernadine's gown. She washed her face of blood and dirt and they sat together.

'Where did you find the gold to free me?' she said.

'Where did you find the silver to buy your maid's dress in Melksham?'

Madlen laughed and bit her lip. 'We mayn't reach Calais as lovers but that we go as whores.'

'I'm no whore,' said Will. 'I fucked the king-mother at her bidding and she gave me a gift.'

Madlen laughed harder and shook her head.

'They beat you and left you thirsty and now you mirth like a girl,' said Will.

'I mirth that you found what I always knew, that you're my loveman.'

'I'm not your loveman. I'm your friend and I lacked you.'

The rain beat on the reeds and the walls swayed in the wind.

'We mayn't stay here,' said Will. He began to take the wings of his back. Madlen stayed him with her hand.

'Keep them,' she said. 'It likes me to see you winged.'

'We mayn't stay,' said Will again. 'We must find the others before night.'

'We go on together?'

'Yeah,' said Will. 'As friends together.'

Madlen looked to one side, as if it needed her to mark something there. 'You may buy me of a gnof like Cockle for gold,' she said. 'To keep me you must spend more dearly.'

'You told me you wished to come with me.'

'I do. But you' —and she dight his lips with hers— 'must spend' —she dight his lips again— 'more dearly. Your mouth is cold.'

She kissed him once more, and this time put her tongue in his mouth. Will let her in, and their tongue-tips hunted each other.

'I'm tired,' said Madlen. She put her head in Will's lap and shut her eyes.

LAURENCE AND HIS man Raulyn rode down the road to Edington, against the flow of carts. They wore their swords and their faces were grave. Laurence guided Berna's horse on its reins to his rear. Berna was in the saddle, still in her Warm Welcome clothes, her back curved in a pose of such abasement that it appeared she might plunge to the ground. Laurence turned and demanded she take care. She ne replied.

'We mayn't delay,' he said.

The air trembled and for an instant the sombre obscurity through which they journeyed was illuminated. Gross pearls of rain penetrated their garments and glazed their faces. Laurence halted, passed the reins of Berna's horse to Raulyn and placed Berna in front of him on his horse. They continued. They mightn't search for refuge, said Laurence, as they were surely pursued, and must join the archers and press on regardless of time.

'May the rain lave my father's blood of my shirt,' said Berna.

'I anticipated gratitude at your salvation, given how ardently you desired to be rescued of marriage to the ancient,' said Laurence.

'I ne desired that you murder my father.'

'I ne murdered no one. I cut his arm. He'll recover.'

'His face when he regarded me, his proper daughter, and realised I was a traitor. He supposes I encouraged you to violence against him. Now I may never return. I shall never embrace him again, or my sisters, or lay flowers on my mother's tomb.'

'It was necessary to demonstrate my readiness for violence, persuade them that if they resisted, one of them were seriously injured. I wouldn't that this were no fatal venture, but I would make the hazard credible.'

'His face!' said Berna. She ne let of sobbing. 'I despised him so long and travelled so far of my family. I considered myself liberated of the influence of filial emotion. It required but a cut of your sword to let the malice of him. He appeared so surprised, as if he ne comprehended until that moment how profoundly I resented the arrangement. And now I scrutinise my memory, and demand of myself, did I really explain? Exercise all power to convey to him how unjust his conduct was, that he might amend it, and we be reconciled?'

'You do him too much justice.'

'Why could you not have defended me there, at the pageant? Observed their approach, and ravished me away without combat?'

'You saw how humiliated I was by the arrivage of that beastly pig. All the credit I might have won by my performance was endangered were I unable to prove my valour in a different sphere.'

Berna turned her entire body round to put her face in Laurence's. 'Am I to comprehend that your decision to rescue me was inspired by a requirement to save your reputation?'

'What difference does it make?' said Laurence. 'The result is that the purity of my honour is restored in every angle; in respect of them, and in respect of you.'

'I would prefer to exist in a manner not entirely relative to your honour.'

'I would prefer a more generous recognition of my role as the agent of your salvation.'

They crossed the pasture where the pageant had been enacted, where brown pools were forming, their surface agitated by the rain as if the water boiled. They encountered the archers at the base of the escarpment, in a place where an ouverture in the trees led to a dark, abrupt ascent. All were there except Will. None had seen Madlen.

Laurence and Raulyn had secured Berna's possessions and placed them in the cart. She went in, where it was dry, and changed from her wet costume into the marriage gown. Cess silently gave her bread and cheese and ale, then regarded her while she ate.

'Were you injured?' asked Cess.

'The blood was my father's,' said Berna.

Cess pulled something out of a basket, invited Berna to open her hands, and filled them with raisins.

'Let no one see I gave you them,' she said.

The ferocity of the tempest had receded, and the rain was now a regular gentle clicking on the cover of the cart. The archers sat under the trees, water dripping of their hoods. Laurence spoke with Hayne, but it ne appeared that Hayne replied to him.

Hayne put his hand on Laurence's shoulder, and at the same moment the archers rose as one. A figure approached, water pouring of the white feathers of his wings, carrying a sleeping maid in his arms who wore a ragged double of Berna's gown.

As if Will were sent some craft of binding, none shifted nor spoke until he'd lain Madlen in the back of the cart. He straightened, and beheld Softly like to he was ready to fight him. All stood back, and stiffened, but Softly only nodded his head.

'Fill my cart with your stolen women,' he said, 'but ne chide me for aught I've done.'

Hayne said it was time to go. The captain's man Raulyn knew a stead up on the downs where they might shelter.

'It's dark,' said Thomas.

'We mayn't linger here,' said Laurence Haket. 'My lady's kin will come again more thickly.'

The bowmen began to go. Holiday led the cart and Thomas, Laurence Haket and Raulyn likewise went on foot and led their horses. Hayne bade Will lead the lady Bernadine's horse.

'I'd get my gear,' said Will. 'I wouldn't go further as Venus.'

'Your gear's in the cart,' said Longfreke. 'There it'll bide till we reach the top, to learn you. And ne cast off your wings. They as choose wings must show how well they fly.'

Mad and Sweetmouth went beside Will.

'What kind bird is it?' asked Mad.

'A cuckoo,' said Sweetmouth.

'White feathers,' said Mad. 'Thinks me a swan.'

'True,' said Sweetmouth, 'for the swan's a royal bird, and wasn't this one seen going in the king-mother's tent?'

'One gives you ten our swan lacks a feather or two,' said Mad. 'I'll lay, as often the queen says her cunt tickles, that's how many feathers our swan lacks.'

'But what of the maid in the wedding gown?'

'Oh, this swan sheds feathers like an old hawk in moult.'

The road was a steep hollow way. Though the rain had lessened, a stream of water ran down the middle, and in the darkness they had to steer their feet by mud and small sharp stones and swaths corven through it. Men and horses tripped and fell. They must stint to lift a great tree that had fallen athwart the way, and again to take bracken and sticks to fill holes that the cart wheels might run over them.

They reached the top and came of the trees. The rain had ended and the moon shed the clouds that had hidden her. Before them lay a wold spread with wrought fields and the swell of downs and barrows. In a vale a mile away a great fire burned red. There weren't no other lights.

'I can't see no one about that fire,' said Will. 'There's a barn nearby, or maybe a church.'

'That's Imber town,' said Raulyn.

'Why do they set such a great fire in the middle of the night?' said Hornstrake.

'It burns hot after such rain,' said Mad.

'I ne know what they do,' said Raulyn. He led them to a threshing barn and bade them bide inside while he sought leave and board of the owners. He rode away.

The women bode in the cart. Cess doled out the bowmen's gear and woollens and the last of the bread and ale and the men did on dry clothes. Thomas and Laurence Haket sat away of the others with their bags and saddles. Laurence Haket stripped to his breech and wrapped himself in a woollen and bade the proctor do likewise, but Thomas shook his head, and wrapped himself in his thin riding coat.

IN THE CART, in the dark, in a bass whisper, Berna demanded to know of Madlen the explanation for her disappearance. 'As far as I may perceive,' said Berna, once Madlen had given her account, 'your salvation was the result of a money bargain.'

Madlen said she ne comprehended 'salvation', 'money' or 'bargain'.

'Will bought you,' said Berna, 'whereas I was saved by combat, by my courageous paramour. When I say saved, I intend ravished, and considerable violence applied to my father.'

Madlen ne comprehended.

'My point is, Madlen, that when a demoiselle suffers the grandeur and horror of ravishment, an experience as potent as any romance story, she does not anticipate an attempt at competition from an inferior, particularly one to whom she provides protection from the gallows.'

Madlen asked how she'd offended Berna.

'I judge it the height of presumption on Will Quate's part to continue his performance in the pageant to the point of carrying you to us in his Venus costume as if he were some version of an angel, and you a form of martyr,' said Berna. 'And in my gown, as if portraying me! Was that your intention? Because I may assure you that were I to be seen carried home by an angel I would make a more powerful impression on the company than you and your ploughboy. Why do you still wear my gown? Remove it instantly! Take it off!'

Madlen said she hadn't nothing else to wear.

'Cess, lend my servant a gown,' ordered Berna.

Cess, who was couched in the fore part of the cart, ne replied and ne moved. Berna went to rouse her, and discovered her vigilant, regarding the night, her arms crossed across her chest. She ne responded to Berna's demands, even when Berna spoke close to her face; a peculiar rigidity afflicted her.

'Cess, aid me,' said Berna impatiently. When Cess persisted in her open-eyed silence, Berna became alarmed and passed her hand across Cess's face, but the Frenchwoman ne appeared feverous.

'Let me be,' said Cess.

Berna pulled at her lip. 'Is it of my story?' she said.

Cess's eyes filled. Her hand darted to them, she absorbed the tears with her sleeve and concealed the sleeve in her crossed arms, as if it carried a dangerous sign.

Berna gently demanded her pardon, and kissed her. 'I had no choice but to escape my father,' she said.

'I mayn't choose to see mine again,' said Cess.

Berna returned to where Madlen had made them a place to couch, lay down and pulled a woollen over her.

She heard Madlen ask in a whisper if she might come with Berna to Calais.

'To Calais, I suppose, and afterwards, until a more suitable candidate presents herself.'

Madlen lay down beside her with her back to Berna. Berna might lay her body against hers, she said, if she would, if she were cold.

'I require you to keep a proper distance from me,' said Berna, 'even if it be no more than an inch.'

Madlen said she had heard from Will about Berna's encounter with Enker.

'He is a noble pig,' said Berna. 'I wonder who keeps him now.'

Madlen said he would find his way home again.

WILL WAS THE first of the score to wake. He'd writhen himself into a bow by the barn doorway and the early light fell on his eyes. He rose and did on his shoon and went with his shaving knife to find water. The barn stood in a mean little town with a few whitewashed cots and their yards and one ox-shed. There were daisies in the graze and ripe corn drooped in the wet, weed-spotted fields. The new-risen sun was wrapped in mist like to a spider's egg. A mile away on the far side of an open coomb stood the houses and church of Imber and by the church a spire of black smoke reaching into the sky. No living thing stirred out-take Will and the horses. Raulyn's horse was gone.

Will dipped his knife in the water of a trough that stood near the ox-shed and began to shave. He smelled coal on blaze, dried the blade on the hem of his shirt and followed his nose to where Madlen had set a kettle to boil over a fire in the yard of one of the cots.

'Where did you find a kettle? And coal?' he asked.

Madlen blew on the fire. 'I took them of the house,' she said. 'And the firestones to tind with.' She nodded to the door, which stood open. 'I've been to every house.' She opened her hands and counted six fingers. 'Six houses. There's nobody here. All the folk have gone, with all their cattle and all their fowl and tools and clothes.'

'You ne owe to steal what folk mayn't bear with them. They'll come again.'

'You ne know the shed between "steal" and "borrow". The lady must have warm water. Come with me.' She took Will's hand and led him to the northern edge of the town. The land fell away down the cleeve they'd clamb the night before, but instead of Wiltshire spread out for their sight, a wold of downy cloud stretched as far as they could see.

'See? We're in heaven,' said Madlen. Her neb was lit by the strengthening sun. The bruise on her cheek was a purple bloom and the cut on her eyebrow a small black mark. 'We look down on the clouds from above and we're alone, you and I.' They kissed and held each other tightly.

'Does it like you?' whispered Madlen.

'I wouldn't do it otherwise,' said Will.

'It needs you to say it likes you out loud, that I may hear it.'

'It likes me to hold you,' said Will.

'And to kiss me?'

'I would that we weren't seen.'

'Why?' Madlen took a small step away, bit her lip and held Will's fingers.

'When I was a child my dad said my whys vexed him more than bee stings.'

Madlen laughed. 'Would it like you to sleep with me?' she said.

'Yeah,' said Will.

'Like to we were man and wife.'

Will was still a handwhile. 'How?' he said.

'We'll make a way. I wish that I might make you glad to the end of your life.'

'And I to the end of yours.'

'Truly? As glad as now? I ne know how I might be gladder.'

'Truly. As my friend. As my dearest friend.'

Madlen wrapped her arms round Will again. 'What is your greatest other wish?'

'To be a free man.'

'You might have had your freedom now if not for me.'

Will ne answered her but took her by the wrist and led her toward where she'd left the kettle. 'I'd borrow a stop of your warm water to shave,' he said.

He shaved and bade Madlen bide till evening, when he would see they were alone together.

When he came again to the barn, he found all the bowmen awake out-take Hornstrake. Laurence Haket's man Raulyn had run away in the night. For days he had threatened to go home to his kin in Somerset, and now, against his lord's will, he'd left.

Hayne Attenoke, too, was gone, with all his gear, out-take the rood he wore around his neck and the key to the score's strongbox, both of which he'd left by Longfreke's side. The bowmen sought all over town, but Hayne wasn't to be found, only the mark of his giant feet in the mud, heading south.

'HAS THIS HAPPENED before?' said Laurence Haket.

Longfreke said that for Hayne to go away without a word was like to the roof of their house were stolen overnight.

'God's teeth, it's his score the Berkeleys hired, not some lesser man's,' said Laurence Haket. 'Do you bowmen read among yourselves who you'll have as master until Hayne comes again, and read quickly, for I'd be on the road.'

'Do we ne bide on Hayne?' asked Thomas.

'This stead ne likes me,' said Laurence Haket, and left them.

The bowmen hung Hayne's rood with the likeness of the pined Christ on a nail on the barn wall and stood beneath it while they read which one of them would be the leader. Holiday said he'd have Softly as the vinter, for he was the best fighter, and had the nimblest brain, and had the eldership, and should by rights have had the rood Hayne took for his own in Southampton.

'It must be Longfreke,' said Sweetmouth. 'Softly's only out for himself.'

'Then you can bear your own gear and not burden my cart,' said Softly.

'You wouldn't have no cart without that your even-bowmen drove it through the mud up the hill,' said Longfreke.

They bickered and chid till it all but came to blows. Mad said they owed to ask Thomas to help them settle it.

Thomas said each one of them should make their choice, and he who was chosen by most should be as master while they bode for Hayne to come again.

'You're short one bowman,' he said, and showed Hornstrake with his finger.

Sweetmouth strode over to where Hornstrake still slept, bundled in his woollen. He kicked him.

'Get up, idle lump,' he said. 'You're lacked for the first time in your life.'

Hornstrake groaned and turned on his side. Sweetmouth kicked him again.

'It's old,' Hornstrake croaked, and coughed.

'What's old?' said Sweetmouth.

'Apples in my shirt,' said Hornstrake. 'Your games are stale.'

'I ne put no apples in your shirt.'

'Liar. Under my arms. I feel them.'

Sweetmouth kneeled and felt under Hornstrake's arms. He put his hand inside Hornstrake's shirt, felt about, withdrew and stood. His face had lost all hue.

'A botch in each armpit the bigness of a hen's egg,' he said.

'Ne look in his eyes!' yall Longfreke. All turned their backs, out-take Thomas, who left the barn, Will, who stared at Hornstrake, and Holiday, who went to him, knit a cloth over his eyes and began to feel him with his fingertips. '"Whatso evil you be",' he spelled, in a steven like to a housewife soothing a chicken before its neck was wrung,

> *In God's name be bound to me.*
> *I bind thee with the holy rood*
> *That Jesus was done on for our good.*

251

I bind you with nails three
That Jesus was nailed upon the tree.
I bind thee with the most dear blood
That Jesus showed upon the rood.
I bind thee with wounds five
That Jesus was pined by his life.

Holiday took dry worts of a purse on his belt. He bade Softly bring him a stop of hot water, and the others to go out, and he would come later and tell them what ailed their brother.

I USED THE opportunity presented by Softly and Holiday's absence to communicate with Cess. I did not attempt discourse face to face, but inclined my back against the cart, as if resting, and uttered my salutations in French until I heard her respond through the cart cover, in subdued, fatigued tones.

I advised her that Hornstrake exhibited pestilential symptoms.

Did I expect her to pray for him? she inquired.

Hornstrake had participated in the crime against her, I said, and I mightn't force her to absolve him. But he now faced the conclusion of his terrestrial existence, and his spirit's transmission to its final habitation, and her judgement was the difference between his salvation and damnation. I had previously advised him to seek absolution from her, and desired to discover her response.

Hornstrake had come to her, said Cess, and she had recommended he appeal to a cleric. As a victim she had no power to absolve him.

I was convinced, I said, that her personal absolution might save him. Hornstrake was a virtual imbecile, a man of flaccid intellect and tenuous morals, super-persuadable. He was not the instigator of her rape. It had not been he who alienated her from her virginity.

Did I consider, Cess said, that the primary justification for her existence was as a sanctuary for her virginity, and that once the sanctuary was violated and her virginity raped, she became a ruin, through whose fractured portals any man might pass with a pure conscience?

I initiated a response, but she interrupted. It was obvious to her, she said, that I considered myself different from and superior to the archers, because I was capable of imagining the suffering she experienced at their hands. But my powers of representation were debilitated.

I invited her to assist me in a more perfect comprehension of her torment.

She declined. She was capable, she said, of describing to me each instant of her father's extermination, her rape and captivity, and of conveying to me how it had not sufficed for the archers to use her for their sexual satisfaction, but that they must demonstrate their masculine ability to dominate her according to their will; how it had pleased them to restrict, diminish and confine her spirit to the dimensions of a minute mental cloister, constructed according to the limits of their own malicious reason. She was capable of such description; but would not attempt it, for to do so would be to permit me to imagine myself entering her mind, and consequently, given my intellectual vanity, encourage me to assume I might express her situation more effectively than she. A spiritual violation would occur, subsequent to, and aggravating, her actual rape, in which I would forcibly enter her consciousness, raping her of her experience, emerging to distort it and redescribe it according to my own intentions.

(That I liberally translate her objections into our clerkly Latin should not deflect from the originality and ingenuity of her proposition.)

Irrespective of her attitude towards me, I said, Hornstrake's immortal spirit was in peril. I urged her to relent, and if, when communication between us was impossible, she should resolve to exercise clemency, she might simply let drop an iron pan by way of a signal.

Were she to absolve Hornstrake, said Cess, she would simply conform to the doctrine of Softly and Holiday, which was that they might commit whatever crimes they pleased in the terrestrial domain, providing they confessed at the final moment.

That opinion was as heretical as the equally incorrect supposition that certain crimes were too grave to be absolved, I said. But she should consider the radical effect her absolution of Hornstrake and the other archers would have. On their post-mortem deliverance to the celestial empire of Christ they would have such gratitude towards her that they would inevitably intercede with the Deity for her own salvation.

Why, inquired Cess, would she be in need of intercession? She had no crime to confess. Her conscience was pure.

She had procured the blankets, I said.

Cess pretended incomprehension.

She had acquired the blankets from a ship in the port of Bristol, I said, at so minimal a price that they might has well have been offered gratis. Which in probability they were, from a deserted ship, its complement of mariners perished of plague.

Cess insisted on her ignorance of the sense of my accusation.

I could readily comprehend, I said, her desire to inflict a fatal justice on those who'd committed such a terrible crime against her and her family. But how could she justify to God the infection of those archers who had not participated in her rape? How could she justify the infection of Will Quate?

Cess repeated her denial, but commented that of all the archers, Will Quate was the most repugnant and the most reprehensible.

Before I could interpret this stupendous observation, Softly and Holiday emerged from the barn, and I moved to put distance between myself and the cart.

Judith, now that the plague has come, and I sense, rather than merely imagine, my imminent separation from you and Marc, memories revisit me of another separation — the day I left home, over my parents' protests, thirty years ago, and never returned, not because of a familial rupture but because I moved far away and always discovered some cause to avoid revisiting. Is it absurd to characterise the epidemic of young people rejecting familial domesticity in favour of mundial ambition as a kind of plague? Not absurd to my parents. They presented my departure to England as a form of mortal calamity.

☽

'HE HASN'T NO qualm,' said Holiday. 'It's an unorny fever is all. Folk's armpits swell up that way in a fever. I gave him worts and spelled him a craft. Let him sweat it out in the cart.'

The archers looked at each other unsikurly.

'I know fevers. I never saw such swellings,' said Sweetmouth.

'You ne know aught of sickness but your own when you're overdrunk,' said Softly.

'Here's what, though,' said Longfreke. 'Damp air. A south wind. Six homes without no folk nor cattle. The swelling right like the Malmesbury doctor said it would be.'

'Any of you ne true my read, go feel him with your own hands instead of standing about like a heap of old women.'

'Whatever ails your brother, we owe not to leave him here, nor bide here no longer,' said Thomas. 'Here there's no priest, bed nor food.'

Sweetmouth told Softly Longfreke would be their leader in Hayne's stead, and they bode on Softly's wrath, but Softly smiled and said he'd gladly yield a handwhile, and then they'd see.

He took the rood of the nail, hung it round Longfreke's neck and thacked Christ's legs lightly against Longfreke's chest. 'There,' he said. 'Our new leader.' And his smile widened, and would have looked sweet as a girl's, had his teeth ne been all of gold.

BERNADINE RETRIEVED THE book from the saddle pocket where she kept it and turned the pages to ensure they hadn't suffered no damage in the rain. She went in search of Laurence and discovered him on the far side of the village, sat on a log placed in such a manner as to survey the plain to the south, towards Imber. He regarded the view with his chin cupped in his hands, his elbows on his knees. Berna approached and touched his shoulder. Laurence instantly rose and attempted to embrace her. She pushed him away.

'Your persistence in denying me the reward of intimacy when I have proved my love for you in perilous action is very annoying,' said Laurence, his voice high and impatient. 'I commence to doubt the vigour of your sentiments towards me.'

'Hold my hand,' said Berna. 'You have demonstrated a care for me, and though I would have preferred it done without violence, Mama liked to say Papa would have benefited from a simple bleed when the planets were in their proper house.'

Laurence accepted Berna's hand, drew her brusquely to him and attempted to kiss her. She averted her face and he sat miserably down again.

'Be patient,' she said. 'I require to accustom myself to the magnitude of my dependence on you.'

Laurence took *Le Roman de la Rose* of her and regarded it closely. 'This is probably quite valuable,' he observed. 'It's not a grand dowry, but it adds to our substance.'

'You speak as if our future were settled.'

'I would you concede it is.' Laurence sat close to her and clasped her hands in his. 'We'll be married by the next priest. We'll journey on to Dorset and embark at Melcombe for Calais, where my manor house and enfeoffed estate lie vacant, in anticipation of my arrivage. It's a fine estate, with forests and a mill and part of a river, and the house has chimneys, with mews for horses, dogs and falcons. The local curate is mine to appoint. We shall employ servants. My English companions will join me and we'll go on the chase together. Our villainage will labour in our fields and we shall be enriched. We'll create a new English line there. I'll be made knight, rise in the favour of earls and the king, and when time has passed and we and our French cousins are amicable again, we'll invite our families to Calais, and visit Paris together. May I suppose you at least partially satisfied by this vision?'

'The dubious conceit of partial satisfaction is a lamentable statement of your sentiments towards your future spouse. The estate pleases you — but you were just as pleased had they offered you a different one, quite similar. The mill in a different place, the forest perhaps less filled with beasts of venery, but the river more fishous. Is this not the case?'

'I suppose so.'

'I sense that your sentiments towards me are similar. That you find me perfectly acceptable, even pleasing, but not uniquely so. As one estate or house or horse is as acceptable as another, so you are

257

content to marry me, but were equally content to marry any of a thousand others, should they have presented themselves to you.'

'I consider my desire to pass the remainder of my life with you to be sign sufficient of absolute love.'

'Were that sufficient, you would be a younger and more attractive figure of the odious Sir Hennery.'

Laurence would reply, but they were interrupted by Madlen, who brought them a little bowl of pottage she'd made of scraps found in the empty houses. Longfreke and Thomas arrived, and Longfreke told them that while Hayne ne returned, he would lead the archers.

Before he could complete his report, Laurence hushed him. He stood and pointed down to the Westbury road. A band of mounted men, their arms reflecting the sun, travelled towards the crossroads. They were a mile distant.

'The lady's father has found more men,' said Laurence. 'I reckon twenty of them.'

'Mother pure, defend me,' said Berna.

'You may outride them,' said Longfreke.

'It's too late,' said Laurence. 'Your bowmen must shield the town.'

Longfreke flinched. 'We mayn't, captain,' he said. 'We wouldn't be outlaws in our own land.'

THE BOWMEN SAW the horsemen come and guessed they came to take the bride Laurence Haket had stolen. They readied their gear to go, and bode on Longfreke's bidding.

At the meeting of the roads the horsemen turned and made for the town where the bowmen stood.

'The captain will give her up,' said Holiday.

'He'll fight,' said Softly. 'No man worthy of the name owes to steal a woman if he won't fight for her.'

'If he fights he loses,' said Sweetmouth. 'They are many and he is one. They know the maid's here. You may see her gown a mile away. They were better to outride her father's men.'

'They're right to come for her,' said Holiday. 'A maid owes to do as her father bids.'

'Five to one they ride away,' said Sweetmouth to Mad.

A horse ran out of town with the lady Bernadine on its back, her white dress throwing in the wind of her flight. She rode to the east of the horsemen, back toward Imber, where a smit of smoke still darkened the air.

'Fivepence to me,' said Sweetmouth.

'How so? She goes alone,' said Mad. 'He would give her up, but she'd rather be free.'

'She's more man than him, Fiend fetch their bones,' said Softly, and spat.

'She hasn't no hope,' said Sweetmouth. 'She must go by them to go beyond them.'

In going by the riders, the lady Bernadine dight a stretch of rough thorny ground between her and them, and they must come of the road and climb to overtake her.

'They near her,' said Sweetmouth. He turned to Will. 'How well does your lady ride?'

'I would she got away,' he said.

Longfreke came up to them and bade them go. They'd fare athwart the road, he said, while the riders were led astray.

'Astray?' said Holiday.

'Pick up,' said Longfreke, and the bowmen began to walk. Holiday led the cart.

Thomas's and Laurence Haket's horses swung out before them,

259

but while Thomas rode his horse, Laurence Haket led another rider on his, a knave wrapped in a woollen.

'Who rides the captain's horse?' said Will. 'Where's Madlen?'

'Take this,' said Longfreke. He gave Will a littlewhat of calfskin folded and bound with cord. 'There's your freedom deed. That was what you yearned for, was it not? Come on! Step it up!'

'I ne gave no fee for this deed,' said Will.

'Another gave it for you,' said Longfreke.

He who rode Laurence Haket's horse turned her head. It was the lady Bernadine in her Warm Welcome clothes. 'Your sweetheart spent dear to buy your freedom,' she said to Will.

Forthright, Will began to run. The bowmen beheld him lengthen his stride on the way to the meeting of the roads, for he took the straightest way to Imber. He lagged far behind the pack of horsemen, who'd all but overtaken the maid in the wedding gown. All now understood that maid was Madlen.

'She overheard Laurence Haket talk,' said Longfreke. 'She said she'd lead them away, did Laurence Haket but give Will Quate his freedom.'

Thomas offered the two high-born folk his horse, that they dight more miles the sooner between them and they that hunted them; he might walk, he said, as far as Heytesbury. Straightway and thankfully the lady Bernadine sat on Thomas's mare and Laurence Haket took the saddle of his own horse again. The captain bade Longfreke lead the bowmen and the proctor safe to the far side of the downs, and they would meet in Heytesbury that afternoon. And they rode quickly on ahead.

The bowmen found a rough way for the cart along the side of a great hay-meadow. As they went they kept an eye on Madlen's hight to outrun the riders and Will's hopeless work to overtake them.

'She stints,' said Mad.

'They have her,' said Sweetmouth. 'Why ne rides she on? Is the horse lamed?'

They saw far away by the Imber church how Madlen clamb down of the horse and stood beside the bonefire which now no longer made no smoke. They who hunted her were right near.

'She knits her arms around the horse's neck,' said Mad.

The riders rode up and gathered round Madlen, hiding her of the bowmen's sight.

'Now they'll know they've been swiked and their quarry's elsewhere,' said Sweetmouth. 'They will take it out on her, poor little maid.'

'She wasn't but a thief,' said Holiday.

A VIGOROUS GALLOP put Bernadine and Laurence out of view of those who would arrest them. They reined in their horses and continued at a more gentle pace.

'Low thief though she be,' said Berna, 'it troubles my conscience that my servant so endangers herself to my benefit.'

'She ne acted to aid you, but to please him,' said Laurence. 'His actions reflect ingratitude. He won't enjoy the liberty she presented him for long if he attempts to defend her. He'll be cut to pieces, and her sacrifice lose all value.'

'You confuse sacrifice with a payment for a service.'

'On the contrary, I have sacrificed a document priced at five pounds, you have sacrificed a fine horse, and the material consequence is that once again you have escaped capture.'

'Laurence, can you sincerely compare your renunciation of a future payment with a woman's exchange of her life for her lover's liberty, and her lover's immediate rejection of that liberty in favour of an attempt, certain to fail, to rescue her? Didn't you observe how instantly, without calculation, each of them acted, guided by love?'

'If by "love" you mean the noble sentiment that inspires us, it were ridiculous to credit such people as your father's thralls and villains with its possession. They act as they do because they lack the power of anticipation. They are moved by the desires of the moment. And ne assume I intend base desires. A good peasant is like a fine dog – loyal, brave, honest, delighting in serving his master till he dies, but constantly distracted by corporeal desires. The dog would chase a rat, but his head is turned by a mutton bone, and again by his master's affectionate caress, and again by a passing bitch. So he chases the bitch, inflamed by his natural passions. And what does she pursue? Some strange scent entices her, alluring but beyond her comprehension. It is the gown she stole of you. She stole it in desire to resemble you as if the gown, rather than your blood, were the source of your nobility, and now she suffers all the fever and delusion of the paramour without any of the measure and regard to the grander course of affairs by which we gentle people moderate our hearts.'

IT WAS IDLE for Longfreke to bid the bowmen go more quickly, for they mightn't draw their gaze of the cluster of horsemen in Imber, and the struggle of Will to reach them. When the horsemen gathered round Madlen, the riders were still. All at once, like to each had been stung, the horsemen started. They pulled wildly at their horses' harness. The stots reared and the sound of their frightened neighs reached the ears of the bowmen over the fields. The horsemen turned as a body and rode again the way they had come as if the Fiend and all his hinds snapped at their heels. The white shape of Madlen stood where she had, as before, her arms around the horse's neck.

'They ne laid a hand on her,' said Sweetmouth. 'Maybe truly she's a witch.'

The riders flew by Will without stint. As they went by the bowmen, barely two hundred yard away, they ne looked to the right ne left, only stood in the stirrup and egged on their horses with wild yells. Soon they were gone.

'Now there's a wonder,' said Holiday. 'You ne know who God will lift a finger to help, and who he'll turn his back on when she needs him.'

WILL CAME TO Imber and went to Madlen. She ne let go the neck of the lady Bernadine's horse. She stared at Will with dismal cheer, her cheeks pale. Ash was minged in the ground with the mud of the night's rain and the lower deal of the gown was stained black.

'Look,' she said. She showed with her finger a spot on the church steeple where the smoke of the fire had darkened the limewash. 'They marked the church on their way.'

Will put his arms around her. 'Who?' he said. 'Did the riders hurt you?'

Madlen ne answered. Will beheld over her shoulder the leave of the bonefire. In the middle was a great whirl of white ash, and about the sides the bones that hadn't burned through. They were the limbs of men made coal and one scorched skull. It seemed the bodies had been lain with their heads to the middle; that one head must have rolled out in the bonefire's blaze. There were shrivelled feet, black as pitch, all about the brink.

THE END OF THE WORLD

WILL BEAT ON the church door. None answered. He rattled the handle but the church was locked. In the churchyard were five fresh graves. Work had begun to dig a great pit; the shape was marked out, but only a little earth had been dug. They heard a moan of the far side of the town, and walked through the streets, which were still, out-take a few cats and hens, till they came to a yard with an unmilked cow. Will and Madlen took it in turns to milk it while the other lay on the ground beneath the udders with their mouth open. They drank till they were full. When the cow was settled and ne moaned no more, they heard a groan of a nearby house with an open door. Will went to the threshold and called inside.

'Ne come in would you not sicken,' came an old man's dry steven. 'Bide there a handwhile.' There was a rustle of straw and the scrape of earthenware and a can was thrust out of the doorway into the light.

'Fill it with milk for me and lay it here again,' he said. 'Ne feel it with your naked fingers, let there be cloth between your flesh and the clay.'

Will pulled dock leaves of the old man's yard and used them to hold the can while Madlen milked the cow into it. When it was full, Will laid it at the door again and saw it drawn into the darkness. He heard the old man drink. It must have slipped of his hands for he heard it hit the ground and break.

'What else may we do for you?' said Will.

'Nothing, thank you.'

'What ails you?'

'Four nights ago it was sent us. They as might took their goods and cattle and went to hide in the woods, like to that would help them.'

'Where's your priest?'

'He was one of the first to sicken, and the deacon with him. I ne know how we might fare further in this world now we've lost so many. My son and his wife are gone, and his three children, and the smith and most of his folk, and the greater deal of them with their yards on the back road that look south, which was what did for them when the wind blew of Dorset. I know all Danny Green's kin gave up their ghosts for I laid them together on the bonefire, the smallest in the middle and the longest on the outside, as seemed meet. You saw the fire?'

'Yeah,' said Will.

'Was all burned to ashes?'

'Almost,' said Will. 'As near as made no shed.'

'But you might know the bones that burned were mankind?'

'Barely.'

'You ne saw no child's bones.'

'None.'

'Good,' said the old man. 'I ne would that aught of them were left out in the air for any outcome churl to see or fox to gnaw. I said I'd dig a pit for the dead after the leave had gone, for I knew I was already sick. I thought me I had the strength to work it, but no sooner had I marked the pit and begun to dig than I weakened and my brain began to whirl. So I thought me I'd make a bonefire, for if we make one anywise each year to clean the air, might it not hurt the Fiend to send our folk to heaven in a foul breath of smoke? The priest and deacon weren't there to ask, for we'd already buried them, and the freke we sent to the next parish for help ne came again. So I drew all into a heap and tinded them, and they burned hot, God bless them, for they were good folk, even they that swiked you and overbeat each other. I barely might with it, and by the end I myself burned with such a fever I couldn't stand. Then God sent the rain, and I thought me at first it was a token I'd done ill to burn my even-Christens instead of burial as I behest. But the rain ne quenched the bonefire, and it cooled me, and I took it as token I did right.'

He was taken by a fit of coughing. Madlen came up to Will and laid her hand on his shoulder and her cheek against his.

'I'm Danday,' said the old man. 'Thanks that you milked old Hurryhome. She was set to burst.'

'Will and Madlen,' said Will. 'We're Cotswold folk.'

'I thought me I heard horsemen.'

'We've one horse between us. We're with a score of archers, bound for Melcombe, but lost our way.'

'I never saw Cotswold. I heard it's fair. You're of the land?'

'I was bound. I'm a free bowman now. I have a deed.'

'I lived bound,' said Danday. 'I reckon by this time tomorrow I'll be free. The priest shrove us all. He knew his end came and he said we were a heap of foul sinners, but he would see us all right with the Redeemer. And then he told us we must shrive him.'

'I ne knew that might be done.'

'And I. We were astoned. He told us how he'd swiken us on our tithes with a false weight, and before we could gather our wits, he swallowed Christ's body like to it were a shive of bread and bacon and laid his eyes together.' He coughed again. 'Warned you your priest this death would come?'

'We thought it were a new wile to make us buy more masses and candles.'

'Yeah, we too.'

'And those as believed him thought England shielded, for our land is girded by the sea, and it mayn't overgo the water, and God loves the English more than the French.'

'Yeah, son. We too.'

'Must we all die?'

'I ne know, son. I hope it be otherwise. Be bold and go on meanwhile. Ne linger here. The air's bad.'

'It ne likes me to leave you alone without no friend or kin.'

'I'm not alone, son. I have my Sarah here. She sleeps and won't wake again. She's the dearest of my son's children and I couldn't bear to burn her.'

Will asked again if there was aught else he might do. There wasn't nothing, and they bade each other farewell, and Will led the lady Bernadine's horse on toward Heytesbury, with Madlen riding it that the gown not be worse befouled.

IT HAS FREQUENTLY been noted by those more familiar than I with calamity that one cannot determine one's reaction to extreme situations in advance. Distance having been placed between the young nobles, the posse comitatus pursuing them, Will Quate and Madlen, and the remainder of the company – i.e. our constituent parts being dispersed over the elevated plains of Wiltshire – I was obliged to examine my consent to accommodate the aforementioned gentlepeople with my horse. Had I been required to predict my response to the discovery that a paucity of hours remained to me before the plague extinguished my terrestrial consciousness, I would have fixed on the probability of my directing my horse, with the maximum possible velocity, to the most proximate infirmary, and abandoning my companions to their fate – not so much in expectation of a cure as in the desire to discuss my conclusive personal history in the relatively congenial circumstances of clerical assistance and abundant provision of wine. In place of which I traversed as a pedestrian – a virtually senile pedestrian – the five miles from an area obviously abandoned by its inhabitants at the first sign of pestilence towards one I assumed was equally infected. The route was rendered more intolerable by the conviction among the archers, based on their unaccountable confidence in Holiday's medical art, that Hornstrake was not exhibiting plague symptoms, but an acute form of a more customary febrile state.

I inquired of Holiday why he had insisted Hornstrake was not suffering from the pestilence.

'YOU DEEM THE lack of folk in that town tokens it's qualm-ridden,' said Holiday.

'I do,' said Thomas.

'Whoreish quick for your pestilence to get such a hold on Hornstrake in so short a time.'

'We don't know where the sickness first went in him,' said Thomas. 'He might have breathed in the evil a week ago, and it sit and bide in him till now. Who's to say he found it here? Who's to say he didn't bear it with him from Bristol?'

'Hornstrake's not a Bristol man,' said Holiday. 'He's of Nailsworth, far from any haven. Only I, Softly, Dickle and Hayne were in Bristol these days.'

'When was Hayne there?'

'Nine days back. He came to bid Softly cleave to the score again and go with him to Calais. They spoke a few hours, then Hayne went back to Gloucester.' He spat. 'You goad your ox up the wrong furrow, proctor. There's no pestilence in England, and I'll tell you why.' With his first fingers on either side of his noll he made the token of the horns. 'Jews,' he said. 'France, Italy – all the lands that have the pest are thick with them, and they've always yearned to spill the Christens. But old Edward, the king's eldfather, he kicked them out sixty winter ago. There's not been a Jew in England since, and as long as we keep them out, they mayn't work their pestilence on us.'

'You truly ween the Jews have all the guilt for the plague?' said Thomas.

'All with a smit of kind wit know it.'

'But there aren't no grounds,' said Thomas. 'The Pope himself made it a sin to lay it on them.'

Holiday widened his eyes and proked Thomas in the chest with his finger. 'There's your witness show's the Pope's not but a tool of the horned folk. And maybe more than a tool.' He looked about him and lowed his steven. 'Why's he got such a long hat, if not to hide horns under it?'

'You deem the Pope a Jew?'

Holiday stuck out his lip and nodded. 'If he'd show himself otherwise, let him die of the qualm himself. Then I'd worth him as a good Christen man.'

EVER SINCE THE excitement in the deserted village I have detected an alteration in the relations between us – i.e. between the nobles, the archers, and me, the simulacrum of a cleric. A familiarity, a diminution of habits of respect and subservience on the commoners' part, and a degradation of comfortable assumptions of superiority on mine and Bernadine's and Laurence's. Even Holiday, in his state of denial, addresses me with a novel directness, not so much insolent as revelatory that if, previously, we treated them with open contempt for their minds and spirits, they, secretly, manifested an equal contempt for us. Are we now more inclined to regard each other according to our humanity, rather than to our civil status? Was it in this spirit that I spontaneously ceded my horse?

Here in this new sense of community it is facile to delude ourselves that universal fraternity is an inevitable consequence of a greater equalisation of social status. I suspect the majority, if required to celebrate this novel harmony of cleric, commoner and aristocrat, would consider the occasion ideal for persecution of the Jews.

Judith, Marc, would it not be the most atrocious of fates for you to survive the plague, only to be exterminated by the ignorant because you are kin to Moses? Is it not incredible that even as we are menaced by a disease that may eradicate the majority of humans, the military men with whom I travel are prepared to contemplate future conflict with the survivors?

WILL AND MADLEN fared by fields of ripe barley that lacked weeders and children to scare the birds. Sheep without shepherds wandered at will among the crops, where they foreswallowed their own weight in men's food. Will ne bore the sight and must look away or drive the sheep of the fields himself. About them above the wrought land were old barrows made by the folk that lived in England long ago.

They came to a wood and saw men and women with scythes reaping corn that grew near the trees. When they saw Will and Madlen they ran away into the wood. Will called to them but they ne answered, and when Will and Madlen went by, these frightened folk beheld them from the shadows, still and staring like deer at the sound of a hunter.

They came to the brink of a cleeve that let on a great wold sprad out to the south, and at the cleeve's foot, the roofs of Heytesbury. They met the other bowmen, and told them what they'd seen.

THEY CAME DOWN into Heytesbury, their nebs pale and their cheers grim. None spoke to no other, out-take that they bade Thomas go on the horse, for it wasn't meet for no learned old man to go on foot while a hired maid rode, but Thomas said it liked him to stretch his legs. Madlen wouldn't ride no more anywise, so she clamb down, and the horse was led riderless into town.

No sooner had they come to the high street than they heard the priest's bell, and all fell to their knees, for the priest came by bearing Christ's body and singing the paternoster. Behind him went a knave with a great candle half burned through, the flame hardly seen in the sunlight, and a crock of smoking reekles. Beside the knave a crookbacked man of forty winter, in a threadbare shirt and overworn breech, drove a handcart. Last came a small boy who rang a bell with one hand and bore a likeness of the mother of the maker of all things in the other. All four looked weary. The priest hadn't shaved and though his neb and hands were washed the hem of his greasy kirtle was fouled with dust and mud.

As the priest went by they saw a wonder thing. A woman came between two houses bearing two buckets of water on a yoke. Her head, mouth and nose were hidden so only her eyes showed. She overwent the road ahead of the priest-gang. She turned her head to look at the priest, but instead of going on her knees and bidding a bead in sight of Christ's flesh, she ne stinted, and went on her way, through a gate in a wall, into a yard and out of sight. The priest-gang ne heeded the woman and went into a house at the far end of the street that had a cloth hung of an upper window. Cloths of other hues hung of many windows in the street.

Hornstrake wouldn't wake. His breath was shallow and his forehead hot and clammy. He whispered in his fever of a dog he'd befriended outside Calais that had run away, and of how he'd cast God's breath upon a fire in Melksham.

They went to bide in the churchyard, where there were many new graves and an open pit. Last night's rain had begun to wash away the new earth and in spots the winding sheets of the heaped dead showed through white. When they saw this the bowmen ne would bide among the graves but went into the church. There they found a few folk on their knees before the rood or being led in beads by a lewd man with a little knowledge of the gospel. These folk were ware at first of the uncouth bowmen, and made fearful by the sight of Longfreke's cleft neb, but it came out Laurence Haket and the lady Bernadine had come to town already, and, before going to the bailiff's house for food and rest, warned that the bowmen were on their way.

'Imber folk aren't right in the head,' they said when they learned what Will and Madlen had seen. 'They're ungodly up on the downs.'

The death, as they called it, had come to Heytesbury five days before, and already slain forty folk, men, women and children, a third of the town. None would go to their neighbours' houses no more for fear they'd sick. Folk would hang cloths of their windows, one to send for the priest, two to ask for food and drink to be left for them, three to have a body borne away. The priest and the bell-ringer had gone to and from the homes of the sick so often none paid them heed no more. The inn was shut, none came to town to buy the cloth they made, the crops were ripe but none would harvest them, and half the cattle lacked a master.

The priest-gang came again. The crookbacked man, whom they called Stucken, drove the cart before him with the body of a tucker, Ed Sutton, in his winding sheet. All made the token of the rood athwart their chests and the priest blessed them while his knave shook holy smoke at them of the can of reekles. In the midst of his blessing the priest stinted to cough and when he was done the townsfolk melted away.

'It needs one of our men to be aneled,' said Longfreke to the priest. 'And we'd have you hold a mass for us. We have silver.'

'I held mass this morning. I haven't slept two days,' said the priest. 'I've three more houses to go to. I must see to my own folk first, and lay poor Ed in the ground. And your captain would have me wed him to his burd.'

'Have the wedding and the burial at the same time,' said Sweetmouth. 'Afterwards we'll leap in the pit together, bride, groom and guests, and there'll be less work for the cooks at the feast.'

'Anele our man,' said Longfreke to the priest. 'He's an English Christen too.'

Thomas took the priest by the wrist and led him over to the cart, where he spoke with him a while. The others heard Thomas speak, though they ne could make out the words, and they heard the priest cough, and Cess let fall an iron pot onto the ground.

Thomas and the priest came again, and Thomas said the priest would anele Hornstrake, and bury him in a hallowed spot in the churchyard, were he to die before they left town in the morning. Before nightfall, the priest would hold a mass for them, and shrive them, if they would.

The bowmen asked where they might eat and drink, and the priest said even without the harvest, the town had more food than it knew what to do with. The cattle couldn't be milked fast enough, and what milk there was sat spoiling for lack of use. Hens and pigs ran free. They lacked bread, for the baker and his knave had died, and none knew how to work the ovens hot enough. Instead of bread and pottage the children ate pancakes and shives of sheepflesh the thickness of their fingers. So many houses stood empty the bowmen might hire one each for the night and sleep alone.

Thomas, Longfreke and Madlen would seek Laurence Haket and the lady Bernadine.

Will said he would go with Madlen, and Longfreke wrathed.

'Would you break your bowman's oath a second time, and not yet drawn a bow in anger?' he said in a high steven. 'You're sworn into the true and only score of Hayne Attenoke of Gloucester, where I now rightly spell as leader, and by all the hallows, you'll hear what I bid you. You're a soldier, and a soldier's not free to have his will, but works with his fellows at his leader's bidding, like one ox in a gang. Now bide here till I come again. Do you understand me?'

'Yeah,' said Will.

'I'm Master Gilbert to you.'

'Yeah, Master Gilbert.'

Longfreke, Thomas and Madlen went on their way. Madlen led the horse and as she went she turned and blew a kiss to Will.

For a handwhile the others were still and there wasn't no sound but the scrape of Stucken's spade in the earth and the mild snores and coughs of the priest, who'd writhen himself up like a baby on the grass and fallen asleep.

'Longfreke ne frighted the priest much,' said Sweetmouth. 'I ne reckon our Player much frighted neither.'

'How to make men fear your strength when death's come to town to play the same game?' said Mad.

Sweetmouth wrinkled his nose. 'To call seven men a score, and one of them at grave's brink, Lord keep him. And why should Will not be with his maid till we leave?'

'Madlen's my friend,' said Will.

Sweetmouth and Mad laughed. 'We know what you'd get of that friendship,' said Sweetmouth.

'As Death said to the old man who finished his house on the day he died,' said Mad, '"Better late than never."'

The priest opened his eyes and sat up.

'Your man Stucken looks ready to let that one be buried,' said Sweetmouth, nodding to where the crookback had drawn Ed Sutton's body to the brink of the pit. 'Why do you call him Stucken?'

'It's short for Stuck-in-the-bushes,' said the priest, yawning. 'He's always stuck in the bushes near where the children go to swim.'

Sweetmouth laughed, then shifted his cheer to one more meetly dismal. 'We wouldn't be merry here,' he said.

'I'll tell you a thing,' said the priest. He brushed grass of his clothes. 'I've learned much of our kind these last days. How those who speak most loudly of man's wickedness as the root of this sickness, they most eager to buy candles and masses and hallows' likenesses against it, are the slowest to help their fellow when he sickens. How those like Stucken, deemed low and foul and cursed by heaven, found hidden in the bushes with their breech around their ankles beholding young folk, who mayn't stand straight, stake their lives five times a day handling the bodies of the dead, when no one else would. And how that which seems wondrous may with daily use become stale and old. And how we may laugh even in the midst of this.'

The priest bent forward to cough. A gobbet of dark spit came of his mouth and he wiped his lips with the back of his hand and went on. 'Ed Sutton and the other tuckers, when they heard the death was truly come, they knew they had but a short time left to drink. Every night they'd be awake till the ale they drank barely stopped in their bladders long enough to turn to piss. Two days ago we went to fetch one of them of his house, Gibby, dead as a doornail. I aneled him, we wound him in a sheet, and buried him. He was the first to go in the pit. We'd barely walked ten yard of the hole when we heard him yelling he was either in hell or in Heytesbury, and if it were Heytesbury, the town had a priest too many. When we saw him there stood in the pit, his head stuck out the end of his winding sheet, cursing us, we laughed, Stucken and I. We mightn't help ourselves. He'd drunk so much his wife had taken him for dead.'

He shook his head and wiped his hands on his kirtle. 'Mind you,' he said, 'yesterday he died again, for good this time, and that wasn't so merry.'

ALL DAY I have been afflicted by perspiration, jugular discomfort, a dolour located in the cranial region and a powerful desire for liquid refreshment. I am percussed by conflicting desires: to proceed rapidly to a private place where I might examine myself and discover the nature of my symptoms, or alternately to ignore the signs of tribulation in expectation of their natural increase and disappearance, like the ordinary febrile manifestations to which all men are subject.

Longfreke and Madlen were silent adjuncts on alternate sides as we ambled through the vill, Madlen conducting the horse. Surreptitiously I observed their faces for signs that they, too, experienced febrile symptoms whose existence they would not admit.

Longfreke requested that Madlen distance herself from us, as he had personal matters to discuss with me; and Madlen, increasing her pace, separated from our company.

We continued in silence for some moments. I am so accustomed to the profound cicatrix dividing his face that it no longer prevents me detecting other indications of change in his appearance. Our eyes coursed over each other's features for signs of inquietude, and our lips trembled, as if each recognised something risible in our vulnerability, as if only respect for the surviving inhabitants of Heytesbury prevented us from collapsing in uncontrollable laughter there in the way.

It occurred to me that, as a military man, he was well acquainted with situations when not only he but all those around him perceived the limits of their mortality.

As if my ruminations were transparent to him, he said he would prefer to die in combat. He said he desired to conduct the archers at least to the littoral, that they be securely transmitted to France. His conscience was the clearer, he said, for our previous conversations. And as if to re-examine his actions for malificent qualities he had failed to perceive, he commenced for me an account of the origins of Hayne Attenoke's company.

HAYNE FIRST GATHERED his score ten year before, said Longfreke, after the French burned Portsmouth, and the southern havens lacked walls and men to man them. When Hayne set up in the George and Worm in Gloucester and called for bowmen, he told them it was to help the folk of Hampshire, who might seem like outcome churls, but were as English as they were. He told them a tale of how grim the French and hard-hearted, how they slew the guiltless, stole English folk as thralls, reft maids of their maidenhoods and burned whole streets to blue ashes. Hayne would lead bold men to shield the Hampshire havens, to ward the weak and old and children of the wicked French. He made it sound as if his score would fight with a red rood on their chests against an un-Christen foe, like to Englishmen in Palestine two hundred year before.

Longfreke nad five and twenty winter then, a cooper's son in Gloucester, and Dickle and Softly young Bristol knaves who wrought the Severn ships and hung about the George between fares. None knew who Hayne was or where he came from, and if folk said he'd fought the Scots at Halidon, and fought for the king's father against his queen and Mortimer, it was they said it, not he. What drove them to cleave to Hayne were his fair words. Dickle and Softly had clean hearts then. Them thought Hayne might lead them to be great fighters in another's song, a song folk would sing long after they were fallen.

Hayne led the score to Southampton. The burghers of the town wouldn't hire them and bade them leave, but on the day they were to go home again, the French landed and burned the town. Hayne and the score fought to shield Domus Dei sickhouse of the foe, and Softly, with a wonder shot, killed the French captain who led the other side against them. Afterwards, when the French left, folk in the town showed their thanks to the bowmen in silver and gave Hayne the rood he always wore on a chain about his neck. Softly said the rood should be his, for he shot the arrow that slew the French captain. But Hayne wouldn't yield it, and Softly ne forgave him never.

When the score came together again eight year later to fight for the king in France, the fight that ended with Crécy and the take of Calais, Hayne was the same, and Longfreke ne thought himself shifted, but Softly and Dickle had become other. Softly had his gold teeth and Dickle had the rood on his forehead and the marks of nail-wounds on his hands and feet, and each of them had a devil in him. It had been in the gleam of their eyes. On the way to

Crécy and Calais the score burned French towns and took French goods. All King Edward's men did that, as they were bidden by the king, and the king's captains. It was war. It wasn't no sin. But Softly and Dickle also killed the guiltless, and ne worthed no Frenchwoman's soul higher than a fly's.

'Cess,' said Thomas, 'and her father.'

'Yeah,' said Longfreke.

'Why would Hayne take such a man as Softly with him to France now?'

'To pine him for his pride,' said Longfreke. 'And Softly the same on his side. Hayne thought to bring Softly to a land rotten with qualm where he would die with all his sin unshriven and be damned in hell for ever. But Softly thinks he won't die. Him thinks he'll show Hayne how God loves him, and always meant for him to have the rood. Softly would that Hayne see how he may reave a woman of her maidenhood, kill her father and steal her of her kin, and instead of striking him down, God speeds him and helps him win. Softly would that Hayne see how he, Softly, go over the qualm-lands without hurt, and go unshriven, day after day, and ne fall sick, but go him rich to Bristol, and have a great shrift at home when he is old and ready.'

'Why did you come?' said Thomas.

'I'm a soldier, and Hayne is my master.'

'But what said he to you when he came again of Bristol, after he saw Softly about this fare to Calais?'

'The same as he said to Sweetmouth and Mad,' said Longfreke. 'He said: "I go with Softly and his woman and his friends to Calais. I would you come with me, but it were better for you that you ne come."'

'And yet you ne heeded his warning. You came.'

'I'm a follower,' said Longfreke.

They reached a great house that might only be the bailiff's. They stinted by the gate. Longfreke furrowed his brow. He looked down and shook his head. 'I held Hayne a right handy man and good,' he said. 'I ne know why he'd leave us now, when we're in plight.'

THE BAILIFF OF Heytesbury had gone to visit his lord, who had his residence at a different manor a journey away, and Berna and Laurence were received by the bailiff's wife, Matilda. She interrupted their explanations by offering chambers in her house for the night. She was a long, powerful, red-cheeked dame in a rude white apron and kerchief, constantly in movement as she attempted to rally the village against distress, issuing orders to servants and villagers, then commencing execution of the very action she demanded of them in the same instant, which obliged her servants to press on in rapid imitation – measuring infusions of feverfew, dispersing rue and vinegar, arranging search parties in houses that appeared deserted, delivering supplies to sufferers, consulting with the priest, registering vacant properties in the manorial record book, praying, chanting and lighting incense. Matilda ensured that orphans were placed with families to nourish them and abandoned beasts were transferred to heritors. She had converted part of the stable into an infirmary for those with none to care for them.

All afternoon, Laurence and Berna attended in Matilda's hall to hear that the priest had attained the leisure to marry them. With Madlen's help Berna laved and adorned herself and Laurence, too, found clean garments, while Madlen put away the marriage gown in favour of a lamentable old smock that had been the property of Matilda's sister. Matilda's surviving servants, her cook having perished two days previously, were occupied with their mistress's endeavours to combat the effects of the pestilence. When Thomas arrived, he went immediately to rest, and Longfreke only remained long enough to report that Hornstrake would soon receive the final sacrament, and that the remaining archers had found lodging in an abandoned house by the church.

Outside it rained. In the hall, hung with poorly fashioned Flemish tapestries, Madlen came and went on the duties assigned her by Berna and Laurence, which consisted principally in shoe-cleaning and the carriage of water. A mutton roasted on a spit over the fire. Every so often Laurence gave the spit a turn. As the meat browned he cut slices and laid them on a wooden platter on the grand table in the centre of the hall. He and Berna had already consumed more than they desired.

In the distance they heard the sound of the priest's bell. As if roused from sleep, a woman in the stable who had fallen silent recommenced her piercing lamentation. She appeared to be pronouncing a name, but they couldn't perceive whose it was.

With tender care, Laurence cut a large slice of mutton of the thigh and held it up to demonstrate to Berna how it wasn't no denser than a piece of cloth.

'I was inducted into the art as a page at my lord Berkeley's table,' said Laurence. 'I may cut it meagre like this, or in pleats, or in gross morsels, or daintily for ladies. But usually I had a trencher to cut onto. I ne comprehend why they ne carry bread of another village.'

Berna raised her face from a basin of warm rose water infused with cloves and zedoary.

'I marvel you may view the mutton to cut it in this sombre light,' she said. 'What did they say when you went out for candles?'

'I was addressed with considerable impertinence and familiarity by a peasant of the village,' said Laurence. 'I shall not repeat the terms the insolent beggar used.'

'They have their troubles,' said Berna.

'I'm quite sensible that their suffering is terrible. It's no reason for them to treat their superiors with less than the proper reverence. If one of them fronts up to me like that again he'll receive the flat of my sword on his back.'

'I demand of myself whether I ne owe to aid Matilda in some manner. Like a Christian.'

'Like a saint?' said Laurence. 'Lave their plaguey feet?'

'Like a saint before she were a saint,' said Berna cautiously.

'You owe to not go out,' said Laurence. 'Our best defence is to not respire the same pestilential air the poor spirits of this village are accustomed to. These maladies must course through the poor like a forest fire, and the tall trees go untouched.'

'You heard what passed in Imber, and now half this village has perished and one of your own archers is in his final hour. Can't you comprehend the grandeur of this change? For all we know half of England has already departed.'

Laurence came to her, cupped her chin and wiped away her tears with his thumbs. 'Outen Green is far to the north, and high, and the air is pure there. Your family is secure.'

He attempted to kiss her. She pushed him away.

'When we're married,' he said.

'When we're married,' she said, and smiled at him, her eyes red and moist with grief and fear.

Madlen returned with fresh water and Laurence demanded a melody English, that the lady ne be tormented by sounds of suffering. Madlen stood by the window and sang:

> When the nightingale sings,
> The woods wax green,
> Leaf and grass and blossom spring
> In April, I ween
> And love is to my heart gone

> *With one spear so keen,*
> *Night and day my blood it drinks,*
> *My heart does me wring.*
>
> *I have loved all this year,*
> *That I may love no more.*
> *I have sicked many sicks,*
> *Loveman, for your ore,*
> *Me ne's love never the nearer*
> *And that me rues sore.*
> *Sweet loveman, think on me*
> *I have loved you yore.*
>
> *Sweet loveman, I bid you,*
> *Of love one speech.*
> *While I live in world so wide*
> *Other ne'll I seek.*
> *With your love, my sweet love,*
> *My bliss you might eke*
> *A sweet kiss of your mouth*
> *Might be my leech.*

Madlen respired for a new verse. She was interrupted by the entrance of Matilda, a group of her attendants, and a man in rain-soaked travelling clothes carrying an infant in a blanket. The man, a gentleman by his appearance, laid the infant on the table. It was a boy aged three or four in a fine white linen shirt, his face pale, his eyes half open. He coughed and called for his mother. The man who had carried him in bit his knuckle and caressed the boy's cheek.

'Mama,' said the boy clearly, opening his eyes wider, and the gentleman murmured in his ear.

Berna aided Matilda in making the boy comfortable, arranging the blanket underneath him and positioning a cushion to support his head. The boy was Robert, nephew of the lord of Heytesbury, and the gentleman his father, the lord's brother Alan, who held a manor on the Warminster side.

'I heard you people brought some sort of French doctor with you,' said Alan to Laurence. He had a silver beard, fine lines at the corners of his eyes and an air of one who considered it generally accepted that not only his but humanity's patience was exhausted.

'I regret . . .' said Laurence. 'Thomas is ordinarily resident in France, and erudite, and possesses a marvellous amount of Latin, but he's no doctor in no sense medical.'

'Is he a doctor or not?'

'He's a proctor, not a doctor,' said Berna.

Alan insisted that Thomas be summoned, and he came, more uncertain and absent than usual, his sombre clothes creased.

'D'you know aught of medicine?' said Alan. 'They say you aren't no doctor but I suppose with your Latin you've gained some science of the ancients.'

Moving rigidly, as if suffering some discomfort, Thomas went to the boy and lifted his open hand over him. It appeared he'd touch him, but he hesitated and moved his hand away. 'No ancient ne endured this malady,' he said. 'If you'd comprehend the course of the pest you should make your demands of the dame who invited us. I've only just arrived. She's resisted the disease here since its first appearance.'

ALAN TURNED TO Matilda. She laid her hand on Robert's forehead. 'The fever's not so high,' she said, and asked the knave how he fared.

'I'm hungry,' said Robert.

Laurence gave him a shive of mutton and he ate it quickly.

'He's not as bad as yesterday,' said Master Alan. 'Two nights ago he burned like to he was on fire. He wouldn't eat, but drank as if there wasn't no bottom to him. He had two botches between his legs more than his bollocks, and now they're less.'

'You've ground for hope,' said Matilda. 'In our town some that overlived the first high fever are already on their feet.'

'What do those that overlive have in mean?' asked Master Alan.

'Not goodness,' said Matilda. 'There's a fellow, Stucken, who bears the bodies and buries them, who was known as a wicked churl. He was one of the first to sicken, and now he's heal again. We mayn't know what drives the Almighty to choose. All should go to mass and bid their beads, light candles, keep dry and cool, drink right worts, spread holy water on their threshold, keep out of the south wind, but at the last, it comes to God's send.'

'And the worth of your friends,' said one of the townfolk who'd come with Matilda.

'That's right, and kin,' said another.

'Where's the need to speak of that to guests?' said Matilda. 'What use is it now?' She turned to Thomas, then to Alan. 'Some folk think them fewer would have died had their nearest been more kindly.'

'Abby Fisher died of thirst after her husband ran away and left her,' said one of the town women. 'I know he's a beater and a swiker and an idler, for they're my neighbours, but if he'd said he meant to go I'd have fetched her ale, were she ever so sick. Poor thing, she lay there behind a shut door and none knew.'

'There are folk in two rooms with the sick in one and the heal in the other too feared to go in and help their own and too ashamed to tell a neighbour,' said another.

'That's enough,' said Matilda. 'Get out, the lot of you, you've work for three times as many. Remember your lord's nephew in your beads.'

The townfolk left, and when the thud of their boots was gone, a sound was left like to a man who fought for breath. It was Master Alan, who'd sunk to the floor and sat there with his legs spread out, his back against the table, his body shaken by sobs. A whine rose of the deep of his chest and he began to howl of sorrow.

Laurence Haket kneeled beside him and put a hand on his shoulder. 'Master Alan, your son will surely recover of this.'

Master Alan ne let of weeping. Young Robert rolled over on his side and looked down of the edge of the board at his father and told him he felt better. The boy let his hand down and Alan groped for it, held it tight and sobbed the more.

Matilda leaned towards Berna and whispered that the boy's mother, Master Alan's wife, had died that morning.

LATER, BERNA AND Laurence were solitary in the hall again. Thomas had returned to the chamber he would share with Laurence. Matilda had departed. The rain had intensified, the fire was extinguished, the basin of spice infusion and the mutton cold. Berna kneeled, hands clasped, and said a prayer Thomas had given her. She signed the cross over her chest, prostrated herself and repeated the process while Laurence paced up and down.

'Sancta Maria, Mater Dei, ora pro nobis peccatoribus, nunc et in hora mortis nostrae,' said Berna again. She went down on the flagstones.

'I hate this place,' said Laurence. 'It reminds me of Berkeley in autumn, sitting in solitude in the grand hall, attending a place at some event I was unsure I'd been invited to.'

'I ne comprehend what you mean by solitude. I'm here.'

'You won't even permit me to kiss you,' said Laurence. He came to where Berna kneeled on the floor and seized her hands. She stood but ne attempted to release herself.

'I'm defenceless,' said Berna. 'I can't prevent you were you to treat me as the archers treated Cess.'

Laurence threw down her hands, took several paces away and struck the basin with his fist. The force of the blow pulverised the vessel against the wall.

'It appears there's no injury to my honour you consider too severe,' he said.

'I ne apprehend it no cruelty on my part to demand restraint on your possession corporeal of my person. With a little patience we may be married properly and have it entered in the rolls.'

Madlen came into the hall and silently commenced collection of the pieces of basin. Laurence observed her labour meditatively. He turned to Berna and said: 'You're unreasonable. You're aggrieved I ne ravished you previously, yet now I've made it impossible for you to return to your family by the very act of ravishment, you are aggrieved by that too. Yes, I see it ne pleases you to hear that I have comprehended you, for if there's one thing more injurious than not to be comprehended by your amour, it's to be comprehended too well.'

'I never insisted too fiercely on my reasonableness,' said Berna.

'I only demand that you consider my position. You have a family whose fate inquiets you. I have none except my brother, who possesses my family property and won't part with a penny; and he has sons. I have no place to return to save the humid chamber in my lord Berkeley's house I share with three other younger sons, as poor as I. All that's promised me I gained in war. All my fortune, all my family, is in the future.'

'I'm here now,' said Berna.

'Not in no sense complete,' said Laurence. 'Regard.' He searched inside his shirt, took out a wallet and displayed for Berna the grant of fief of the manor near Calais and the tally stick for the boat. 'These are real,' he said. 'Our property, our inheritance.'

'We mayn't be sure we'll see this property,' said Berna.

'To the very point,' said Laurence, approaching close to her without touching. 'Master Alan is deprived of his spouse, and he can't be sure he'll survive either, but their son has endured the pestilence and emerges. Remember the Romance. Nature demands with urgency that we engender a family.'

'It is marvellous that you and I should have been present at the same scene and remember it so differently,' said Berna. 'What appeared most noticeable to me wasn't the survival of the boy, though that is very touching, but the abandonment of the woman who perished of thirst. I would that were you and I in solitude, without no servants and affected by this pestilence, we demonstrate our love by carrying water to each other rather than succumbing to a second fever to populate a vacant universe.'

A bell sounded of the church tower and ne let of ringing.

'It's the appeal to attend our marriage,' said Laurence. They roused Thomas, who said he would go at his own pace. Madlen pleaded that she might be present, but Laurence gave her money and ordered her to search the village for wine and pastries, and to ensure Berna's chamber was in a proper condition.

The rain had ceased, and the marriage couple departed on their horses. Berna's gown appeared to radiate whiteness in comparison to the ordure of the street. Accompanying the sound of the bell and of the horses' hooves was the drip of water of the town roofs and of the cloths hung impregnated of the windows.

WHEN THE BOWMEN came first to Heytesbury, late on Sunday morning, it seemed to them the town was gripped by madness, as if it weren't the qualm that astoned the townsfolk with its grim speed, but that folk had lost their wits early and made the sickness worse than it owed to be by their giddiness. As evening nighed, the bowmen's mood shifted. When they saw for themselves how cruel the pest was, it ne seemed no more the townsfolk were mad; it seemed they weren't mad enough. The bowmen ne understood how the living of Heytesbury kept themselves in wield when so many of their near and dear had laid their eyes together in so short a time. They felt it was they, the bowmen, who must lose their minds, while the townsfolk seemed wonder even. It was like to you spoke to your child, and turned away, and turned again a stound later, and the child was gone.

The priest had barely aneled Hornstrake, and fed Christ's body in his mouth crumb by crumb – with Will holding the priest's wrists that he ne shake and spill a speck of the flesh of the Lord of Life – when he, too, fell. He ne woke no more, and within an hour both Hornstrake and the priest stinted to breathe.

Otherwhiles, Longfreke had sickened, with a high fever, dulled eyes and dry mouth. He shat blood. They laid him on a bed in the house they'd taken near the church and the bowmen took shifts to bring him water and ale. He wouldn't eat, though there was much to eat. They laid baked chicken and lamb's liver under his nose and he turned away.

Stucken rang the church bell for the deaths. It was long before any of the townfolk came. The first to come were Laurence Haket and the lady Bernadine, clothed for their wedding, and it was grim to see their nebs fall when they heard the priest was dead, and Hornstrake, and Longfreke sick.

'How could he weaken so fast?' said Laurence Haket.

'It goes other with other folk,' said the deacon. 'Some speedy, some slow.'

Longfreke lay in a room in the house he'd hired of a widow who'd lost her husband and eldest daughter. The widow had gone to bide with her kin on the other side of town. She brought the bowmen food and ale and water and linen, but wouldn't go near Longfreke, and it fell to Will to clean him and handle his piss-pot. The bowmen bought candles in church, lit them and set them around Hayne's rood on a shelf in the nook where the widow had kept her hallow-like-nesses. There wasn't no lavender nor roses to sweeten the air so they seethed a handful of gillyflowers and seeds of heaven in water and dight it in a can on the floor near Longfreke's head. Holiday would have him drink a treacle, but Longfreke said it hadn't done Hornstrake no good, and bade the bowmen work a burial and dig a grave for their friend, for no man of Hayne Attenoke's score wasn't going to be laid in no pit.

'Dig another for me,' he said. 'I'm about to hit the mark.'

His steven came to them as if from behind a thick wall. He bade them all go, out-take Will, and to send him a priest if they found one, and lacking a priest, to send Thomas.

'My eyes are like to red-hot needles were pitched in them,' said Longfreke when he and Will were alone.

'You'll be heal again,' said Will.

'This arrow sees its mark, son. The Almighty ne lifted his bow too high when he shot me, nor struck the string too hard.'

'I'm sorry I played Venus to the high-borns.'

'Hush, son. I was weak to let you cleave to the score. I owed to have seen you bide at home with your burd and your plough.'

'I'm glad you took me.'

'For God's sake, shut your mouth. Hayne said: "Let him come if he hears what Noster tells him. Let it be of his own free will, if he knows who we are, and what we've done, and where we're going." I would I hadn't listened. You hadn't wit enough to understand the stake. I ne knew myself what Hayne meant for us. Maybe all of us are to be deemed guilty, that we ne fought harder to set Cess free. And now Hayne has left us, and I'm near to gone, and Softly's heal. He wins.'

'When I met you on the road near my home, I thought me the qualm was a tale,' said Will. 'I ne thought me the world would end in summer, under the sun in a clear sky, with the leaves new and the birds in song and loving-Andrew in the hedgerow.'

'Who calls it a tale?'

'Sweetmouth, for one.'

'Sweetmouth likes to speak of fair maids.'

'Yeah.'

'Tell me, which maid's fairer, Hope or Truth?'

Will lowered his eyes.

'Ne pine yourself, son,' said Longfreke. 'You fare to fight, and now to follow your sweetheart too.'

'Madlen is my friend.'

'You understand that when I'm gone, Softly will be master of such of the score as is left?'

'I would it were another,' said Will.

'Softly's the oldest, and has the right, and he's nimble, be the Devil ever so deep in him,' said Longfreke. 'You have the captain to lean on. Maybe he will hold Softly back. But it ne likes the captain to look too nearly at what goes on between bowmen. He ne cares much for our sins before God as long as we do as he and his masters bid. All I ask is that do you reach France you help Cess go to her own folk again.'

'I swear on my life,' said Will.

Longfreke's neb furrowed on either side of its great wem. He hid his eyes with his hand. 'Only this morning I nad no need of shameful help,' he said, and turned on his side. Will helped him squirt shit into the pot, cleaned him with straw, pulled up his breech again and took the filth away to the dung-heap.

HEYTESBURY SHOULD HAVE been rich in priests. As the deacon informed Laurence, the grand church of Peter and Paul was a church collegiate, and the rector the dean of Salisbury Cathedral. But the rector hadn't never visited Heytesbury, nor Salisbury. He was an Italian who had his principal habitation somewhere between Rome and Avignon, and the dimes of Heytesbury's peasants and drapers journeyed to him as silver via the deanery. Usually spiritual care was furnished by one of two vicars and two chaplains, but since the arrivage of the pest, there was a grave mortality among the clerics, and each parish pleaded with its neighbours for aid ecclesiastical. And ne simply pleaded; money was offered. One of their vicars had gone to Warminster to assist, and hadn't returned. One chaplain had journeyed to Swallowcliffe, a village in Heytesbury's care, and hadn't returned. The other chaplain had travelled to Salisbury in search of a replacement, and hadn't returned. It was possible the chaplains had succumbed to the malady, but equally possible they'd succumbed to the temptation to take up residence elsewhere for double the pay and the promise of a benefice. So in Heytesbury a single priest remained, Father Simon, and now he was departed to the life eternal, they ne comprehended how they might continue.

Laurence stood with the deacon by a column in the centre of

the nave. 'Aren't you fit to shrive and absolve?' he demanded.

The deacon crossed himself and shook his head. 'I mightn't shrive Father Simon himself just now,' he said. 'He died unshriven.'

'What, you refused to hear confession of your master in his final hour?'

The deacon looked miserable. He appeared on the verge of tears.

'I haven't the power,' he murmured. 'Father Simon did such good these days, and wasn't never without Christ's body near to hand, and said so many masses, and drank so much of the Almighty's blood, I hope he may go swiftly to God's house without shrift nor aneling. I ne ceased to pray for him.'

'Well, you mayn't receive confession, but you may marry me to my lady Bernadine.'

'Marry you?' said the deacon, his face changing.

'Yes. It's a lesser sacrament, I believe.'

'How can you think of a wedding at a time like this? Have you lost your wits?'

'On the contrary, I feel it is I alone whose mind is unspoiled by the madness of these events. Who will rule and defend the common people in future if we nobles ne procreate? Producing the next generation is a matter hardly less urgent than attending to the spirits of the departing.'

The deacon respired. 'Your tongue's got the sleight of French, sir, which I ne understand well, but they learned me some Latin. Produco, producis, producit; generatio, generationis. I think me you're about this.' He circled the thumb and forefinger of one hand and moved the forefinger rapidly in and out.

'You impudent harlot,' said Laurence.

The deacon shrugged and pointed to where the churchwardens and other common people of the village were preparing space close to the altar for the priest to be placed for a vigil. 'I mayn't wed you to your burd,' he said. 'I haven't been given such powers. I've too much else to do while so many are sick and dying. I go to work. Do as you will without my help. Go forth and produce the next generation.'

ALL THE HEAL bowmen, Softly, Holiday, Sweetmouth, Mad and Will, crowded into Longfreke's room, together with Thomas, who wasn't his even self. None had seen him write a word all day, his skin was ashen, his lips pale, and it seemed to like him to keep his eyes shut when he could. He wouldn't stand in for a priest again, he told them, in a thin dry steven like to when a ploughman frots an ear of corn between his hands to know its ripeness. But the bowmen told him he must, for such was his bond to them, and he was the nearest to a priest they had, and if he'd have a penny of each of them for his work, that wasn't no woe.

So Thomas sat on a milking stool by Longfreke's bed and held the bowman's thick wrist in his bony hand. Laurence Haket came and said his farewell, and said Longfreke was a good bold soldier, and behest to buy a pound's weight of candles for him, and to have his chaplain-to-be say beads for him when he was in his manor in Calais. And he left to be with his lady.

'You all owe to go,' said Longfreke. His steven was so small it mightn't be heard out-take that all were still. 'The air in here is rotten.'

'We aren't women like the men of Wiltshire,' said Softly. 'We're western men and soldiers. We ne fright so lightly.'

'I say yet it's not no qualm nor pest nor plague nor whatever outcome shit likes you,' said Holiday. 'I know towns near Bristol

297

where the ague slew half the folk. It happens somewhere every year.'

'Thomas,' whispered Longfreke, 'I'm near to done.'

Thomas nodded to the rood in the hallow nook. Mad took it down and handed it to Will, who held it up at the foot of the bed.

'Open your eyes,' said Thomas, 'and look on your redeemer.'

Longfreke opened his eyes and looked on the body of Christ. There was a stir at the door and Cess shoff her way through. Softly looked at her astoned. His mouth gaped before he got himself in wield and said in his soft steven: 'Go to the cart again. I ne gave you leave to come here.'

'I have the right,' said Cess.

'A bowman leaves this world,' said Softly. 'This has not to do with you. The longer you stand there, the worse it'll be for you later.'

'In France, at the end, the one who dies must forgive and be forgiven,' said Cess. 'Are they another kind of Christen here?' She spoke wonder boldly, with her head up, and looked Softly in the eye.

'Let her be,' said Longfreke.

'It was the fake priest told her she might come,' said Softly, showing Thomas with his finger. 'He'd make this death-time a deem of what was done in France. He seeks to draw it out of our mouths that we were wicked in France and must be pined on earth for it.'

'I ne asked Cess to come,' said Thomas, 'but here she is, of her own will.'

'She's my woman, and she hasn't no will but as I let her,' said Softly.

'Longfreke's is the need,' said Thomas. 'He'd have her here.'

Softly looked round the nebs of his even-bowmen, but none would speak for him.

'It were better for all of you to let me drive her out,' he said.

'Why did you come?' said Longfreke to Cess.

'To know if I might see God's work in your sickness,' she answered, 'that the Almighty be wreaked on the wicked, and harm you, as me and my father were harmed.'

'He ne hurt you,' said Sweetmouth. 'He fought for you against Softly.'

'Hush,' said Longfreke. 'She means I ne fought long or hard enough. She means I was of this fellowship.'

'Is he right?' said Thomas.

Cess ne answered, but gazed on Longfreke. She stood next to Will at the foot of the bed.

Longfreke asked her: 'Well, see you God's work wrought in me, in this sickness?'

'Maybe it's there,' said Cess. 'I ne see it. I see a poor soldier with a done-in face dying in another's bed, far from home, ne knowing who's to keep his endless soul.'

'I would I'd done more to help you,' whispered Longfreke.

'Where's your pride?' said Softly. The bowmen hushed him.

'I'm sorry,' came of Longfreke's lips.

'I believe you,' said Cess. 'I would that the devils step away and let you fare to a better stead.'

'Bring the rood nearer,' said Thomas. He bade Longfreke repeat after him: 'God, I ask forgiveness, and of your mother St Mary and all the saints of heaven, of all the sins I've wrought, in work, word and thought, with every limb of my body. With sore heart I ask God forgiveness, and in the lack of a shriftfather, I ask God to hear me, and shrive me of my sin.'

Then Thomas bowed his head and spoke in Latin:

'God omnipotent, in the profound humility of my ignorance, which exceeds that of any veritable ecclesiastic, I commend the spirit of Gilbert Bisley, alias Longfreke, to your benign clemency. Malificent acts have been committed by the military society of which he was part, yet he was not complicit directly in their commission. He attempted to ameliorate the consequences, and has been absolved by the enduring victim. Reveal to him your grace, and accept him into the territory celestial, and to eternity vital. May I observe, oh Father, that in securing Bisley's absolution, I incurred hostility from the most violent individual in the society, and I request that you consider this at the moment of my own spirit's migration, an event I anticipate imminently. In nomine Patris, et Dei, et Spiritu Sancti, amen.'

Spellbound by Thomas's bead, the bowmen ne saw Cess slip away. Soon afterward, Longfreke laid his eyes together, and when Thomas held a feather under his nose, it ne stirred. Softly took the rood of Will's hand and dight it about his own neck.

IT WAS IN wone among the bowmen to bury their own quickly when they were on the road, the dead man in his fighting gear, in a bare sheet with the ashen rood drawn on it, with his own bow broken in half and knitted into a rough rood with twine. Thomas egged the deacon to let Hornstrake and Longfreke be buried in the graves the bowmen had dug for them in hallowed ground, all but Longfreke wasn't rightly shriven, and with Thomas's fair speech and a handful of silver, the deacon said it might be done. Thomas wrote letters to be borne to the priests in the dead men's home parishes, that their kin might know what had befallen them. By nightfall, Hornstrake and Longfreke were in the ground, and the bowmen drank to them with wine and ate their fill of brad chicken. Afterward they went to sleep, for none would stint in Heytesbury a stound longer than they needed, and Laurence Haket was for setting out at dawn.

In the night Sweetmouth woke Will and bade him follow. Will got up and Sweetmouth led him to the church. Inside folk sat in wake about the body of the priest. Dear candles burned bright and steady at each nook of the board on which the body lay. Sweetmouth went up to the light and Will saw he had all his gear with him, his pack laden, his unstrung bow in his hand.

'A penny candle, brother, for our men,' said Sweetmouth to a churchwarden. The warden fetched it and Sweetmouth lit it.

'Better say your beads in here,' said the warden, who saw that Sweetmouth meant to take the light outside. 'It ne likes folk to have lights and speech among the graves at night.'

'We nad no time for a right wake, like your priest,' said Sweetmouth. 'We shan't be long, and then we'll come inside again.'

'Mind the pit,' said the warden.

Sweetmouth and Will sat on the grass between Longfreke and Hornstrake's graves and Sweetmouth set the candle on a pewter plate he took of his pack. It was warm and still and the light ne flickered. The sky was thick with stars.

'You owe to fetch your gear,' said Sweetmouth. 'Do we leave now we may be in Warminster by morning. I ween this a good time to buy a cheap horse. If we ride hard we may be home again by Wednesday.'

Will ne understood.

'You wouldn't be a bowman under Softly, with this death sent to the world?' said Sweetmouth. 'Does he live, he'll turn to thieving of the dead, and drive you to thieve with him.'

'But if you bide, you and I and Mad and the captain are more than they.'

Sweetmouth shook his head. 'It seems this qualm's no tale. I would be near my wife and children now.'

'What of our oath?' said Will.

'Longfreke's dead, and Softly wears the rood. If the oath means aught in this tide, why has Hayne forsaken us?'

'To show us we can steer ourselves without him.'

'Ne be wise, Player. Come with me. You've a mother and brothers at home, and a betrothed. You'll go up into Cotswold and plough again, and be wed, and drink on the holidays.'

'I found a friend on the road. I mayn't leave her, and she mayn't go home again.'

'Come now. A friend you make on the road's not like kin. You may always leave them. She's but a kiss and a swive on the way.' He took Will's cheek in his hand. 'We're Englishmen. For us the road always goes home again. We mayn't live in some other land beyond the sea. We go there, we fight there, we swive there if God sends, we make some silver and come home again.'

'I found another road,' said Will. 'One that bears me away and ne comes again.'

'There's no such road,' said Sweetmouth.

'How might Mad let you go?'

'I haven't the heart to tell him. He'll find it hard to bear. I lack the strength to look him in the eye and say I must go.'

'Would you have me tell him?'

'Not if you come with me.'

'I told you, I shan't.' Will's steven broke. 'It's right hard after Longfreke to have you go. It's like to you die too.'

'Then come.'

'No.'

Sweetmouth stood and pitched the candle in the earth at the foot of Longfreke's grave. 'Farewell, Longfreke and Frongleke,' he said. 'Do devils take one, the other may go with the angels.'

The candle cast its light now on the edge of the pit, and both men looked there. Will wiped his eyes.

'She was right fair to look on,' said Sweetmouth.

'Who?'

'Cess. I saw her in the stoneyard in Mantes. I would sorely have others know how fair she looked to me and I must open my mouth and tell Softly. If I hadn't spoken, hadn't said how sweet her neb and lickerous her body, they wouldn't have sought her out.'

'But you weren't among them that took her.'

'No. I have no guilt for that. I ne did nothing.' He was still, then said again: 'I ne did nothing.'

The two men held each other in their arms a stound and said their farewells. Then Sweetmouth left for Westbury along the dark road, and Will went again to the house.

BERNA LAY VIGILANT in her bed in the bailiff's house. The chamber was obscured in the profundity of night. She called out to Madlen, who lay on the floor by the door.

'Are you asleep?' she said.

'Yeah,' said Madlen.

'Are you afraid?'

There was a moment's silence. 'You mean afeared? Yeah.'

'Of the pest.'

'Yeah.'

'You ne appear afraid.'

'Appear?'

'Seem.'

'I ne understand, my demoiselle.'

'I mayn't rest. My heart beats furiously and hard. I contemplate and think on my death and mortality over and over. I see myself covered and ended by darkness. But you seem calm and even, like

to you are untroubled and unhurt by the possibility of fatal and
deadly malady and sickness.'

'Possibility?'

'Let's say "speed". Or "hap". That which may be, or may not.'

'I never had no possibilities, my demoiselle. I have what I have.
I mayn't do nothing about what's to come. I'm afraid of the pest,
that it take my loveman before me, for I mayn't live without him.
Otherwise I'm blithe enough. I've a full belly, and a roof over my
head, and I'm heal. I have love now, and mayn't do aught today
to shield myself of death tomorrow.'

'Is it of your faith?'

'I ne know aught of God and he knows aught of me. He's too
much else on his shoulders.'

'Ne fear you for your brother, as I fear for my family at home?'

A curious noise issued of Madlen, like to a sneeze or a suppressed
laugh. 'I fear for my brother least of all,' she said. 'He's one no
pest may reach.'

I WOKE WITH a spasm and a sense of terror. Query: why terror?
Miraculously, my state had been transformed from febrile to lucid.
My dolour was removed. My humours were restored to their ideal
temperament. It appeared possible that I had not suffered from the
plague, but from some vulgar, innocent contagion, or had been
divinely credited with a corporeal nature resistant to this particular
morbidity. I repeat: why terror, in the face of such extraordinary
good fortune?

Because I had provoked Softly. Why had I provoked him, in full
cognisance of his violent nature? Because I expected to perish of

plague. Now it appeared I would not perish of plague, but by homicide.

It was dark. A young person's respiration was audible. I examined my memory. I had been accommodated by the local administrator, apportioned space in a cubicle with Laurence Haket. I had regressed from the interment of the archers exhausted, convinced that I, too, would succumb. The situation necessitated prayer, meditation, a final accounting, a preparation to face my fate with dignity and resignation. Instead I fell asleep remembering my mother clamouring my name when I had concealed myself in some secret place where she could not discover me.

I became conscious that I had not, as I initially assumed, been roused by an internal stimulus. A figure occupied the doorway, illuminated solely by the lunar radiance from the window. The horrible suspicion that it was Softly caused me to rise, and I was about to wake Haket when I noticed that the form of the intruder was less substantial than my presumed homicide. Inspecting his features more proximately I apprehended that it was the Welsh archer, Mad. Indicating digitally that I should be silent, he conducted me outside, to the area in front of the house by the principal portal.

'THERE'S NO SCORE no more,' said Mad. 'It's no breach of my oath to leave, and I'd go home to Merioneth.'

'Now?'

'Yeah.'

'And leave young Will to may alone with Softly?'

'He'll have Sweetmouth. I can't bear to tell them. It ne likes me to see a man weep out-take it be of a tale I sing. You speak for me in the morning. Tell them you begged me to bide, but I ne yielded.'

'I would beg you, but I know you won't yield.'

'That's right. I go on foot to Warminster, and buy a horse there.'

'It's a lonely road by night, and thick with ghosts this tide. Bide till morning.'

'I must go. I'm full of song. I'd sing it in Merioneth before I die.'

'What song?'

'The song of the bowmen. Of Hayne and Softly, and how they fell out over a dear gift. How Softly and his men came again to Hayne to fight with him for the king, and each brought a holy thing, one a golden rood, one a book, one a ball of Christ's breath, one a rood on his forehead and nail-holes in his hands and feet, but none was so fair and holy as Hayne's rood. How they fought the French at Crécy. How Softly stole the fair Cecile and Dickle slew her father. How Longfreke the bold was cloven atwain and made whole again. How death was sent to the world on the wind, and the bowmen gathered again to go to France, and Softly staked all, for if he lost he would be damned, and if he won he would do as he chose and get the rood. How love came to the world in the shape of two young men, and how one of these men helped the other out of plight, and how love wrought it that they might know each other as man and man and wife and wife.'

'I'd know more of what you sing in your song.'

'Then come with me to Merioneth, forget you can read and write, and learn Welsh.'

'I guess I'm not in your song.'

'No. I ne sing of no Latin writers.'

'Ne fear you to fare alone and die unshriven on the way?'

'No.'

'You too are of this score. You ne hurt Cess as Softly did, but ne helped her neither.'

'I'm but the bard. I mayn't be in my own song.'

'Then all that betides is stuff for the song?'

'Only in Merioneth are true things. Only there is the world true and for ever. Here, or in France, everything is a tale. All shifts. Everything haps once, no more, and then it's gone, out-take that some bard like me minds it.'

'And if a writer like me writes it down?'

Mad waved his hand and blew a puff of wind. 'It's not the same. Your written words are but ash-to-be.'

'What is it about Merioneth that makes it true?'

'Folk there mind everything, and everything has a name, each stone and tree. All know what all are, and who they were, and who their kin were and their forefathers. Nothing shifts and all that seems new is another side of what was there before.'

'And that's why you ne need shrift. Your everlastingness is there.'

Mad ne answered, and it was too dark to see his cheer. They bade each other farewell. Mad went away into the darkness and Thomas went to bed again.

JUDITH, I AM a solitary man. What may my desire for the security of your unconditional love be except the desire of an exile to be restored to his original state? How ridiculous I was, liberating myself from the love of my family in Scotland only to attempt to recreate that love two months' journey away in France, with the difference being that while in both places I expected unconditional love, I sought to exchange my submission to their authority for your submission to mine.

LAURENCE HAKET WAS wrath in the morning to find he had three
bowmen left of the ten behest, and more run away than dead. Yet
he was drawn to some other care the bowmen ne knew of, and
Softly outdid him in anger, cursing Mad and Sweetmouth as chicken-
hearted sons of bitches and, which was worse, women. He fingered
the rood about his neck while he spoke.

'Why did you ne wake us when Sweetmouth came to you?' he
said to Will.

Will ne answered. He was stricken by the loss of his friends.

'And how might Mad walk out without that no one saw?'

None spoke.

'Captain,' said Softly, 'let me go with Holiday and Player to
Westbury and I swear I'll bring you those harlots on a rope, and
if not them, two better bowmen. We'll meet in Mere tonight.'

But Laurence Haket wouldn't be left without one bowman. So
they read that Will would go with him to the castle at Mere, where
the captain knew folk, and Softly and Holiday would seek the
runaways.

It was early. The sun was barely up. Softly led Will over to the
cart, away from the others, and showed him where he'd knit two
loops of rope on one side.

'New masters shift old ways,' he said. 'Marked you how Hayne
ne learned you no bowmanship?'

'Yeah,' said Will.

'Under me you'll get the lore. It begins of strength in the arms.
Let's see how strong your arms are. Put your wrists in those
loops.'

Will did as he was bidden and Softly and Holiday tightened the
ropes. 'See if you can heave the cart over,' said Softly.

Will hove with all his might. The cart rocked a little but he ne might throw it over. He would draw his hands of the ropes but they were held fast.

'Good,' said Softly. 'You've learned you aren't as strong as you thought. Now I'll learn you another thing. You mind how if you broke Hayne's law, one without guilt would be hurt? That wasn't no good, for you shamed us in Edington by going about as a woman, and you shamed us again by letting Sweetmouth go. Under me, if you break my law, I hurt you.'

Holiday took Will's shirt and bared his back. Softly took a whip of the cart and struck Will athwart the back with it, leaving a wale a foot long. He struck him twice more, then Holiday threw a stop of water over him, and they set him free.

'Hayne ne told you his laws. He let you find them as you broke them,' said Softly to Will, who sat on the grass half witless. 'I'll tell you my law. It's one: Do as I bid you.'

Will got to his feet.

'Now we may fulfil the behest of our first meeting,' said Softly. 'Do as I bid and we win together. Softly and Player will be the freest of men.'

He clapped Will on the back with his hand. Will gasped.

'Get your burd to dight some grease on that,' said Softly. 'Go, ne make the captain bide.'

WILL HADN'T NO time to do aught but let that he was heal, for Laurence Haket had bought two horses and harness cheap of folk who'd got them after their kindred's qualm death and lacked the means to keep them. The captain would that Will and Madlen rode

them as far as the sea at least, to get there quicker. The horses
were no gift, he said, but a loan, and the fees to feed and house
them would come of silver they had yet to earn.

The sun was two fingers of the brink of the world when they
rode out of Heytesbury, Laurence Haket, the lady Bernadine,
Thomas, Will and Madlen. Drops of dew lay on every leaf and
mist stood thick as milk in the hollows. Sheep's fleeces glew gold
of the morning and the cattle stinted to graze and beheld the
riders going by as if the days of Adam's kind were long gone
and they hadn't never seen no man before. The riders went by
hollow ways through dim woods where the birds sang loud as
children achatter in the church, and by fields of ripening corn
that hadn't been weeded a week, bright with red, yellow and
blue blossoms. They came of their horses and led them on foot
down the steep road into the dean of the Wylye, between still,
sleeping towns without no smoke nor bells, and up a wild road
on the far side onto high green downs, nearer to the sun, thick
with bees and butterflies, where the grass grew so rich the horses
trod without no sound. By mid-morning they came to the top
of a hill that looked down on Mere, with its mighty castle, and
beyond the town a great wold that glimmered with the water of
the Stour, and beyond that, blue and far, the downs of Dorset,
so Thomas said.

'THE ESSENCE OF the matter is,' Laurence remarked to Thomas
as they descended towards the castle, 'marriage is imperative.
Once married, do I perish, she inherits the property; does she
perish . . . of course one can't be sure, but it is reasonable to

have esperance of an heir. Of all the problems I anticipated in choosing the course of ravishment, the general extermining of the clergy just when their services are most in demand wasn't one.'

'A priest is ideal,' said Thomas, 'but in the most recent cases I've heard argued, not essential.'

'Berna!' called Laurence. 'He says we ne need no priest.'

'There was a scholar in Paris,' said Thomas. 'Lombard. His ideas have been generally adopted by the canon lawyers. He maintained that a marriage is acceptable if each of the two parties, without compulsion, says to the other "I will marry you."'

'That's it?' said Berna.

'The presence of spectators to confirm the voluntary nature of the arrangement were desirable. And in your position some form of testimonial document, which I would be delighted to provide, by way of a marriage present.'

'That's all?'

'There must then be consummation.'

'Will! Madlen!' shouted Laurence. The archer and the servant rode up.

'The ecclesiastical authorities may still punish you for this,' said Thomas, 'but none may say you aren't married.'

Accordingly, Bernadine Corbet and Laurence Haket exchanged their marriage promises on the hill in front of the proctor Thomas Pitkerro, the archer Will Quate and the maidservant Madlen of Outen Green.

Laurence took a golden ring of his grandfather's of his finger and put it on Berna's. They kissed, and Madlen crowned each with a chaplet of daisies. They rode on to the castle, crossed the moat, and discovered that the great door was open. They passed through into the castle courtyard, dismounted and searched for a person to accept their request for hospitality.

THE COURTYARD WAS immense, haunted by pigeons, invaded by weeds erupting of the pavement, encumbered with ruined and half-repaired and half-constructed objects, blanched with the ordure of the birds. The heaped material was placed so closely that although the entrance to the stables was visible it was difficult to trace a way for the horses past the wheel-less cart with the five-level pigeoner attached, the pile of half-mended troughs, the sheaf of rusted lances fixed to a cratch, and the ploughs with barrels joined to the handles, barrels that for some reason leaked salt. Rusted gaffs, saws, mallets, chains and pincers lay on the ground, alongside mounds of blocks, traves, pulleys, bars, cases, cages, hutches and kennels, the old and the damaged mixed with the fresh and the unused. In one part of the courtyard, lines of dead trees in basins stood in perfect array, their leaves brown, the soil in which they were planted parched.

A small door, the lower edge scraping the stones of the pavement, was opened with a series of kicks. An old man emerged carrying a pot of grain. He had a disorderly beard and was negligently clothed in a once-expensive purple velvet tunic now blemished by wine, paint, grease and the necessaries of pigeons.

He moved rapidly towards them, dispersing grain as he went and exclaiming excitedly how fortunate it was they'd arrived. Each gesture of distribution summoned a furious tempest of competing birds and the detail of his expressions of joy ne might be comprehended until he stood among them. He set down the pot, now void of its contents, and clasped Laurence's hands.

'My liege lord,' he said, 'I ne doubted you'd relieve me. I urge you to order your people to commence charging the carts immediately. The French army lies concealed not far of here and they outnumber us. I'm informed they have war engines in their train, and elephants of India.'

'Our business is with the castellan, father,' said Laurence.

'I! I! I am the castellan!' said the old man, jumping in place and jabbing his chest with his finger.

'Sir Walter?'

'I! I!'

'It's Laurence Haket.'

'Of course you're obliged to pretend,' said Sir Walter, pressing his hand on Laurence's shoulder and lowering his voice. 'If the French knew a member of the king's family were here they'd assault the castle immediately.'

'You've confounded me with another,' said Laurence. 'I'm no relative royal. I'm Laurence Haket. I shared a chamber with your son at Berkeley.'

'Pay attention, sir. My sons aren't loyal to your line.'

'Surely that's false. I was in combat with Lionel against the French on the Crécy campaign.'

'He's a traitor. All my family and servants are traitors. They abandoned me. I mayn't defend the castle unaided. We must move the armaments and the royal property north, to a safe place, where we may reassemble our forces and give battle to the enemy.'

Laurence turned to Thomas, then said hesitantly to the castellan that he doubted the presence of an enemy army in the vicinity.

'Why would my pigeons lie?' said Sir Walter.

'There's no sign of war in England,' said Laurence.

'No sign? Corpses on every side! Each day I hear the bell toll in the village. Of that high tower' —he pointed to the castle's highest turret— 'I espy how they must dig a pit to inter the soldiers, the mortality is so severe. Why would my servants and family abandon this castle if they ne feared the assault of a foreign army? What might this be save signs of war?'

'Signs of plague?'

Sir Walter's mouth turned down at the corners and he beat the air dismissively with his hand. 'People of vile habits are always subject to vile diseases. This idea of a plague universal was imagined by the Pope to deceive the enemies of France.'

'Do you know me, sir?' Thomas said to Sir Walter.

'Of course,' said the castellan impatiently. 'My lord archbishop.'

'As you say, our position is grave,' said Thomas. 'The king is rallying the barons near Oxford.'

'Excellent.'

'He will hardly may without these potent armaments. Do I perceive a vehicle for the transportation of your pigeons? An engine of your own devising?'

'Aha!' cried the castellan, winking furiously and tapping the side of his nose. He regarded the cart with the pigeoner mounted on it and appeared momentarily uncertain. 'I suppose your people will be able to reattach the wheels.'

'Certainly,' said Thomas, 'but our baggage train is delayed. Our fifty carts won't arrive till Vespers.'

'Fifty?' said Sir Walter in disappointment.

'Did I say fifty? I intended one hundred and fifty.'

'Aha! Possibly sufficient.'

'Until then, I regret that my companions and I are too tired for reasonable discourse. Have you places where we may retire to rest and refresh ourselves?'

'For you, sir, and your consort,' said the castellan, indicating Laurence and Berna, 'the chambers royal, on the first floor, where the lion rampant is portrayed. And for you, my lord Norfolk, and your consort' —he turned to Will and Madlen— 'the chamber rose, on the second floor. You'll see the flowers. My lord archbishop in the chaplain royal's chamber. As for your servants— Where are your servants?'

'We outpaced them,' said Thomas. 'I only pray they've not been captured.'

Berna regarded Madlen, and appeared to be on the verge of demanding some service, but Laurence seized his bride by the wrist and drew her towards the door.

'Consider yourself at liberty for the present, until I should summon you,' called Berna to Madlen over her shoulder. The newly married pair disappeared into the castle. Thomas went to recall them, to remind them of the necessity to prepare a marriage contract in advance.

THERE WEREN'T NO grooms, and Will saw to it that the horses were put in stalls and watered and hayed. Madlen took a bundle of her horse and she and Will went into the castle and through a hall scattered with deerhides and horns, sheets of calfskin thick with writing pinned to the horn-tips, and as they walked they must heed their feet, that they ne overturn no cans of ink with feathers pitched in them, all but the ink was dry. Along one wall was a great heap of shields, swords, spears, axes and helms, all broken and blunted and rusted, driven together hab-nab like leaves in a yard. Another wall was hung with calfskins stuck together to make much sheets, inked on with the likenesses of gins throwing bolts at castles, or shooting fire, or snapping ships atwain, each strike against the foe drawing a cloud of pigeons to swoop on the eyes of the fallen. The hall stank of stale bread and ale and other fouler, slower-rotting things.

On the far side of the hall they found the bottom of a stairway that clamb to a long dark narrow way with doors leading of it.

The doors stood open, and as they went by they looked inside. Some rooms were bare. Others were stopped with gear, the dear, the badly made and the broken all minged together any old how; here a heap of gitterns without strings, there folded horse-cloths laid one upon the other, with a set of horse-helmets on top, the eye-holes empty like skulls. There were reed baskets filled with clapperless hand-bells and dented horns, headless stone likenesses of men and women on their backs on the cold floor, a maypole corven into firewood, a table stacked with pewter plates, a score in each stack, and on one plate, a chewed old sheep bone busy with flies.

At the end of the narrow way was a shut door that bore the likeness of a gold lion on the wall above it, stood on its hind legs, its mouth open and its great red tongue wagged out. Another stairway led further up. Will and Madlen clamb the stair and came to a doorway framed by the likenesses of red roses, with their green stems, leaves and thorns.

They went into the room and Will shut the door behind them. There was a bed like to the king-mother's bed in Edington, with a ragged old cover that had once been dear, sewn with the likenesses of babies with bows and arrows and naked maids stood with their hands hiding their tits and cunts. The room smelled of dust and gillyflowers.

Madlen went to the bed and stood with her neb to Will. Will took her head between his hands and kissed her till their chests hove and their limbs shook. Will thud the floor with his foot, broke his mouth of hers, took the hem of her gown and lifted it of her head. They fumbled with their own and each other's clothes, shivering like to they sicked, until they were naked and held each other's hard pintles in their fists and kissed again, Will with his free hand gripping the back of Madlen's neck. Will came first, on Madlen's hand, and she licked it clean while Will looked on her with bared teeth, then shoff her on the bed on her back and took her pintle in his mouth and sucked it and tongued the knob till her seed gushed into his mouth and he swallowed it and looked at her and laughed.

Madlen lay quaking, breathing hard. 'Who learned you that?' she said.

'None. It seemed right.'

Madlen sat up and leapt to him on the bed on her knees. She found his whip-wounds, and cursed Softly, and hunted about till she found a flask of foggy green glass with a greasy sweet-smelling oil inside. She smeared it on Will's wems. When she was done she took his limp pintle in her hand, kissed it, dight it between her lips, ran her tongue around it, let it fall long enough to say 'I'd know the smack of yours,' and took it in her mouth again.

'FEOFFEE,' SAID THOMAS, his pen suspended over the line he wrote. 'It signifies one who benefits of a fief.'

'"With all appurtenances and easements",' chanted Sir Walter of the rear of the chamber, where he endeavoured to cut open wine bottles with a sword.

'But what of the dower?' said Laurence.

'The dower only matters if the decedent leaves an heir. This instrument supersedes the dower. "Sans",' muttered Thomas, '"encumbrances".' A pigeon settled on his shoulder and Berna shooed it away.

ON A WOODEN stand in the rose room stood a bowl of green ore with a hole in the bottom that led by a pipe to a hole in the floor. Over the bowl hung another pipe in the shape of a firedrake's head of whose open mouth trickled a steady stream of clear water, like wine of a tap in a barrel.

'How may it run?' said Will. He drank of the water. 'It's sweet and cold. How may it run up so high?'

Madlen ne answered. She stood and looked at a moth-eaten cloth hung on the wall that bore the likeness of two high-born young men. One showed, with his hands, a rose bush, while the other kneeled beside it. To one side stood a smaller figure, a maid with wings in a red gown, drawing a bow nocked with an on-blaze arrow.

'It's you,' said Madlen. 'How might they know so long ago when this was made that you would go about in a red gown with wings, and fire an on-blaze arrow?'

Will splashed water on her bare skin and she ran to the bowl and fetched water to cast at him. They ran around the room and laughed till they were wet and out of breath. They went to stand at the small window, barely bigger than a head, that overlooked the fields of the vale of Stour. The sun shone in at the window and lit Madlen's neb, and Will stood tight behind her, left arm across her chest, his right hand on her pintle and her bollocks, his pintle tucked in the cleft of her arse.

'Would you see Hab again?' said Madlen.

'Only were Madlen there too.'

'That can't be.'

'Then let him bide wherever he be, if it's not too hard for you.'

'Are you afeared to die?' said Madlen.

'No,' said Will.

'I will be,' said Madlen. 'I will be afeared to die, do I live. But I'm not afeared now, in this room, with you.'

'I too.'

'When we were small, before they bishoped us, they said were we good we'd go of this world to the next when we die.'

'Yeah.'

'But it's like to there's another world, of us here in this room. It were lighter to die than to go of being with you, and you alone, in this stead, to that world of other folk where we used to live till a handwhile ago.'

'I've had more bliss in a stound with you than I've known my whole life. Ne shadow it with your thoughts of going down the stairs again.' He wiped a tear of her cheek and led her to a lesser room that led of the much one, where rich clothes lay in chests. They too were moth-eaten and smelled of damp winters but must have been right dear when they were new.

'Choose me some clothes,' said Will. Madlen chose him breech and a coat of deerhide dyed black, and a belt of soft red cloth, and red boots once fit for a lord.

'Now you're ready to hunt with the king,' said Madlen.

'I wouldn't go without you.'

'You'll bring me a fresh haunch of deer meat. Now you choose for me.'

Will clothed Madlen in a gown blue like to the sky, hemmed with black and gold and sewn with black and gold bees the muchness of pennies. Will asked how it liked her, and Madlen said it wasn't for her, but for him, and Will said she looked so fair he wished she could see herself. Then they found at the back of the room a looking glass three foot long with enough glass unbroken that they might see themselves together. They stood a while to stare in wonder at these two, who looked so like the high-born

319

folk who came to bide with Sir Guy at the manor house in Outen Green. Afterwards they took off the clothes and shifted them so each wore the other's. They wore many other clothes, some women's, some men's, and stinted their play to kiss and feel each other, until Madlen wearied of the game and stripped naked again, and bade Will do likewise.

'These clothes are of the world below,' she said. 'Let's swive again. Fuck me, loveman. Fuck me as you fucked Ness Muchbrook.'

'I mayn't, for you haven't no cunt. But I may fuck you as the king's father once fucked the king-mother.'

'I wish you did.'

'They told me if I breathed a word of what happened in the queen's teld I'd be killed, but I ne care.' Will lifted Madlen and lay her neb down on the bed and bade her raise her arse in the air. He pitched his finger slowly in her arsehole. 'Would I be the first?' he said.

Madlen laughed. 'I met some stern kindly men at Melksham pig-fair last year who learned me things.' She rolled over on her back and lifted her legs. 'That this is better, for one,' she said.

'The hole's small, and the pintle's thick,' said Will. 'The queen had a pot of sweet grease to slicken it.'

'I'll be still while you pitch it in,' said Madlen. 'I'll hold my breath.' Will pitched his pintle in and got deep, and Madlen gasped, but it was tight and dry, like a wet cotter-pin in a cold pinhole, so Will dripped some of the green flask oil on his pintle, and put it in again, and it went slicker. He took Madlen's hip-bones in his hands and drew her onto him and away and on again while she wielded her own pintle and bade him not to spare her.

When they were done and still, and the sounds that came of their throats ne rang in their ears no more, Madlen said: 'The bourne wasn't never so deep as we go now.'

'We go to the sea,' said Will.

'I never saw the sea neither,' said Madlen. 'I dreamed I were in it, free to dive as deep as it liked me, and to rise again to the light, endless.'

'With me?'

'Yeah.'

'This isn't no dream.'

'No.'

'They'll seek us soon.'

'Oh,' said Madlen. 'Let's play with their clothes once more, and find some fair things to hight my hair.' She took of her bundle the wedding gown Will had redeemed of Cockle and dight it over her head.

BERNA TOOK A towel of the pile close to the bed and pressed it between her legs. Holding it there she got up and went to the basin through which pure water flowed. She laved herself, then rinsed the towel, frotting the fabric against the metal of the basin to remove the blood. Unsure where to put it, she placed it flat on a ledge in the privy.

Laurence coughed and she went to kneel on the bed next to him. He lay naked and uncovered, still resplendent with the perspiration of their coupling, his eyes closed.

'My lord,' she said.

Laurence opened his eyes and regarded her.

'I shan't always call you my lord,' said Berna. 'I desired to test it in my mouth.'

'How was it?' said Laurence. His voice was guttural.

'I prefer Laurence,' said Berna.

'I meant . . . I ne intended to be so ferocious,' said Laurence. 'My injury is incurable, but not serious.'

Laurence examined the cover of the bed, blinking, and passed his hand over his eyes. 'Have you soiled it grievously? I suppose it not impossible some corpus royal may eventually touch this linen.' He coughed again and let himself fall back on the bed. 'We're guests.'

'If that is your principal anxiety, I may call Madlen to clean it.'

'Would you?' said Laurence. 'In a few moments. I've a dolorous head. What a pleasant manner to fatigue oneself. And you have fatigued me. Would you bring me some water?'

'Was it so fatiguing?' said Berna, searching for a cup. 'I found it a brief pleasure.' She discovered a maselin adorned with an ursine motif and filled it with water. 'I was surprised by the violence of your initial approach, but you tempered your savagery, and I commenced to enjoy it, and suddenly I found you'd completed your labours.'

Laurence drained the cup and demanded more. 'My desire compelled me,' he said. 'Consider that I've pursued you since April.'

'An interrupted pursuit,' said Berna.

'The interruption only increased my desire.'

'And now the pursuit is over.'

'Gloriously so! And life proper commences.'

'Tell me,' said Bernadine, pulling on her tunic, 'when you arrive at the end of a chase, and your quarry lies sanguine at your feet, do you proclaim to the beast that thence commences the proper life?'

'Berna, Berna!' said Laurence, and sat up. The effort caused a fit of coughing. He recovered and continued: 'Your comparison is unreasonable, even for you. The erasure of virginity isn't death, or the death of love. It's a stage.'

'You never see,' said Berna calmly. 'I never desired to be the conclusion of no pursuit. Can't you imagine a life in common where we jointly pursue a joy that rests just beyond our power to apprehend?'

'That sounds more ecclesiastic than familial, my angel.'

'You're impossible.'

'You're a stranger to reason.' Laurence gazed at her, but appeared to have difficulty maintaining the fixity of his vision, compressing his dry red eyes as if attempting to draw out their natural moistening humours.

Berna got up and put on a plain brown gown of one of the royal closets. 'I'll call Madlen,' she said, and went out.

BERNA DISCOVERED THE rose chamber. The door was closed. She listened for a moment, and pushed the door. It opened silently, revealing the entire chamber to her view.

Two figures stood with their backs to her, partly illuminated by an elongated diamond of fierce sunlight of the window that traversed their forms and created its own secondary light of the reflection of their garments. On its way to its target the solar ray acquired solidity, like a transparent vessel imprisoning, gilding and setting in motion an infinite number of grains of dust to turn in space.

They were a young man and a young woman, who were evidently, by their clothes and by the tranquillity and affection expressed in their posture, of gentle birth. He, broad and powerful, with dishevelled blond hair, wore an old-fashioned red tunic and embroidered white belt and parti-coloured hose of black and white. She wore a marriage gown identical to Berna's, and her hair, dark, long and undulating, was semblable, though her figure was more meagre.

Each had one hand around the other's waist. They appeared to regard their reflection in a mirror in the closet, but from where she stood Berna might not perceive the reflected image of their faces.

The couple turned to each other with simple grace, and with a movement that was at once eager and restrained, they kissed.

They turned towards Berna with amicable surprise. Their beauty, as two people and ensemble, and the sincerity of their affection, was irresistible, and Berna smiled.

In a moment, her smile perished. The gentle lovers of high estate and noble countenance who regarded her with such frankness did so in complete coincidence with the forms of Will Quate, the former bondman who used to dung her father's fields, and Madlen, the felon sister of the village pigboy. None might simply judge whether the stolen gown lent its splendour to Madlen, or the reverse.

Bernadine's eyes narrowed and her nostrils flared. She charged at Madlen and pushed her with such force that Madlen tumbled over. Will, taken by surprise, ne knew whether to assist his amour or to restrain Bernadine, and while he hesitated, Berna hurt his face furiously with the back of her hand.

Madlen rose, and man and maid regarded Berna. They were peaceful and curious and silent, as if at a marvel, while she defied them, respiring profoundly, her teeth bared, her muscles tensed.

'You've been permitted the most outrageously excessive liberties,' she said, 'but this charade of gentle matrimony in stolen garments is a violation too extreme for heaven to endure.' Her mouth trembled, and she departed.

'I barely understood one word,' said Will when she was gone. 'Why wrathed she?'

'I ne understood neither,' said Madlen. 'Maybe her new husband fell short in the swive.'

HAVING PROBED THE castellan for information on the fate of the castle's other inhabitants, without success, I was content to be interrupted by Berna, her face, as usual, disturbed by emotion. Her presence balances our company: it is beneficial to have one less fatalistic than the archers and less inclined than me to repress personal anxieties. All we have sustained should not be received in passive silence, and if I, the miserable substitute for an actual cleric, do not articulate our reactions, we can depend on the dissatisfied Berna to voice our sense of affliction.

I remembered I had advised her and her spouse to indulge in sexual congress to validate their spousal contract, and it occurred to me that some related calamity had occurred: Laurence was impotent, or incompetent in the act, or Berna's hymen impenetrable, or the sanguinary aspect of the transvirginal moment had perturbed her. Or the pestilential circumstances had detracted from the felicity of their nuptials. Certainly my injunction to urgently consummate the marriage was artificial – had they simply declared publicly that they desired each other as man and wife in the present rather than in the future tense, any canon lawyer would accept their marriage as instantly formed. It was a minor deception on my part, and justified. These are amorous young people, naturally possessed by carnal desires, and to legitimise them was no crime. On the contrary, it was necessary. The tension between them required resolution, were they not to suffer permanent alienation.

'THOMAS,' SAID BERNA, sitting on the rim of a cartwheel opposite the proctor, who had made himself comfortable in the upturned fragment of a ruined arch, 'I have a troubling matter to recount. I'm obliged to tell you that the archer Will Quate and my maid-servant Madlen practise deceit on us.'

Thomas exhaled. 'You're not obliged to tell me anything,' he said. 'Especially on your marriage day.'

Berna was trembling. Her colour was high and her respiration rapid. 'You are my confidant,' she said.

'The usual course is for the marital bed to acquire the lease on your confidences, for a year or two at a minimum,' said Thomas. 'Surely this is not the moment to concern yourself with the faults of a servant?'

A tear appeared on Berna's cheek. She wiped it away and sniffed. She regarded Thomas with great seriousness. 'The priests say that violations of the divine order are connected to the appearance of this pestilence,' she said. 'How may I be silent when I observe such very violations, now that the pest has arrived in England?'

Thomas narrowed his eyes. 'Well, offer your complaint against these people. What are the facts of their deceit?'

'They deceive us that they are noble,' said Berna.

'I ne comprehend you,' said Thomas. 'You refer to Will and Madlen? In what manner have they represented themselves as noble?'

'You haven't noticed?'

Thomas caressed his chin. 'Were this a court of law,' he said gently, 'it were at this point the case might be dismissed for default of evidence.'

'Is it or is it not part of the divine order that the quest romantic is the preserve of the gentle-born? Consider: since my departure from Outen Green, those two have mocked, imitated and attempted to surpass my every noble lover's action, in my escape from the manor, in my journey to my paramour, in my appearance in the pageant, in my escape from captivity, in mutual sacrifice between lovers. Did they attempt to dissuade the castellan of his delusion that they were a baron and his consort? No. While Laurence and I enjoyed the initiation of our marriage, they were upstairs, imitating us, abling themselves in rich garments they discovered in those fine chambers. I came across them playing out the roles of earl and countess as if they, too, had just been married. A bondman and a thrall! Will you not agree that this presumptuousness is an affront to order, and a danger to all?'

'I ne judge it such terrible damage,' said Thomas apologetically. 'If they can find refuge from this calamity for a little space of play, I ne see no offence. Nor do I comprehend how it injures you, or how at this moment of fulfilment of your desire for Laurence, in the midst of an epidemic, your interest can be diverted to something so trifling. Unless your sentiments towards your spouse have changed. Surely that is not the case?'

Berna regarded the circle of sky above their heads, surrounded by the castle battlements.

'This place has such a melancholy savour,' she said. 'Why does the castellan preserve this refuse? It's all either useless or unused. And why do the pigeons not move to some more beauteous place? Surely the open sky invites them.'

'Most creatures prefer the comfort of the familiar,' said Thomas.

Berna turned her head downwards, clasped her hands and respired deeply. 'I ne love Laurence Haket,' she said.

'Incredible that such an extreme transformation in your sensibility could take place so rapidly.'

'It is not so rapid,' said Berna. 'It has been plain to me for some time that he is a junior form of the fiancé I took such pains to evade. But it were simpler for me to take comfort in the pretence Laurence and I were habitueés of a poet's romance did I not have the love of these two commoners to set against it. It were a story I might have cherished for some years, don't you think – my two escapes, my pageantry, my ravishment – in fine compensation for my loveless marriage, were it not that I'm outdone by my inferiors, grander than me in my own clothes, more noble than the nobles?'

'If they are noble, they are unconscious of it,' said Thomas. 'Nothing could be more noble than your sense that there is a nobility in them of which you and Laurence fall short.'

'You are generous to me. I have tried to simulate credence in the idea that people such as Will and Madlen might not, by birth, approach my stature, but I have failed. I wish I were more blind. I wish I ne resented them.'

'You are severe to yourself, and them. It appears to me that you and Will and Madlen are entirely dissimilar to each other except in your desire to put distance between yourselves and your native soil. Now attend.' Thomas frowned, wrinkled his nose and frot his face with his hands. 'I advise you to cease these statements of distaste for your situation.'

'Even privily, to you?'

'You may damage yourself in a fashion you appear not to have anticipated. It's marvellous how you're so attentive to relations with Laurence that you ne remember what occurs in the world. Can't you imagine the effect on your conscience were Laurence to sicken now, after you'd openly declared you ne love him?'

Berna fell silent, the colour disappeared from her face, and her eyes seemed to cease to see. She jumped up and ran into the castle.

Sir Walter's voice came of the high tower, proclaiming the arrivage of the carts.

THREE CARTS CAME to Mere Castle of the west and drove into the yard. One was Softly's old cart that he got in France. Cess drove it. She had a black eye of a beating Softly gave her that she durst come to see Longfreke die without Softly's leave. The other two carts were driven by Wiltshire men Softly had found. They were called Fallwell and Miredrum. They'd shown him they knew how to use a bow, Softly said, and he'd sworn them into the score all but they weren't Gloucestershire born.

Softly rode a long fair horse with a gleaming black hide, dearly dight with gear of oxhide and brass, and he wore a new red coat and new blue shoon. Holiday had a new horse too, a handy brown mare with a white star on her forehead, but he ne rode it. He lay on his elbow in the back of the old cart, for he'd drunk spoiled ale, he said, and must rest out of the sun a while.

Will came of the castle in his bowman's clothes to greet Softly. Sir Walter hopped about the carts, rubbed his hands, laughed and egged them to make fast to load up the king's goods, for the foe was near the gates. Softly was quick to understand the old man's madness, and bade Will and his new hirelings scour the castle for whatever was best to take, and load it up, only leaving the rooms where Laurence and the lady Berna would spend the night.

'Where's the captain?' said Softly.

'In the lion room,' said Will. 'He's sick.'

'Well, get to work.'

'You ne saw Mad and Sweetmouth on the road?'

'Had I seen them I'd have dragged them here on ropes. Fiend fetch them, they're weak men. This isn't no time to be held back, son. This whole land's opening up for the heal and nimble to take what it likes them to. Over there, that length of walnut: throw it in the cart. That's sixty-pence worth, and we wouldn't have the foe get his thieving hands on it.'

INFORMED OF LAURENCE'S condition, I went to see him. At the entrance to his apartment I was intercepted by Madlen, acting as custodian, who reported that neither Laurence nor Berna would be disturbed. I was impressed by how confidently Madlen made this statement. Berna had complained to me of Madlen's presumptuous competition in romance, but here was a different power. Had Madlen increased in authority with the propagation of the plague? In this pestilential period, aristocratic status is conferred on the plebs by the singular virtue of their survival when their superiors succumb. In a mobile community such as ours, the serf may become commander in the absence of those above him; ultimately the slave girl, if she remains when all others disappear, must be queen under God. And if she should have a rival — one, like Bernadine, more superficially suited to the exercise of power — were it not possible that the former slave would triumph, as one more accustomed to adversity? And were experience of adversity to be the rule that determined who flourished in the post-pestilential dispensation, was there not a third woman among us, yet to be permitted a voice by he who subjugated her, capable of exceeding them all?

Oh, Bernadine! I would never have described the possibility of Laurence being infected did I think it had already occurred. A few hours prior, when they exchanged their promises, he had seemed luminously vital. And if we observed a particular ardour in him, was that not natural in one fervent to possess Bernadine corporeally? And now, in my negligence, I had compounded the misery of her situation. If without my intervention she would have secretly accused herself of desiring his destruction, now I had fashioned the accusation into a damning public one, as if God, so deaf to all pleas for clemency in the face of the pest, would instantly open his ears to a plea for malice.

I revened to the central area of the castle, where Will, Softly and the new complement of archers, two individuals of desperate appearance, were adding spoils to their carts. I'd intended to collect items removed from my horse when it was stabled, and retire to my apartment, but as I passed Softly's original cart, I heard Holiday cough and call my name.

He reclined on his elbow at the rear of the cart, on a blanket, with a container of ale in his hand. His face, humid with perspiration, had a mortal pallor, contrasting with the ruby tincture of his ocular margins. It was evident he desired to communicate.

Addressing me with an effort, he said he was not ignorant, as if I had expressed the contrary. He was literate, he claimed, and by way of evidence produced a legendary he carried on a cord round his neck. The pages, I noted, were tainted with desiccated blood. He repeated that he was not ignorant, and added that he was a veritable Christian – again, as if responding to an accusation I had made, although I had voiced no opinion on his piety.

'WHO'S HAYNE TO tell us where and when we list our lives before a priest?' said Holiday. 'Softly and I will have a great shrift next year in Bristol, when we come of France again and are ready, and have the silver. We'll hire St Augustine's for it. A thousand candles will be lit and the abbot will be our shriftfather. You can hire him and the church together for twenty pound a day, and they throw in a heap of singers, and enough reekles to choke a coalman. It'll be bare winly. You have to make a wonder if you'd have God heed you. And afterwards we'll bake twelve sheep for poor folk, one for each of Jesus's men, and open five barrels of wine, one for each of the Deemer's wounds.'

'You would that the world know how free you are in your humbleness.'

'We shan't go down in no beshitten outcome barn, or tell our sins to no Scottish proctor who thinks him he's Tom Aquinas. Yeah, grin if it likes you, you wouldn't have me know the names of great doctors. You take me and Softly for green uplandish gnofs who ne know how to read nothing. That we be fools to think us we may go to France and ne fall sick of this qualm, this pest. I'll tell you something you ne know. When Hayne bade us go to Calais with him, we already knew the pest. We knew it in Bristol.'

'Knew it?'

'Cess sickened of it. There was a French ship bore wine to Bristol and Cess thought she'd creep aboard and go back to her own land. But Softly found her and took her home again. And she sickened, for those French seafarers were lousy with it. Great much botches in her armpits like to Hornstrake had, skin hot as a foundry. And she got well, thanks to Softly, who cared for her till she was heal. And I too, a little, for we all shared one house.'

'And Hayne ne knew this.'

'We ne told no one. Hayne was like you. He took us for fools, always did. He weened that in our pride we staked all our endlessnesses on a throw. He deemed himself nimble, but we japed him. We made out we were so bold in our hopes that we'd got some pest-ridden woollens of a French ship, and would take them along with us, that the stakes be yet higher.'

Thomas put his head in his hands and wrothe his cheer in riddle.

At the other end of the cart Cess had clamb down and washed clothes.

'Do you say,' said Thomas, 'that Hayne was ready to have the whole score sicken and die of the pest, of these woollens if not otherwise, to make you, Softly, Dickle and Hornstrake die a bad death on the road?'

'To him we're all guilty. I, Softly, Sweetmouth, Longfreke. Will Quate. The captain and his burd. You. All who've yoked themselves to this score of bowmen. I ne say Hayne hadn't no wit at all. He was nimble to get you, for you're no use to help a dying man get to heaven, but you've got the sleight of ask to wring the shame of his deeds out of him for all the living to hear. What Hayne ne understood was that I and Softly ne feared the pest. We ne feared the woollens, for there wasn't no pest in them. Softly got them last year in the thieves' riot in Bristol. They're clean. We ne feared the pest in England, for we've no Jews. And we ne feared the pest in France, for we'd lived three weeks in a house with a pest-sick French harlot who got it of a French ship, we breathed the same air, and we ne sickened.'

The mirth of minding how they'd swiked Hayne stirred Holiday, but he wearied, the flesh of his neb fell, and he was racked by coughing. He reached up and dight a cloth to shield the back of the cart from anyone looking in.

'You ne seem well,' said Thomas.

'Look,' said Holiday. 'Come nearer.' He drank a mouthful of ale, which wasn't no light swallow for him, and opened his shirt, baring his chest. His flesh was blackened, like to he'd been beaten from within.

'Do you know it?' said Holiday.

'God's tokens,' said Thomas. 'They spoke of it in Heytesbury. Not all who sicken of the pest have them.'

'And those that do? Tell me the truth.'

'It ne bodes well.'

'Would you hear why I have this?'

Thomas looked at his feet and ne answered.

Holiday lowered his speech to a whisper. 'It's her, the French whore. She's one of the Fiend's folk. A devil's made a nest in her cunt and Softly's bewitched. Hers wasn't the first maidenhood he reft but it was the first maid he took away with him. That devil had him by the pintle, and he mightn't let her go. She even made him seek to wed her, then turned him down to madden him more, and still he keeps her. She sent the devil into the goat that killed Dickle, and made Longfreke and Hornstrake and the captain and me sicken. It's she, all she.'

THE APARTMENT ROYAL was extensive, consisting of a bedchamber and privy, several closets, two separate chambers for servants, and a private dining room. Berna, attempting to avoid the assistance of Madlen, found the presence of what Thomas called 'plumbing' to be of inestimable assistance. By ingenious artifice water ran continuously of a spigot. The water was cool, fresh and clear and served as well to drink as to lave with. Berna pressed wet cloths to Laurence's forehead to ease his fever and responded to his constant complaint of thirst. He passed of lucidity to raving and to clarity again. In the most terrible moments of fever he demanded a male servant be summoned to assist him to the privy. He called for Raulyn, then said he would accept Madlen as the closest to a knave they had.

Madlen had already made attempts to visit Berna, offering to serve. Each time Berna dismissed her peevishly, but now she was obliged to accept her aid. Together the two women raised Laurence's trembling body of the humid linen and together they discovered indisputable signs of the pest between his legs.

Laurence slept. Berna sat on a chair by the bedside and caressed his face. 'I ne expect you to remain in these chambers,' said Berna to Madlen. 'It would be unjust for you to be infected. Go to your Will for now, lest the qualm spread to you.'

'We wrathed you, lady,' said Madlen. 'You saw us in the rose room. We ne understood what you said but maybe it ne liked you to see me in the gown I stole of you and Will got up like a high-born.'

'It ne liked me to see you look so well in clothes you have no right to wear,' said Berna. 'It ne liked me to see you do so well in deeds I never bode on you to do. You and your loveman went to each other without no doubt, when in the hours of my marriage to a heal and handy young man doubt was all I had. Now he's punished, and I'm punished by losing him.'

'I ne understand the meaning of "doubt" or "punished", like half the words you use,' said Madlen. 'It ne helps you nor him to talk about yourselves to me like I was your friend. I'm but your hire, and I'll do right by you as best I can.'

'How can you speak so?' said Berna. 'This very day I saw you and your love so sweet and joyous and stately together, and now it's as if you desire to deny these attributes and the emotions we have in common, and the perils we face.'

'Too many French words again for me,' said Madlen. 'You turn to me to say what's on your heart for that you haven't no other near to hand more like yourself. As for Will and I, we are as we be, not as we're seen to be by some other.'

'I wish it were I who sickened.'

'And I wish I might drink and hop at my own burial,' said Madlen. 'You may better help your husband do you hold his hand

and speak to him. I'll do the leave. If we're to fare tomorrow we owe to be ready.'

IN THE EVENING Thomas came to the chamber. Laurence's fever had decreased and he lay supported on cushions with his eyes large and staring like a bird's, his hair pointed and dishevelled with perspiration. Berna sat on a chair beside him while Madlen passed in and out. There wasn't no bread in the castle nor fresh food, but Madlen had found nuts, bacon, hard cheese, apples and wine.

Laurence affirmed he was capable of riding, and Thomas recommended that next day the party attempt to reach the infirmary at Cerne Abbey. It was a long journey, but the infirmary was excellent, the air and water pure, and Thomas was personally acquainted with the abbot. Once Laurence had recovered, they might travel on to Melcombe at leisure.

'There's no leisure,' said Laurence. 'Our ship departs finally on Thursday morning. I consent to ride to Cerne tomorrow, but do my condition ne improve, my spouse must fare on alone.'

'I refuse,' said Berna.

'You'll change your mind,' said Laurence. He turned to Thomas. 'How do you estimate the new archers?' he demanded.

'Unreliable,' said Thomas. 'Holiday won't survive long. Softly is attentive to the castellan's instructions to charge the carts. He pursues his second profession here, as if already in France. He perceives the plague as an opportunity for enrichment.'

'Half the archers at Crécy were criminals in quest of a pardon,' said Laurence. 'We may have over-encouraged their tendencies.'

Thomas regarded Berna, and Laurence turned to her.

'You consider me as if I were an additional problem,' said Berna.

'I'm strong enough to mount a horse, but too feeble to fight,' said Laurence. 'And you mayn't defend her.'

'You'll recover in my care,' said Berna. 'You'll rest at Cerne and we'll find a different ship.'

'I haven't no money for no second ship,' said Laurence.

'There appear to be two choices,' said Thomas. 'One, the course of personal security for yourself and your young spouse: to abandon the archers, ride with the greatest rapidity to Cerne, hope for treatment from the monks, and attempt to catch the ship before it sails. Two, the course that reflects the promises you made to your commanders, to deliver archers to them, and the promise to the archers themselves, to ferry them across the sea: travel with them to Melcombe via Cerne, but less rapidly.'

'For Berna's sake, the first,' said Laurence. 'It's not my fault the pest arrived in England. I mayn't be blamed that the score I ordered has ceased to exist.'

'As I indicated, there appear to be two choices,' said Thomas. 'Unfortunately this is an illusion. For you, there are no choices, only preferences. Although you are the captain, and the most senior here, the choice falls to another. We pray and contest against the malady that affects you, but we owe not to delude ourselves that even if we attain Cerne tomorrow night your recovery is certain. If you insist your spouse travel on to France, she must be accompanied; she owes not to be no solitary voyager. Madlen ne suffices. Bernadine must have one with her who's both honest and capable of defending her. There's only one such in our party.'

'Well, let's take Quate,' said Laurence. 'That's the reason I bought him a horse.'

'He's promised to the archers,' said Thomas. 'He also made promises to Longfreke regarding the prisoner.'

'Wasn't it to Hayne he promised loyalty? And Hayne has gone. I'll tell Quate he's finished with archery for now.'

'Have you the power to enforce such a command?'

'He's decent enough to know his place.'

'There are only two places now, sick and heal,' said Thomas.

Laurence pushed himself up in the bed. He regarded Thomas defiantly, then sensed the air on his white chest and clutched the ouverture of his shirt to close it. 'Place isn't simply a matter of degree, to be erased by pestilence,' he said. 'It's a matter of the particular terrain that unites persons superior and inferior in a sense familial. Will Quate is the lady's father's man. There are obligations of loyalty between peasants and their patron that urbane clerks such as you fail to comprehend.'

THEY SENT MADLEN to get Will. Madlen found him in the darkening yard, lit by hornlights glimmering under the cerecloth telds of the carts. He was hungry and weary of the load of goods. There wasn't room in the carts for a hundredth deal of the castle gleanings, and each time a cart was full, Softly would find another thing he worthed more dearly, and bade Will and the new hires unload and stow again of the beginning. To make it worse, Sir Walter hopped about, found keys to rooms he'd forgotten, showed Softly new gear to take, like a thief's knave, and chid them for working too slow.

Softly gave Will leave to see the captain, bidding him not to dally, and he followed Madlen into the castle. On the stairs she took his elbow and would keep him.

'Let's go,' she said. 'Let's take our horses and go.'

'Where?'

'Anywhere. God drives folk of the world that he might have free hold of it again. We'll find a town where all have left or died and bide there together until he comes for us. Hayne went, and your friends Sweetmouth and Mad had the wit to go. We're bound to sicken soon and I'd spend my last days with you and not work for these gnofs no more.'

'I'm a sworn bowman. I must go on.'

'You told me you'd be a free man.'

'I am free, and I freely choose to be a bowman, as you freely choose to work for the lady Bernadine.'

'I ne chose her. I'm her maid only to better follow you. But now we may be truly free.'

'I shan't break no oath,' said Will.

Madlen shoff him in the chest. 'You think you they're so true? They're up there now reading how to swike Softly and run to France without him. They only need you for your strength, to shield the lady on the fare when her lord gives up the ghost. They think them you must choose their way or Softly's. They ne ween we have another road without them.'

Will shook his head and went on up the stair. 'I shan't break my oath,' he said again. Madlen stood and looked forlornly after him, then ran behind.

Before Laurence, Bernadine and Thomas, Will kept to his word. He ne need be no archer, said Laurence. Go speedily with them, and he might be the Hakets' reeve and bailiff in the new manor, and Madlen their housekeeper.

'I shan't break my oath to the score, sir,' said Will.

'An oath to a body of men led by Hayne and Longfreke loses its weight when another becomes the head,' said Thomas. 'More so when that new leader is as other as Softly. He leads you into guilt. He drives you to steal.'

'I do as I'm bidden,' said Will. 'Longfreke held all of us steeped in guilt already for the take of Cess. They as did it, and they as let it be done. It seemed to me you thought so too.'

Thomas opened his mouth to speak, then shut it.

'I swore a second oath to Longfreke,' said Will, 'to help Cess go to her own folk again.'

They mightn't lead him to another way of thinking, and in the end they read that they must go to Cerne together next day, to reach the abbey before dark.

SOON AFTER SUNRISE they left the castle. They thanked the castellan and told him they would strike the French a blow from behind, by going over the sea to France, which was true, in a way.

The castellan clapped his hands and said it liked him. He gave the lady Bernadine a white dove in a wicker basket and a bag of corn and said she should let it go when they reached Calais so it would fly home and he would know England was won of the foe. A little water and a small handful of corn a day, he said, no more, or it would grow too fat to fly. When they went through the castle gate, the castellan wouldn't leave the yard, still heaped with his broken old things, and in the bright light of day outside the castle walls, they couldn't see, looking back into the shade within, if there were anybody there.

They came into Dorset and fared through the long hot morning by the Stour vale meads in a cloud of dust kicked up by their cartwheels and horses' hooves. The dust made it seem to those they met that they were more and higher than they were, and they were shunned, as if they brought new hardships to folk who already had more than they could bear. They saw friars stooped over one of their own who'd fallen by the roadside, a whole town on the run with its geese and pigs and children — but to what haven? — and the sights that tokened the old life: reapers in the cornfield, old men outside the alehouse, women hanging out washing, maids with stops of milk, a moleman with hide like oak rind skinning moles in the sunshine on a board before his house.

They weren't far inside Dorset when Bernadine saw that Laurence must be taken of his horse, for he hadn't the strength to ride. They shifted him to Fallwell's cart, where the softest goods taken of the castle were, and Bernadine sat with him there. They went on and ne stinted till noon. By then Thomas proctor had also sicked.

DEI GRATIS, MOTION has ceased. I rest. Will perceived I was afflicted, assisted me from my horse, put me under a tree out of the sun and offered me ale, which I accepted. We have travelled halfway to Cerne but I have the impression we have been moving for eternity. Dolour has penetrated my bones. Each pace of my horse creates a violent prickling sensation in my joints and muscles. My trachea is in agony. The condition I assumed had disappeared after its manifestation on Sunday has returned with terrible intensity. I cannot postpone the manual examination of the symptomatic area. I must momentarily put aside my scribal implements.

Is this legible? My hand is not stable. They are there, as I suspected: two oval protuberances on opposite sides of the groin.

It is marvellous how one's speculations on the destruction of humanity are transformed when the most familiar specimen to be destroyed is oneself. Death is universal, and yet it arrives to each individual, even in a period of terrific mortality such as this, as a sort of miracle. How might all that is this mind and memory cease? In place of imagining a universe without people, I imagine a universe without me, and it might as well be silent and void if I am not present. Let us all perish simultaneously, or not at all! In place of a fervent spiritual preparation for divine judgement and eternity, there is a terror exactly proportionate to my corporeal presence – i.e., small enough to establish my insignificance in the universal scheme, vast enough to obliterate me.

More than anything there is a desperate interest in the actions of those in my vicinity apparently unaffected by the pestilence, as if horror of infection by plague has been replaced by avarice for a quasi-infection of life. I perceived Fallwell and Miredrum as brutes, but they are healthy; I observe their movements voraciously as they attend to their horses. How I desire that the vitality they exude diffuse through the air and condense on me. Madlen and Bernadine tend Laurence. And there is Cess, under the supervision of one who violated and continues to violate her, Softly, obliged to care for her other rapist, Holiday, now dying. Cess, under so crude a malediction, apparently ignored by God, yet in secret from all except me and her abusers the most vital of any of us, the only one to have contracted the pestilence and survived. She is hope. She is the future, held captive by the dying past of Holiday and the malign present of Softly, and the rest of us do not care enough about her to save her from them.

Will persists as if indestructible, solid, beauteous, candid, with the frigidity of marble and the calor of blood, with the mysteries of his benignity and purpose. Rarely have I been in such proximity to one so unlettered and ignorant of universal matters who offers such capacity for alteration. The servile rural existence inclines towards the completion of a man when he is barely adolescent, to sate him with violence, crudity, primitive prejudice and practical agricultural doctrine and to occupy whatever remains with labour such that there is no space for intellectual discovery. After they are fourteen you may introduce them to Canterbury, Oxford, Paris, Rome, romance, power, law, but the magnificent social structures, the captivating possibilities of ideas, will be invisible to them; they will only be stupefied by magnitudes of gold and ornament. Will is different, unfinished; the nature of his ignorance is not of mental capacity already replete with hostility, acerbity and complacency before his twentieth year, but of a liberal vacancy for future occupation by the cognitive sciences — or by a more depraved form of meditation.

Our minor local authorities now contest for Will. Superficially it is his corporeal attributes they desire — Madlen his vitality, Bernadine and Laurence his resistance to the pest, Softly his strength. But from my position under the tree on the riverbank, my spirit emerging into the light from the obscuring enclosure of my carnal self, I perceive that what they most require is his capacity for transformation into a more potent and significant creature. Softly desires a companion in malifcence not, to be charitable, that he might cause more damage or even acquire more lucre, but to dilute the singularity of his culpability, to make his perversions more acceptable to himself by the certainty they are duplicated in an attractive companion. Laurence and Bernadine would exploit Will's honesty and his capabilities for the acquisition of new disciplines to induct him into the sphere of administration — as much their social inferior as presently, but equipped with letters and arithmetic, and better clothes. Madlen's intention, I suspect, is the most radical: to accept the inevitable mortality of all humanity, to transmute all Will's potency into the materials of young love — dulcet verdure, incandescent flame — and to consume it with him in the numbered hours before they, like me, succumb.

Judith, I wish it were possible for me to offer my imminent demise as an alternative to your own. My best effort at a true and final confession to you is that I came to Avignon a fugitive from my inability to love the place and family into which I was born. In attempting to recreate in France the conditions of domesticity I abandoned in Scotland, I ascribed the abandonment to the place and the family, rather than to my inability to love. I request your pardon for this. I hear your voice informing me that the pardon I require is not yours or Marc's, but another's.

I shall care for you to the end.

With all my love, Thomas Pitkerro

THEY STINTED A mile short of Sturminster, where the road went nearby Stour stream and they might fetch water for themselves and the horses. They set Thomas under the shade of a willow, where there was a break in the reeds that otherwise grew thick along the bank. He lay on his side on a horse-woollen and wrote. Cess made food for the bowmen, but Softly wasn't hungry. He went to sit in the shade of his cart with his back against a wheel and drank alone. He had a great can he drank of, and it was full, and he lifted it to his mouth, and it shook, and most of the ale spilled on his new red coat. He cursed, drained the leave and fell asleep.

There was a hot sleepy stillness in that stead, where the bees hummed in the blossoms, the horses cropped the clover, spoons tapped against the sides of bowls, and Bernadine murmured to Laurence. Madlen, in a dull blue gown Bernadine had chosen for her in the castle, went down to the river to fetch more water, and

Will went after her, saying they might find time to talk. But Madlen was wrath and ne would speak to him.

The stillness was rent by Cess, who screamed for help in Softly's cart. With her screams came a sound like to the roar of a dog, a roar of which man might know Holiday's steven, yapping that Cess was an outcome witch and owed to die.

Softly leaped up, reached into the cart, drew Holiday out with one hand and drew his bollyknife with the other. Holiday flew of the cart, struck the ground with his shoulder and lay there writhen in the shape he'd fallen, his eyes closed and his neb atwitch.

'He would kill me, were he not so weak of his sickness,' said Cess. 'He took the butcher's knife.'

Softly came to where Holiday lay.

'You overstep, my friend,' he said.

'How else might she live and I die, had she not some craft against us?' whispered Holiday, like to his steven trickled through chines in a wall. He opened his eyes, but ne beheld Softly. He coughed. His hand rose to hill his mouth but lacked the strength to go so far and his blood and spit were sprinkled in the dust. Will, Madlen and Cess beheld from the shade of the carts a few yards away. The lady Bernadine looked out of the teld of the cart she was in with Laurence, and drew her head inside again, like to the weather were foul. The new bowmen beheld all with empty cheer.

Softly bent down, gripped Holiday's shirt and lifted him to his feet.

'Stand and look me in the eye,' he said.

'I'm sick,' said Holiday.

Softly let go and took a step backward. Holiday swayed and stackered. The flesh had fallen of his bones, his cheeks were sunken and his skin was as dry and thin as last winter's leaf.

'She bewitched you,' he said. 'You owed to leave her behind like the others.'

'You won't take what's mine.'

'I wouldn't take her, but rid you of her,' said Holiday. He drew back his lips and showed what was left of his teeth. 'I mayn't stand no longer. Buy me a mass. Buy me a mass in old Augustine's, with some sweet singers and a heap of candles in my name. Make it worthy.'

'Hush,' said Softly. 'I'll heal you.' He pitched his knife deep in Holiday's belly. When it was in up to the hilt he took it with both hands and reared Holiday of the ground till the life was gone of him.

MADLEN CRIED OUT when Softly slew his friend, and she took grip of Will's arm. Will swallowed his spittle. Their nebs fallowed, yet they couldn't take their eyes of the mark that grew over Holiday's guts. Cess knit her arms fast, bent her head, turned and went quick inside the cart. Softly let the dead man fall, cleaned his blade on the grass, pitched it in his belt again and dragged Holiday to the stream, where he threw him in the brown water. He shoff him out away of the bank till he floated neb-down among the lilies.

Will had followed a few steps behind Softly, one arm half held out, like to he ne knew whether to help his leader or hold him back. He stinted short of the stream and when Softly cast Holiday's body away his mouth worked, but no words came of it, and his body twitched, but he went no nearer.

The brim of the water wasn't smooth again before a long, narrow boat came swiftly down the middle of the stream. It was white, with eyes and a prow and sides hight in the likeness of a swan, and rowed by six oarsmen in black, with white coats bearing the

tokens of an owl and an oak leaf. In the stern of the boat, in an
open coffin wrapped in clean white cloth that shone in the sun, lay
the body of a man in armour, his hands folded over his chest on
the hilt of a longsword. At his feet sat two young knaves in long
white shirts who sang sweetly in Latin. The steersman was a long
fair freke in rich gear of gold and red. As he went by, he turned
to the bowmen and called to them, ne seeing the hump of Holiday,
who'd become a new step for frogs hopping of one lilypad to
another.

'Bow your heads!' called the steersman. At the sound Berna
looked out again. 'Sir Lionel de Hammoon goes home to his people!
Sir Lionel, the hero of Crécy! Pray for his soul to find everlasting
peace in the love of our Lord Jesus Christ! Pray for him!' The
boat sped on and was soon out of sight behind the reeds at the
next bend in the stream.

WHEN THE BOAT was gone, Softly seemed to wake and turned to
Will, and to Madlen, Fallwell and Miredrum, who'd come up
otherwhiles.

'You're witnesses,' he said. 'He'd kill my Cess.'

He sat on his haunches, kneaded his eyes with his fingers and
shook his head. 'My friends aren't true,' he said in his old soft
steven. 'Why won't they follow me? Why do they begrudge me a
woman of my own?'

He rose and turned to Will. 'Would you worth me were I a
giant like Hayne?' He gripped the rood about his neck, his fist dark
around the pale flesh of Christ's legs. 'I'm stronger than any. I ne
ran, and I ne sicked. I'm true. All I ask is that you follow me and

worth me and let me keep my woman.' He grinned. His teeth shone bright in the sun. 'Thinks you Holiday's dead? He's well. He won't die so lightly.'

Softly went to the stream's brink and slipped into the water. It came up to his shoulders. He began to go, half walking, half swimming, to where Holiday floated.

'The bottom's soft,' he said. 'The Dorset streams are full of filth. I wouldn't eat no pike of no Stour.'

He came to Holiday, laid his hand on his back and shook him. He called his friend's name and bade him wake. He trundled him over on his back, pulled a lick of weed of his neb and thacked him on his cheek. Holiday's body drifted a little but otherwise ne stirred. All his middle was dark of the wound of Softly's knife.

Softly took the book of saints' lives of his friend's neck, left the body and came to the bank again. He hove himself up, then fell back, and Will helped him out onto the grass. Softly stood. He shivered and his gold teeth clacked together.

'You need a woollen,' said Will. 'You'll catch cold.'

'In manus tuas, Domine, commendo spiritum illum; redemisti illum, Domine, deus veritatis. Amen,' said Thomas, on his elbow under the willow tree.

Softly came up to him and asked what he had said.

'"I give that soul into your hands, Lord; redeem him, God of truth."'

'How fare you?' said Softly.

'I'm sick, as you.'

'I'm heal.'

'It's hot, but you shiver.'

'The water is cold.'

'Your eyes are red.'

'I weep for my friend.'

'You lacked the strength to climb of the stream without help.'

348

'I'm weary of the fare.'

'You staked all to go to France with Hayne, and you have lost. You won't see Bristol again.'

'I shall see it. God shields me. If God would hurt me, he would have sent me the pest in Bristol, when my Cessy sickened of it, but he ne sent it. If God would hinder me, he would have helped Cess when I took her two year ago, like he helped the maids in this book when the heathens would have them against their will.'

'Now you've slain your friend, you mayn't read that book no more.'

'I mind it, every word. How God broke the wheel they'd pine St Katherine on, and hid St Agnes in light that the gnofs mightn't reave her maidenhood. I ne need no book.' He bent down and took the calfskin Thomas wrote on. 'I'll burn your words,' he said. 'You're Hayne's hire and now he's gone we ne need you. You're too sick to ride and I shan't have you in my carts.'

'We owen't to leave him,' said Will.

Thomas looked fearful. 'The captain and his wife are my friends,' he said.

'They haven't no carts,' said Softly. 'You bide here and rot. You aren't no Englishman and you aren't no priest. You've no stead in this world. You're not but a lawyer's harlot.'

'I ne make myself out to be no priest,' said Thomas.

'You go about in black. You're always there when one of us is near his end. But instead of hearing all our sins, like a priest owes to, you'd only hear of one. You're a tell-tale. I ne need you. God loves me.'

'You ne slew Holiday for harming Cess. You slew him in your pride, that it be by your will he die, and not of the pest. For if you let Holiday die of pestilence, it were as much as to say you will too. And you can't bear that truth. You'd be false to yourself a little longer and believe yourself beloved of God.'

349

Softly threw himself on the proctor, who curled up with his hands hilling his head, as he'd done in Chippenham. But Will Quate took hold of Softly's shoulders and dragged him away.

Softly turned to Will, amazed, and took his knife again.

'Truly?' he said. 'Would you? Truly?'

Will bade him let Thomas alone.

'I'm sorry I must carve your fair neb open,' said Softly. And he swung his knife-arm at Will's throat. But by the time his blade reached it, the throat wasn't there, and Will's strong hands gripped him. In a stound, the foreboding that Will would be speedily hurt or slain shifted, and all could see how Softly had weakened. With that grip, Will's first, Softly was beaten, and the mastery went to Will. Softly would fight back, but he barely had the strength of a small girl. In the wink of an eye, Will laid Softly mild-heartedly down on the ground like a mother putting a fretful child to sleep.

Softly shut his eyes in shame. 'Why won't you help me?' he called to Miredrum and Fallwell. They ne heeded him.

'Thomas and him to the carts,' said Will to Miredrum and Fallwell. 'Thomas first.' Softly lay still as stone on the grass. Will took Softly's knife and cast it into the Stour. He took the rood in his hand, then turned and saw that Madlen beheld him. He set the rood back on Softly's chest.

'You may be master yet,' he said, and went to help bear Thomas to a stead in one of the carts.

THEY STOWED SOFTLY in Holiday's stead in the old cart, and Thomas in the cart Miredrum drove, so each cart bore a sick man. Will went to Cess and told her she was free. 'I shan't let Softly hurt you no more,' he said. 'If you will, you may take Softly's horse and go where it likes you. Or you may bide with us, and fare with us to France, and we'll see you on your way back to your kin.'

'A woman alone mayn't be free in this world,' said Cess.

'Will you drive the cart?' asked Will.

'Yeah.'

'And help Softly in his sickness, for now?'

'Yeah.'

'Only if it be your will.'

'Yeah.'

Cess ne gave no thanks, and her neb ne tokened no feeling of blitheness that she was free. She kept a hard stern cheer, and her gaze wouldn't meet Will's. It was like to she hated him.

They drove on. Some towns along the road had set watchmen to keep wayfarers out, and Bernadine, Will and Madlen between them had to use nimble speech to shift them. They ne hid that they had sick folk with them. Then and then, outcome townsfolk helped them. Otherwhiles they weren't trusted, or were feared, and help came grudgingly, or with some new law these folk had made, like that if a pot were used by a sick man it ne owed never to be used again, or that no wayfarer come within ten yard of any doorway. In one town they were bidden to wear blindfolds, and were led through to the other side. In another, an old man bade none of them sneeze or cough, or he'd kill and burn them, though he looked like he lacked the strength to harm a mouse, never mind a man.

In the towns where the pest was worst, folk were most reckless, and barely heeded them.

When the sun was hottest, they saw a great hill. Miredrum said it was Bulbarrow, and marked the beginning of the Dorset downs. They must follow the road up to the downs, fare a few miles west, and they would come to Cerne. They broke their journey there to rest, near a bourne that ran through a wood.

Madlen went to fetch water and Will followed. They came to a spot where the bourne ran fast. It fell of rocks, and beyond the rocks, hidden from the road, was a deep pool, golden green on top and black below. Will kissed Madlen and reached under her gown and held her pintle in his fist. They swived there quickly, like to knaves who do a small wrong they know they'll be beaten for if they're caught, which is half the mirth, then stripped and dived into the pool. They followed each other underwater, grabbing at each other's heels, and floated neb to neb, keeping in their stead with sweeps of their arms.

'You left the others,' said Madlen. 'I thought me you were leader now, and must vex yourself about carts and horses and what those other bowmen do, and look to Laurence and the Frenchwoman.'

'Softly's still leader.'

'I feared him before. Then when I saw how lightly you beat him it was you I feared.'

'What's to fear?'

'That we shan't die soon. That you're drawn to leadership and husbandry and I lessen in your life and we grow old. I mayn't be your old woman, or you my old man.'

'You look too far ahead.'

'I wouldn't look so far!' Madlen ran her fingers over Will's jaw. 'As long as the world's about to end I ne fear nothing.'

They went back to the others. Cess had made a fire and boiled water. Madlen went to Bernadine and Laurence, and Will to Thomas. Afterwards Madlen came to sit near Cess, and in a while Will came up and sat there too, but a little further away. He plucked at grass and looked at the ground like to he knew he must be there but ne knew why.

'Why do you hate my loveman Will?' said Madlen to Cess. 'It wasn't he who reft your maidenhood and stole you.'

Cess said: 'For two years I hoped God would help me from

these men who stole me. I listened to the tales Holiday read of his book of saints, of angels who helped the women martyrs. I thought me how an angel might be, fair and strong. One day one was sent like to that angel of my imagination. I guess you ne know what imagination tokens.'

'The lady Bernadine learned me,' said Madlen.

'Well. So, one day, there he was. Fair and strong. But he ne came to help me. He came to help them. To be theirs. He deemed them bold and handy. He knew what they'd done to me and my father, yet he'd be one of them. He'd be their fair face to the world.' She turned her eyes to Will. 'How can they be wicked, folk ask, when they have among them a young man so kind, so like an angel? They ne know. He who does a fair face on wickedness is wickedest of all.'

IT WAS A hard climb to the downs and a rough road west against the sun along the spine of the hills to the abbey, all but they were above the heat and dust of the lowlands. To the north they could see sprad out the way they'd come along the Stour, and south to the hills that lay between them and the sea, though the sea itself was hidden.

At the abbey the Vespers bell rang. A heap of folk stood outside and sought to go in. Some were sick, some pilgrims, and some local folk who'd buy beads or candles or holy likenesses. But the gate was shut, and the lay brothers who warded it said none might come in till morning. The lay brothers' brown kirtles could hardly be seen for the weight of tin saints' tokens they wore, that shone on them like fish scales in the half-light.

They wouldn't let the carts through, for all the lady Bernadine's asks, until she bade them come to where Thomas lay awake. Thomas told the brothers to give his name to the abbot, and after a while they came again and opened the gates, and what was left of the score came inside to the abbey yard. The sky had darkened, and the light of many candles came of the great windows of the abbey, and the sound of song.

BERNA SAT WITH Laurence in the hospital. The infirmary was full, but since the arrivage of the pestilence, many lodgings in the hospital had been vacated. It was night and the window was closed. A single candle lit the plain chamber. An iron cross with an unpainted wooden Christ was fixed to one wall. Their words rang against stone.

'You must be very uncomfortable,' said Berna. 'This mattress is no more than a double blanket on a board.'

'After a day in the cart on the road, it's paradise,' said Laurence. His head was supported by a small square cushion. His voice had changed since morning. It was both diminished and more confident. His skin was dry and colourless, his eyes enlarged, his cheekbones more prominent. Berna combed his savage hair with her fingers.

'I would prefer you maintain a certain distance,' said Laurence. 'This malady catches of people like fire.'

'It's in the air,' said Berna. 'Distance is no defence. Even if it were, you mayn't separate me now, little spouse.' She kissed his forehead.

'They'll care for me here,' said Laurence. 'My condition improves. You must go on to Melcombe tomorrow and secure passage to Calais. Once I've recovered I'll join you there.'

'I shan't leave you.'

'It's my desire and my command that you do.'

'Married a day, and you'd separate already?'

'For your security and mine. For a measure.'

'You're terribly unjust. Tell me, when you went to France last time, in Lord Berkeley's entourage, did you know one Lionel de Hammoon?'

'Hammer Hammoon!' said Laurence. 'We were of an age. A knight by birth, but he treated me equally enough. Amusing fellow. When I was fresh in the company he sent me to the gunners with a sealed pot of gunpowder. "Ensure it remains level, or it will explode, and you will be vaporised," he said. I walked to where the ordnance was. It was only a mile, but it took me an hour, I was so cautious. Trembling, I conveyed the pot to the master-gunner's hand. He took it, regarded it a moment, then removed the cover and drank half the contents. It was wine! Completely valiant, Hammer, knew no fear. Terrible swordsman, excellent taste in clothes. We charged in the same line at Crécy. He had a drum, too, he used to beat. Dancing outside the tent without no women. We were young and judged ourselves the most brilliant warriors a king ever arrayed. That morning, when we buckled up and were mounted, and the knaves ran from horse to horse polishing our armour, and we entered the mist, a train of plumes and steel, facing mortal combat, we were so vulnerable and felt so indestructible. We so desired to make each other laugh – it seemed so proper to be grave and serious. Few of us had fathered children and most of us had lost a parent or two. We were like a family of all brothers.'

'Why not speak to me before of your soldier days?'

'I desired to demonstrate I wasn't foreign to your terrain – your terrain of gentler virtues, I mean, of flowers and verse and music. For completeness of honesty, frankly, I doubted my power to play the valorous man. I regarded my comrades when they recounted their war histories to their amours, and sometimes recounted another's story as their own, and I noticed how the same stories altered according to the tellers and the audience. One esquire descrives how he decapitated an enemy, and his amour finds him marvellously courageous; another esquire recounts exactly the same story, and his amour judges him a boaster sanguinary. One knight descrives discovering the corpse of a young page who rode into battle on his master's mount, and his amour is touched by how this cruel vision must have made the knight suffer; the same knight tells the same story to a second lady, and she's disgusted he should have been party to such carnage.'

Berna draped her arm over Laurence and laid her head on his chest. 'I needn't know each joint of your battle stories,' she said. 'You must have been awfully valorous at Crécy for them to have conferred on you such a generous fief.'

'Oh, the manor wasn't for my valour at Crécy. I was there certainly, but Berkeley induced them to grant me the manor in the days preceding. They cited my captaincy of the archers at Mantes. I had such a paucity of men, and the city was so damnably difficult to put to fire, my commanders were terribly impressed I managed to arrange as much destruction of French property as I did in so brief a time. Difficult, you know, but not valorous, nor enjoyable. Women and children crying everywhere, old men singeing their beards attempting to extinguish the flames issuing from their houses.'

'I see,' said Berna, in a diminished voice. She swallowed. 'I assumed . . .'

'The fault was mine. I permitted you to assume. I mean it might equally well have been for courage at Crécy. It just arrived differently. That's war, I'm afraid. One's enemy isn't going to give battle unless he feels one's hand in his pocket, and the pocket, in this case, was the taxpaying citizen of Mantes.'

Berna commenced to whisper: 'Might it not have been possible for you . . .'

'I wasn't in that place,' said Laurence testily. 'I saw they'd stolen a cart, and that was permitted, and it wasn't until next day I apprehended they'd ravished a woman too.'

'They murdered her papa.'

'A man of fighting age. He owed to have concealed her. I know, I know, it introduces a taint.'

'But . . .' Berna ceased. Both were silent for some moments.

'I would that I'd been clearer in my orders,' said Laurence. 'I commanded them to show mercy to the church, not to kill women and children, and that was all. I said "Otherwise I ne care what you do." I gave licence. I owed to know how they would comprehend me.'

'Open your conscience when you confess.'

'Yes, but . . .' He clasped her hand so firmly it was clear he judged himself more enfeebled than he was. 'It's a cold ritual. My confessions tumble through the priest and on to the Almighty without no return. I'd confess to you. You reply. There's a frankness to you I ne perceive in others.'

'What would you confess?'

'That I mentioned to you the places I was courageous, and omitted the places courage failed me. I ne know if I had the power to command the archers to release Cess, but I ne attempted the command. How people admire the courage of the chevalier in the field, charging the enemy, when true courage is the knight who defies his friends.'

'I ne know how a priest may perceive very repentance, but surely it's semblable to regret,' said Berna.

'Cess presents herself more clearly to my conscience when so many others have died. I suppose she desires to return to Mantes. Her people may reject her. Should she suffer to remain, I would you aid her to find some new existence in Calais.'

357

'I'll convey your words to her, and aid her as I may,' said Berna. 'I pray God will pardon you if she does not. I discover you ne please me less for what you've said.'

'I suppose Hammer would be a decent marriage for you once I've gone,' said Laurence. 'He's nicely provided for in England but he wouldn't turn his nose up at a manor in France.'

'That wasn't my reason for mentioning his name. We passed through his land today.'

'Whether I survive this or not, it is essential that you arrive in Melcombe port by Thursday, to secure the manor for us, or to render yourself marriageable to my successor.'

He was agitated, and his voice trembled, and he began to cough. Berna urged him to rest, and gave him water, and assured him she would ride to Melcombe next day regardless of his condition, and sail to France, and travel to their manor, and insist on her immediate, unconditional occupancy.

'I'll go first to the priest and make his acquaintance and apprehend the disposition of the people,' said Berna. 'He may be suspicious initially, but he can't dispute our documents, and he must expect the arrivage of the new lord's tenant from England. We'll go together to the manor house, and he'll introduce me to the servants. We'll go round the house, opening the shutters, permitting light and fresh air to enter, and I shall take an inventory of everything, and ensure each lock has an accompanying key. I shall discover the mews, and the stables, and the kitchens, and the buttery, and the cellar, and the bedchambers, and the dining hall, and the parlour, and how the poultry is maintained, and the pigs, and the quality of the milk. I shall demand fair payment of the people to use our mill, our forests, our river, our fields and our stone. I shall enforce their duties and their privileges. I shall ensure payment of their rents in silver and in services. I shall choose honest men as my principal officers. I shall be just, yet firm. I shall avoid debts and honour the Haket name and livery in our domestic adornment. My initial priority, of course, will be the harvest, and if God sends, the proceeds will suffice for some modest expenditure on plate, costume and the establishment of a mute of hounds for the chase.'

In the course of Berna's prognostications, Laurence fell into a gentle sleep. Not long afterwards, they were visited by the infirmarer.

BERNA FOUND THOMAS in a more comfortable bed in another part of the abbot's residence, where he was attended by various surviving members of the abbot's retinue. He sat up with his back supported by a pile of cushions. Flasks of wine and water stood on a table by his hand, and he had his scribal equipment out on his lap. The chamber was brilliantly illuminated by a multitude of candles.

He had aged, and his face, like Laurence's and the archers before they succumbed, was desiccated and colourless. He had attained the same stage of the malady as Berna's husband, of a fragile alertness, of accommodation to physical frailty, of the corporeal surrendering its meagre remaining resources to provide the spirit with powers and senses to conduct its final business in this world. He smiled at Berna and inquired after Laurence.

'He has esperance of recovery,' she said, 'but the infirmarer . . .'

'The infirmarer is excessively disposed to increasing the population of paradise, in my opinion,' said Thomas. 'I feel my condition has improved, yet he advised me to prepare for the priest.'

Berna's eyes filled with tears. 'He said the same regarding Laurence.'

'We shouldn't be too severe towards him,' said Thomas. 'He's lost many friends. He told me he'd observed some remarkable returns from the borders of eternity. If Cess might survive the pestilence, why not Laurence? He's young.'

'He desires that I travel to Melcombe tomorrow, regardless of his condition. He put it to me in terms of a command. I promised to obey, but how may I?'

'The manor in English France represents your sole security, and paid passage on the ship departing Thursday your sole reliable form of transportation. No doubt Laurence would rather have your company. To demand your separation is his sacrifice.'

'I endured so much to marry him, and now I must abandon him, when he's dying? I should appear to the world as a sort of monster whose only desire were property.'

'If your primary concern is for the world's opinion, of course you must remain.'

'Why are you so horrible to me? Does the fact my husband is departing this world offer me no protection of your moral judgements? Let me savour these hours with him. And if, God save him, the worst— What would become of his memory and remains without me?'

'I compose my final testament,' said Thomas. 'Do I survive, I'll ensure he's cared for in your absence; do I perish, I shall ensure the abbey adopts the duty. If necessary, I shall endow a chantry, at the expense of my estate. I have no heirs.'

'You are generous. Pardon me my acerbity. I know your condition is as severe as Laurence's and I am touched that you should remember him when you must compose yourself for the same journey. And here I am, as ever, with my confidences. If my most noble and courageous course is to obey Laurence's command and abandon him prematurely, I confess to an ignoble lack of courage. I have already disgraced myself by pretending to imagine with him my arrivage in our new domain, as if I cared about anything except his condition.'

'It took more courage to commence your journey than most knights display in combat,' said Thomas.

THE MATINS BELL sounds. Avian chorus, solar light. Aqueous blue permeates my quarters. My temperature is elevated. I have no strength to write, yet my mind continues to generate sequential phrases. I am a sheet of Italian paper in the process of inscription, kept from igniting only by the fractional cooling power of the ink. The retention of lexical capacity signifies the persistence of vitality. New clauses form with the regularity of a pulse.

The excessively young student, Hugo, has returned. The abbot placed him at my disposal yesterday. He has already completed his first year at Oxford. The abbey sent him there, hoping to secure for itself a portion of the fruits of the new scholarship, but it has simply equipped him with the means to categorise the disadvantages of the monastic life.

We speak in a curious dialect, the locution, I suppose, of the privileged young of the south of England, in which popular English and the French-English of the gentry is augmented by liberal use of Anglicised Latinisms.

'The archer Quate came to pay his respects while you were asleep,' says Hugo.

'He departed?'

'He promised to pray for you, and light candles for you in France, and expressed the hope you would remember him.'

'And the others?'

'They left, except the lady Bernadine and her husband. She bade her maidservant to travel with the rest, and she would join them when she could.'

'And Softly? The sick archer?'

'They took him, against the advice of the infirmarer, who said he wouldn't suffer a journey. His woman, the Frenchwoman, insisted on his being carried with them.'

I experience a sense of solitude and abandonment. I am deprived of the conclusion of their journey. And yet I would not endure another moment in the back of a cart.

'Who is the French prisoner?' asks Hugo.

I narrate the history of Hayne's company. The clauses issue from me of their own impetus, and I feel the history expand into a chronicle composed as much of interpretations and imaginings as facts.

'I ne understand,' says Hugo, when I describe the reformation of the company for the Crécy campaign, 'why this Hayne would be reunited with such criminals.'

'There was in Softly's insistence that he merited the precious cross some element profoundly repugnant to Hayne,' I say. 'Softly's pride, his rejection of Hayne's supremacy as creator of the company, made Hayne decide to transfer punishment into divine hands. He perceived, in the assurances of the clerics that England's war was just, an opportunity to tempt Softly to transgress beyond the boundaries of what was permitted. His preference was not a secular penalty, but that they be damned to hell of their own volition.'

'I doubt such brutes as these archers are capable of such fine moral reasoning,' says Hugo.

'The journey to France with Hayne became a contest. Softly would prove to Hayne that he was God's favourite, that it was his destiny to possess the cross and survive the pestilence. Hayne would demonstrate to Softly that his pride was misplaced, that in the final hour he would attempt repentance, and be humbled, and cry for mercy in Hayne's hearing.'

Hugo's face expresses disgust and fascination at once. 'What was the result?' he asks.

'Dickle died unconfessed of a demonically possessed goat. Hornstrake perished of the pestilence, having pleaded for Cess's mercy. Holiday caught the plague, but was murdered by Softly before he could die of it; and Softly's condition promises imminent misfortune.'

The gravity of Hugo's face is replaced by serenity. 'Well,' he says, 'I have rarely heard such decisive proof of divine justice.'

'Justice?' I say. The effect of the sudden application of intense emotion to my voice, combined with my feeble condition, is to create a sinister tremor in the word, like the afflatus of some funereal reed instrument. I am gratified that Hugo blushes, genuflects and stammers an apology.

'Pardon me, master,' he says. 'I ne intended to suggest there was any punishment associated with your . . .'

'We're all sinners,' I say. 'Your notion of the pestilence as divine punishment is uncontroversial. My impression is that on this occasion God has decided to increase the quantity of Noahs who will survive to repopulate the world. This has consequences. He has divided humanity for ever into two sorts, the guilty and the proud. The first will be tormented by the notion that they, the survivors, are less deserving than those who perished. "My children were innocent," parents who have lost sons and daughters will say. "They were punished for my sins. I should have died in their place." The second will take their survival as confirmation that they are God's

363

favourites. Whatever doubts they may have had over their own conduct will disappear; their every action will be validated. The definition of virtue becomes their own gratification. To be is to be good.'

I pause, becoming conscious I have moved from my subject, and how nothing is more miserable than the digressions of a dying man. And no sooner do I think this than it occurs to me that nothing is more expressive of human vitality than the mind's power to wander in the face of such a powerful call on its attention as its own extinction.

'I digress,' I say. 'The fact is that to speak of justice in respect of Hayne's company is problematic. Removing my own situation from the history, there remains the case of another archer, Longfreke Gilbert Bisley, who succumbed to the pestilence on Sunday. Of all the archers, it was he who attempted most vigorously to secure the release of Cess.'

'But perhaps he made a satisfactory confession?'

'What does "satisfactory" signify here? Is it more satisfactory for an expiring sinner to repent, confess and be absolved by God through the agency of a priest, or to make their penance to the person they sinned against?'

'A priest,' says Hugo, without hesitation.

My heart beats irregularly. I sense that were it to fail the words would continue to emerge, regular, precise, expressing the absent consciousness of a non-existent being. 'But there was no priest, only me. And I reasoned that were God to hear an archer sincerely request Cess's pardon, it would assist in his appeal for entry to paradise.'

I have noticed a certain disgust, a certain impatience, form on Hugo's face. Now it erupts. 'I ne comprehend your concern with the consciences of these people,' he says. 'They are an inferior sort. Brutal, savage, emotionless. And the French virgin, had she been of gentle origin and virtuous, I doubt they would have considered her vulnerable to their purpose. They've gone. Be grateful you no longer need concern yourself with them.'

'Were I a doctor of philosophy, I suppose I would take as reasoned an attitude as you,' I say. 'As it is, in my irrational way, I cannot put them out of my mind, or regard them as unimportant. Oblige me. Let me tell you what I find most difficult to comprehend.

'To Hayne, any archer who travelled to France this time was as guilty as any other. Each accepted the abuse of Cess as if it were normal. In Hayne's eyes even young Will Quate acquired guilt by entering the company's service. When I joined their company I think Longfreke made a distinction between his own conduct and that of Softly's; he preferred to see himself as a warder conveying Softly and his confederates to their place of punishment. But finally he concurred with Hayne, that they all progressed to the same destination. Do you observe what is absent from this portrayal?'

What gentility Hugo has demonstrated so far has been more from his notion of appropriate personal conduct than from compassion. The old autodidact's fastidiousness is tedious; only custom requires. Now his scholarly mind engages.

'If Hayne judged the entire company of archers to be mortal sinners for their complicity in the treatment of Cess, where does that place him?' he says.

'Exactly. It was in his power to control the archers in Mantes. It was he who mediated between the careless command of Haket to make destruction in Mantes and the archers who would give form to that destruction. It was he who tolerated the abduction of Cess, when he could have forced Softly to release her.'

An unexpectedly penetrating look of realisation, as gratifying to me as it is agonising, appears on Hugo's face. 'Do you mean that you reproach yourself for not perceiving the importance of Hayne's responsibility earlier? Is that the source of your obsession with these people?'

'I was preoccupied with Hayne versus Softly, instead of attending to the arena of Hayne's contempt for Cess.'

'There's nothing you can do now.'

'The giant survives, I'm certain. He is present. He persists. He menaces. If I rode furiously . . .'

'For what purpose?'

My fingers make contact with the cup of wine. He has identified the obstacle. 'A second part of my confession concerns the fact that I am a veritable coward,' I say. I drink.

Hugo is pleased to be placed in the position of reassuring a man older and more experienced than himself. 'You're too feeble to consider a journey to the cloister, never mind Melcombe,' he says.

I am lachrymose. Why? Hugo assumes I weep for the archers, for Cess. No. I weep for Will and Madlen and Bernadine, for their courage in abandoning their former lives.

More honestly: I weep for those they abandoned.

More honestly still: I weep for my own courage, that I dared relinquish the country of my birth.

With absolute honesty: I weep for the brutality of the courage, the courage of the brutality, of he who steals himself away from his origins.

Oh mother, forgive me!

WILL AND MADLEN, and the three carts driven by Cess, Fallwell and Miredrum, left Cerne on Wednesday morning. The rim of hills about the abbey shifted to gold in the early light. Softly lay sick in the old cart. They went south over the tops of green downs that trundled in tight waves like to a great woollen in its spring shake. In the narrow vales below them bells rang, the toll of the church's, the ring of the priest's as the gangs hastened to the dying, and the steady tinkle of cowbells as cattle shifted their graze.

They came on a shepherd with his flock in a high bare spot. A small girl lay on the ground next to him, writhen in the sun. The sheep tore at the weeds that grew at the roadside. The shepherd beheld a town far below, half in shadow, half in light. One line of smoke rose of a smithy, white and straight in the windless air. When the carts and horses stinted they could hear from far away the sound of the smith's hammer.

Will came down of his horse, went to the shepherd and greeted him.

'Heal?' asked the shepherd.

'Out-take one in the cart,' said Will.

'We lose many, but the smithy ne lets,' said the shepherd. 'I haven't been down there since folk began to sicken. I keep watch from here.'

'How white this land is.'

'It's chalk,' said the shepherd. 'What's yours?'

'Cotswold lime,' said Will. 'Good for dykes, hard on the plough.'

They spoke of husbandry a while. Down in the valley the smith stinted his hammering and a knave led a new-shod horse away down the street.

'How clear the sound,' said Will.

'Sometimes I make out what they say, all but it's further than a mile,' said the shepherd. 'Last night I saw the priest go to the butcher's, and later a body was borne away. I thought me, be it so to sit in heaven, to see all that goes on down below and lack the means to help? I looked for heaven to give me rest, but how might I rest there if the plight of those I left behind be always before my eyes?'

Cess came up to them and greeted the shepherd. They heard Softly call her name of the cart. Will asked after him.

'He's weak,' said Cess. 'He mayn't stand nor lift his arms. It won't be long.'

She asked the shepherd what ailed the girl.

'Nothing,' said the shepherd. He knelt and shook the girl's shoulder mildly. She rubbed her eyes, opened them, looked about and got quickly to her feet. Cess stroked her hair and asked her name.

'Trude,' said the girl. 'Where do you go?'

'France.'

'Take me with you.'

'You must bide at home,' said Cess.

'I shan't go home again,' said Trude.

'Her father was taken to Christ last week, God keep him,' said the shepherd. 'He used to beat his Trude when she vexed him. Some old fool told the mother she owed not to be soft on the child out of mild-heartedness over these wretched times, else the girl would be spoiled. So her mother, who was always kind to her before, began to beat her too, and ne knows how to mete it right, so it's either too much or too little.'

Softly cried for Miredrum and Fallwell to help him learn Cess her stead. But the new archers ne stirred.

Cess bade the shepherd care for Trude till she was ready to see her mother again. She said: 'Her mother owes to know that if she loses her daughter to the wide world now she'll be spoiled too deep to be right again.'

'I told her so,' said the shepherd. 'I'll take Trude down tomorrow. I mayn't bear to stand aside up here another day.'

'Bide your time,' said Cess to Trude. 'A bad home's better than none.'

'I'll find another. Take me with you.'

'I mayn't take no one's child away,' said Cess, shaking her head.

I<small>N THE MIDDLE</small> of the day they came of the high downs to a ford over a stream that ran down the middle of a shallow valley. Cess drove the cart over the ford and steered it upstream to a clump of alders. The others followed. She bade Fallwell and Miredrum lift Softly and lay him under the most alder and folded a woollen under his head.

'Let me go,' croaked Softly to his new men. 'Do as I bid. I shall be borne to the haven and take the ship.'

The new bowmen ne heeded him. They laid him down where Cess showed. Madlen and Will rode up, came down of their horses and stood with their hands on the bridlethongs, like to they ne knew whether to listen or to ride away.

'The alder's an evil tree,' said Softly. He made to rise, but lacked the strength, and only trundled on his side and again on his back. 'Judas hung himself of it.'

'Was he your friend?'

'Set me in the cart again, or I'll give you such a beating you'll not have one white spot.'

'You're too weak to beat me, John.'

Softly took in breath and grabbed her wrist. Will would help her but there wasn't no need. Cess looked down at Softly's fingers, which were grey and thin like to bird's claws, and lightly pulled them of her. Softly's arm fell on the ground again like to it were already reft of life.

'You die, John,' said Cess.

'I'm not ready,' said Softly.

'No one ever was.'

'I shall be ready,' said Softly. 'I'll be shriven in the great church in Bristol.'

'That's no shrift, John,' said Cess. 'More like a wedding. But you won't be wed now.'

'You ne know aught of how worthy folk are shriven,' said Softly. 'Shrift is when a man lists the wrongs he's done, and shows he's sorry, and begs forgiveness.'

'Of Christ alone,' said Softly. 'I shan't beg of no other.'

'And yet you die. It's time.'

'I mayn't die, for there's no priest to shrive me.'

'And yet you die.'

'Would you have me list my life to that fool proctor?'

'Thomas is gone, John.'

'Who's left? The green knave who sold me, Player Will? I'll not tell him no wrongs of mine.'

'There's only me, John. Cecile de Goincourt.'

Softly was still a while. Then he would call Will's name, but couldn't lift his steven higher than a croak. 'Help me,' he said. 'Ne leave me with this witch. Were I shriven by a woman at the last I were stripped of all my worth.'

'Come now,' said Cess. 'We've been together long, you and I. Let me help you confess.'

'I'll have none of your beshitten "confess". Let me be shriven like an Englishman.'

'We're all Christen, John, be we English or French. Shrift and confession are two words for the same thing. I know your wrongs better than I know my own. Let me make it light for you. I'll confess like to I were you and you need do not but say it's true, and beg forgiveness.'

'Christ shield me,' whispered Softly.

'You mayn't ask Christ to shield you of yourself.'

'I must be aneled,' whispered Softly. 'Where's the oil?'

'There's no oil,' said Cess. 'Yours is a poor man's death.'

'I'm not poor,' said Softly. 'My mouth is full of gold.'

'A good stead to begin. Listen now while I speak as you. Jesus Christ Almighty, Lord of Life, maker of all things, who bought us on the cross, forgive me, John Fletcher of Bristol, Softly by ekename, my sins. Forgive me that in my lust for wealth and holy things I slew the hermit Alan Weston, took his book of saints' tales and golden cross, and had that holy rood melted down and made into teeth, for my own were rotten. I'm truly sorry I slew him while he prayed, while his back was turned, and that he died in fear, for my first blow wasn't true, and I struck him again when he lay on his side, and his eyes were open, and he begged me to spare him. Forgive me that I struck that second blow, for I ne feared him alive nor dead, but I feared him wounded by my hand, and I would that I hadn't struck him, but I had, and I ne might make him whole again, and besides, I would have the cross. Forgive me that I put stones in his clothes and cast him into the sea. Forgive me that afterwards I gabbed of what I did to my friends and to Cecile de Goincourt, the woman I stole, that they fear me and worth me as a strong man and grim.'

'He behest me those things,' said Softly.

'You've no use of your pride no more,' said Cess. 'It's left behind with your body and your lies when you fare to the next house. Speak the words. Say "Yeah, that's how it betid, I'm truly sorry, and I beg forgiveness."'

'If it were to Christ I might.'

'He hears.'

'He never hung about no beshitten field in Dorset to hear no French cow swike her master into saying unworthy things.'

'Time's short, John, fare on. Forgive me, Lord, that I yielded to my lust on king's service in France. I knew I did wrong to lead my friends to the mason's yard in Mantes. I hadn't no right to find nor take no maid against her will. I would be free to dight anyone as it liked me, reckless of their wishes, and that was wrong. I

371

would find a maid, any maid, and have her. Were she fair, so much the better, for it would show me and my friends what good hap I was sent. Should she yield to me without no struggle, good, for it would show she saw I were strong and handy, even as it show she fear me, which were good, for it show my might. And if she ne yield, but fight, so much the better, for it would show I had the strength to turn all to my will, and I'd win the mirth I love that comes of the pine of soft mild beasts – for it likes me when they ne know which way to run. It likes me to see in their eyes how they ne understand what drives me to hurt them.

'Forgive me, Lord, for I'm not wicked all the way through, and now I know I did wrong, and am truly sorry. What's worse, and makes my need for forgiveness great, is that I knew when I went to the mason's yard I'd tell you I was sorry one day, and believe it. As much as it likes me to have against her will a maid I choose, so it ne likes me to be unworthed by my fellows for doing it. I'd have all worth my manhood as one who may take any maid by strength, and all worth my manhood as one who ne needs to take no maid by strength. Forgive me my pride.

'Forgive me that when I came to the yard I ne heeded the fullth of holy likenesses of saints and angels. Forgive me that I ne bade my friends turn and go again the way they came when we saw the stead was dight for God's work. Forgive me that I let my friend Dickle stab to death the good and worthy master-mason Maurice. I ne heeded his body, and took his daughter, who was bent over him crying "Papa, Papa", and dragged her away. Forgive me that I ne heeded the life-blood come of him, and his legs kick twice as he lay on the ground, in full sight of his daughter. Forgive me that this man, whose hammer and chisel quickened fair flocks of angels out of stone, was slain and left without no priest to send him forth.

'I knew she was afeared, and it pined her horribly that she lacked the means to shield herself against me and my friends. Her helplessness made me bold. Each freedom we took with her made us thirst for another. We knew we were strong, right and handy men and would not dare to dight an English maid so. We made a stead in our rightness to do wickedness in and having made that stead we'd know how deep our wickedness might go. Her helplessness made us feel mighty but even so we helped each other hold her down. We felt bold but even so we cursed and mocked her and made each other laugh at her to make us feel the bolder. Forgive me, Lord.'

'Enough,' whispered Softly.

'Will you take these words as your own, every one?'

'No.'

'I go on. I am John Fletcher, and I have sinned. In the beginning a spot of shame was left in me, but in the end there wasn't none. I would slake my lust on Cecile de Goincourt, but the more I took what I sought, the more I hated her. Forgive me, Lord, for I've lied. I made myself out to love England and to hate the French when Hayne led me to shield Southampton. I called the French un-Christen when I saw them be free with the Hampshire maids. But in the dern hollows of my heart I envied them. I yearned to have such freedom. Again, when Cecile de Goincourt lay half dead and blooded after me and my friends shifted to have her, I made out that my heart softened, and I minded my mother, and took her under my wing. Forgive me, Lord, for it was a lie, and the truth was that in my heart I envied my father, who took my mother against her will. I would be that grim and ruthless freke who used my mother, and I would be the stepfather who took me in, all at once. I was all lies, lust and pride. Proudly I raped her, and proudly I came forward as the man who'd shield her of rape's cruel afterclaps.'

'I ne learned you English that you might talk to me in French words I ne know. What's "cruel"? What's "envy"? What's "rape"?'

'Cruel is grim. Envy is nithe. Rape is to reave a maid of her maidenhood against her will and steal her of her kin.'

'I cared for you when you sicked. I brought you water and cleaned you and shifted your linen. It were lighter for me to let you die. Maybe it were of helping you then that I sick now.'

'I sickened in your bonds, far from home. You beat me before I sicked, and you beat me after.'

'I beat you to help you that you ne misstep. I offered to wed you.'

'Why would I wed you, John?'

'None might live if each day they minded each blow they ever took. You owe to learn to forget. I thought me you forgot. You bore arrows for us at Crécy. I learned you to shoot with a bow when you asked. I said you had a good arm.'

'Let him go to hell,' said Madlen.

Will bade her be still.

'I, John Fletcher, am truly sorry for my sins,' said Cess. 'I've been a wicked man. Forgive me, Lord. Bring me to you. Will you take these words for your own, John?'

Softly looked at Cess. For a stound a keener light came into his eyes. 'You ne care if my next house be heaven or hell,' he said.

'I wouldn't say so,' said Cess. 'I wouldn't be made to answer your wickedness and hardness with vengeance. I wouldn't be driven to match your break of my life by speeding your damnation. I would that I might believe you know what you have done, and feel at last the hurt of others, and chose your punishment.'

It was like to Softly ne heard, only beheld her with the new light in his eyes. 'You ne care how Christ deems me after,' he said. 'You'd only have me beg forgiveness of you.'

'Well?' said Cess with fresh strength, meeting his gaze without fear.

'I take your words as my own,' whispered Softly. Something caught in his throat and the light in his eyes began to fade. 'Out-take one truth I'll tell you. Believe me, Cess, and let Christ hear if he will. It's true I am not wicked through and through. But as I did to you in Mantes, so I would do the same to you again. I'm not sorry that Dickle slew your dad, I'm not sorry I took you against your will. I would have you, and I did. That's the truth.'

'It ne lessens your wickedness to know you're wicked and say so,' said Cess. 'Won't you give me more?'

'You?' said Softly. 'This is for Christ. I shan't tell nor give you nothing.'

'You'll bide on Christ for ever. But that ne tokens you should bide with us no more.'

Cess rose to her feet. She took her eyes of Softly, turned and walked away to the cart. As she went by Fallwell and Miredrum, who bore a spade, she said: 'Take your fee.'

Softly had shut his eyes. Miredrum bent down and took of Softly's neck the rood and the key to the score's strongbox. He held them out to Will, who took them.

'Is there life in him yet?' said Will.

Fallwell dight the sharp end of the spade gently between Softly's lips, then set his right foot on the spade. He shoff his foot down hard, with all his weight, and the spade went clean through Softly's jaw and neck.

'No,' said Miredrum. And when the gush of blood was done, he and Falwell went on their knees with their knives to work out the gold in Softly's teeth.

Cess, Will and Madlen left them there and went on southward with the one old cart. None spoke for miles, though Will and Madlen rode nigh to Cess, who held herself upright and looked about her.

She broke the stillness, though she ne beheld Will nor Madlen when she spoke.

'I am Cecile de Goincourt,' she said.

BERNA CLOSED THE door gently and returned to Laurence's bedside.

'Was that the chaplain?' said Laurence, with effort.

'He'll return after noon,' said Berna. 'Unless you feel . . .' She mightn't complete the condition.

'If only it were possible to evade my journey out of this world by concealment from the priest.'

'We may hide under the bed,' said Berna.

Laurence's respiration rasped in substitute for laughter. 'As Earl Dungeness told his jester when he lay mortally wounded, "Keep me amused till the chaplain arrive, but not so much I die before he get here."'

'It pleases me to make you laugh,' said Berna. She caressed his face. 'I wonder if you appeared as you do now, at once so courageous and afraid, when you faced the French at Crécy. It is like to a grand, terrible power is present, visible to you directly, but to me only reflected in your eyes. I oughtn't to have imagined you as both a man-at-arms and a courtly lover.'

'I failed you. Not in the matter of Ness, I mean, not that I avoided to ravish you from your father's manor . . . a more general default. That you find me too domestic in my interests, too occupied with material affairs. That you travelled to me and married me because you had no choice.'

'Have I been so cruel?' demanded Berna.

'I ne reproach you. It gives me a certain joy to be the instrument by which you broke open the wells of your courage and escaped your family.'

A tear fell on Berna's smiling lips as she pressed his hand. 'I ne comprehend how this may be an end when it appears so like a beginning,' she said. 'You are fresh and new to me in your frankness.'

Laurence shook his head very slowly. 'Too late for frankness,' he said. 'I were unreasonable to insist on your honesty now. I were quite content to hear you say you love me now, true or not.'

'With frankness and honesty,' said Berna, 'I say there's very love between us. Having considered your painful words I'll tell you its nature. Not the love of gentleman and lady, nor man and wife, nor dreamer and rose. It is the love of one knight for another. Of a knight who loves her comrade because her comrade, despite going astray, is ready to be recalled to his duty, and remains loyal thereafter, in the face of the first knight's resentment that he falls short of her ideal.'

'Of a knight who loves his comrade,' said Laurence, 'because she's more courageous than any other, and for all her disappointment in him she ne abandons him, no matter how great the danger. She is his Warm Welcome.'

'And the Rose . . .'

'. . . is elsewhere.'

'They quest for it together.'

'Until the hour she must go on alone,' said Laurence.

Berna mounted the bed, lay down beside Laurence and embraced him closely.

THE DORSET DOWNS swalled yet and dipped about Will, Madlen and Cecile, but their height wasn't so much as before. The air was brighter, like to the sun had nighed the earth. The soft warm wind bore an outcome smack of otherness.

'I would that you ne took that rood for your own,' said Madlen to Will. 'I would that you ne wed no life but mine.'

'We may not love but if we eat,' said Will.

The two white swaths of the road wrothe and clamb to a height, then fell away. Will stinted his horse. Far away on the brink of sight lay a mighty blue rock that stretched into the sky. Will sat in the saddle astoned. The rock, a kind of great hill, seemed not only to reach into the sky, but to float on it. Beneath the hill, instead of land, lay an endless even field of blue, of almost the same hue as the sky, only a little darker. The mark where the two lines met was misty and the field, like the sky, seemed to have no end.

'I ne know what I see,' said Will.

'The sea,' said Madlen. 'It's the sea.'

THEY WENT DOWN toward the hill and came to the haven of Melcombe. The streets were still and the shops shuttered. An old woman who sat on her doorstep and twisted rope told them the pest had set in a month before, of a ship from Brest, and ne slackened, out-take there were fewer souls left for the Maker to pick.

Will asked were the cog *Welfare* there, and the roper beheld him with a sour eye and said he wasn't the first to ask. She told them to look for the ship at the haven wharf.

The wharf stank of salt and fish. Great white birds of the muchness of lambs wandered about. Shrill cries came of their beaks. The dark seawater clapped the stones and timbers of the wharf, and the greater sound of the endless sea was in their ears, like the woods threshed by the wind. Many small ships were moored there, and one greater, with a castle at the back end and a thick high mast. All along its upper side were likenesses of great fish and deer and birds and cats dight with spots and bars. A long-haired knave, bare-chested in a straw hat, sat on a board hung over the side and wrought with a brush the likenesses of some grey cattle with much ears and long horns of their mouths. The knave had a gold pin in one ear and an outcome token branded on his shoulder.

Will said he sought the master of the *Welfare*.

'The old master's buried in the churchyard,' said the knave. 'He was my father, God keep him.'

'God keep him,' said Will.

'Thanks that you say so like it were fresh,' said the knave. 'I and my brother are the leave of shipmen now, and we share the cog with my mother and my brother's wife.' He took a second brush of a second can and gave the cattle eyes. 'All four of us overlived the pest. We lost my father and two mates.'

'We lost many.'

'It ne gives time to mourn for one before it takes another.'

'Have you bode on us so long as to write these likenesses?'

'Dad ne let us hight the ship brightly as we would.'

'May you bear us to Calais?'

'Why would we?'

'You're bound to bear Hayne Attenoke's score,' said Will.

'Not without the tally stick.'

'It comes.'

'We sail tomorrow, with you or without you,' said the shipman. He beheld them over his shoulder and laughed. 'I see no score,' he said.

'I'm the last.'

'You're not,' said the shipman. His eyes looked beyond them. They turned, and Hayne was there.

'MASTER HAYNE,' SAID Will. 'We feared for you.' He smiled.

Hayne ne answered. The giant stood still and beheld him without no light in his cheer.

Will took the rood of his neck and gave it to Hayne, who took it and dight it on himself.

'I thought me I was the last,' said Will. 'You left without a word.' He told Hayne what had befallen the others.

'You alone overlived to come here before the ship sailed,' said Hayne.

'Was I wrong to come?' asked Will.

'He means you were wrong not to die,' said Cecile.

Hayne beheld her like to he ne knew of where came the sound of woman's speech. He turned to Will again.

'You would that I take you to France as a bowman,' he said.

'Yeah,' said Will.

'I warned you not to come. I warned you not to leave your town. You knew what my other bowmen had done, yet you cleaved to them like to you ne cared. As if however they'd be damned, you'd willingly be damned with them. Now here you are, heal and well, like to you think yourself better than the others.'

'Sweetmouth and Mad went away free,' said Will. 'They weren't harmed.'

'Maybe they were harmed.'

'By you?' said Cecile.

'Ne speak,' Hayne told her.

'I'll speak,' said Cecile. 'You drew your men to damn themselves by hurting me and killing my father. You ne hindered them. You led them to their deaths in steadings where they ne lightly found absolution. All this you did in my name, in the name of the deeds against me and my father, the deeds you allowed. And you tell me not to speak?'

'I work in no one's name,' said Hayne. 'I work for right alone.'

He beheld Will. 'We'll go to France. But mind my law. One who's not guilty will be hurt.'

He grabbed Madlen by the arm and dragged her to him, pinning her to his chest. Will sprang at him but Hayne dealt Will such a blow with his free arm that the young man fell to the ground. While Will gathered his wits and got to his feet again Hayne drew his long knife and made to hew open Madlen's throat.

The air rushed aside. Two rows of goose feathers were pitched in Hayne's shoulder. The iron head stood out of Hayne's shirt at the back. Blood dropped on the stones.

Cecile had taken Softly's strung bow of the cart, nocked a war arrow and shot it from ten yard away.

'Who learned you to shoot?' said Hayne. He let Madlen go. She ran to stand by Will.

'My foe learned me,' said Cecile.

'He owed to have learned you to have another arrow ready did the first miss its mark.'

Will drew his knife.

'It ne missed its mark,' said Cecile. 'I wouldn't kill you, for I wouldn't be like you.'

Hayne put his knife back in its belt, went to Cecile, took the rood of his neck and offered it to her. She shook her head.

'Were I to take it I would throw it in the sea,' she said. 'It's your burden.'

Hayne went to where he'd left his gear and took his great bow, seven foot long. He went to the shipman, who'd beheld from his board without stirring, and gave him the bow.

'Have you all the hues?' he asked.

'Yeah,' said the shipman.

'Dight a bar of each on my bow. I ne need it no more. The days of right are over.' He said to Will: 'Fare further without me.' And he walked away northward, as heedless of the arrow stuck out of him as if it were a thorn in his hand.

'I thought me you hated us,' said Will to Cecile.

'I fairly did,' said Cecile. 'But Softly and Hayne made that hate. Be it ever so right for me to keep, I wouldn't have nothing of theirs no more.'

THE NEW WORLD

THE SHIPMEN WOULDN'T let them go up into the cog without the
tally stick that showed the fee had been given. The leave tide was
at noon next day, they said. They'd bide no longer.

Madlen, Cecile and Will went to the strand and sat there to
behold the sea and hear its crash and hiss. Will stripped to his
breech and swam in the waves. The water had a saltier smack than
any broth. Cecile and Madlen walked in up to their knees. They
drank ale and ate dried fish they bought of a huckster, who told
them the great hill that stood over Melcombe was called Portland.

They went through the goods in the cart. There were many rich
old clothes that Softly had stolen of Mere Castle, a heap of arrows,
bowstrings, clubs, wicker shields, iron caps and the strongbox. Will
opened it with the key. Cecile told the pennies, for there were too
many for Will and Madlen to tell: two hundred and seven.

'They're ours now,' said Madlen.

Will asked Cecile to teach them to tell things greater than a
hundred. Madlen said it was a waste of time, and would Will not
walk with her, and leave Cecile a while? Will said he would come
later. Madlen went to sit by herself near the water while Cecile
showed Will how to work arsmetrick with shells and strokes in the
sand. Each answer to 'How many?' was a number, she said, and
Will minded he'd heard the priest and Anto the reeve use the word
'number' in Outen Green, but hadn't known what it meant.

Will coughed and Madlen came again. She laid her hand on his
forehead. 'You're hot,' she said. 'Are you dizzy?'

'A little,' said Will.

'Does your throat hurt?'

'Yeah.'

'Are you weak?'

'Hayne's mightier than me, but when he hit me it seemed I went down lightly.'

'I'll care for you, loveman,' said Madlen.

'You said it made you bold to know all must die soon.'

'I thought me I'd sicken first,' said Madlen. 'Besides, now you sick, I know what I ne knew then, that I wouldn't never have you die.'

When the sun was low the lady Bernadine rode into Melcombe. She wore a set of Laurence Haket's clothes, and had shorn her hair short, and sat astride her horse like to a man. Her face was dirty with dust and dried tears, for Laurence Haket's ghost had shifted house. They sang for him in the abbey, and would sing and bid beads and burn candles till his brother came to fetch his body. Thomas gave the silver for it.

Will asked after Thomas.

'He bade me wish you well before he laid his eyes together,' said the lady Bernadine. 'He said he was as ready for the next world as a man could be. He was shriven to his bones, they aneled him. He said his farewells. I have his writings in my bag, though I ne know where to send them. When I asked him he said "Avignon, Edinburgh".'

She told them she wouldn't fare further as no widow, for she was weary of the way folk dealt with lone women on the road. Until they reached the new manor, she said, she would go as a man, and bade them make out to all that she was Laurence Haket, a noble young man-at-arms, in mourning for his bride, the fair Bernadine. When she spoke these words, 'the fair Bernadine', she fell weeping into Madlen's arms.

They went to the ship. Laurence gave the shipmen her half of the tally stick. They took out theirs and the two halves matched.

Will's strength held out long enough to help load the horses and cart on board and fill the ship's casks with ale and water. They gave him a stead to rest in, a straw bed shaded by a stretch of cerecloth against the castle at the back of the ship, and he fell into a long feverish dream.

He dreamed he came to Outen Green at Martinmas, when the trees were black and bare, when the ground and the roofs were white with frost and smoke rose of all the smoke holes. The day dwined and lights glimmered through each shutter, like to even the poorest had found the means and need to burn candles at home before sunset.

He stood by the frozen pond. Whichday Wat lay under the ice with his eyes shut. Will would break the ice and free him but Ness put her hand on his arm and held him back. 'Ne wake him,' she said. 'He dreams of you.'

Will went to his house to find his mother. Inside the house had grown to the muchness of the lord's hall and all the town sat at board. Half the folk were blithe and red-cheeked and mirthy and half were not but bones. The live folk ne heeded the still eyeless fleshlessness of their neighbours, and feasted on rich fare Will hadn't never seen in his house: piglet, pike, pigeon, baked deer. His mother was at the head of the board with her new husband, Anto the reeve.

In the shadows at the side of the hall stood Sir Guy, who called that Anto behest him gold for his deer, but Anto ne heard him.

Will sat at board. Athwart him were the bones of a girl whose name he thought him he should know, but he ne minded. Her jaw opened and words came from between her teeth.

'Buy me a foot of red band at Brimpsfield fair,' she said.

'I must hedge tomorrow,' said Will.

'I have work too,' said the girl. 'I owe to throw myself on the bonefire. They bade me fetch my weight in bones but all I found were my own.'

Will lifted a gobbet of pigflesh to his mouth. The girl's fingers fastened white on his wrist.

'You ne bade farewell,' she said. She led him outside and showed him the top of the hill, the shortest way to the Rodmarton road. Will saw folk walk away southward there, outlined against the sky, yellow after the sunset. The evening star shone. The folk were far but Will knew them: Madlen, Hab, Enker, the lady Bernadine, Cecile, Thomas and his own self, Will Quate.

'I would go with them,' he said.

'Your other self is there already,' said the girl. 'You may bide here for ever. You're needed for the harvest.'

'I would go,' said Will.

He woke and opened his eyes. Beyond the shade of the cerecloth the light was blindingly bright. The ship rolled. He was wet with sweat. A great sail hung of the mast, and Hayne's bow, many-hued in bars, was nailed up there. He lifted himself on his elbows. In the middle of the ship he saw three folk: Cecile, and a fair young knave in high-born gear who was Hab, and Bernadine in Laurence Haket's clothes who was bent over the ship's side.

Bernadine-Laurence straightened, wiped her mouth and yelled at Hab, like to she'd already wrathed at him and had only broken off to spew. Cecile put her hand round Bernadine's waist and helped her back to the side, where she spewed again. At their feet the wicker basket for the castellan's dove stood empty.

Hab saw Will was awake. He ran to him, kneeled beside him and gave him water.

'What ails the lady Bernadine?' asked Will.

'You mean Laurence Haket?' said Hab. 'We ne call her Bernadine no more. Seasickness ails her, and the lack of Madlen. I hope it ne vexes you that Madlen's gone.'

'You were my friend longer than she,' said Will. 'I told you I would see you again.'

'Loveman,' said Hab. He looked behind him, and with his back to the ship quickly kissed Will on the lips.

'Ne catch it,' said Will.

'Aren't you better?'

'I feel other.'

'But you're better?' Hab frowned.

'Death ne needed me,' said Will, 'and now I ne know who I am.'

Acknowledgements

I'D LIKE TO thank Francis Bickmore, Leila Cruickshank, Natasha
Fairweather, Sophy Geering, Caroline Gillet, Duncan McLean,
Matthew Marland, Kay Meek, Daniel Orrells, Adèle Smith, Eugenie
Todd, and everyone at Canongate.

Much of this book was written in libraries and cafés, and some
in library cafés. I'm grateful in particular to Espresso and Bread
Source in Norwich, to the Zealand, Pavilion and Recharge in Bethnal
Green, and to UEA and Tower Hamlets libraries.

Parts of Thomas's exegesis of the Malmesbury carvings are taken
from the Wycliffe Bible. The chant of the Outen Green villagers
on their way to the bonefire is from E. J. Dobson and F. Ll.
Harrison's *Medieval English Songs*. The song 'When The Nightingale
Sings' is from the Harley lyrics in the British Library. Holiday's
spell against the plague is from Eamon Duffy's incomparable master-
piece, *The Stripping of the Altars*, which was both source and
inspiration. I drew on the translation of *The Romance of the Rose* by
Frances Horgan, who was kind enough to respond to a question of
mine.

Three quite different books, all called *The Black Death*, by John
Hatcher, Rosemary Horrox, and Ole Benedictow, provided priceless
background on the plague. Caroline Dunn's *Stolen Women in Medieval*

England was invaluable, as was H. J. Hewitt's *The Organisation of War Under Edward III*. Mad's description of the battle of Crécy is based on various sources but I found the account given by Richard Barber in *Edward III and the Triumph of England* persuasive. I particularly appreciated Barber's appendix in that book where he listed the royal tournaments of Edward III, showing that the king's last pre-plague tournament was in Canterbury on 14 July 1348.

I must acknowledge the work, now spanning three centuries, of that great scholarly enterprise, the *Oxford English Dictionary*. Without its online version it is difficult to see how this book could have been written.

London, 2019